About the Author

Sarah Mallory grew up in the West Country, England, telling stories. She moved to Yorkshire with her young family but after nearly thirty years living in a farmhouse on the Pennines, she has now moved to live by the sea in Scotland. Sarah is an award-winning novelist with more than twenty books published by Mills & Boon Historical. She loves to hear from readers, and you can reach her via her website at: sarahmallory.com

T0312494

Regency Secrets

Regency Secrets:

Saved from Disgrace

SARAH MALLORY

MILLS & BOON

First Published in Great Britain 2023
By Mills & Boon, an imprint of HarperCollins*Publishers* Ltd,
1 London Bridge Street, London, SE1 9GF

www.harpercollins.co.uk

HarperCollins*Publishers*
Macken House, 39/40 Mayor Street Upper,
Dublin 1, D01 C9W8, Ireland

ISBN: 978-0-263-31912-5

THE TON'S MOST
NOTORIOUS RAKE

For TGH, as we stand on the edge of
another great adventure.

Chapter One

'Molly! Molly!'

She held her breath, balanced in her leafy eyrie and peeping down at the path below her. Edwin would never think to look up into a tree. Her brother did not think girls could climb trees. He was four years older and at school now and he did not think girls could do *anything*. True, her skirts had been a hindrance in scrambling up into the branches and Mama would be sure to scold her when she saw the tear, and Papa might beat her for it, too, and make her learn another tract from the Scriptures, but it would be worth it. She would wait until her brother had passed beneath her, then jump down behind him. That would give him a scare.

'Molly, where are you?'

'Where the *devil* are you?'

The voice had changed. It was no longer Edwin and suddenly she was no longer six years old and hiding in a tree. She was in a dark place, bruised and bleeding, and waiting for the next blow.

'Molly. *Molly!*'

It was a dream. Only a dream. She shook off the fear

and panic, clinging to the fact that it was her brother's voice dragging her from sleep. She opened her eyes, but remained still for a moment to gather her thoughts. She was safe here. It was the vicarage garden and she was lying on a rug beneath the shady branches of the beech tree.

'So there you are, sleepyhead.'

She sat up, rubbing her eyes. 'I beg your pardon, Edwin. I came out here to do some sketching and I must have fallen asleep.'

'Well, if you will go off at the crack of dawn to help out at Prospect House.' He threw himself down beside her on the rug, grinning at her and looking far more like the errant elder brother she had grown up with than the sober Reverend Edwin Frayne, vicar of the parish. 'There is no need for you to visit more than once a week, you know. Nancy and Fleur are very capable of running the place.'

'But I like to help when I can and today is market day when they sell the surplus from the dairy and the kitchen garden. There is always so much for them to do to pack up the dog cart, deciding on a price for the eggs and butter, and—'

He threw up a hand, laughing. 'Enough, enough, Molly. You do not need to convince me. You are a grown woman and may do as you please.'

'I know they could cope without me,' she conceded, smiling. 'However, today will be the last of those early mornings. With the days growing shorter I shall go to the house on a Tuesday. We will prepare all we can in advance so that Fleur and the others have only to pack up the cart in the morning.'

'If you must.'

She reached for his hand. 'I like to do it, Edwin. I like to help. It makes me feel necessary.'

'You are very necessary, my dear. You are necessary to my comfort, keeping house for me here.'

She took his hand and squeezed it, wanting to say how grateful she was that he had taken her in when she was so suddenly widowed, but the memories that stirred up brought an unwelcome lump to her throat and she did not wish to embarrass either of them with her tears, so she pinned on a bright smile and asked him where he had been.

'I called upon our new neighbours at Newlands.'

'Oh.'

Edwin spread his hands, 'I could not ignore them, Molly, you must see that. And I admit I was pleasantly surprised. Sir Gerald is really most gentleman-like. He was most accommodating.'

'One would expect him to be, to a man of the cloth.' Molly bit her lip. 'I beg your pardon, Edwin, I know one should never listen to gossip, but from everything I have heard, Sir Gerald Kilburn and his friends are everything I most despise...'

She tailed off and Edwin looked at her with some amusement.

'You must learn not to attach too much importance to the gossip our sister writes to you. She has inherited our father's abhorrence of anything frivolous. Sir Gerald and his guests all seemed very pleasant. He introduced me to his sister, too. Miss Kilburn is to keep house for him here. She has with her an elderly lady who is her companion. Their presence and that of other ladies suggests this is not a party of rakish bucks intent upon setting the neighbourhood by the ears.'

'Not all of them, perhaps,' said Molly darkly. 'But Louisa wrote to warn me that one of the party is sure to be Sir Gerald's oldest and closest friend, Charles Russington. Even you will have heard of his reputation, Edwin. Louisa says the gossip about the man is no exaggeration. He is the most attractive man imaginable and no lady in town is safe.'

'If the fellow is so attractive, perhaps it is *he* who is not safe from the ladies.'

'Edwin!'

'I beg your pardon, I did not mean to be flippant, but I think you are making too much of this. Yes, I have certainly heard of Beau Russington, but I did not see him today.' He grinned suddenly. 'If the fellow is as rakish as they say, then perhaps he is coming into the country for a rest! No, no, do not rip up at me for that, my dear. Forgive me, but I think you are too quick to judge. It is our Christian duty to give these people the benefit of the doubt, at least until we are a little better acquainted with them. And we shall soon know what our neighbours think of the newcomers. Sir Gerald told me they plan to attend Friday's assembly at the King's Head. His party comprises five ladies, excluding the elderly companion, and six gentlemen, so just think how that will liven things up!'

Molly was still digesting this news when Edwin coughed.

'I thought we might go this time. Just so that you might meet the Newlands party, you understand. Miss Agnes Kilburn is a quiet, well-mannered young lady, about your age, and your situations are quite similar. I think you might get on very well.'

Molly said nothing, but her doubts must have been

plain in her face, for Edwin said earnestly, 'I really should like you to meet her, my dear.'

She narrowed her eyes, a sudden smile tugging at her mouth. 'Why, Edwin, I do believe you are blushing. Have you taken a liking to Miss Kilburn?'

'No, no, of course not, we have only met the once.' His ears had turned quite red, which only increased Molly's suspicions. He said, 'I am merely concerned that we do not appear unfriendly. And I thought you would prefer that to my inviting them here.'

'There is that,' she agreed. 'Very well, we shall go. I admit my interest has been piqued. In meeting Miss Kilburn, at least.'

'Molly.' Edwin tried to look stern but failed miserably. 'I will not have you making Miss Kilburn feel awkward.'

'No, of course not,' said Molly, her grey eyes twinkling. 'I shall be the very soul of discretion!'

Molly decided that if she was going to attend the assembly then she would need some new gloves, since she had noticed at their last outing that her old ones were looking decidedly shabby. Thus, on the morning of the assembly, she sallied forth to the high street to make her purchases. Hebden's was by far the most popular shop for the ladies of Compton Parva. The business had begun as a haberdasher, selling everything one might require for sewing such as ribbons, thread and needles, but as the number of families in the area increased, the business had expanded to include such necessary items as ladies' bonnets, scarves, reticules, stockings and gloves. The shop was now run by Miss Hebden, who had inherited the business from her parents, and when she saw Molly, she came immediately to serve her.

'Ah, Mrs Morgan, good day to you,' she greeted Molly with her usual cheerful smile. 'How may I help you today?'

'I need a pair of white gloves, but I can wait, if you have other customers.'

'No, no, those ladies are shopping together and Clara is looking after them very nicely. She does not need me always looking over her shoulder.'

'She has settled in well, then?'

'Oh, yes, indeed, very well. She is a quick learner and not afraid to ask if there's something she don't know.' She turned slightly away from her assistant and lowered her voice. 'I admit I was a little reluctant, when you first suggested I should take her on, but she's a good girl, very polite, and the customers like her, which is important.'

Molly smiled. 'I am very glad.'

'Yes,' Miss Hebden continued. 'And she's company, too. In fact, I have grown very fond of her.' She hesitated, then said in a rush, 'I think what you are doing at Prospect House is a very fine thing, Mrs Morgan, taking in those poor girls and giving them a second chance. What Clara has told me about her last employer, trying to take advantage of the poor maid and then turning her off without a character when she refused—well, it makes my blood boil, so it does. And him a gentleman, too, so she says. There's some wicked folks in this world, Mrs Morgan, and that's a fact.' For a moment, Miss Hebden's countenance was unusually solemn, then she gave herself a little shake and smiled. 'But I mustn't keep you talking all day, ma'am. It's white gloves you want, isn't it? Now, then, let me see… Yes, here we are. You are in luck, it is the very last pair. We've had quite a run on them this week and on ribbons, too. Everyone wants to look their best for tonight's assembly, I shouldn't wonder. I understand the new owner of Newlands intends to be there, with his friends, so everyone will be out to impress them.'

Molly stifled the urge to say that she did not wish to impress anyone. More customers came into the shop at that moment, so she paid for her gloves and left. She felt a little spurt of indignation that the arrival of a fashionable gentleman and his friends could arouse such interest in the town. Well, she for one would not give them another thought.

Alas for such hopes. Molly had not gone a hundred yards when she met up with Mrs Birch and Lady Currick, two highly respected matrons of Compton Parva. Since each of them had a daughter of marriageable age, Molly was not surprised when they told her they would be attending that evening's assembly.

'All of Compton Parva will be there,' remarked Mrs Birch, nodding sagely. 'Everyone is agog to see the new owner of Newlands. Have you met him yet, Mrs Morgan? No? Ah, then we have the advantage of you.'

'Yes,' averred Lady Currick, interrupting her friend. 'Sir William lost no time in visiting Newlands and invited them all to join my little card party last night. Was there ever such a man! Not a word to me until it was too late. I asked him how he thought I would accommodate another eleven guests, which, of course, he could not answer. But somehow I managed to squeeze in another table and it passed off very pleasantly, did it not, Mrs Birch? What a pity you were not able to join us, Mrs Morgan, for you could then have met the whole party.'

'I vow I was a little in awe of them to begin with,' said Mrs Birch, 'but I needn't have worried, they were all so pleasant and obliging. Sir Gerald is a most engaging young man, very genial and even-tempered, despite his carrot-coloured hair! And wait until you see the ladies' gowns, Mrs Morgan. London fashions, one can tell at a glance.'

Molly listened in good-humoured silence while the ladies went into raptures over the cut and quality of the various gowns and giggled like schoolgirls over the handsome gentlemen, saving an especial mention for Beau Russington.

'Oh, now there is a handsome gentleman,' said Lady Currick, sighing. 'One can quite understand why ladies are constantly throwing themselves at him. He is so very tall and with such an air of fashion about him!'

'And those *eyes*, ma'am.' Mrs Birch sighed gustily. 'So dark and intense, and that way he has of fixing his gaze upon one, as if you were the only person in the room. La, I think if I were not a happily married woman I might succumb to the beau myself!'

'Indeed, I think you are right, my dear, I have always had a soft spot for a rake, even one as notorious as Beau Russington.' Lady Currick gave another little giggle before becoming serious. 'But with so many personable young men in town, and all of them renowned for being a little *fast*, we must be sure the girls are properly chaperoned. No more than two dances, if any one of these gentlemen should ask them to stand up.'

Molly stared at them. 'You acknowledge the gentlemen to be libertines, yet you will allow your daughters to dance with them?'

'Why, of course, my dear, it would be a great honour to stand up with a fashionable gentleman. And I have no worries that they might attract the gentlemen's attention beyond the dance, for I think Mrs Birch will agree with me that our girls cannot hold a candle to the fine ladies staying at Newlands. But you will see for yourself, Mrs Morgan, if you are coming to the ball this evening.'

The ladies strolled off and Molly went on her way, wondering if it was too late to cry off from tonight's assembly, but it was not really to be considered. She would be obliged to meet the Newlands party at some point, so it would be best to get it over.

It was with the feeling of one doing an onerous duty that Molly went upstairs to change later that evening. She had no intention of dancing at the assembly and she chose to wear her grey satin gown with a demitrain, but when she tried to add a lace cap to the ensemble, Edwin protested, saying it made her look like a dowd.

'Nonsense, it is perfectly proper for a widow of my age.'

'Anyone would think you were forty rather than four-and-twenty,' retorted Edwin. He added, 'Covering your head like that is the sort of thing Father would have approved. He was ever the puritan.'

That made her laugh. 'That is certainly a strong inducement to me to remove it.'

'Which is my intention, little sister! Now, go and take that thing off.'

Molly capitulated, realising that her brother was very much displeased, and ten minutes later, she presented herself in the drawing room again, her unruly dark curls almost tamed by a bandeau of white ribbon.

The public entrance to the King's Head assembly rooms was at the top of a flight of stairs, leading up from the yard. When Molly and Edwin arrived, the Newlands party were about to go in, and Edwin would have hurried Molly up the stairs to meet them, but she hung back.

'There can be no rush, Edwin, and I would like to take off my cloak and tidy myself first. Even that may take some time, though; I so rarely come to these dances that I can already see several of our acquaintances waiting to speak to me.'

'Very well, go and talk to your friends, my dear, and I shall meet you in the ballroom.'

Molly happily sent him on his way and went off to the cloakroom to change into her dancing shoes. She tried not to dawdle, acknowledging her reluctance to meet Sir Gerald Kilburn and his guests. The presence of a party of fashionable gentlemen and ladies in Compton Parva was bound to cause a flutter and, while the young ladies present this evening had the advantage of their parents' protection, her girls, as Molly called the inhabitants of Prospect House, were very vulnerable.

Molly had set up Prospect House as a refuge for young women who had lost their reputation and had nowhere to call home. Some were of humble birth, but many were young ladies who had been cast on to the streets and left with no means of supporting themselves. Molly provided them with food and shelter, and in return, her 'girls' helped out in the house and on the farm attached to it. Molly tried to find them suitable work and move them on, but she knew there would always be more destitute young women to take their place.

Molly had worked hard to overcome the doubts and prejudice of the townspeople, but she knew that such a house would attract the attention of rakes and libertines, who would see its inhabitants as fair game. Molly was afraid that some of her younger charges were still innocent and naive enough to succumb to the blandishments of a personable man and that could have catastrophic consequences, not only for the young woman, but also for the refuge itself. In the five years since she had set it up, Prospect House had become self-supporting, but its success relied upon the continuing goodwill of the local townspeople.

She was thus not inclined to look favourably upon the newcomers, and when she went into the ballroom and saw her brother chatting away in the friendliest style to a group of fashionably dressed strangers, she did not approach him. Surmising this must be the party from Newlands, Molly moved to a spot at the side of the room and took the opportunity to observe them.

Sir Gerald was soon identified, a stocky young man with a cheerful, open countenance and a shock of red hair. Molly guessed it was his sister standing beside him. The likeness between the two was very marked, although Agnes's hair was more golden than red, and in repose, her countenance was more serious. Her glance quickly surveyed the rest of the party. She had no doubt the local ladies would be taking note of every detail of the gowns, from the uncommonly short sleeves of one lady's blossom-coloured crape to the deep frill of Van-dyke lace around the bottom of Miss Kilburn's gossamer silk. By contrast, the gentlemen's fashions appeared to be very much the same—dark coats with lighter small clothes and pale waistcoats—but Molly was obliged to admit that she was no expert on the finer points of male fashion.

There was one figure, however, who stood out from the rest of the gentlemen. It was not merely his height, but a certain flamboyance in his appearance. His improbably black hair was pomaded to a high gloss and brushed forward to frame his face with several artistic curls. His countenance was handsome, in a florid sort of way, with thick dark brows and lashes that Molly thought suspiciously dark. His lips, too, appeared unnaturally red, even from this distance. The points of his collar hid most of his cheeks and the folds of his cravat frothed around his neck. His black tailcoat was so broad across the back and nipped in at the waist that she suspected the shoulders were padded. He was gesticulating elaborately as he talked and the ladies around him appeared to be hanging on to his every word. Molly's lip curled in scorn.

'So *that* is Beau Russington.'

'I beg your pardon?'

The startled voice at her shoulder made her look around. A tall gentleman in a plain blue coat was regarding her. She did not know him, but recalled seeing him talking to Mr Fetherpen, the bookseller, when she came in.

'Oh, dear, I did not mean to speak aloud.' She smiled an apology. 'The gentleman over there, holding forth to the group standing before the mirror. He has been described to me as an—' She stopped herself from saying *an infamous rake*. That would be most impolite, and for all she knew the man at her side might well be one of the Newlands party. 'As a leader of fashion,' she ended lamely. She saw the amused look on the stranger's face and added quickly, 'That is what the epithet *beau* denotes, does it not?'

'It does indeed, ma'am.' The stranger looked across the room. 'You refer to the exquisite in the garish waistcoat, I presume?'

'Yes.'

'That fribble,' he said, a note of contempt in his voice. 'That painted fop.'

'Yes,' said Molly, glad to discover he shared her opinion.

'That is *not* Beau Russington, madam. It is Sir Joseph Aikers.'

'Not?' She looked at the stranger in surprise.

He gave a slight bow. *'I* am Russington.'

'You!' Molly's first impulse was to apologise profusely, but she held back. It was not her intention to pander to any man. Instead she gave a little gurgle of laughter. 'I thought you were a book salesman.' His brows shot up and she explained kindly, 'I saw you talking with Mr Fetherpen, you see. And our assemblies are open to everyone, as long as they have a decent set of clothes.'

Had she gone too far? She saw the very slight twitch of his lips and was emboldened to look up at him. There was a dangerous glint in his dark brown eyes, but that thought was nothing to the danger she perceived as she studied him properly for the first time. He was tall, certainly, but well proportioned with broad shoulders and a powerful frame. His black hair was too long to be neat and curled thickly about his head and over his collar. In repose, she thought his lean face might look saturnine, but with that smile tugging at the corners of a mobile mouth and his dark eyes laughing at her beneath their black brows, a bolt of attraction shot through Molly and knocked the air from her body.

Quickly she turned away. Lady Currick had in no way exaggerated this notorious rake's charms and Molly felt a stab of alarm. If *she* felt this way, what effect might he have on her girls?

'A book salesman?' he murmured, dashing hopes that he might have walked off. 'I suppose I should be thankful I was not talking to the butcher.'

Another laugh bubbled up inside Molly, but she resolutely stifled it and with an incoherent murmur she hurried away.

Oh, heavens, was there ever anything so unfortunate? Molly moved quickly around the room, smiling but not stopping when Lady Currick beckoned to her. That lady would have seen Molly talking to Mr Russington, but Molly was not ready to discuss it. She would dearly like to go home, but that would only cause more speculation. Instead she made her way to Edwin's side, bracing herself for the introductions she knew he would be eager to make.

Her nerves were still raw, but she achieved a creditable appearance of calm as her brother presented Sir Gerald and his friends to her. They were all genial enough, clearly willing to be pleased by the provincial company in which they found themselves. Even Sir Joseph, the painted fop, bowed over her hand and paid her a few fulsome compliments.

Molly made her responses like an automaton, her thoughts still distracted by her recent encounter with Mr Russington. However, she forced her chaotic mind to concentrate when Sir Gerald presented his sister. Agnes Kilburn was handsome rather than pretty, and during their short conversation, Molly gained the impression that she was an intelligent, thoughtful young woman. In any other circumstances, Molly would have been delighted to make her acquaintance, but she had no wish to give Sir Gerald and his friends any reason to spend more time than necessary in Compton Parva.

Suddenly Molly was aware of a tingling down her spine and she heard a deep, amused voice behind her.

'Ah, Mr Frayne, will you not introduce us?'

'I'd be delighted to do so! Molly, my dear, may I present Mr Russington to you? M'sister, sir. Mrs Morgan.'

Steeling herself, Molly turned, her smile pinned in place. She could not recall putting out her hand, but within moments he was bowing over her fingers. It was ridiculous to think she could feel the touch of his lips through her glove. That must surely be her fancy, but she did not imagine the little squeeze he gave her hand before releasing it.

'Mrs Morgan and I, ah, encountered one another a little earlier.'

She thought angrily that he might expect her to apologise for her mistake, but when he lifted his head and looked at her there was nothing but amusement in his dark eyes. A faint smile curved his lips and she felt the full force of his charm wrap around her.

She could hear music, but it took her a moment to realise the sweet strains were the sounds of the musicians striking up for the first dance. She was vaguely aware of Edwin leading Agnes Kilburn on to the dance floor, but for the world she could not tear her gaze away from Beau Russington's laughing eyes.

'Would you do me the honour of dancing with me, Mrs Morgan, or does that privilege fall to your husband?'

She felt dangerously off balance and his amusement ruffled her. It was as if he was aware of her agitation.

She said coldly, 'I am a widow, sir. And I do not dance tonight.' She moved towards the empty chairs at the side of the room. When he followed her, she said crossly, 'Surely, Mr Russington, you should dance with some other lady. There are plenty without partners.'

'Ah, but none to whom I have been introduced. Besides, the dance is now started. I shall have to wait for the next.'

When she sat down, he took a seat next to her. Could the man not take a hint?

'Pray do not feel you need to remain with me,' she told him. 'I am sure there are many here who would prefer your company.'

'I am sure there are,' he agreed, not at all offended.

Her agitation disappeared, ousted by a desire to shake him from that maddening calm.

She said, 'When I was a child, Mama had a house cat, a very superior being that had the unfortunate trait of always making for the visitor who liked him least. You are displaying a similar trait, Mr Russington.'

'You liken me to a cat?'

Molly hid a smile. She murmured provocatively, 'A tomcat, perhaps.'

A tomcat?

Russ glanced at the lady beside him. She was fanning herself as she watched the dancing and looking quite unconcerned. Did she realise what she had said, at the insult she had just uttered? Of course, she did. From their first exchanges he had had the impression that she was trying to annoy him. Well, perhaps not at first. Not until she had known his identity. He wished now he had not spoken, but when he had heard her speak his name and had seen her looking with such contempt at Aikers, he had not been able to help himself.

He remembered how she had turned to him, a smiling apology upon her lips and in her frank grey eyes. Then, when she realised who he was, the look had changed to one of unholy amusement and soon after that, sheer dislike. He was used to ladies fawning over him, or teasing him in an attempt to gain his attention. Never before had one been so openly hostile. A tomcat! He felt a momentary shock, until his sense of humour kicked in and he laughed.

'I fear a longer acquaintance with you will do my self-esteem no good, madam!'

'No good at all,' she agreed affably.

She rose and, with a nod of dismissal, she left him. Russ watched her walk away, noting the proud tilt of her head, her straight back and the soft, seductive sway and shimmer of her skirts as she glided across the floor. Perhaps it was a ruse to pique his interest. Perhaps he might indulge the widow in a flirtation. After all she was pretty enough, although nothing like the ripe, luscious beauties that he favoured.

He decided against it. Compton Parva was a small town and she was the reverend's sister. In his experience it was better to dally with dashing matrons who could be relied upon to enjoy a brief liaison without expecting anything more lasting, and then, when the time came to part, they would do so amicably and with never a second thought. No. Much better to leave well alone.

Edwin and Molly strolled home from the King's Head once the dancing had ended. They had decided against using the carriage for such a short journey and the full moon and balmy summer night made it a pleasant walk, but for Molly the enjoyment was dimmed as she waited for the inevitable question from her brother.

'Well, sister, what thought you of Miss Kilburn?'

Molly was cautious. 'She appeared to be a very pleasant girl, although we did not have an opportunity to speak a great deal.'

'You would have had more if you had not insisted upon spending all your time with the old ladies such as Lady Currick.'

'Edwin!'

'Well, you must admit, Molly, you are young enough to be her daughter.'

'But I could hardly sit with the young ladies who were waiting for partners. It was embarrassing to watch them all making sheep's eyes at the gentlemen.'

'You might have stayed with the ladies from Newlands,' he suggested mildly. 'Then you might have had more opportunity to become acquainted with Miss Kilburn.'

'Perhaps, but these things are never easy at a ball.'

Edwin patted her hand, where it rested on his sleeve. 'Never mind. All is not lost, my dear, we have been invited to Newlands for dinner next Tuesday. I am going fishing with Sir Gerald during the day, but I will come home to fetch you for the evening.'

Molly's heart sank, but before she could utter a word he continued, 'I know you usually visit Prospect House on Tuesdays, but if you take the gig, you will be back in plenty of time to change. And you will have saved yourself a tiring walk.'

'Well, that is the clincher!' She laughed. 'Especially since I tell you that I am *never* tired.'

'There you are, then. It is settled, you will come!'

She heard the satisfaction in his voice and said nothing more. It was clear that Edwin wanted her there and, after all the help he had given her, how could she refuse?

Chapter Two

Molly had never visited Newlands and as Edwin's carriage rattled along the drive she leaned forward to catch a first glimpse of the house. What she saw, glowing golden in the sunlight, was a rambling stone house in a mix of styles. Its previous, ageing owner had not used it for years, so she could understand the excitement that had erupted in the town when Sir Gerald bought the hunting lodge. The gossip had started several months earlier, when workmen had descended upon the property. Word soon spread that Sir Gerald was a bachelor of substantial means who was planning to bring a large party to the house at the end of the summer. Molly's sister, Louisa, soon provided even more information, writing to inform her that Sir Gerald was a familiar figure in London and numbered amongst his acquaintances many of the fashionable rakes and Corinthians who flocked to the capital each Season.

Now those fashionable acquaintances were here, staying only a couple of miles from the town and far too close to Prospect House for Molly's comfort. Beside her, she heard Edwin chuckle.

'You look disappointed, Molly. Were you hoping Newlands would be so ugly and uncomfortable Sir Gerald and his friends would quit it within the month?'

'Something like that.'

'Do not fret, my dear,' He patted her hands. 'Sir Gerald has made it very clear he and his party are here for the sport. Why else would he have bought a hunting lodge?'

'But if the area's hunting, shooting and fishing do not live up to the party's expectations, might not Sir Gerald and his louche friends look elsewhere for a little entertainment? And a house full of what they would consider to be "fallen women" is certain to attract their attention.'

'Now you are being unreasonable,' exclaimed Edwin. 'You cannot deny that at last week's assembly the gentlemen from Newlands behaved impeccably. You have no reason to think ill of them.'

'I have Louisa's letters,' replied Molly darkly.

'Louisa has nothing better to do with her time than pass on salacious gossip, for the most part untrue or exaggerated. Come, Molly, you are being unfair to Sir Gerald and his friends. When people are disparaging about the inhabitants of Prospect House, you tell them that one should not make hasty judgements, yet here you are doing just that.' Edwin squeezed her fingers, pressing home his point. 'I am sure our new neighbours will have no interest at all in Prospect House, and if they do...' He spread his hands. 'You cannot keep your charges locked away for the duration of Sir Gerald's visit, my dear.'

'I know that,' she admitted, as the carriage pulled up before the house. 'But even if the gentlemen have no designs upon them, I very much fear one or two of the girls might find the presence of such handsome and fashionable gentlemen in Compton Parva...distracting.'

'My dear, if they are ever to make their way in the world again then they will have to learn to withstand the attractions of personable gentlemen.'

'Of course.' Molly clasped her hands together. 'But you saw how the ladies at the assembly reacted. Such fashionable young bucks, with all the glamour of the town clinging to them, are particularly attractive to susceptible young women.'

Edwin laughed. 'Do you really believe that, Molly?'

She thought of Beau Russington with his dark looks and careless charm and felt her stomach swoop.

'Oh, yes,' she whispered, her mouth suddenly dry. 'I really do.'

Sir Gerald and his friends were waiting for them in the drawing room. With the exception of Mrs Molyneux, Miss Kilburn's aged companion, they had all been present at the assembly where introductions had been made. As greetings were exchanged, Molly took the opportunity to study the company. She had been reassured at the assembly to see that Mrs Sykes and Lady Claydon were homely matrons, while Agnes Kilburn and the Misses Claydon had soon been at ease and mixing with the young ladies of the town. They were all very lively, but not at all the dashing sirens she had feared. This second meeting appeared to confirm her view, which was a relief, and she turned her attention to the gentlemen. Their host, Sir Gerald, was the most genial looking of them all, while Sir Joseph and Mr Flemington were the most flamboyant in their dress. But there could be no doubt they were all very fashionable—the cut of their clothes, the number of fobs and seals and the intricacies of their cravats had made them stand out at the recent assembly.

All except Beau Russington. She had been too agitated at their first encounter to appreciate why he was considered a leader of fashion, but here, in the elegant drawing room of Newlands, she had the opportunity to make a calm appraisal of the man. It did not take her long to realise that although he was not as showily dressed as his friends, his style was far superior. At least to her inexperienced eye. There was a simplicity to his dress, but nothing shabby in the superb cut of his clothes. Not a wrinkle marred the perfection of the dark evening coat stretched across his broad shoulders. It fitted him so well she wondered how many servants it had taken to ease him into it.

A plain white waistcoat was buttoned across his chest and she refused to allow her gaze to linger on the close-fitting breeches that sheathed narrow hips and powerful thighs. She quickly raised her eyes to take in the snowy neckcloth, intricately tied and with a single diamond winking from amongst the exquisite folds. The study of his cravat took her eyes to the countenance above it. A lean face, darkly handsome with a sensuous curve to the mouth. At that moment, as if aware of her scrutiny, the beau turned to look at her and her cool assessment came to an abrupt end.

Even from the other side of the room she felt the power of his gaze. Those dark, almost-black eyes skewered her to the spot and caused her pulse to race. Not only that, excitement flickered deep inside, like flames licking hungrily at dry tinder. She looked away quickly, shocked to realise that he had awoken sensations she had never wanted to feel again.

Sir Gerald was addressing her and she forced her mind to concentrate on his words. She exchanged pleasantries with his sister and then joined in a conversation with Mrs Sykes and Lady Claydon while the gentlemen discussed the day's shooting until dinner was announced.

Molly found herself seated at Sir Gerald's right hand, with Sir Joseph Aikers beside her. Mr Russington, she was relieved to see, was sitting opposite her brother at the far end of the table. She did not think she would have enjoyed her meal half as much if the beau had been sitting beside her. Sir Joseph might be a fribble and a painted fop—as some people so cruelly described him—but Molly soon discovered he was exceedingly good-natured and assiduous of her comfort, ensuring her glass was filled and that she had her pick of the succulent dishes on offer.

The food was excellent and the conversation interesting. No awkward subjects were broached and Molly began to relax. These were cultured, educated people who knew how to set a guest at ease. Perhaps she had been magnifying the dangers they posed. Just as that thought occurred to her, Edwin laughed and she glanced down the table towards him. After his day of sport, her brother was clearly upon easy terms with the gentlemen. Mr Russington was looking her way and he caught and held her gaze. Molly's heart began to race again. She felt trapped, like a wild animal, in thrall to a predator. With an effort, she dragged her eyes away, realising the danger was all too real. At least where one man was concerned.

Her appetite was quite gone and she was relieved when Miss Kilburn invited the ladies to withdraw. Molly intended to sit with Lady Claydon and Mrs Sykes, but when they reached the drawing room Miss Kilburn and the Misses Claydon were determined that she should perform for them.

'Your brother was eager that we should hear you play upon the pianoforte, Mrs Morgan,' explained Miss Claydon, opening the instrument and beckoning to Molly to sit down. 'He told us you are most proficient and that you sing, too.'

'Such praise,' murmured Molly, vowing to give Edwin a trimming as soon as they were alone. 'I am very much afraid I shall disappoint you.'

Harriet Claydon gave a trill of laughter. 'I doubt that, ma'am. Judith and I are both hopeless, despite Mama insisting that we have the best of teachers.'

'Sadly that is very true,' agreed Lady Claydon, shaking her head. 'We spent a fortune upon their education and they can neither of them do more than play a few simple pieces. Miss Kilburn, however, is very accomplished.'

Molly drew back in favour of her hostess, but Miss Kilburn was quick to decline.

She said shyly, 'We should very much like to hear you play, Mrs Morgan.'

Molly took her place at the piano. Perhaps it would be as well to play now, before the gentlemen came in. She played a couple of short pieces and, when urged to sing, she rattled off a lively folk song, before concluding her performance with an Italian love song. Her audience were generous in their praise, but when she could not be persuaded to play more, Agnes Kilburn took her place and Molly retired to sit with the older ladies, relieved that she was no longer the focus of attention.

She hoped that might be the case for the rest of the

evening, but it was not to be. When the gentlemen came in, the conversation turned towards Newlands.

'Many of our friends were against my purchasing such an out-of-the-way place,' said Sir Gerald cheerfully. 'Including the beau here. Ain't that right, Russ?'

'I was.' Mr Russington moved a little closer to the group. 'After all, there are good places to hunt that are much closer to London.

'Aye,' declared Mr Flemington, coming up. 'These provincial towns can be the very devil for entertainment. Not Compton Parva, you understand,' he added hastily, with a bow towards Edwin and Molly. 'The assembly at the King's Head last week was as good as any I have attended outside London.'

'Well, I do not regret my choice,' declared their host. 'It may be a long way north, but what is a few days' travel, compared to the sport that is to be had here? No, I am delighted with my new hunting lodge and glad now that I did not allow myself to be dissuaded.'

Edwin laughed heartily. 'Did you expect to find only savages in Knaresborough, Kilburn? I admit I had the same reaction from my friends and acquaintances when I accepted the living here. But I am very much at home, you know. And I vow it provides some of the best riding in the country.'

'Yes, I grant you, if your taste is for rugged grandeur,' put in Sir Joseph Aikers, waving one hand. 'You cannot deny the weather here is less clement than the south. And the mud.' He gave a comical grimace that made his companions laugh.

'In the main we are very favourably impressed,' declared Mrs Sykes. 'It is true the journey was a trifle wearisome. But Kilburn has made the house very comfortable and the townspeople of Compton Parva are most welcoming.'

'We are relieved to have Newlands occupied at last and not only for the enlargement of good society,' Edwin told her with a smile. 'It provides occupation for local people and business for our tradesmen. That must always be welcome.'

'There is one thing that surprised me,' remarked Lady Claydon. She hesitated and glanced towards the pianoforte, where her daughters and Miss Kilburn were engaged in singing together. 'I had not expected to find a house here for females of a *certain order.*'

'My wife means the magdalens,' declared Lord Claydon. 'I admit I was surprised when I heard of it—one usually associates Magdalene hospitals with the larger cities. But I suppose small towns have the same problems, what? It's a way of keeping that sort of female off the streets.'

Molly stiffened, but Edwin caught her eye and gave a slight shake of his head.

'You refer to Prospect House' he said calmly. 'It is a refuge for unfortunate women who have suffered at the hands of men. It is not a house of correction.'

'However, it is a little disturbing to think there is a need for one in Compton Parva,' remarked Mrs Sykes.

'The sad fact is we need more of these places,' said Edwin. 'Since Prospect House opened its doors, it has always been full, taking in residents from far and wide.'

'Ah,' cried Mr Flemington, rolling his eyes, 'So it is not that this area has more than its fair share of Lotharios.' He cast a laughing glance around at the gentlemen standing beside him. 'At least, not until now!'

There was much good-natured protest from his auditors

and Mrs Sykes rapped his knuckles with her fan, telling him to behave himself.

'This is no laughing matter,' she said. 'I would assure Mr Frayne that we are great supporters of the Magdalene houses. After all, someone has to help these poor women and show them the error of their ways.'

'Error of their ways?' Molly was unable to keep silent any longer. 'None of the women in Prospect House are prostitutes, ma'am, although that might have been their only way to survive had they not been taken in. However, I admit it was set up on the *precepts* of the original Magdalene hospital,' Molly added, 'to provide a safe and happy retreat for women of all classes.'

Molly knew her words would bring the attention of the group upon her, but it could not be helped. She sat up very straight, holding her head high. A couple of the gentlemen had raised their eyeglasses to regard her and Beau Russington, too, was watching her, but Molly ignored them all.

'Do you mean there is no attempt to reform them?' asked Lady Claydon, her brows rising in surprise. 'Is this not merely pandering to vice?'

'The women at Prospect House are the *victims* of vice, ma'am, not perpetrators,' Molly told her. 'Some have been seduced, others come here to escape seduction or because their reputations have been ruined by men who sought to use them for their own ends. As for reform, they are taught suitable skills in order that they may support themselves.'

'You appear to be very well informed about the business, Mrs Morgan,' remarked Mr Russington.

'I am,' said Molly, tilting her chin a little higher. 'I set up Prospect House.'

Her words brought a flutter of gasps and exclamations.

'Oh, good heavens,' murmured Mrs Sykes, fanning herself rapidly.

Molly kept her head up, prepared to meet any challenge, but she could see no condemnation or disapproval in the faces of those around her. Some of the gentlemen looked amused, the ladies merely surprised and then, to her relief, she heard Edwin's cheerful voice.

'Yes, and I am very proud of my sister. She purchased the property, provided a small annuity to fund it and then set up a committee of local people, knowing it was important to have the goodwill of the town if the house was to survive.'

'Most commendable, I am sure.' Lady Claydon responded faintly.

'It is proving a great success,' Edwin continued. 'They have a small farm which provides most of their food and any surplus of eggs, butter and the like is sold at the weekly market.'

'Quite an enterprise,' declared Sir Gerald. 'You must allow me to contribute to your fund, Mrs Morgan.'

'Thank you, sir.' Molly smiled, warming to him, until in the next breath he suggested they should all visit Prospect House to see it for themselves.

'I am afraid not,' she said quickly. 'With the exception of the doctor, they admit only women to the house. All deliveries and callers are directed to the old farmhouse.'

'But a house full of women, that is quite a temptation.' Mr Flemington sniggered. 'To, ah, uninvited guests.'

'We have seen to it that they are well protected,' replied Molly. 'Their manservant, Moses, is a fearsome fellow. A giant. He has orders to keep all unwelcome callers at bay.'

Her fierce stare swept over the gentlemen.

'Well, well,' declared Sir Gerald, breaking into the awkward silence. 'Shall we have some dancing?'

The gentlemen jumped up with alacrity and began to move back the furniture from the centre of the room and roll up the carpet. Hoping to atone for making everyone feel uncomfortable, Molly immediately offered to play. This was robustly contested by Mrs Sykes and Lady Claydon, who both expressed a willingness to perform this duty and persuaded Molly that as a guest she must take her turn on the dance floor.

'Now, now, Mrs Morgan, I hope you are not going to say you do not dance tonight,' said Lady Claydon, moving towards the pianoforte. 'Lord Claydon does not dance, since his accident, and if I play for you all, everyone else has a partner. Is that not splendid?'

'And as our guest, the honour of leading you out falls to me,' declared Sir Gerald, coming up. He held out his hand. 'Come along, let us show the others the way!'

Molly felt her heart sinking. She had not expected that there would be any impromptu dancing, but a very quick calculation told her there were just enough gentlemen and ladies to make six couples, if one excluded the pianist and Lord Claydon, with his bad leg. It would look odd, therefore, if she refused to dance, for that would leave only one gentleman without a partner. She had not even the excuse that she was not dressed for dancing, because her green muslin evening gown with its moderately flounced hem would not be any hindrance at all. She accompanied her host to the floor, pinning her smile in place.

Sir Gerald's good humour was infectious and Molly's smile became genuine. She loved to dance, although she did not indulge in the amusement very often, and she was soon lost in the music. She skipped and hopped and turned as the lively, noisy, country dance progressed. They began to change partners and Molly was moving from one gentleman to another and another, and by the time she was standing opposite Mr Russington her smile was wide and brilliant. As they joined hands and began to skip down the line she looked up into his face. He caught and held her eyes, a glinting amusement in his own, and in that moment everything changed. She could hear the piano, the other dancers clapping in time, but it was as if she and her partner were in a bubble, contained, connected. Her mind was filled with images of him pulling her close, holding her, kissing her, undressing her...

The familiar patterns of the dance saved her from humiliation. She danced like an automaton, moving on, smiling at her next partner, on and on until Sir Gerald claimed her once more and the dance was ending. She joined the others in applauding, but inside she was in a panic. Everyone was changing partners for the next dance. From the corner of her eye she saw Beau Russington looking at her. She could not dance with him. Would not! Quickly she grabbed Edwin's hand.

'Pray dance with me, brother. It is an age since we stood up together.'

'Dance with you?' Edwin sent a quick look over her head. 'Oh, I was hoping to ask Miss Kilburn to stand up with me again.'

'Please, Edwin.' She hoped her tone was not too beseeching, but she clung to his hand, and after a moment, he capitulated.

For this dance she had only the smallest contact with

the beau as the dancers wove in and out of one another. It was a mere touch of the fingers and this time she was prepared. As they crossed one another she was careful not to meet his eyes, but just his presence made her body tingle. Every part of her was aware of him, as if there was some connection between them, and it frightened her.

When the music ended Molly made her way to the piano, where Lady Claydon was leafing through the sheet music.

She said, 'My lady, I know the music for "The Soldier's Joy" by heart. I beg you will allow me to play.'

'Oh, but surely you would prefer to dance, my dear. You so rarely have the opportunity.'

'I think I sprained my ankle a little in the last dance, ma'am, and would prefer to rest it for a while, but that would leave a gentleman without a partner, and besides, my brother would fuss so if he knew of it.'

Lady Claydon was immediately full of sympathy. That made Molly feel a little guilty, but they exchanged places, Lady Claydon going off to join in the dancing, and Molly's guilt eased a little when she saw how much the lady was enjoying herself.

She remained at the piano for two dances, then Miss Claydon suggested 'Dancing Hearts' and Molly was obliged to search through the sheet music. She had just found the piece when Beau Russington approached and that nervous flutter ran through her again.

'Would you not prefer to dance, Mrs Morgan? I am sure one of the other ladies would play for us.'

Without looking at him she waved her hand towards

the music. 'No, no, I am quite content, thank you. I am not familiar with the steps of this dance.'

He leaned closer. 'I could teach you.'

Her mouth dried as, inexplicably, her mind filled with images that had nothing to do with dancing. It was his voice, she decided. It was too low, too deliciously seductive.

'No. I—that is, I turned my ankle in that first dance and prefer not to dance again this evening.'

'Ah, I see. So you do not trust yourself to dance? I quite understand.'

His tone suggested he did not believe her and Molly felt guilty colour rushing to her cheeks. She busied herself with straightening the sheet music on the stand, trying to concentrate on the notes she would have to play, and after a moment he walked away.

'Well, if he understands that I do not want to dance with *him*, then so much the better,' she muttered, running her fingers over the keys. 'And if he is offended enough to leave me alone then that is better still!'

She played two more dances, which were very well received, then Sir Gerald announced that refreshments awaited everyone in the dining room. There was a general move towards the door and as Molly got up from the piano, she found Beau Russington beside her.

'Allow me to give you my arm, ma'am.' When she drew back he added, 'It is best you do not put too much weight upon your foot.'

'My—oh. Oh. Yes.'

He offered his arm, and as her fingers went out he grasped them with his free hand and pulled them on to his sleeve.

'I am perfectly capable of walking unaided,' she told him, panicked by his firm grip.

'But what of your ankle, Mrs Morgan?'

'It is well rested now, thank you.'

'I think you are afraid of me.'

'And I think you are teasing me.'

'Well, yes, I am. Your reluctance for my company is intriguing.'

'It is not meant to be. A gentleman would be able to take the hint.'

He sucked in a breath. 'Cutting. You do not consider me a gentleman, then?'

'Oh, no,' she said with deceptive sweetness. 'I know you for a rake, sir.'

If she had hoped to offend him, she was disappointed.

'Do you think you are being quite fair to me, madam?'

'Oh, I think so. Your reputation, and that of your friends, precedes you. And it is not mere gossip, I assure you. The information comes on good authority and from more than one source.'

Molly felt exhilarated by the exchange. She could not recall speaking so freely to any man before.

'The devil it does!'

She laughed and was immediately aware of the change in him. Through the fine woollen sleeve beneath her fingers she could feel the muscles tighten. And she suspected she had angered him. When he spoke his voice was soft, smooth as silk, cold as steel.

'But all this is hearsay, madam—what do you really know of me?' They had reached the hall and with practised ease he whisked her away from the crowd and into the shadowy space beneath the stairs. 'Well, Mrs Morgan?'

He had turned her to face him, his hands resting on her shoulders, very lightly, but she found it impossible to move. Even in the shadows, his dark eyes glowed with devilish mischief. She had the strangest feeling that invisible bonds were wrapping around them, tightening, forcing her closer. She could feel him, *smell* him, a musky, spicy, lemony scent that she wanted to breathe in, to close her eyes and give in to the desire burning in her core. She fought it, curling her hands until the nails dug into her palms, using the pain to stop her from reaching out and pulling him towards her. To stop herself surrendering, as she had done once before to a man. A rake who had taken everything and left her to suffer the consequences. Desire was replaced by panic and she fought it down, struggling to keep the terror from her voice.

'You go too far, sir. I beg you will let me go.'

His hands tightened. 'Are you afraid I might kiss you?'

I am afraid I might not be able to resist!

'You would not dare.'

Russ felt her tremble, saw the uncertainty in her eyes and knew she was weakening.

He murmured softly, 'But you said yourself, madam, I am a rake and rakes are very daring.'

Her eyes widened, he saw the pink tip of her tongue flicker nervously across her lips and for a moment he was tempted to carry out his threat. To pull her close, capture that luscious mouth and kiss her into submission. Then he saw the apprehension in her gaze and something more, a fear that was not warranted by the threat of a mere kiss. She was terrified.

What the devil were you thinking of, Charles Russ-ington? Are you such a cockscomb that you think no woman should be able to resist your charms?

He took his hands from her shoulders and stepped away. This was no way to treat a lady.

'You are right,' he said. 'I beg your pardon for teasing you.'

The look of terror had lasted only a moment and it was now replaced by anger. She glared at him.

'I would expect nothing else from a libertine.' Her voice was shaking with fury as she put up her hands to straighten the little puff sleeves of her gown that had been flattened by his grip. 'Your disgraceful behaviour proves that the reports I have heard about you do not lie. The sooner you and your...your *friends* remove from Compton Parva, the better!'

With a toss of her head she turned and hurried away. Russ watched her go, but he made no move to follow her back into the laughing, chattering throng that was slowly making its way into the dining room. He knew he had been wrong to tease her, but she had made him angry and he had forgotten himself. His lip curled in scorn. The great Beau Russington, famed for his sangfroid, his charming manners, had allowed his temper to get the better of him.

He raked his fingers through his hair. Damn the woman, she should not have this effect on him. Why, she was not even his type—too small and dark for one thing, and a sanctimonious reformer to boot. No, his original instinct had been right. *Leave well alone!*

Two days of rain followed the dinner at Newlands and Molly was relieved that the bad weather deterred visitors.

She thought—hoped—no one had seen that brief interchange with Beau Russington, but had no wish to discuss the evening with anyone, not yet, when she was still so unsettled.

On Thursday she took the carriage to make her belated visit to Prospect House, thankful for the inclement weather. The house and its farm were situated on the opposite side of the valley to Newlands and she knew Sir Gerald and his guests rode out frequently beyond the bounds of the park, but it was much less likely that they would do so in bad weather.

Prospect House was a stone-built dwelling standing tall and square on the landscape. It had belonged to a gentleman farmer who had built himself this house in a style more fitted to his dignity and it now boasted large sash windows and a pedimented front door. The new dwelling had been built at a suitable distance from the old farmhouse and separated from it by the stables and a kitchen garden.

Prospect House was now home to ten women of various ages and stations in life. They tended the house and garden with the help of one manservant, who also looked after the farm. It had taken Molly years of hard work and determination to turn Prospect House into a successful and self-sufficient refuge, and as the carriage turned in through the gates she felt an immense pride in the achievement.

The door was opened to her by Moses, the only male servant, whose size and somewhat bovine countenance belied a sharp intelligence. He had worked at Prospect House all his life, and when Molly bought the property, she had kept him on, recognising that his knowledge of farming would be invaluable. This had engendered

Moses with a fierce loyalty to his employer and made him protective of the house and its female residents. Molly greeted him cheerfully and made her way to the office at the back of the house. The pretty blonde poring over the accounts glanced up as the door opened and flew out of her chair to hug her.

'Molly! I did not expect you to come here in all this rain.'

'But as patron I must call at least once a week to see how you go on, although I was certainly not going to *walk* here.' Molly laughed and returned the hug. 'But, Fleur, I am interrupting you.'

'Not a bit of it, I had just finished totting up the money we took at market yesterday and I am pleased to say we sold everything, which was a surprise, given the heavy rain.'

'I am glad of it and only sorry I did not come over to help you—'

'There is no need to apologise, Molly, we tell you time and again that we can manage.' Fleur took her arm. 'Come along into the drawing room, and we will take tea.'

Molly accompanied Fleur out of the office, reflecting that the happy young woman at her side was a far cry from the frightened girl she had taken in all those years ago. Fleur Dellafield was a childhood friend of Molly's. She had grown up to be a beauty, but when her widowed mother had married again, life had become a nightmare. She had been thrown out of her home after thwarting her stepfather's attempts to ravish her. Molly had found her, destitute and starving, and brought her to the newly opened Prospect House. She had settled in well and shown such an aptitude for organisation that Molly had been delighted to make her housekeeper. She had protested at the time that Fleur was too pretty to languish for long at Prospect House, but Fleur had been adamant.

'I met plenty of gentlemen at my come-out in Bath,' she had told Molly. 'I found none of them more than passable, and after what happened with my step-papa, I have no wish to meet any more. No, Molly, I want only a comfortable home and to be *needed*.'

So Molly had installed Fleur as housekeeper and seen Prospect House flourish. Now, as they entered the drawing room and she saw the welcoming bowl of fresh flowers on the highly polished drum table, Fleur's words came back to her.

'I like to come here, Fleur,' she told her friend. 'I like to feel I am needed.'

'Then do, please, call as often as you like, for there is always something to be done!'

Fleur tugged at the bell pull and a few moments later a maid in a snowy cap and apron entered. Molly smiled at her.

'Good day to you, Daisy. How are you?'

'Very well, ma'am. Thank you kindly.' The maid dropped a curtsy, her cheerful face creasing into smiles. 'Between Miss Fleur and Miss Nancy, I am learning how to run a household and to cook.'

'And your son?'

'Ah, Billy is doing very well, thank you, ma'am, although he don't much like his lessons.' She gave a sigh. 'Twice this week I left him practising his letters and he escaped through the window.'

'He does prefer to be working out of doors,' remarked

Fleur. 'He is a great asset in the garden and Moses says he has an ability with animals.'

'Perhaps we should let him help out on the farm more,' suggested Molly. 'Although I think it imperative that he learns to read and write, at least enough to get by.'

'Then I shall tell him that if he works for an hour at his lessons every morning he may spend the rest of the day helping Moses,' said Fleur. 'Will that be acceptable to you, Daisy?'

'Very kind of you, Miss Fleur, and more than we have a right to expect.'

'Nonsense, you have worked very hard since you have been here and we would like to help you and Billy to find a home of your own. Now, perhaps you would be kind enough to fetch tea for Mrs Morgan and myself, if you please.' Fleur waited until the door had closed behind the maid before sighing. 'I wonder if we did the right thing, taking in Daisy Matthews and her son. We have none of us any experience of ten-year-old boys.'

'But where else would they have gone? Daisy's employer had thrown them on to the streets upon discovering that Billy was her natural child. And Edwin tells me the vicar who applied to us had tried to find them another home, with no success at all.'

'It is such a cruel world,' said Fleur, her kind face troubled, but then she brightened. 'However, Daisy is quick to learn, and I am already looking about for a suitable position, although I fear Billy may not be able to go with her. However, if all else fails he can stay here and help Moses.'

'A very sensible idea,' agreed Molly, 'but we can make no decisions until we have procured a position for Daisy. Which reminds me, I was in Hebden's on Friday last and saw Clara at work. You will be pleased to learn that Miss Hebden is delighted with her, so I think we may write that down as another success. Now, you must tell me how everyone else goes on here.'

Molly listened carefully while Fleur made her report. It did not take long and they had finished their business by the time Daisy returned with the tea tray.

'Which means we may now please ourselves what we talk of,' declared Fleur, preparing tea for her guest. 'And I very much want to know what you think of our new neighbour at Newlands.' Molly did not reply immediately and Fleur shook her head at her. 'You cannot think that we would remain in ignorance,' she said, handing her friend a cup of tea. 'Everyone at the market this week was talking of Sir Gerald and his friends. I would like to know your opinion.'

Molly made a cautious reply. 'They are all extremely fashionable.'

'They spend a great deal of time in London I believe,' remarked Fleur. 'Six men, I understand. Are all of them libertines, do you think?'

Molly was surprised into a laugh. 'Good heavens, Fleur, that is very blunt. Why should you think that?'

'Nancy told me.'

'Ah, of course.'

Molly sipped her tea and considered the woman who was now cook at Prospect House. Nancy, or more correctly Lady Ann, was the youngest daughter of an eccentric and impoverished earl who had tried to force her into a marriage with a man old enough to be her grandfather. Molly should have remembered that she was still in contact with one of her sisters, a terrific gossip, who kept her well informed of the latest London scandals.

'So, Molly, tell me what you think,' Fleur prompted her.

'Edwin thinks them all very gentlemen-like.'

'But you, Molly. What do you think?'

With her friend's anxious blue gaze upon her, Molly could not lie.

'I suspect one or two of them might have a...a roving eye.' She saw Fleur's look of alarm and hurried on. 'They know of Prospect House, of course, but there is no reason to think they will call here. I gave them to understand you were very well protected.'

'That is all very well, but we cannot remain within the bounds of Prospect House for ever!'

'No, indeed, and I see no need for you to do so, as long as you never go out unaccompanied. These are gentlemen, Fleur, they would not force their attentions upon an unwilling female.'

'Would they not?' Fleur gave a little shudder. 'That has not been our experience.'

Molly was silent, remembering the loud voices, the blows, the pain. Fighting back the memories, she said quietly, 'The horrors we experienced happened in private, at the hands of men with power over us.'

'But Nancy says Sir Gerald and his friends are known for their wildness.' Fleur turned an anguished gaze upon Molly. 'We both grew up in one small market town in Hertfordshire and now live in just such another. You were married at eighteen and I have never been further afield than Bath. What do we really know of rakes and libertines and the fashionable world?'

Molly sighed. Fleur was right and it was useless to ask Edwin for advice. He insisted upon seeing the best in everyone. Unlike their father, she thought bitterly. He had only seen the worst in everyone, especially his youngest daughter. The truth, she suspected, was often somewhere in between. She put down her cup.

'Come along,' she said, rising. 'Let us go and talk to Nancy. She knows far more about these things than we do.'

They made their way down to the kitchen where they found the earl's daughter beside the kitchen table, sitting in a most unladylike pose with her feet up on a chair. Nancy was large, loud and brash, but she had a heart of gold and a surprising flair for cooking. She had explained to Molly that she had learned the skill from her father's French chef, a tyrant with a soft spot for a child so ignored and unloved by her parents that she might disappear to the kitchens for days on end without question. Now Nancy ruled the kitchen at Prospect House and was something of a mother hen to all the residents. She greeted Molly and Fleur cheerfully and invited them to join her at the table.

'I don't suppose you want more tea,' she said, swinging her feet to the floor and turning to face them.

'No, thank you,' said Fleur, disposing herself gracefully on a chair. 'We have come to talk to you about the people at Newlands.'

'More especially the gentlemen,' added Molly, taking a seat beside Fleur. '*My* sister has already hinted that they were…er…gentlemen of fashion, and I understand yours has sent you similar information.'

'Yes, only in far less mealy-mouthed terms,' said Nancy, not mincing matters. 'Sir Gerald Kilburn's set are infamous in town. Young men with too much time and too much money and spend both on flirtations, affairs and outrageous wagers.'

'Oh, heavens,' murmured Fleur.

'But Newlands is a hunting lodge,' said Molly. 'Sir Gerald told Edwin they are here for the sport.'

Nancy gave her a pitying look. 'Sir Gerald's party will be made up of rakes and Corinthians. They regard pursuing women as *sport*. But you have met them, Molly. What is your opinion?'

'They all appeared very amiable. Two of the gentlemen are accompanied by their wives, and Lord and Lady Claydon have also brought their daughters. Miss Kilburn acts as hostess for her brother and she has brought a companion, to give her countenance.'

Nancy shrugged. 'Perhaps we are misinformed, then. But rich, idle men are always a threat to women. Who else is in the party, what single gentlemen are there?'

'Apart from Sir Gerald?' Molly tried to sound unconcerned. 'There is Mr Flemington, Sir Joseph Aikers and Mr Russington.'

'Kilburn's closest cronies,' exclaimed Nancy. 'I remember them all from when I was in town. Flemington and Aikers were notorious womanisers even then, at least my father would not countenance them making me an offer, but that may have been more to do with their station than their reputation. He was determined that I should marry an earl at the very least.'

'And Mr Russington?' asked Molly, tracing a crack in the table with her finger.

'Ah, yes, the beau.' Nancy rested her chin on one hand, a smile on her lips and a faraway look in her eyes. 'He is more notorious than all the rest. I remember him very well. He and Kilburn are of an age, I believe. They must be, what, eight-and-twenty now.'

'The same age as yourself,' put in Fleur.

Nancy nodded. 'They came to town after my come-out. My sister tells me Russington is a friend of Brummell, although unlike Mr Brummell, he is also a noted sportsman. A Corinthian rather than a dandy.' She cast a mischievous glance across the table. 'We danced once, at Almack's, you know, I remember it because he is taller than I! And so handsome. All the ladies were in love with him, but he soon earned a reputation for being dangerous, because any woman who threw her cap at him was likely to be indulged in a wild flirtation. Wise mamas keep their daughters out of his way now, but it may be that Kilburn has Russington in mind for his sister. I believe he is exceedingly wealthy.'

Fleur shuddered. 'He sounds exceedingly dangerous, if he is so very attractive. What did you think of him, Molly?'

'I?' Molly gave a little laugh, playing for time. 'I had very little to do with him.'

'Was he one of those gentlemen you said had a *roving eye*?'

She did not know how to answer Fleur's question. She had not noticed the beau's dark eyes on anyone but herself and then with devastating effect. Just the thought of it sent a shiver along her spine.

'I am not sure the beau needs one,' said Nancy, meditatively. 'From what my sister says he does not need to look about him. Women fall over themselves to gain his attention.'

Molly gave a little huff of despair. 'Oh, how I wish Sir Gerald had never come to Newlands!'

'Too late for that now,' said Nancy, 'they are here and we must deal with it. We must make sure the others are aware of the dangers.' She began to list the girls on her fingers. 'Daisy is hopefully too old to attract the attention of these gentlemen. She has Billy to look out for, too, which should make her wary. Elizabeth and Bridget are young and pretty, but as the daughters of gentlemen they already know what a dangerous combination that is and will be anxious to avoid repeating the mistakes that led to their being cast out of their homes. Marjorie is near her time now and her condition should make her safe from any unwelcome advances. That only leaves the two housemaids. They are still young and silly enough for anything. I shall keep an eye on them and make sure they do not step outside without Moses or one of us to accompany them. I shall also ask Moses to inspect that all the doors and windows are fastened at night.'

'Perhaps we should get a dog.' Fleur suggested.

'That is a good idea.' Nancy agreed. 'I shall tell Moses we must have a guard dog, although knowing his soft heart he is likely to bring back the first mongrel he sees that needs a home. In the meantime we must all be vigilant to keep the girls safe from predatory men.' She sat up straight, folding her arms across her ample bosom. 'As for you, Fleur, you must *always* take one of the girls with you when you go to market, for with your golden hair and blue eyes, you are quite the prettiest of us all and the most likely to attract the attentions of a rake, especially such a noted connoisseur of women as Beau Russington.'

Molly was aware of a little stab of something that felt very much like jealousy and quickly pushed it aside. She did not want the beau's attentions, so why should she be jealous? It made no sense at all.

'You flatter me, Nancy,' said Fleur, blushing. 'And I really do not wish to attract any man's attention, or unwelcome advances.'

'They will not harm you, Fleur,' said Molly, catching her friend's hand. She frowned and added grimly, 'I shall not allow them to harm anyone here.'

Chapter Three

Despite her brave words, Molly came away from Prospect House knowing there was very little she could do to protect its residents. It was unlikely that any of the gentlemen would actually come to the house, but it was very possible they would see the girls when they went into town to fetch supplies or to sell produce on market day. However, when she mentioned her worries to Edwin, he was sanguine.

'I believe your charges have little to fear from the gentlemen at Newlands,' he told her. 'There is enough sport to be had to keep them hunting, shooting or fishing for weeks, and apart from the assemblies there is little to bring them into Compton Parva. Why, it is quite possible they will never set eyes upon your girls, as you call them!'

With that Molly had to be satisfied. Since Edwin had no wife to help him, she took it upon herself to visit the sick and distribute clothes and food to the poor of the parish. This, combined with her role on various committees, including that of Prospect House, kept her busy most days and she was able to put her worries about the Newlands party out of her head until the following Sunday.

* * *

When she accompanied Edwin to the morning service at All Souls, Sir Gerald and some of his guests were already occupying the box pew allocated to Newlands. She spotted Mr Russington's tall figure immediately, but Sir Joseph and Mr Flemington were absent.

The residents of Prospect House were amongst the last to arrive. They were all most soberly dressed, with the ladies heavily veiled, and they were accompanied by Moses and little Billy Matthews, scrubbed and dressed in his best coat. The whole party slipped into their usual seats at the back of the church and, although they quickly settled down for the service, Molly found it difficult to concentrate. She rebuked herself for her inattention and told herself there was no reason at all why Sir Gerald or his friends should have occasion to look back at Fleur and her companions, but she did not relax until the service was over and the Newlands party had gone out without sparing a glance for the rest of the congregation. She hovered at the church door and watched them exchange a few words with Edwin and only when they had climbed into their carriages and driven away did she turn her attention to her friends.

'Everything is well at the house,' Nancy told her, in answer to Molly's anxious enquiry. 'We have had no unwelcome visitors and Moses has found us a guard dog.' Her eyes twinkled. 'He brought home the prettiest little terrier! Not a mastiff, I know, but he has a good bark, which is what we need, and Moses tells me he will be useful for keeping down the rats in the barn.'

Molly laughed. 'He sounds perfect.'

'Why not come back with us and you can see him for yourself?'

'I would love to do so, but I am helping with the Sunday school today, and tomorrow I have promised to call on Mrs Calder at Raikes Farm. Edwin tells me she has not been well and asked me to visit her. No matter, I shall see this new addition on Tuesday, when I come over to help you prepare everything for the market. If the weather is as fine as today, I shall walk.'

'And you will bring your maid?'

'Of course. I intend that Cissy shall go everywhere with me from now on, whenever her other duties allow. Having recommended that you must all be circumspect, I must lead by example!'

Alas for such good intentions. On Monday, when Molly went below stairs to collect the basket of food for Raikes Farm, she found that the upper housemaid, who also acted as her dresser, was in tears, having received word that her mother was very ill.

'Then you must go to her immediately,' Molly decided, quickly revising her plans. 'Gibson shall take you in the gig. He is waiting for me at the door now.'

'Ah, no, ma'am, I couldn't possibly,' sniffed Cissy, mopping her eyes with her apron. 'You and the master is too good to me already, taking me in, and me without a reputation—'

'Nonsense,' said Molly briskly, handing Cissy her own handkerchief and shepherding her up the stairs. 'Reverend Frayne and I know very well that you were too young to be blamed for what happened to you. But I hope you know better now than to walk out into the gloaming alone with a young man.'

'Aye, I do, ma'am, and it won't ever happen again, I

promise you. I am much wiser now.' She managed a watery smile. 'And the baby is doing very well.'

'You have no regrets about sending him to live with your sister and her family?'

'Oh, no, because I wants to become a lady's maid and I can't do that if I have my baby with me, so I was very happy when my sister offered to have him. No, he is very happy where he is. They quite dotes on him.'

'I am very glad of it,' said Molly, 'and you are proving to be a very good dresser, Cissy. As soon as we can find another housemaid to take your place, I shall promote you to my personal maid.'

She cut short Cissy's effusive thanks and instructed her to run up and fetch her cloak. 'I will tell Gibson there is a change of plans and he is to take you to your mother. And you must remain with her at least until tomorrow. Promise me.'

'Very well, miss, if you say so, but what will you do about delivering your basket?'

'Mr Frayne shall drive me to Raikes Farm in the carriage.'

Having seen the maid off, Molly went in search of her brother, only for him to tell her that he had made other arrangements.

'My old college professor is on his way to Ripon and is breaking his journey at Compton Magna tonight,' he said. 'He has invited me to join him at the White Hart for dinner.'

His face clouded when she explained she had sent her maid off in the gig and he immediately suggested he could cancel his engagement, but Molly stopped him.

'No, indeed you must not do that,' she said, smiling. 'You will be passing the turning to Raikes Farm on your way, so if you set off a little earlier you can drop me off there. Now, please do not argue, Edwin. It promises to be a fine afternoon for me to walk back. I do not intend to stay above an hour and it is barely two miles from here cross-country, so I shall be back in good time for dinner.'

The arrangements having been agreed, Molly collected her basket and set off with her brother in the carriage. The inclement weather had not let up for the past week, but at last the skies had lifted and although the sun only showed through intermittently, there was every promise of a fine afternoon and evening.

Molly's visit to Raikes Farm was much appreciated. Mrs Calder was the wife of a hard-working farmer and the young family had been struggling to cope while their mother was ill. They fell with delight upon the basket of food, with its bread and pies and cakes. Molly soon ascertained that Mrs Calder was on the mend and after spending an hour talking to them all, she set off to follow the footpath back to Compton Parva.

The sun was peeping in and out of the clouds, but there had been so much rain over the past week that the footpaths were thick with mud. Molly did not mind. She had taken the precaution of wearing serviceable boots and she would be able to change as soon as she reached the vicarage, so she strode away from the farm, determined to enjoy her walk.

The highway to Compton Parva followed a circuitous route, but the footpath was much more direct, ascending between enclosed pastures until it joined the stony cart track running along the ridge. A solidly built drystone wall ran along one side of the track and separated the farmland from the moors that stretched upwards to the skyline. To avoid the thick, glutinous mud that covered large sections of the lane which had not yet dried out, she walked along a narrow grassy strip at the side.

The view from here was unrivalled. Looking across the valley and the road that ran through Compton Parva, she could see the lane leading to Prospect House, while directly ahead was the dark green mass of Newlands's Home Wood. At this distance she would see immediately if anyone was riding out from the Park, but all was quiet and she knew she would shortly be cutting back down towards the town, so she had little fear of meeting anyone while she was alone and unprotected. She gave a little sigh. Before Sir Gerald and his rakish friends had appeared, she had never worried about walking unaccompanied in the town or in the surrounding countryside. Now she was aware of the constant danger.

As if summoned by her thoughts, her eye caught a movement on the lane ahead of her. Someone was approaching from the opposite direction. The gentle curve of the lane meant she could not see the figure clearly above the walls, but she could make out it was a man, carrying a long staff. Most likely a farmer, checking his stock. A shepherd, perhaps, looking for a stray sheep.

Distracted by trying to peer into the distance, Molly missed her footing. Her boot slipped off the uneven grassy bank, and she lost her balance. Her left foot flew forward, but landed awkwardly amongst the stones of the rutted lane and she gasped as the impact jarred her ankle. The next moment she found herself measuring her length along the ground.

Bruised and shaken, Molly pushed herself up, feeling very cross. Her skirts and spencer were filthy and she suspected that her face, too, had not escaped the mud. As she tried to stand a sharp pain shot through her ankle and she fell back. She took a couple of moments to compose herself, then struggled to her feet, but one tentative step was enough to tell her that the pain was too severe for her to walk unaided.

She hobbled to the wall and leaned against it, considering what she should do. The farmer, or shepherd, had by this time reached the junction and turned to follow the footpath down to the road in the valley bottom. A glance each way along the cart track showed her that it was deserted. She might sit there all day in the hope of someone driving past. Molly bit her lip, knowing she had no choice but to shout out and ask the only other person within sight for help.

She called, then called again. The man stopped and she waved to attract his attention. He started back up the path, but it was only as he turned into the lane that Molly realised he was no farmer, despite the long staff he held. As he strode along the lane towards her she could see the embroidered waistcoat and the tight-fitting buckskin breeches he wore beneath his country jacket and his mud-spattered top boots had the cut and fit only obtained from a first-class bootmaker. With a sinking heart she raised her eyes and looked into the lean, handsome face of Beau Russington.

It took Russ a few moments to recognise the bedraggled figure leaning against the wall and he was aware of a most reprehensible feeling of satisfaction. So the widow who had so plainly shown her dislike of him, who had been so contemptuous, now needed his help.

'Mrs Morgan.' He touched his hat, all politeness. 'How may I be of assistance?'

Her cheeks were flushed with a mixture of annoyance and chagrin.

'I think I have sprained my ankle.'

'Indeed?' He could not help it, his lips twitched. 'Possibly fate is paying you back for your using the excuse the other night. I should be flattered that you were prepared to go to such lengths to avoid dancing with me.'

She bit her lip and glared at him, but he noticed she did not deny it.

She said icily, 'I thought, perhaps, if you would lend me your staff, I could manage to walk home.'

'Don't be ridiculous.' He rested the staff against the wall and came closer.

'Wh-what are you going to do?' She shrank back, putting her hand out as if to hold him off.

'I am going to carry you.'

'B-but you can't.' She looked horrified.

'Oh, I think I can. You do not look to be too heavy.'

'But I am covered in mud. Your clothes—'

'The mud will certainly test my valet's skills,' he agreed, scooping her up into his arms. 'However, we must risk that.'

'And it is too far,' she protested.

'Flack is waiting with my curricle at the bottom of the lane.'

'What about your staff?' she objected as he began to walk.

'I will send someone back to collect it later.' He settled her more comfortably in his arms and set off towards the footpath. They had only gone a few yards when he stopped and looked down at her. 'I think you will be more comfortable if you allow yourself to lean against me,' he said. 'And you might want to put your arm about my neck to support yourself.'

Her cheeks flamed, but one dainty hand crept around his collar.

He grinned. 'That's better.'

She did not reply, neither did she look at him, but Russ did not mind. He was enjoying himself, bringing the haughty widow down a peg or two. That might be an ignoble and unchivalrous sentiment but it was damned satisfying. After all, he was only human.

The curricle was soon in sight and Flack showed no surprise when Russ came up with a woman in his arms, merely watching in wooden-faced silence as Russ deposited his burden on the curricle seat. She winced as her foot touched the boards and he frowned.

'We had best ascertain the damage to your ankle. May I?'

She did not protest, but pulled her skirts aside to reveal her footwear. As Russ untied the laces, he reflected wryly that he was more in the habit of removing satin slippers than serviceable half-boots, but such thoughts disappeared when he looked at her ankle.

'I do not think you have broken any bones, but it is already swelling,' he muttered. 'We must get some ice upon that as soon as we can.'

Molly was beginning to feel a little faint, and she clung on to the side of the curricle as the beau jumped up beside her and they set off at a smart pace along the road, the groom swinging himself up into the rumble seat as the vehicle shot past him. Her ankle was throbbing most painfully and she was content to sit quietly as the curricle bowled along, but when it slowed and turned off the main road she sat up, saying urgently, 'This is not the way to Compton Parva.'

'No. I am taking you to Newlands.' He glanced at her. 'Do you have any ice at the vicarage?'

'No, but—'

'We need to reduce the swelling, and thus the pain, as quickly as possible. Newlands has an ice house. Not only that, but it is considerably closer.'

Molly was silenced. She knew she was not thinking clearly and all she wanted was for the pain in her ankle to be over. She gave a sigh of relief as they reached the door of Newlands and made no demur when her escort lifted her into his arms to carry her indoors. Miss Kilburn was crossing the hall as they entered and as soon as she realised the situation, she sent a footman running to fetch some ice before instructing Mr Russington to follow her upstairs to one of the guest rooms. However, when she directed that Mrs Morgan should be laid upon the daybed by the window, Molly was roused to protest.

'No, no, my clothes are far too dirty.'

She was dismayed to find her voice broke upon the words, but no one remarked upon it. Agnes pulled a cashmere shawl from the back of a chair and spread it over the couch.

'No one will worry about a little dirt, ma'am, but you shall lie on this, if it makes you feel better. Oh, goodness, you are looking very pale.'

'Shock,' said the beau, removing Molly's gloves and beginning to chafe her hands. 'Perhaps we might find a little brandy.'

'Yes, yes, of course.'

Agnes hurried away and Molly thought she should

protest at being left alone with a gentleman who was no relation, but she did not have the energy to complain and the way he was rubbing warmth into her hands was so comforting she did not want him to stop, so she lay back against the end of the daybed, watching him from half-closed eyes, thinking idly that it was quite understandable if ladies threw themselves at such a man. He was very attractive, in a dark and rather disturbing sort of way...

Molly knew she must have drifted off to sleep, because the next moment, she felt a glass pressed gently against her lips and heard a deep, soothing voice urging her to drink. She became conscious of being cradled against a man's chest. The smooth softness of a waistcoat was against her cheek and when she breathed in her senses were filled with a heady mix of citrus and spices and something very male. There was something familiar about that scent, but at the moment she could not place it.

Obediently she took a sip from the glass and coughed as the sharp and fiery liquid burned her throat. She struggled to sit up and immediately the strong arm around her shoulders released her. For the first time she saw Agnes Kilburn standing on the other side of the daybed, looking down at her with concern. Molly was relieved at her presence and even more so when she looked back to Mr Russington, kneeling beside the daybed, and realised he was in his shirtsleeves.

His eyes were full of amusement, but also understanding.

'I beg your pardon for removing my coat, ma'am, but it had picked up rather a lot of mud from your clothes, and I did not want to rub that into you.'

Molly murmured a faint thank you and looked past him as a footman hurried in.

'Ah, the ice at last,' exclaimed Agnes. She removed the bucket of ice and towels from the servant and brought them over. 'Mr Russington, will you see to it, if you please? You have much more experience in these matters than I. That is, if you do not object, ma'am?'

'I think Mrs Morgan might prefer you to remove her stocking,' the beau remarked. He smiled at Molly and held out the glass to her. 'You might like to finish drinking your brandy, for it may hurt a little.'

Molly was relieved that he turned away while Agnes began to untie the garter and roll the stocking down over her damaged ankle. Cautiously she sipped at the brandy. He was right, it did hurt, but she was also mightily embarrassed. She had never liked to be the centre of attention and now she sought for something to distract the gentleman from what was going on behind his back.

'It was fortunate for me that you were walking on the moor, Mr Russington,' she said at last. 'Although I am curious as to why you had left your curricle at that particular spot.'

'I have formed the habit of walking the moors every day before breakfast. There are golden plover up there, did you know? I have been watching them. It was not possible to make my usual walk this morning, so I stopped off on my way back to Newlands. No doubt you thought my only interest in birds was in killing them. For sport.'

She flushed guiltily. 'I did not think that at all, sir.'

'There, it is done,' said Agnes.

Molly was relieved that the soft words brought an end to their interchange. The beau turned his attention back to her ankle and she clasped her hands about her glass, biting her lip as he used towels to pack the ice around her foot.

'It is exceedingly swollen. Are you sure it is not broken?' Agnes asked him.

'I inspected it earlier, when I first came upon Mrs Morgan, and I am sure it is merely sprained,' he replied. 'However, if you would feel happier we will send for the doctor.'

Molly quickly disclaimed. 'I am sure I shall be well again very soon,' she assured them. 'Although I may have to trouble you for the use of your carriage, Miss Kilburn, to take me home. My brother has gone off to Compton Magna and will not be back until very late, if at all tonight.'

'Then it would be best for you to stay here,' said Agnes. 'We will send a carriage to the vicarage to tell them what has happened and to bring your maid— You look distressed, Mrs Morgan, have I said something amiss?'

'No, no, it is merely that I gave my maid the evening off.'

'Then on no account can you go home,' declared Agnes. 'You must stay here, where we can look after you.'

In vain did Molly protest. Shy, quiet little Agnes Kilburn proved immovable.

'There is no time to fetch your clean clothes before dinner, so you shall dine here,' she told Molly. 'And afterwards, if you feel well enough, my maid shall help you change and you can be brought downstairs to rest on a sofa in the drawing room. I know everyone will want to assure themselves that you are recovering well and the evening will pass much more quickly in company, do you not agree?'

Molly did not have the strength to withstand such common sense. With Edwin out for the evening, and Cissy looking after her mother, she knew there was no argument she could put forward that would not sound ungrateful.

'Very well, then. Thank you, Miss Kilburn. You are too kind.'

'Call me Agnes, please,' said her hostess, smiling. 'And, if I may, I shall call you Molly.'

'Then it is settled,' said Mr Russington, picking up his coat. 'We will leave you in peace now, ma'am, and I shall return after dinner to carry you downstairs.'

'I am sure that will not be necessary, sir,' said Molly swiftly. 'I might be able to walk by then, or, if not, one of the servants—'

'Oh, but I insist,' he interrupted her, his eyes teasing her in a way that made Molly want to hit him. 'As your rescuer, I think I have earned that privilege.'

He followed Agnes out of the room and Molly was alone. She felt exhausted, and not a little homesick, despite the undoubted comfort of her surroundings. She glanced at the small table beside her with its glass of water, the vinaigrette bottle in case she should feel faint and the little hand bell that Agnes had urged her to ring, should she require anything at all.

She closed her eyes, allowing her thoughts to drift. Nothing could have exceeded Agnes Kilburn's kindness, but Molly could not help thinking that she was in the lion's den. The people in this house stood for everything she detested: wealth, privilege and a lack of moral restraint that she could not condone. But even as the idea formed she rebuked herself for being unfair. Sir Gerald had not brought a party of single gentlemen and their inamoratas to Newlands. The ladies were all perfectly respectable and if any of the gentlemen had a reputation for loose living, it was up to the mothers of Compton Parva to protect their offspring from these dangerous individuals.

Molly stirred restlessly. It was one of those dangerous individuals, Beau Russington, who had come to her aid that afternoon and she had come to no harm. Now that she was alone with time to reflect, she realised that what disturbed her most was that when the beau had lifted her into his arms—as if she weighed nothing!—she had not felt at all afraid. In fact, she admitted now with great reluctance, she had never felt safer. Not that *that* made the man a jot less dangerous!

'So, Russington, you have been rescuing damsels in distress.' Joseph Aikers helped himself to more brandy before pushing the decanter towards his neighbour.

'I could hardly leave her sitting in the lane,' said Russ, refilling his own glass. 'It was fortunate that my curricle was nearby.'

He kept his tone neutral. The ladies had withdrawn and Gerald had dismissed the servants, so there were only the gentlemen left in the dining room and Russ knew from experience that at this stage of the evening the conversation could easily degenerate, and somehow he did not want Molly Morgan to become the object of any lewd discussion.

Flemington gave a coarse laugh. 'I'd wager the beau would have preferred to find a pretty young gel languishing at his feet. I saw a few that I wouldn't mind trying at the assembly last week.'

Gerald met Russ's eyes as he took the decanter from him.

'Seducing innocents has never been the beau's way,' he remarked. 'He's like me—too afraid of the parson's mousetrap.'

There was general laughter at that, but it was Lord Claydon who answered.

'I know you young bucks think yourselves awake upon every suit,' he said, shaking his head in mock severity. 'But let me warn you that one day you will find yourselves in the suds and I hope when you finally make a fool of yourself that you have the sense to choose a good woman.'

Gerald chuckled. 'I am not sure a *good* woman would suit the beau.' He grinned at Russ. 'If I thought that, I'd have suggested m'sister as a match for you, my friend, but your roving ways would break her heart and I would have to call you out.'

'Then it is fortunate for everyone concerned that Agnes and I regard each other as siblings,' Russ told him. 'You may be assured, though, that when I do eventually decide upon a wife, my…er…*roving ways*, as you call them, will be at an end.'

A ripple of laughter went around the table and cries of disbelief.

'Is that why you have remained single for so long, Russington?' called Sykes from the far end of the table. 'It can't be for lack of opportunity. Your lineage is impeccable and your fortune is so vast you have the pick of the *ton*.'

'Aye, you lucky dog,' cried Flemington, the suspicion

of a sneer in his voice. 'You can have any woman you want for a bride.'

'But I do not want any woman,' drawled Russ. He lifted his glass and stared at it, as if inspecting the contents. 'If, *if* I marry, it must be based on mutual affection and respect. A marriage of true minds, as Shakespeare calls it. Nothing less will do.'

'Ha, you are searching for a mare's nest,' declared Sykes, reaching for the decanter. 'Believe me, it doesn't exist. You'd be advised to give up such daydreams and find yourself a good-natured woman who will make you a comfortable wife.' He gave a shrug. 'Mrs Sykes wasn't my first choice, nor was I hers, but we have rubbed along very nicely for the past twenty years, which is more than many couples can boast.'

'Sound advice,' agreed Claydon. 'Best to leave love well out of it, my boy. Look what happened to your own father, hardly out of mourning before a beautiful woman got her claws into him. Never seen a man so besotted. Pity it wasn't mutual. She almost ruined him.'

'Quite.' Russ's fingers tightened about his glass as the familiar pain sliced into him, but he said lightly, 'I want a wife who will love me for myself, not my fortune.'

'And if you don't find her?' asked Gerald.

'Why, then, I shall continue to enjoy my bachelor life.' He drained his glass. 'Which reminds of a promise I have made. If you will excuse me, gentlemen, I offered to carry Mrs Morgan down to the drawing room.'

'Oh, ho!' cried Sir Joseph. 'Stealing the march on us with the widow, are you, Russington? I wouldn't have thought she was your type.'

Russ paused at the door to look back, unsmiling.

'She is not at all my type, as you so crudely put it,

but she is safer in my arms than anyone else's, because she has made no secret of the fact that she detests me.'

Mindful of propriety, he went to find Agnes and ask her to accompany him when he collected the invalid, but when he entered the drawing room, he found that Molly was already downstairs and resting on a sofa. He had to admit she was looking very much better, dressed in an evening gown of lavender silk trimmed with silver lace and with a fine silk shawl thrown over her feet.

'So, you are here before me, Mrs Morgan.'

He was surprised that he should feel so unaccountably annoyed, as if he had been denied some treat. It was a ridiculous idea and it exacerbated his temper even further, but he forced himself to speak cheerfully. Her bright smile was equally false.

'Yes. I managed to walk downstairs, with help from Miss Kilburn.'

His brows snapped together. 'That was rather reckless of you, ma'am.'

'I did not wish to inconvenience anyone.'

'It will be more of an inconvenience if you have further strained your ankle! If you will permit me to check?'

'No!' Her hands came down quickly on the shawl. 'I assure you there is no need. I am quite well.'

'Fie, Mr Russington,' cried Mrs Sykes, coming up, 'Would you be so indecorous as to expose a lady's ankle in public? Come away, sir. Mrs Morgan assures us she is quite well and needs only to rest, is that not so, my dear?'

'Yes, it is.'

She was looking up at him, her grey eyes defiant, and Russ hesitated. He wanted to argue, but at that moment the rest of the gentlemen spilled noisily into the room.

'I pray you will go away, sir, and not draw any further attention to me.'

Her words were quiet but heartfelt, and he moved away. Gerald and the others descended upon the widow to enquire after her health. Mrs Sykes went to sit near Molly, and Russ was drawn into a discussion about the following day's shoot, but all the time part of his mind was racing.

Had she walked downstairs rather than have him carry her? He could hardly believe it. He had known women to throw themselves at his feet, feigning an injury to gain his attention, but never one so determined to reject his help. Ungrateful creature!

He turned to glare across at the petite figure reclining on the sofa. As if he could have designs upon such a thin drab of a woman. He recalled that moment under the stairs, when he had been tempted to kiss her, but that meant nothing. It was merely the result of too much wine. True, there was something appealing about her elfin face, but her mouth was far too wide for beauty and those unruly curls would not stay beneath her bonnet. They had tickled his chin as he had carried her down the hill this afternoon. Damned annoying that had been, too!

And her eyes, a cool grey with an unsettlingly direct gaze. What man would want that? He preferred cerulean blue, or deep chocolate brown. Eyes that a man might drown in. He tried to name one of the beauties of his acquaintance, as evidence of this assertion, but could think of none. Russ shook his head. What did it matter? He dragged his mind back to the conversation, agreed that if the weather was fine tomorrow, they might enjoy an afternoon's shooting, and kept his back resolutely turned towards the sofa for the rest of the evening.

* * *

However, when the tea tray was brought in, he could not refuse Agnes's request that he carry a cup across to Mrs Morgan. She watched him approach, such a wary look upon her countenance that his bad mood evaporated and he could not help the smile tugging at his mouth.

'Am I that alarming, Mrs Morgan?'

She relaxed a little. 'No, of course not, but I feared you might be going to scold me again.'

'I would not dare,' he murmured, handing her the cup. 'You have made your opinion of me perfectly clear, Mrs Morgan.' Everyone else had moved towards the tea table, so there was no one to overhear him. 'You likened me to a tomcat, if I recall correctly.'

Her chin lifted a little at that. 'I was trying to convince you that I did not desire your attentions.'

'As you did when you feigned an injury rather than dance with me the other evening. Although I rather think you have been paid back for that little deception, do not you?'

She looked away, spots of colour staining her cheeks. 'It was not just you. I did not wish to…to dance with anyone else.'

'Why was that? You seemed to enjoy your first dances.'

'I have already told you. The reputations of the gentlemen staying at Newlands are well known in Compton Parva. I have no wish to encourage such persons.' She met his eyes, but only for an instant. 'I am extremely grateful for your assistance today, sir, but one such act is not enough for me to make a sound judgement of your character.'

'I think your judgement of my character has already been formed,' he retorted, nettled.

Molly's spirits dipped as she watched him walk away, but she rallied them immediately. It should not worry her that the gentleman did not like a little plain speaking. If he ignored her in the future, then that would be a good thing. And if he and his friends thought Compton Parva too dull for them and decided to quit the area, that would be even better!

She finished her tea and put the cup down on the little table Agnes had thoughtfully placed within easy reach. The party was now seated around the room and cheerful conversation flew back and forth. She was grateful for their efforts to include her, but she felt very tired and her ankle was throbbing most painfully. The clock chimed midnight, but no one seemed in the least inclined to bring the evening to an end. Molly was just wondering if she could attract her hostess's attention and ask for help to retire, when the beau rose from his chair.

'I fear we have fatigued Mrs Morgan with our chatter.'

'Goodness, yes,' exclaimed Agnes. 'You are looking very pale, ma'am. How thoughtless of me not to notice sooner. We must get you to your room.'

'Allow me.' Before Molly had realised his intention, he had lifted her into his arms, the silk shawl still wrapped around her skirts. He said, 'Perhaps, Agnes, you would have someone light our way with a candle?'

'Really, there is no need,' Molly protested, but with no conviction at all.

'Do not fret, Mrs Morgan,' said Sir Gerald, opening the door for them, 'You are perfectly safe and you must not deny Russ the chance to show how chivalrous he can be!'

He called to a hovering footman to precede them up the stairs, bade Molly a cheerful goodnight and shut the door on them. Molly swallowed, uncomfortable with the silence.

'I am sorry to give you so much trouble, sir.'

'Think nothing of it, ma'am.'

He paused on the stairs to shift her more comfortably in his arms and she slipped one hand around his neck, her head dropping against his shoulder. Suddenly she felt too tired to fight. When they reached the guest room they found a maid dozing in a chair. She jumped up as they came in.

'Miss Agnes has instructed me to wait on you, ma'am. I'm to fetch you anything you need.'

'First, light the rest of the candles,' the beau ordered. 'I need to see what damage Mrs Morgan has done.'

He put Molly down upon the daybed and pulled the shawl away. For the sake of propriety she had managed to put on silk stockings and a pair of lilac satin slippers, but although she had fastened the left shoe very loosely about her ankle, the bruised flesh was already pushing against the ties.

'Go and fetch more ice,' he commanded the maid. 'Immediately.'

He sank to his knees beside the sofa and began to loosen the ribbons.

'I really thought it would do no harm,' she murmured, watching him. 'I made sure I did not put my full weight upon it.'

'No, you merely hobbled along the corridor and down a full flight of stairs.' She gave a little gasp as his fingers touched her skin and he said quickly, 'Forgive me. Did I hurt you?'

'No more than I deserve,' she said contritely. 'You must think me very foolish.'

'Yes,' he retorted. 'And obstinate. You should never have walked downstairs. Risking your health to avoid me. The utmost folly.'

Gently but quickly he removed both her shoes and dropped them on the floor. Molly held her breath as he pushed her skirts above the knee and began to unfasten the garter. Then his hands stilled.

'I beg your pardon, I—'

'No, no, go on.' Her voice was little more than a croak and she tried to clear her throat of whatever was blocking it. 'The...the stocking needs to be removed for you to examine my ankle.'

'Yes.' He was staring at her leg, his voice devoid of all emotion. 'Of course.'

Molly sat very still, clutching the sides of the daybed as he dropped the garter on the floor and reached for the stocking top. The throb of her ankle was eclipsed now by her racing pulse. Her heart banged painfully and erratically against her ribs as his fingers brushed her skin. No man had touched any part of her leg since...

She blocked out the thought. She would not succumb to the fear and panic that came with those memories. She would not.

Molly sank her teeth into her lip and forced herself to watch as he began to roll the silk over her knee. Her fear was subsiding, replaced by the thought that no man had touched her with such tenderness. Ever.

Not even the love of her life. The man who had sworn to love her until death.

Her hands slid protectively over her stomach, but her thoughts could not be distracted from the man beside her.

She looked at his dark head, studied the handsome profile while his long fingers moved gently down her leg and another emotion began to grow inside her. A warmth, a yearning that tugged at her loins. He had reached her ankle. Molly sucked in a breath, anticipating pain, but he stretched the stocking wide before easing it with infinite care over the swollen joint.

'There.'

His eyes were fixed on her foot as he dropped the stocking on the floor and she noted that his breathing was ragged and uneven.

'Should you not remove the other stocking, too?' She was shocked to hear herself suggest it. 'That you may better compare the ankles,' she ended lamely.

'No, no need for that. It is quite clear where the damage lies.' He pulled the skirts more decorously over her legs and gave an impatient huff. 'Where is that girl with the ice?'

'I doubt there was any in the house at this late hour,' said Molly, desperate to keep talking. 'They will have had to go to the ice house and that could be some distance away, most likely in the park. It is most likely locked, too—'

'Stop it, for heaven's sake!'

'I beg your pardon?'

'You are prattling because you are afraid of me. You have no reason to be nervous, Mrs Morgan. I assure you. I have no designs upon your virtue.'

'No. Of...of course not.'

'Respectable widows are not my type.'

Molly flinched. 'You make that sound like an insult.'

'It was intended merely as the truth. I thought it might set your mind at rest to know that I do not seduce every woman I meet.'

'It does. Thank you.'

The door burst open and the maid hurried in.

'Here you are, sir, another bucket of ice. An' I beg your pardon for taking so long, sir, but we had to send out to the ice house for it.'

Just for an instant the beau's eyes met Molly's, a glinting smile in their black depths.

'That is what we thought,' he said gravely. 'Come along then, girl, bring it here.'

Ten minutes later Molly's ankle was once more soothed by an ice pack. The beau gave instructions to the maid before turning back to Molly.

'Under no circumstances are you to put your foot to the floor again tonight, madam. Do you understand me? The maid will help you with everything and now you have both seen what I have done, you can pack it with fresh ice in the morning, if the swelling has not reduced. Is that clear?'

'Yes. Thank you, sir.'

'Then I will bid you goodnight.'

'Mr Russington!' Molly held her hand out to him. He took it, his brows raising a little. 'You are wrong, sir,' she said. 'You are wrong to think my evasive actions are aimed solely at you. I have learned to be wary of all gentlemen.'

He stood, looking down at her for a moment, his face unreadable, then with an almost imperceptible nod, he went out.

Russ closed the door of the guest room and walked slowly to his own chamber. He was not sure he believed Molly Morgan wanted to keep all men at bay.

She had seemed happy enough during that first dance, but Gerald was the host and it would have been difficult for her to decline. A wry smile twisted his lips. If he doubted her veracity, might she not doubt his, when he claimed he had no designs upon her virtue? And with good reason.

Twice he had carried her in his arms, and he was well aware that beneath the layers of demure clothing, her body was slim but well formed. Yet it was peeling off the stocking that had confounded him. He had started innocently enough, concerned only that she might have done more damage to her ankle, but rolling the silk down her leg and revealing the soft skin beneath had been strangely arousing. For a brief moment his imagination had run with the idea of undressing her for his own pleasure.

The thought had been fleeting, but the widow had noticed it. She had been tense, almost shaking and he cursed himself for frightening her. He had made it even worse by allowing his anger to show.

He frowned. The dashed woman brought out the worst in him. Over the years he had learned to keep his true thoughts and feelings hidden beneath a cool, polished exterior and created Beau Russington, the epitome of the fashionable gentleman. He was a friend of Brummell, a noted Corinthian. The men sought his company while the ladies sought his bed. He had heard himself described as society's darling, charming to a fault and renowned for his good humour.

So what was there about the little widow that unsettled him? Surely he was not so conceited as to be put out because she did not like him?

'Bah, it is of no consequence,' he muttered aloud.

'Tomorrow she will be gone from here and after that, if our paths should cross, we need spare each other no more than a nod in passing.'

His words were swallowed by the gloomy corridor, but the creak of boards as he reached his bedchamber echoed through the darkness like a laugh.

Chapter Four

By the next morning Molly's ankle was showing great signs of improvement. The swelling was much reduced and, although she took breakfast in her room, she was later able to go downstairs with the aid of a stick. This had been thoughtfully provided by Lady Claydon, who assured Molly that her husband always brought a spare with him.

The gentlemen had gone out, but she found the ladies gathered in the morning room. They all bustled around Molly, Agnes's companion, Mrs Molyneux, insisting she should have the most comfortable seat and the Misses Claydon bringing over a footstool for her use and asking what they might do for her entertainment. She had barely made herself comfortable when the butler announced that her brother had arrived.

Edwin hurried in, looking flustered. In one breath he thanked Agnes for looking after his sister, enquired what had happened and apologised for not coming earlier. He turned to Molly to explain.

'I stayed in Compton Magna last night and did not receive your message until breakfast.'

'Then you saved yourself a night's unnecessary worry,' Agnes told him, smiling. 'You may see for yourself that Molly is recovering well.'

Edwin moved across to kiss Molly's cheek.

'What can I say? If only I had come with you to Raikes Farm.'

'You must not blame yourself because I was foolish enough to slip,' she told him, grasping his hand. 'A few more days' rest and I shall be as good as ever.'

'I hope you do not intend to rush off,' said Agnes, moving towards the bell pull. 'Gerald and the other gentlemen have ridden to Knaresborough to look at the castle ruins there. They will be gone all day so your company would be most welcome, Mr Frayne, and we are about to sustain ourselves with cake and a little wine.'

Lady Claydon spoke up immediately to agree and her daughters added their voices to the request that he should stay. Edwin looked at Molly.

'Well, sister, what do you say? Are you desperate to go home this minute?'

Molly shook her head and disclaimed. After everyone's kindness, how could she say she wanted to quit Newlands before the gentlemen returned? Especially when it was clear that Edwin would like to stay for a while. Besides, it was still early. The gentlemen would not be returning for hours yet. She sank back in her chair, content to let her brother enjoy himself.

She was very proud of Edwin and thought him ideally suited to his calling. Mr and Mrs Frayne had marked their son out for the church from an early age, but Edwin had inherited none of their father's harsh and intolerant religious fervour. He was honest and thoughtful, unfailingly kind and cheerful and at ease in any society, as she was now witnessing. The conversation was lively and entertaining, the wine and cakes brought in for their delectation could not have been bettered and the hours slipped by, until Molly heard the clock chime and gave a little gasp.

'Oh, heavens, Edwin. The time!'

'Goodness, is it four o'clock already? I had no idea. Perhaps, Miss Kilburn, you would summon my carriage. I should be getting Molly home.'

'Certainly, sir, but…' Agnes hesitated. 'Perhaps I might suggest Mrs Morgan should remain here another night? We should be delighted to have her stay.'

'Oh, no, I could not possibly trouble you any further,' said Molly. 'And it is no distance, we shall be home in no time.'

Agnes looked unconvinced. 'But the upset, Molly. After resting your ankle all day, are you sure you should be jarring and jolting it over these rough roads? I believe another night here would be most beneficial for you.'

Molly was about to insist that they leave when they were interrupted by the entrance of their host, which immediately caused a distraction.

'Gerald! I had not expected to see you for an hour or more yet. Is everyone back already?'

Agnes jumped up from her seat, but her brother waved her back. He was smiling and flushed from the fresh air, although Molly thought he looked a little distracted as he made his reply.

'No, no, they have all gone to Knaresborough, as planned, but my horse cast a shoe before we had gone ten miles, so I turned back.'

'And you are only now come in?' Edwin glanced at the clock. 'I trust you did not get lost.'

'Oh, no, nothing like that. I left my horse at the smithy and took the opportunity to explore a little. And as you can see—' he grinned, glancing down at himself '—I did not come in here until I had washed and changed out of all my dirt.'

He turned to Molly to enquire after her health and then joined his sister in pressing her to remain another night.

'And Frayne can stay for dinner, if he wishes,' he declared, turning his cheerful smile upon Edwin. 'I am not expecting the others to return until the dinner hour, so we have already agreed we shall not stand upon ceremony tonight, which means it will be perfectly acceptable for you to sit down to dinner as you are. And there is a full moon, too, Edwin, so you could safely drive home afterwards. And tomorrow, I will bring Mrs Morgan back to you in the barouche.'

'No, no.' Molly was suddenly alarmed. 'That is too kind of you, Sir Gerald, but we really must go.'

Agnes shook her head. 'I assure you it would be no imposition. After all, the guest room is already set up for you, so an extra night would make very little difference to us, but it could mean your ankle will heal all the sooner.'

'Do you know, I think you may be right, Miss Kilburn,' said Edwin. 'And, Molly, perhaps you will be more inclined to remain when I tell you that your maid is not yet returned. She sent word that her mother is no better, so I gave her permission to remain with her another night.'

'Oh, poor Cissy. Of course, she must stay,' Molly agreed, her own worries forgotten.

'All the more reason for you to remain here, then,' Sir Gerald declared triumphantly.

Molly knew it would be churlish to argue and, when Edwin looked at her, she nodded her assent.

'Capital,' cried Edwin. 'I can only thank you most sincerely, Miss Kilburn, for your kindness towards my sister.'

Edwin was beaming broadly and Molly saw that Agnes, too, was smiling and there was a telltale flush blossoming upon her cheek.

Oh, good heavens.

Molly sank back in her chair and lapsed into silence. Not since his schooldays had Edwin shown such a strong preference for any young lady, so why now? And why had his interest fixed upon Agnes Kilburn of all people?

She was immediately ashamed of her uncharitable thoughts. She would be very happy for Edwin to fall in love and settle down. She must not let her selfish concerns get in the way if he and Agnes truly liked one another. But to remain at Newlands tonight, to be in the company of Beau Russington for another evening, how would she endure it? His presence unsettled her. She could not forget how easily he had carried her, how secure she had felt in his arms. When he was in the room her eyes wanted to follow him and if he looked at her she felt the heat rising through her body. It was not to be borne. She did not even *like* the man.

Oh, do not be so foolish, she told herself crossly. *He has told you that he has no amorous intentions towards you.*

Which should have put her at her ease, but instead made her feel very slightly aggrieved and a little unsure of her instincts, because last night, when he had removed her stocking, she had been so sure that he, too, had felt something.

Like a conceited schoolroom miss! And do not forget you have been wrong about a man before.

Molly shifted uncomfortably at the thought, which immediately brought attention back to her. Mrs Molyneux asked if her ankle was hurting and the eldest Miss Claydon offered to bring another cushion to place beneath her foot. She was at pains to reassure them, but she could barely bring herself to smile when Edwin came to sit beside her and murmured that he thought she was very wise to remain at Newlands until tomorrow.

It was not long until the gentlemen came back from their sport. They greeted Edwin with unfeigned bonhomie and were delighted that he was joining them for dinner. When Agnes announced that Molly was staying for a second night, they all agreed it was a wise precaution and appeared quite content with the decision. All except Mr Russington. Molly saw a shadow flicker across his countenance. It might have been dissatisfaction, but she thought it looked more like alarm. It was gone in an instant, but it raised her spirits. Perhaps he was not quite so indifferent to her, after all.

And, strangely, the fact that the thought pleased her shocked Molly most of all.

Dinner was an informal affair. Agnes offered to have a tray sent into the drawing room for Molly, but she insisted that she was well enough to join them, if Edwin would give her his arm. She was given a seat between Mr Sykes and Lord Claydon and nothing could have exceeded their kindness. The conversation ebbed and flowed, it was lively, but there was no hint of impropriety, and later, in the drawing room, there was nothing in the least alarming about the way the party entertained themselves.

Mr Russington and Lord Claydon spent the evening playing piquet while Molly was invited to make a fourth at whist with Mr and Mrs Sykes and Lady Claydon. The others gathered around the piano and took turns at singing duets. Sir Joseph and Mr Flemington flirted with the Misses Claydon. Mr Flemington's high-pitched giggle was annoying, but since neither his nor Sir Joseph's attentions were aimed at her, Molly could relax and enjoy herself.

She felt a slight pang of regret when Edwin went home, but when the party broke up, it was Agnes who accompanied her to her bedchamber and delivered her into the hands of her maid and Molly went happily to bed, thinking that perhaps, after all, she had been too prejudiced against fashionable society. Perhaps it was not all dissipation. At least, not when there were chaperons present. So, she reasoned, staying at Newlands exposed her to no danger at all.

She allowed her thoughts to wander back to Beau Russington, recalling him at the dinner table. He had been listening to something Edwin was saying, his gaze abstracted and his lean fingers playing with the stem of his wine glass. She remembered those same fingers on her skin, peeling away the silk stocking, and once again she felt the hot ache deep within. She curled into a ball and pulled the bedclothes around her a little tighter.

For her, the danger was not with society, she realised, but with one man.

* * *

By the time Agnes took Molly back to the vicarage the following morning in the barouche, they were firm friends. Molly was not surprised when Edwin came out of the house as the carriage drew up. He opened the door himself, following up his words of greeting by inviting Miss Kilburn to step inside and take a little refreshment.

'Yes, please do, Agnes,' Molly added her entreaty, knowing that her new friend's hesitation was from shyness rather than reluctance.

Edwin beamed when Agnes agreed and he handed her out of the carriage before turning to Molly and insisting that he carry her into the drawing room.

'We do not want to undo all of Miss Kilburn's good work,' he said, depositing her on the sofa. 'Now, Miss Kilburn, perhaps you will sit with Molly and make sure she does not move while I go and ask Mrs Rodgers to bring us some tea!'

Molly shook her head as he lounged out of the room.

'Really, there is no need for all this fuss,' she said to Agnes, who smiled.

'Gerald would be just the same, if I were in this situation. You know he was minded to cancel his ride today to escort us here.'

'And we were both adamant that it was not necessary,' said Molly. 'We are fortunate to have such caring brothers.'

'Have you always kept house for Mr Frayne?' Agnes asked her.

'For five years, since he obtained the living here at Compton Parva.'

Agnes's eyes widened. 'You were widowed very young, then.'

'Yes, before I was twenty. And you, Agnes—' Molly was eager to move the conversation away from that subject '—have you always kept house for your brother?'

'Oh, no, I have been living at the family home in Oxfordshire since our father died two years ago.' She saw Molly's sudden frown and added quickly, 'Out of choice. Gerald prefers to live in London, but I do not like the town.'

'I have never been there,' Molly confessed.

'But you were married very young. I wish I had done so.' Agnes gave a sad little smile. 'I was betrothed to a naval officer, a captain, soon after my come-out six years ago. His birth was impeccable and Papa agreed to the engagement, but insisted we wait a little. It was a sensible decision, my fiancé wanted to win a little more prize money with which to set up our own establishment, but it was not to be. He was killed in an action off the French coast.'

'Oh, I am so sorry!'

Agnes fluttered a hand, as if to ward off Molly's sympathy. 'That was four years ago. I am over it now, but I envy you your time with your husband, however short.'

'I pray you will not!' Molly saw that her vehemence had shocked Agnes and she continued more gently, 'What I mean is, we were only married for a few months. It was not a happy time.'

She broke off thankfully when Edwin returned. The conversation became general and remained so until Agnes took her leave an hour later. Edwin accompanied her to the door, and came back beaming.

'What a delightful young lady, is she not, Molly? So kind of her to bring you home herself. Perhaps, once you are better, we should hold a little dinner, invite the Newlands party to come here.'

Molly's response was non-committal. Despite her burgeoning friendship with Agnes, and her conviction now that the gentlemen at Newlands were not as dissolute as she had first imagined, she was still wary of forging closer ties with any of them.

Edwin had been adamant that Molly should rest until her ankle was quite recovered and threatened to summon the doctor if she disagreed with him. She therefore rested dutifully on the sofa until the Saturday, when she came down to breakfast dressed in her green walking dress.

'If I spend another moment indoors, I vow I shall scream,' she told her loving brother when he looked at her in surprise. 'I am going to visit Fleur and Nancy at Prospect House as soon as I have broken my fast. I shall take the gig and Gibson will be with me. He is quite capable of taking the reins should I go off in a dead faint.'

Edwin laughed at that. 'Your constitution is stronger than most, so I do not foresee such an event. No, I am content to have kept you resting for so long. Just remember that we are engaged to dine with the Curricks this evening and do not be late back!'

Fleur and Nancy came running out as the gig pulled up.

'There is no need for that,' Molly said, laughing as Nancy reached up to help her alight. 'I am perfectly well now, I assure you.' She glanced down at the little dog prancing around her feet. 'And this is your new guard dog.' She picked up the furry bundle, laughing as he squirmed in her hold and tried to lick her chin.

'Yes, this is Nelson.' Fleur chuckled. 'I fear he will not offer us much protection, however he is quite noisy when anyone arrives, so that is useful.'

Nancy took Molly's arm. 'But let us not stand out here in the wind. Come indoors, Molly. You must sit down and tell us how it happened.'

'Every detail,' Nancy commanded, as they made themselves comfortable in the drawing room and Daisy came in with the tea tray.

'It is nothing exciting,' Molly told them. 'I was coming home from Raikes Farm on Monday when I slipped and sprained my ankle. Mr Russington drove me to Newlands and Miss Kilburn insisted I should stay for a few days. I hope you did not think too badly of me for not coming to help you on Tuesday and not a word of explanation.'

'Oh, but we knew about your accident by then,' put in Daisy, setting out the teacups.

'I suppose someone told you at the market.' Molly noticed the guilty looks upon the faces of her friends and she looked from one to the other, frowning. 'Fleur, Nancy?'

'Fleur met one of the gentlemen from Newlands on Tuesday,' Nancy explained. 'She was in the orchard as he came along the lane.'

'His stopped to ask directions,' said Fleur, two pink spots colouring her cheeks. 'He was most gentleman-like.'

'It was most likely Sir Gerald,' said Molly. 'He was back before the others, because his horse had cast a shoe.'

'Yes, we introduced ourselves.'

As the blush deepened so did Molly's frown.

'And there is more?' She saw Fleur's anguished look at Nancy and she said sternly, 'Tell me.'

'He and his friends came to our stall on market day,' muttered Fleur. 'There was nothing untoward in their manner, Molly, I assure you. They were merely passing through the market, and he—Sir Gerald—recognised me.'

'So it was purely coincidence.' Molly looked sceptical.

'Let us look on the bright side,' offered Nancy. 'He sent a runner back in the afternoon to buy up the remainder of our produce.'

Despite her concerns, Molly laughed. 'He is certainly very brave, to be interfering in his housekeeper's business!'

The mood lightened and no more was said about the meeting until Molly took her leave. As she hugged Fleur, she warned her to be on her guard.

'You must not worry, Molly. I know better than to be taken in by any gentleman's fine words. Everyone thought my stepfather was the most charming man imaginable.'

Molly felt her shudder and held her closer.

'I cannot fault Sir Gerald as a host,' she said carefully. 'He was most amiable and obliging while I was at Newlands and I have no first-hand knowledge that he is anything but a gentleman. But he is reputed to run with a very fast set and some of them are at Newlands.'

'They are rich and single,' said Nancy. 'Such men think they have the right to do anything they wish, but they will not be welcome here. And we have our protectors. Is that not so, Moses?' she called to the giant, who had brought Molly's gig to the door, and he nodded back at her, grinning.

'Aye, Miss Nancy's right there, Mrs Morgan. I'll keep an eye out for them all, don't you fret about that.'

'And don't forget Nelson,' added Nancy, scooping up the little puppy. 'We shall train him to attack any gentleman who comes within a mile of Prospect House!'

That assurance kept Molly smiling as she drove away. Fleur was far too soft-hearted, but Molly knew she could trust Nancy and Moses to look after everyone at Prospect House.

Dinner at Currick Hall was Molly's first social engagement since her accident and her hosts were anxious to assure themselves that she was fully recovered. Having made her way unaided through the great hall and up the oak staircase to the dark-panelled reception rooms, she was able to reassure them on this point, but she soon realised that no small part of their interest was the fact that Beau Russington had carried her to Newlands. The ladies were all eager to hear more of the rescue and all those who had not yet dined with Sir Gerald were keen to have the house described to them.

Molly did her best to comply, but she was relieved when dinner was announced and everyone prepared to file into the dining room. However, as she rose and shook out her skirts, the squire's daughter, Helen, a bouncy seventeen-year-old, told her in an excited whisper that Papa had a surprise for them.

'He has invited Sir Gerald and his party to join us later! We could not accommodate them all at the table, for it was arranged such a time ago, but Papa thought it would be a great shame not to ask them to come for supper and they have accepted!'

The squire came up, chuckling. 'What's that, Puss,

have you been giving away my secrets? I hope you are pleased, Mrs Morgan. Nell here and the Misses Claydon hit it off very well at the recent assembly and she has been plaguing the life out of me to invite them back, so I mentioned the matter to Sir Gerald when I saw him earlier today and he has sent me word that they are all to come.'

'Is that not marvellous news, Mrs Morgan?' Helen was almost hopping with excitement. 'Papa has said we may have a little impromptu dancing, too.'

'Well, we shall see. We shall see.' His twinkling eyes came to rest upon Molly. 'I have no doubt you'll be glad to see Mr Russington again, will you not, madam? I promise you all the ladies here envy you your good fortune in having such a handsome rescuer.'

He went off, still chuckling, and when Edwin came up to take Molly in to dinner, she muttered angrily that she had become the talk of the town.

'It will pass.' He gave her fingers a reassuring pat. 'It will be eclipsed by other news soon enough.'

'I would not consider my spraining my ankle to be news in the first place!'

'No, it isn't. But being rescued by an arbiter of fashion is. The squire is right, every lady here is wishing it had happened to her.'

Molly gave a long sigh. 'Could we not make our excuses and leave as soon as dinner is ended?'

'No, of course not.' He laughed. 'Cheer up, Molly, everyone from Newlands will be pleased to see you are going on so well. And I confess I should not object to a little dancing this evening, although there is no need for you to join in, if you would rather not. You can say your ankle is paining you.'

It was on the tip of her tongue to retort that she had already used that excuse once, but then she remembered that Edwin knew nothing about that little episode. So she gritted her teeth and held her peace.

Currick Hall was a rambling old house going back at least two centuries and it lacked the spacious reception rooms to be found in more modern properties. The arrival of another dozen people caused a crush in the drawing room, but their host cheerfully assured everyone that once the servants had finished clearing all the furniture, save the pianoforte, from the great hall, there would be plenty of space for everyone, whether dancing or sitting and watching the proceedings.

The crush in the room made it very warm and Molly moved across to one of the deep window embrasures where she knew from experience the ill-fitting casements allowed in plenty of cold air. She stepped past the curtains to where the shadows were deepest. With her dark hair and deep grey gown, she thought she would attract least attention there. The draught from the windows was refreshing and she was happy to breathe it in, allowing the noise and chatter from the room to pass her by.

She was just thinking she should rejoin the crowd when she heard the rumble of masculine voices approaching. They came to a halt and she recognised the squire's genial tones, and the deeper voice of Mr Thomas, the mill owner, who had moved to the area ten years ago, but had never lost his lilting Welsh accent. They had not noticed her and she would have been happy to step out past them, but Mr Flemington's rather nasal voice made her shrink back even further.

'We enjoyed a fine day's shootin' yesterday. Ain't

that so, Aikers? Although Kilburn's land is sadly out of condition.'

'But with good management, that will improve,' replied the squire. 'And even now I am sure it provides some good sport.'

Molly heard Mr Flemington's irritating giggle. 'Talking of sport, we were in town on market day and saw a couple of young women from the Magdalene hospital.'

'You mean Prospect House,' Mr Thomas corrected him. 'And it may well have been the ladies that you saw. They are not above selling their surplus from the farm.'

'Mr Thomas is on the committee,' put in the squire. 'I can assure you, gentlemen, it is a very respectable establishment.'

'Respectable, you say?' Molly could almost hear the leer in Sir Joseph Aikers's voice. 'By Gad, but they are dashed pretty, for all that. Wouldn't mind getting a little better acquainted.'

'Well, you won't do it,' Mr Thomas told him. 'They allow no gentlemen callers.'

'But what about at night?' said Flemington. 'Surely some of the younger fellows would want to try their luck, eh? And mayhap some of the older ones, too!'

'If anyone was to try such a thing, they'd be disgraced,' retorted Mr Thomas bluntly. 'Found out, they would be, you mark my words.'

The squire harrumphed. 'Such behaviour would be very much frowned upon, gentlemen, and in a small town like this, word would be bound to get out.'

'Aye, I suppose it would,' said Sir Joseph. He gave a laugh. 'Still, it might be worth an attempt.'

They moved off but it was some moments before

Molly felt calm enough to leave the shadows. She was shaking with rage. All her effort, all her work to build up Prospect House into a respectable enterprise and it was scorned by a couple of rakehells. She should not be surprised. These were London ways—her sister, Louisa, wrote to her constantly about them.

She left the cool security of the window and went in search of Edwin. He was talking with a group of townsfolk, but as soon as she could draw him away, she told him everything she had heard. He tried to reassure her, telling her it was merely the foolish way men boasted to one another.

'You said Mr Thomas and the squire were quick to warn them off. I am sure nothing will come of it.'

'Are you? I am not. Oh, I wish these people had never come here!'

'Now, Molly, you must not think like that. Despite what your sister writes, the ladies are all most amiable, and as for the gentlemen, they have none of them acted with the least impropriety.'

She swung away from him, saying through her clenched teeth, 'Not yet!'

'Molly, Molly.' He gently caught her arms and turned her back to face him. 'I know you were hurt, my dear, but I pray you will not allow yourself to be prejudiced against all men.'

'It is not prejudice,' she told him fiercely. 'Sir Gerald came upon Fleur in the orchard last Tuesday and the very next day he and his—his *friends* were in the market. Do you tell me that was coincidence?'

'No, I say it was curiosity, nothing more. I spoke to Kilburn about his meeting with Fleur Dellafield and he was most complimentary, even respectful. You know my advice, Molly. You should judge a man's character by his actions.'

'Surely a man should also be judged by his words.'

He gave her a little shake. 'Can you honestly say that Kilburn, Sykes or Claydon have said or done anything to make you think them dissolute? And as for Russ, why, if he had not been on hand to bring you down off the moors and apply ice to your ankle so quickly, your injuries might have been a great deal worse.'

Russ. Even her brother called him by that familiar name now!

'Russ had no choice but to carry you to his carriage, Molly, and Agnes tells me it was he who tended your injury.' He paused and frowned at her. 'But tell me truthfully now, did he at any time offer you insult?'

Her eyes fell. 'If anything it was *I* who insulted him,' she confessed. She raised her head, rallying. 'But what of Mr Flemington and Sir Joseph? What of their outrageous comments just now?'

He shook his head at her. 'Remember what Plato says. An empty vessel makes the loudest sound. You may warn your ladies to be vigilant, but I think you will find that it was an idle boast.'

His attention was claimed by Mr Thomas, who wanted to discuss a point of theology with him. Molly waved him away with a smile, knowing he had done all he could to allay her fears. She wanted more time to think things over, so she avoided Agnes and everyone from Newlands and chose instead to sit with some of the matrons and discuss the rather tedious but much safer subject of their ailments.

* * *

Thankfully the announcement soon came that they should all make their way to the great hall for a little dancing and entertainment.

The squire came up to Molly. 'My dear Mrs Morgan, you are not to attempt the stairs without a gentleman to support you, especially in this crowd. Allow me.'

'Thank you,' she murmured. 'That is very kind.'

'Ah, but here is Mr Russington and in good time, sir! You will provide a much more agreeable escort for my young friend, I am sure! I pray you will give your arm to this lady.'

'I should be delighted.'

The beau held out his arm, all smooth urbanity, but it was all Molly could do not to whip her own hands behind her back out of the way.

'Of course, you would!' declared the squire cheerfully, unaware of Molly's reticence. 'Why, 'tis another opportunity for you to play Sir Galahad, what?'

The squire laughed heartily at his own joke as he walked away. Cautiously, Molly slipped her hand into the crook of the proffered arm and her escort led her towards the top of the stairs.

'Are you actually *touching* my sleeve?' he asked her. 'You may safely lean on me, you know. Perhaps you did not understand our host's reference to Sir Galahad.'

'Of course, I understood it.' She gave a little tut of indignation. 'Anyone would think you had rescued me from a dragon.'

'No, no,' he murmured. 'That would make me Saint George and I am no saint.'

'I can readily believe that,' she retorted.

'Although tonight, for you, I am on my best behaviour,

basking in my new-found fame as a rescuer of helpless damsels.'

Molly gasped. 'Helpless—'

She glared at him. His glance was full of wicked amusement, but his mockery was not aimed at Molly. Rather it invited her to share the joke. Her anger suddenly felt ridiculous and a laugh bubbled up inside her.

'You are quite outrageous,' she told him, trying to sound severe.

'No, no. I am the epitome of chivalry. You heard the squire say so.'

'Nonsense.' She maintained a dignified silence as they began to descend the stairs, but it only lasted as far as the half landing. 'I have always understood Sir Galahad to be extremely pious. Something *you* are not!'

'You do not know that. I have been a soul of propriety since coming to Compton Parva.'

'Why did you come?' she asked him. 'We are a small town, full of bankers and tradespeople. Hardly the society you are accustomed to.'

'Kilburn invited me.' They had reached the hall by this time and he looked up as the scrape of fiddles sounded above all the chatter. 'Ah, so it will not only be the pianoforte accompanying the dancing this evening. Not quite such an impromptu hop, then.'

'We have some talented musicians in Compton Parva,' said Molly. 'I expect the squire requested that they bring their instruments as soon as Sir Gerald had accepted his invitation.'

Russ would have guided her towards the part of the hall that had been cleared for dancing, but Molly held back.

'It is not yet a week since I turned my ankle and I would rather sit out, sir.'

'Then I shall join you.'

'There is no need,' she said quickly.

'But I insist. There are plenty of gentlemen this evening, so I shall not be missed.'

Having heard several ladies gushing over his handsome figure and good looks, Molly did not agree, but she would not pander to his vanity by saying so. She took a seat at one side of the room, not too near to the roaring fire, and tried to look indifferent as he sat down beside her. For a while they were silent, watching the guests milling around, some moving towards the seats at that end of the hall, others taking their places in the sets that were forming nearer the musicians. The squire's wife was looking very pleased to be partnered by Sir Gerald at the head of the first set, while further down the line, Edwin was standing up with Agnes.

'You know,' remarked Russ, following her glance, 'I believe we may be thrown into each other's company a great deal in the coming weeks. It would be as well if we were not always at daggers drawn.'

'Of course not. I can be perfectly polite when it is required of me.'

'Can you?' His quizzical glance made her look away quickly.

'Yes,' she replied, 'if you can assure me that you and your friends are here purely for the sport?' When he did not respond, she mustered her strength to continue as coolly as she could. 'It...it would be a gross outrage if you were to...to try to visit Prospect House.'

'Why the devil should I do that?'

'You might think that they are unprotected and...and I know what many people think of women who are obliged to take refuge there. It was one of your own party who called it a Magdalene hospital.'

'I cannot answer for the others, but I have no interest in chasing such unfortunate women, madam.'

'No, you do not have to pursue women at all, do you, Mr Russington? My sister tells me they fall over themselves for your attention.'

He said softly, 'But not you, Mrs Morgan.'

'Not in the least.'

She kept her head up and managed to hold his gaze. Until he smiled and those little demons danced in his eyes, sending alarm bells clamouring in her head.

'Good. Then to return to my original suggestion, I think we should we call a truce.'

Molly's thoughts were fixed on the sensuous curve of his lips and she was obliged to drag them back, rapidly.

'A…a truce?'

'You have left me in no doubt of your opinion of me, but I think it would be more comfortable for our mutual acquaintances—and your brother—if we could act in a civilised manner when we meet. What do you say?'

'I shall be perfectly civil to you. As long as you do not provoke me.'

'Ah. I thought there would be a caveat.'

'The matter is in your hands, sir,' she told him, feeling more confident of her ground now.

'Then there should be no difficulty.' He eased his long frame from the chair. 'Gerald says we should attend the morning service at All Souls tomorrow morning, ma'am, so no doubt we shall meet there. And we may even manage to be civil to one another.'

He gave Molly the neatest of bows and sauntered away, leaving her to stare after him. *Civil?* Was it civil to set her nerve ends quivering with indignation at his insupportable arrogance, his conceit?

But it is not merely his cool air of superiority that upsets you, is it? It is the fact that you find him undeniably attractive!

'He is a rake, a libertine. He has had mistresses by the score. He is everything you hold in abhorrence,' she rebuked herself sternly, using her fan not only to cool her cheeks but to hide the fact that she was talking to herself. 'He is also part of a group that threatens my friends at Prospect House. If nothing else should make you hate the man, Molly Morgan, it is that!'

Chapter Five

The idea that someone might attempt to gain access to Prospect House during the night remained with Molly, but by the time she reached home that night, it was far too late to send a note. She would speak to Fleur and Nancy at church the next morning.

The day dawned bright and sunny, so she remained near the lychgate, greeting her neighbours while she watched the road, waiting to see the ladies and girls from Prospect House walking to morning service.

The carriages from Newlands were amongst the first to arrive: Sir Gerald and Beau Russington in the chaise with Miss Kilburn, Lord Claydon and his family in a smart barouche and Mr Sykes driving up in his curricle with his wife sitting beside him. Molly's first thought was relief that Sir Joseph and Mr Flemington were absent, because after the conversation she had heard last night she did not think she could be polite to them. It was difficult enough to pin a smile in place to greet the beau. She managed it, but wished he would move on, instead of standing aside while she greeted the other members of the party, and as they strolled away he stepped closer.

'There,' he murmured, 'that was not so very bad, was it?'

His low voice and the smile in his eyes sent a delicious shiver through Molly and made her toes curl, but not for the world would she let him see how much he affected her.

She replied frostily, '*I* have no difficultly in being civil.'

His brows went up. 'What a corker. Admit it, your first thought, when you saw me approaching, was to scurry away and hide.'

It was so near the truth that Molly blushed, but she laughed, too, and shook her head at him.

'That may be the case, but it is very *un*civil of you to say so.'

'Odd, is it not, that we should be able to be so frank with each other? As if we were old friends.'

She looked up at him then. 'My dear sir, how on earth could you and I ever be friends?'

He smiled at her, a strange, arrested look on his face.

'The rake and the reformer? There have been more unlikely alliances, you know.'

He was smiling down at her and Molly's breath caught in her throat. The world tilted, as if every belief she held was suddenly in doubt.

'There can be no question of it in this case,' she managed at last.

She saw Nancy entering the churchyard and with no little relief she gave the beau a dismissive nod and turned to greet her.

'Thank heavens,' she said, holding out her hands. 'I have been waiting for you to arrive.'

'We would have been earlier, but for a little scare that Marjorie's baby was coming,' said Nancy. 'The signs passed off, but Daisy has stayed with her and Moses, too, ready to fetch the midwife if necessary.' She smiled and put her hand on Billy's shoulder. 'So we have this young man for our escort today.'

Molly smiled at Billy and took the time to exchange a word with the little maids, but it was only when, from the corner of her eye, she saw Russ saunter away that she could at last bring her chaotic thoughts into some sort of order. She linked arms with Nancy as they walked towards the church door and quickly explained what she had overheard last night.

'Edwin says it is nothing more than bluster, but you must take care,' she ended, just as they reached the door.

'We have been taking care ever since they came to Newlands, my dear. Moses checks the locks and the shutters around the house every night.' Nancy signalled to the others to go inside. 'But I fear we may have a more pressing problem than night-time prowlers.'

Molly followed her glance and saw that Fleur was coming slowly up the path with Sir Gerald beside her. They were talking earnestly, Sir Gerald in no wise disheartened by Fleur's veil. Neither did he show any signs of self-consciousness when he saw Nancy and Molly waiting at the door. His greeting could not have been more cordial.

'Good morning to you, Sir Gerald,' Molly responded with equal cheerfulness, but shamefully less sincerity. 'The rest of your party are already inside.'

'Yes? Oh—yes. That is, they have gone on ahead of

me.' Another smile, a touch of his hat and he went in, leaving Fleur with her friends. Her veil might hide her blushes, but it could not disguise the defensive note in her voice as she explained they had met by chance at the gate.

'He was waiting for you.'

'Oh, no, Nancy, surely not—'

'How else could it be, when the Newlands carriages have been here for a good half hour? 'Tis a pity Moses did not come with us today—he would have put a stop to it.'

'Perhaps Sir Gerald had something to discuss with his coachman,' said Molly, taking pity on Fleur. She linked arms with them both, saying cheerfully, 'Come along, we had best take our places inside. Edwin will be wanting to begin!'

It was a bright morning and after the service the congregation gathered outside the church, exchanging greetings and catching up on gossip. Molly saw Sir Gerald edging away from his friends, but Nancy was already taking Fleur's arm and hurrying her and the rest of the girls down the path very much like a mother hen protecting her brood from a fox. She wished she could go, too, instead of having to wait for her brother, who was standing a little apart, deep in conversation with two of his churchwardens. Thus she could not escape Miss Kilburn's invitation for her and Edwin to join a little dinner party they were arranging the following week.

Molly demurred, saying that she must confer with Edwin, although she was well aware that the only reason he would decline would be if there was a previous engagement that could not be rearranged. The Newlands party moved off towards the waiting carriages, the gentlemen tipping their hats to Molly as they passed. She acknowledged Russ's polite nod with a faint, distant smile and turned away immediately to greet Sir William, who was coming up with his wife on his arm.

'A good turnout, ma'am,' he observed. 'I am relieved. I did not want your brother blaming our little gathering last night for depleting his congregation.' He glanced towards the line of carriages. 'However, I note only two single gentlemen from Newlands came along today.'

Molly pursed her lips. 'No doubt the others consider the restoration of their bodies more important than their souls.'

'La, Mrs Morgan, that is too naughty of you!' Lady Currick laughed and tapped her arm. 'But it is to be expected from these young bucks, with their London habits. They carouse the night away and then sleep until noon! We must hope your brother can reform them.'

'We must indeed,' said Molly, forcing a smile. 'But one cannot expect a leopard to change its spots, you know.'

'Whoa, Flash.'

Russ brought the big grey hunter to a stand on the edge of a high ridge. He had no idea how long he had been riding, but a glance at the sun told him it was close to noon, so he must have been out for several hours. He had gone out early to try to shake off the unaccustomed restlessness that had come over him the past few days.

Perhaps he should go back to town. There were more entertainments there than at Newlands, but he knew that was not the answer. He had been growing bored with

London life even before Gerald had invited him to come north. A shaft of self-mockery pierced him. He was regarded as a Corinthian, a top-of-the-trees sportsman and second only to Brummell as an arbiter of fashion. He had been indulged since birth, had more money than he could spend, the pick of society's beautiful women and yet, at eight-and-twenty, he felt that life had nothing new to offer.

He knew he should feel grateful. Most second sons had to find an occupation, usually the army or the church, but he had been blessed with a rich godmother, who had left him her entire fortune. He was equally blessed in the fact that along with the investments and estates, he had inherited reliable staff and an astute man of business, who between them looked after his interests, leaving him nothing to do but enjoy himself. But lately he had found all his usual amusements had begun to pall. He had no desire for self-destruction. Gambling to excess held little attraction, nor did he wish to drink himself into oblivion.

He gazed out over the countryside spread out before him. He had ridden down into the valley where Compton Parva nestled and up on to the moors on the far side, so now he could look back towards Newlands with its extensive grounds and woodlands, but even the prospect of more hunting did not excite him.

'Admit it,' he said aloud. 'You are bored. Bored with life.'

He allowed his eyes to travel down from Newlands to the valley below. The houses of Compton Parva straggled along each side of the winding valley road, burgeoning around the town square and the vicarage. He could see tiny figures moving in the square and traffic on the road. Everyone was going about their business, seemingly happy and content. So why could he not be happy?

Perhaps he should marry. His brother, Henry, had made a prudent match just after their mother had died, and now lived in quiet contentment on his country estates with his large family. Perhaps a wife would help to fill the aching void that Russ had become aware of. But he had never met any woman who could hold his interest for more than a few months. And most of—if not all—the women who came into his sphere were more interested in his fortune than in him. His father had made the mistake of falling in love with such a woman and he was not about to do the same.

He had learned much from those early days, when his father had brought home his beautiful new wife, who doted on him only as long as he lavished a fortune upon her. That was why, apart from one or two close friends such as Gerald Kilburn, Russ kept everyone else at a distance. Always polite, always charming, he was equally at home riding to hounds or in the salons of society hostesses. He was accepted everywhere, acclaimed as an excellent fellow and a perfect guest, but he never forgot that he owed his popularity to his wealth. He was happy to oblige any pretty woman who threw herself in his way in a fast and furious flirtation, but when his interest cooled he would leave them without a second thought.

'So why is such a life suddenly not enough?' he muttered.

At the sound of his master's voice the big hunter pricked up his ears and sidled restlessly. Russ leaned forward to run a hand over the grey's powerful neck.

'I must be growing maudlin, Flash, and damned un-grateful, to have so much and yet want something more.' He gathered up the reins and touched his heels to the hunter's flanks. 'Come up, boy. Let's gallop off these fidgets, from both of us!'

Lady Currick might laugh at the idea of carousing rakes, but it did nothing to allay Molly's fears and early the following morning she drove to Prospect House. She found Moses and Billy at work on the flower beds outside the drawing-room window.

'Trampled, they was, ma'am,' Moses told her. 'In the night.'

Molly grew cold. 'Intruders!'

'Nay, ma'am, no one got in. I didn't hear anything, my room bein' at the back o' the house, but *someone* was prowling around last night.'

Molly hurried inside, her imagination running wild with horrid scenes, but she found Fleur in her office, calmly writing up her ledgers. When Molly expressed her concerns she giggled, but refused to say anything more until she had summoned Nancy to join them in the drawing room.

'I must not stay too long,' said Nancy. 'I have left Bridget making a potato pudding, but she will be at a loss to know how to dress the hog's head when it is boiled. But where is your groom, Molly? Surely you did not come alone.'

'The carriage horses needed shoeing and Gibson has taken them to the smith. And before you ask why I did not bring my maid, Cissy's mother is still ailing and I have sent her home again for a few days to look after her.' She waved an impatient hand. 'Tell me quickly now, what happened here last night.'

'Let us say we had visitors.' Nancy went on quickly, 'But the shutters were up and the doors bolted, so there was never any risk of them getting into the house.'

'Oh, heavens!'

'They were not housebreakers, Molly,' Fleur assured her. 'We could make out their white neckcloths and waistcoats quite clearly in the moonlight.'

'You *saw* them?'

'Oh, yes.' Nancy nodded. 'The first I knew of it was when Bridget came to tell me that she could hear someone on the drive.'

'And did the puppy not bark?' asked Molly.

Nancy shook her head. 'He is not yet fully house-trained, so Moses keeps him shut in the cellar at night. Shortly after Bridget had woken me, I heard gravel being thrown against the bedroom windows. Mine and Fleur's. I was thankful they did not make their way to the back of the house and disturb Marjorie, she is so close to her time now she is finding it difficult enough to sleep as it is! It was two of the men—I will not credit them with the label of gentlemen—from Newlands. We had seen them in the market, but we did not learn their names.'

Fleur said quickly, 'Nancy and I both saw them, Molly. It was definitely *not* Sir Gerald.'

Nancy nodded. 'It was the very tall, thin one.'

'Sir Joseph Aikers,' said Molly. 'And…and can you describe the other one?'

'He was much shorter,' said Fleur, 'but he had a horrid laugh.'

'Like a girl giggling?' Molly was aware of an inordinate amount of relief when Fleur nodded. 'That will be Mr Flemington.'

So Russ was not involved. Molly told herself it meant nothing, he might well be aware of this night-time escapade. For all she knew he might have suggested it to his companions.

'I saw their open carriage on the lane,' Nancy went on, her lip curling. 'Heaven knows how they managed to get to us without overturning it, for they were so drunk they could barely stand.'

'Why did you not fetch Moses to see them off?' asked Molly.

'That was not necessary, we saw to it ourselves.'

'Nancy! You did not go down to them!'

'No, no, nothing like that. It is best you do not know, Molly, for it was not at all ladylike.'

Nancy's eyes were positively sparkling with mischief now and a gurgle of laughter escaped from Fleur.

'We put up the window and told them to be off, but they were too drunk to do anything but fall about, crushing all the flowers, which made Nancy very angry, because we had worked so hard to plant them all in the spring.'

'So how did you get them to go away?' asked Molly, intrigued.

'Nancy suggested they should serenade her, under her window, so we persuaded them to move across to the little bay at the end of the house.'

'But that is the landing window,' said Molly, confused.

'I wanted them away from the flower beds,' muttered Nancy. 'Besides, that window juts out over the drive.'

'Is that important?'

'Oh, yes.'

'Oh, for heaven's sake,' said Molly, thoroughly exasperated. 'Tell me!'

'We waited until they were both singing their hearts out, then we emptied the contents of our chamber pots out of the window.'

Nancy and Fleur collapsed into giggles and, after struggling against it, Molly joined them, relieved of her worries, at least for a while. When Nancy had returned to the kitchens Molly went upstairs to visit Marjorie, who was embroidering a little gown for her baby, whenever it should appear. Then she went off with Fleur to speak with Moses about the harvest and talk to the other girls, who were collecting apples from the orchards.

However, when Molly set off from the house it was not Marjorie's imminent confinement, nor the excellent progress that occupied her mind, but last night's occurrence. Nancy might laugh at what had happened and say they were very well able to look after themselves with Billy and Moses to help, but Molly wondered if perhaps another manservant should be hired. Billy was only ten years old and, although he was very useful around the farm, he was far too young to be thought of as a protector.

Indignation welled up inside her as she slowed the gig to negotiate a tight corner. No protector had been needed before Sir Gerald and his friends came to Newlands! As if conjured by her thoughts, she rounded the bend to see Beau Russington sitting at the side of the road, his horse quietly cropping the grass close by. She pulled up the gig beside him.

'Are you hurt, sir?'

He rose gingerly. 'I think not. I was enjoying a gallop

along this stretch of open grassland when the girth broke.' He began to brush off his coat. 'If I had been paying attention, I would not have been thrown.'

Molly had been so intent upon the man that she had not noticed his horse was missing its saddle. A glance showed it lying on the ground a little distance away. She gave Russ another look. He appeared decidedly pale.

'I will take you back to Newlands,' she told him. 'Can you manage to tie your horse to the back of the gig? And I am sure we can find somewhere to put the saddle.'

Five minutes later they had set off, Molly keeping a steady but slow pace.

'I do not want to put your horse under stress,' she explained. 'Nor do I wish to subject you to more jolting than necessary.'

'Your concern is very comforting, Mrs Morgan.'

'I would do the same for anyone, Mr Russington.'

'There is no need to show hackle, madam, I was being quite sincere.'

'Were you?'

Russ observed her sceptical look and his lips twitched.

'I thought we had agreed to be civil to one another,' he remarked. 'That resolution did not last long.'

'As I told you, it was conditional upon you deserving civility.'

'Oh? And what is it I am meant to have done?' He twisted around so that he could look at her, resting his arm along the back of the seat. Several unruly dark curls were peeping beneath her bonnet and he was tempted to tug at one of them, but the frowning look upon her face gave him pause.

'Come, madam, to my knowledge I have done nothing to warrant your disapproval.'

'Not you, perhaps, but your friends.'

'Oh? Would you care to explain?'

'They…called, last night. At Prospect House. They were intoxicated.'

He frowned. He and Gerald had stayed up talking until gone midnight.

'Are you sure it was anyone from Newlands?'

'Oh, yes.' She threw him a swift, angry glance. 'The ladies—and they *are* ladies, despite what you might think!—recognised them. They remembered seeing them with Sir Gerald at the market. Once they had described them to me I knew it was Sir Joseph and Mr Flemington.'

'Damned fools!' He straightened in his seat. 'How much harm did they do?'

'Apart from the inconvenience, and unsettling everyone, very little. They trampled a flower bed.'

Watching her, Russ saw a sudden lightening of her countenance.

'What was so amusing, Mrs Morgan?'

He was surprised when she gave him a look brimful of mischief.

'Nancy and Fleur paid them well for their impudence.'

'Go on.'

'They emptied their chamber pots over them.'

Russ was silent for one stupefied moment, then he put back his head and roared with laughter.

'Well, that explains something,' he said, when at last he could command his voice. 'When I came downstairs this morning the valet was just coming out of Flemington's room with his master's clothes bundled in his arms and there was a distinct smell of the privy surrounding him.'

She shook her head. 'I beg your pardon. It is most improper that I should have told you.'

'It is most improper that they should be skulking around Prospect House at night!'

'Yes.' Her brow furrowed again and he felt a twinge of regret that she was no longer full of merriment. 'It was most reprehensible. And it could be very damaging. You see, Prospect House can only continue here if it keeps its reputation as a respectable establishment. Which is why this escapade of your so-called friends does not help at all.'

He wanted to tell her that they were no friends of his, nor were they long-standing friends of Kilburn, if truth were told. Aikers and Flemington had been on the town for years, but had only recently become friendly with Gerald. Russ had never liked them, but he gave a mental shrug. He was only a guest at Newlands, after all. He could do little about it. He glanced at her, suddenly curious.

'Why are you so passionate about Prospect House?'

'It is impossible not to be touched by the plight of the women there. Not that I expect you to understand that.'

'No?' He turned to look at her again, once more resting his hand along the back. 'I might understand better, if you were to explain it. Believe me, I have no ulterior motive, madam, only curiosity. You say some of them are ladies?'

'Fleur and Nancy's birth is equal to yours or mine, Mr Russington, but circumstances made it necessary for them to quit their homes.'

'Tell me about the others,' he invited, enjoying the animation that lit her countenance when she spoke of these women.

'Well, there is Betty, a gentleman's daughter who was cast out of her home after being persuaded to elope with a plausible gentleman. He took her only as far as the next town, where he abandoned her, and when she tried to return to her family, they disowned her.'

'That is very sad, I agree, but what hope can you give her for the future?'

'She is well educated and I am not unhopeful of finding her a place. In a girls' school, perhaps. For now, she helps out in the charity school my brother has set up. And Bridget, who helps Nancy in the kitchens. She is the widow of a sailor. She was left destitute and found her way to us. Daisy and her son, Billy, were turned out when her employer discovered she was not married. Then there's Marjorie. She was earning her living as a seamstress until an encounter with a so-called gentleman. He promised her the earth and she believed him, until she discovered he had a wife and he left her penniless, alone and with child. Now she makes clothes for the house and for us to sell in the market. She also teaches the others how to sew.' She was at ease now and eager to tell him more. 'One of Marjorie's protégées now works for Miss Hebden, in the town. And a couple more are looking promising—two housemaids who were both thrown on to the streets after being seduced and have horrific tales to tell. One lost her baby and without a character she has been unable to find more work. The other, Ruth, left her newborn son at the foundling hospital—'

'In London!'

'Yes. She was affianced to a sailor, the father of her child, but after he had gone back to sea she discovered he had tricked her and had no intention of returning.

Then she met another man, who promised her if she went with him they would go back for the baby. Instead he brought her here, to the north, and abandoned her in Compton Magna. Her intelligence is not high, but her needlework is exquisite. Marjorie has put a plan to me that I hope the committee might approve—once her baby is born we might set her up in a little shop in one of the bigger towns, such as Harrogate, which is becoming quite fashionable. Then the other two girls could live and work with her. We might even be able to have Ruth's baby returned to her.'

'Quite an ambition.'

'But not impossible. The girls are all hard-working and determined to improve themselves. They merely need a little help.'

She fell quiet and he prompted her with another question.

'Where do these women come from? How do you find them?'

'Some of them find us, but usually Edwin comes upon them through his work. Some, like Ruth, are displaced and the parish will not help them.' She sighed. 'It is much worse in the cities, of course, but even in a small town like Compton Parva there are many who need our help. Cissy, my own maid, for example, was seduced by a travelling man and abandoned. If Edwin had not agreed to employ her she would have had to leave the town.' Molly paused as she slowed the gig. 'Heavens, we are already at the gates of Newlands. I beg your pardon to have rattled on so. You must be thoroughly bored with my chattering about people you do not know.'

'Not at all.' Russ was surprised to find it was the

truth. He added quietly, 'I understand now why you are so prejudiced against our sex, Mrs Morgan.'

'I do not think I am prejudiced,' she responded. 'There are very many good people in the world. The townsfolk of Compton Parva, for example, are in the main very generous. I admit that I am cautious, although I hope I am fairminded. I believe one should judge a man on his deeds.'

'But you judged the party at Newlands before you had even met us,' he challenged her. 'You know very little about Kilburn. Or about me.'

Molly kept her eyes fixed on the winding drive and did not speak until she had brought the gig to a halt at the steps of the house.

'I know you are a dangerous man, Mr Russington.'

'Dangerous?' He sounded genuinely surprised. 'What makes you say that?'

She turned towards him, determined to be honest. 'You are...a danger to women.'

Those sensuous lips curved upwards and she felt the devastating force of his smile.

'I could take that as a compliment.'

She had to fight the urge to smile back. 'I did not mean it so.'

He shook his head. 'I have never forced my attentions upon a woman.'

No, he would not have to, she thought, taking in the dark brown eyes, the curling black hair and the lean handsome face. He had the lithe grace of a cat, the body of an athlete. He only had to walk into a room for all eyes to turn towards him. She had seen it for herself, the way the ladies looked at him and not only the young, unmarried ones.

'Can you also be sure you have never broken a woman's heart?'

'I have never set out to do so. In most cases, the ladies fall in love with my fortune.'

The smile was still there, but it no longer charmed Molly. Now it was full of self-mockery.

She said quietly, 'Then I am very sorry for you.'

She knew she had surprised him. His eyes became dark and unreadable and she braced herself for some withering remark. It never came. Instead he looked over her shoulder and she heard the scrunch of footsteps on the gravel.

'I beg your pardon for keeping you waiting, ma'am, Mr Russington.'

Sir Gerald's butler was hurrying towards them, but he was overtaken by the master of the house demanding to know what had happened. The moment was lost and Molly could not be sorry—the mood between her and Russ had grown too serious.

'I took a tumble when the girth broke, Kilburn. No harm done and Mrs Morgan kindly brought me home.'

Russ gave her a rueful smile and climbed down from the gig while Sir Gerald barked orders for the horse and the damaged saddle to be taken to the stables. Until this was done Molly could not drive off, but she refused Sir Gerald's invitation to step inside, explaining that she needed to get back to the vicarage.

'But surely you can spare five minutes,' Sir Gerald pressed her. 'You must give Russ the chance to thank you properly.'

She glanced at the beau, standing beside his friend and a laugh bubbled up. She said sweetly, 'Mr Russington will need to change out of his muddy clothes, Sir

Gerald, and I really cannot wait while his valet restores him. I am sure it will take an hour, at least.'

Sir Gerald gave a shout of laughter, and Russ's lips formed the word *witch*, although his eyes were gleaming.

'Very true,' he said gravely. He reached out for her hand. 'We have one rescue apiece now, Mrs Morgan. Shall we cry quits?' He added softly, 'Shall we cry friends?'

Her fingers were wrapped in a strong, warm grasp, his eyes were smiling at her. She felt no alarm, no fear, only comfort. She smiled.

'Very well, Mr Russington.'

'If we are truly friends you should call me Russ, but perhaps that would raise a few eyebrows.'

'It certainly would! Out of the question, sir.'

'Quite.' He released her hand, but their eyes remained locked for a moment longer, then he stepped away. 'Off you go, then, Mrs Morgan. I hope you reach home without further mishap.'

She set the gig rolling, urging the horse on until they were trotting away along the drive. She did not look back, but her heart felt lighter than it had done for weeks.

She had just made friends with a rake.

Chapter Six

'Of course, one cannot *really* be friends with a rake.'

Molly uttered the words to the darkness. She had pushed the thought to the back of her mind during the day while she attended to her usual household tasks but now, lying alone in her bed, her mind had returned to her conversation with Russ earlier that day. It was not the same sort of friendship she shared with Fleur and Nancy, and even Agnes, although they had not known each other for very long. But now that she and Russ had cleared the air she believed they could be comfortable together. He would no longer try to flirt with her and cause her heart to beat so erratically. Nor would he fix his eyes upon her and smile in a way that made her stomach swoop with pleasurable anticipation and set her body aching with desire.

She stirred restlessly. She had not felt that for years. Since she had been seventeen, in fact, when she had fallen in love with the handsome Irish soldier who promised to love her to eternity and beyond. Sadly, eternity had lasted only a few months. Since that idyllic summer seven years ago Molly had never experienced that same rush of pleasure, until Beau Russington had arrived with his engaging smile, his flashing eyes and dark looks.

Turning on her side, she snuggled her hand against her cheek and smiled sleepily. It was not Russ's physical presence that attracted her, it was his quick mind, the way they could talk together, laugh together. As long as he behaved himself, she could relax and enjoy his company.

And on this pleasing thought, she finally fell asleep.

Wednesday morning brought a brief note from Prospect House written in Fleur's elegant, flowing hand. Molly put down her breakfast cup with a little cry of surprise that had Edwin looking up from his newspaper.

'Fleur tells me she has engaged another manservant.'

'She is perfectly entitled to do so,' remarked Edwin, 'as long as the costs can be covered by the farm's income.'

'Easily, so there is no need to apply to the committee. I am very pleased, for I was going to suggest it, but it seems she has taken the initiative.'

'Who is the man? Does she say?'

Molly studied the note again. 'No, but she says she discussed the matter thoroughly with Nancy and, since he comes with excellent references, she has taken him on immediately. He is to sleep in the gatehouse.' She smiled across the table. 'It seems an ideal solution. He was most likely recommended to Fleur by Lady Currick or one of the other local families, but I shall find out all the details when I see Fleur this morning.'

'Oh, are you going to the market? I shall walk with you then, as far as the town square, for I have calls to make.'

Molly folded her napkin and set it down on the table. 'Very well, Edwin. I shall go and put on my pelisse and meet you in the hall when you have finished your breakfast.'

It was a crisp autumn morning and the town square was very busy. Molly parted from Edwin and made her way to where Fleur was busy selling a pot of honey to a customer. She was dressed in a sober gown and modest bonnet that covered most of her golden curls, but Molly thought she still looked exceedingly pretty. A shadow of anxiety dimmed her spirits for a moment until she saw that Daisy and Billy were also in attendance.

Fleur waved to Molly and left Daisy serving more customers while she moved to one side.

'You look busy,' Molly remarked, coming up. Fleur nodded.

'Business has been brisk. We have sold the last of the honey and most of the spare apples have gone, as well.'

'That is capital news!'

'Aye, ma'am,' said Daisy, taking advantage of the lull in customers to rearrange what was left of their produce. 'If this carries on, we shall be able to pack up and go home early today.'

Molly nodded. 'Tell me about your new manservant, Fleur. Is he a local man? Do I know him?'

'It is Jem Bailey, the brother of Mr Thomas's mill manager.'

'I thought he was working at Newlands.' Molly caught a look passing between Fleur and Daisy. 'Has he been turned off? Or…heavens, Fleur, have you offered him higher wages to entice him away?'

'No, no, he is to get the same wage he is on now.'

The blush on Fleur's cheek deepened and Daisy said brusquely, 'You had best tell her, Miss Fleur.'

'Tell me what?'

'Sir Gerald brought him to us yesterday.'

Fleur stopped and, following her glance, Molly saw Sir Gerald striding towards them. It was clear his gaze was fixed upon Fleur, but as he drew closer he saw Molly. He missed a step, then came over to her.

'Mrs Morgan.' He touched his hat.

Molly acknowledged him warily. 'I understand Prospect House is in your debt, sir.'

He glanced at Fleur. 'Mrs Dellafield has told you? Perhaps I should have spoken to you or some other member of the committee first, but I wanted to get matters settled as soon as possible. Jem is a good worker and very reliable. You may be sure I made thorough enquiries into his character before recommending him. Mrs Dellafield was reluctant to take him at first, but after the other night—' He shook his head, looking unusually solemn. 'I cannot tell you how sorry I am for what happened, Mrs Morgan. I was most put out to think that any guests of mine could behave so outrageously. I acted as soon as I learned of it from Russ—'

'Mr Russington told you what had happened?'

'Yes. On Monday, after you had dropped him off. I could see it was more than the fall from his horse that was troubling him and when I pressed him he told me about Aikers and Flemington's disgraceful behaviour.' A faint twinkle returned to his eyes. 'He also told me how the ladies dealt with the disturbance. It was well deserved, if you ask me. But you need not fear a recurrence of the incident, I sent them packing that very day and rode over to Prospect House to tell Mrs Dellafield.

Not that I made any attempt to enter the house,' he added quickly. 'I am well aware that you have very strict rules about that.'

'He gave me tuppence to hold his horse while he went to find Miss Fleur in the orchard,' piped up Billy, ducking as his mother aimed a swipe at him and told him to hold his peace.

'Sir Gerald made a very handsome apology,' Fleur put in hastily.

Molly frowned at him. 'Are we to believe you had no suspicion of what your friends meant to do?'

'They are no longer friends of mine, Mrs Morgan. I explained to Fl—Mrs Dellafield that I have not known them that long, although I had seen them about in London. It is true that we kicked up a spree or two together in town, but only harmless fun. Nothing like the outrage they perpetrated the other night. And feeling somewhat responsible, I thought it my duty to do something about it.'

Molly was not wholly convinced, but, judging by the way Fleur was smiling warmly at Sir Gerald and telling him how obliged they were to him, it was clear that she was satisfied. The conversation went on, Sir Gerald declaring that he would not have had it happen for the world, Fleur responding with shy gratitude, until at last Molly interrupted them, bringing to Fleur's attention that the stall was now bare of produce and they could go home.

Molly quite pointedly dismissed Sir Gerald, then waited only to ascertain that they did not require her help to pack up their baskets before making her way back to the vicarage. Whatever she thought of Sir Gerald, there was no doubting his generosity in sending a reliable man to Prospect House. She was also grateful to Russ for informing Sir Gerald of his guests' nocturnal activities. She had not expected that. If he disapproved so much of their behaviour, perhaps he was not quite as rakish as his reputation painted him.

'I am sure his reputation is well deserved,' she argued with herself, 'but he knows the value of not upsetting one's neighbours in a small town like Compton Parva.'

For the rest of the day she found herself wavering between wanting to see Russ and thank him for his intervention, and the thought that if Sir Gerald had set his sights on Fleur, he might want to rid himself of potential rivals. She discussed it with Edwin after dinner, but although he told her Sir Gerald was a splendid fellow and had acted just as he should, Molly knew that Edwin's views were coloured by his growing affection for Agnes Kilburn.

'I see you are still troubled,' he said, when it was time to retire. 'My dear, all you can do is to warn Fleur to be careful. She is a grown woman and is well aware of the risks posed by men like Sir Gerald.' He took her hands. 'Fleur is not you, Molly. You have decided not to trust any man again—'

'And with good reason!'

He squeezed her fingers. 'True, but Fleur must make her own choice.'

He was right, of course, but as Molly prepared for bed that evening she determined that she must spend more time at Prospect House and keep an eye on things for herself.

* * *

Molly had no opportunity to visit Fleur for the next couple of days because she was busy helping Edwin with his parish work and making charitable visits in the town, including a call upon Cissy's mother, who was still very weak from her recent illness. Knowing that her maid would like to spend a little more time with her ailing parent, Molly decided to give her the rest of the day off and walk back to the vicarage alone.

'I have only to call at the post office on my way home and I shall not need you until after dinner this evening, Cissy,' she said, gathering up her empty basket. 'But do be home before dark.'

'I will, ma'am, thank you.'

Molly set off from the little cottage, thinking that the day reflected her sunny spirits, which had been lifted still further by the pleasure she had seen in the old woman's face when she realised her daughter would be able to spend a few more hours at home. Molly felt a bubble of laughter welling up in her. If Edwin asked her to help with a subject for his sermon, she would suggest that this week it should be about the rewards to be gained from such little gestures of kindness.

The idea occupied her until she reached the centre of the town, when she spotted Mr Russington on the far side of the square. He was talking with several local gentlemen, but he excused himself and came across to greet her. When he turned to accompany her, Molly felt obliged to tell him there was no need.

'But I insist,' he replied. 'Unless you think it will do you harm to be seen walking with such a one as me.'

She laughed at that. 'I think my character will survive

a short walk in your company, Mr Russington. In fact, I am pleased we have met.' She became serious. 'I wanted to thank you. For telling Sir Gerald what went on at Prospect House the other night.'

There was a pause.

'I mentioned it, yes. I did not expect Kilburn to be quite so angry about it. He is usually the most placid of men, but he ordered Aikers and Flemington to leave immediately.'

'Perhaps he is removing potential rivals.'

'That is a very cynical point of view, madam.'

'Experience has taught me to be cautious where men are concerned.'

'You are very world-weary, for one so young.'

'I am four-and-twenty.'

'You look younger.'

She disguised her blushes with another laugh. 'Do not be offering me Spanish coin, Mr Russington. There is nothing to gain by it.'

They had reached the post office and she stopped. He was looking down at her, a faint smile playing at the corners of his mouth.

'Now, why should you think I am trying to flatter you?'

'Because you are a rake, perhaps?' She could not help smiling back at him, surprised she could talk to him so easily.

'Even rakes should tell the truth to their friends, madam.'

He touched his hat and strolled away, leaving her to stare after him and remind herself yet again that one could never truly be friends with a rake.

* * *

The news that Marjorie had given birth to a lusty baby girl gave Molly the excuse she needed to visit Prospect House regularly over the next couple of weeks, and it soon became clear that Sir Gerald rode to the house almost every day, stopping to talk to Fleur if she should be out of doors. Little Billy spoke of him as a great gun and told Molly that Sir Gerald always let him look after his horse. When Molly teased Fleur about the number of tasks requiring her attention in the gardens, Fleur flushed, but Molly could not order her to remain indoors. When she mentioned it to Nancy, the cook was philosophical.

'You are not running a prison, after all,' she told Molly. 'And you cannot prevent Fleur from talking to Sir Gerald if she so wishes.'

Molly agreed and in the end all she could do was to warn Fleur to take care and beg Nancy and the others to look out for her. She felt a little guilty, cautioning Fleur against Sir Gerald when she herself was seeing much more of Russ and growing more at ease in his company. It was inevitable they should meet, she supposed, given the good weather. She was out of doors every day, taking the gig to Prospect House or walking in the town visiting her brother's sick or poverty-stricken parishioners. Once she met him when she was on her way to Raikes Farm with another basket of provisions and he dismounted and carried her basket for her.

'Shall I wait to escort you back?' he asked, when they reached her destination. 'I know your propensity for injury.'

She was no longer embarrassed by his reference to her turning her ankle and merely laughed at him.

'But it is not in the least muddy today. No, you must go on with your birdwatching, I do not need you.' She hesitated, giving him a speculative look and his brows went up.

'Well, Mrs Morgan?'

'I wondered if you would be free on Friday morning.'

His eyes narrowed suspiciously. 'Why?'

'I plan to go to Hobbs Lane that day. I want to find greenery from the hedgerows to decorate the church in readiness for Marjorie's baby to be baptised there. I was going to take Cissy, but she is even shorter than I am. Whereas you…'

He laughed. 'You think I might be useful? Very well, madam, I shall be there to help you!'

They parted, Molly feeling only a trifle guilty for issuing the invitation.

Friday dawned bright and when Molly informed Cissy of her plans for the morning, the maid suggested Molly's old primrose dimity would be most suitable.

'You don't want to risk spoiling one of your newer gowns if you are scrambling around the hedgerows, ma'am.'

It was a very sensible idea and Molly agreed, but she voiced a protest when Cissy brought out the russet spencer of fine wool that Edwin had given her last summer. There was a matching hat to go with the little jacket, a frivolous little cap that allowed her dusky curls to cluster around her face and Molly objected that it was far too fine to wear upon such an outing.

'But you never wear it on *any* occasion,' Cissy argued. 'If it sits in the cupboard much longer, it will be quite out of fashion.'

Molly allowed herself to be persuaded and some twenty minutes later she sallied forth. Hobbs Lane was only a stone's throw from the church and she found Russ waiting for her as she turned off the main road. The sight of him in his blue coat and buckskins made her mouth go dry and she wondered if she should have brought Cissy after all, but only for a moment. They were well within sight of the busy road and besides, at this time of year, there was much to do in the house and Cook had asked if Cissy could help her in the kitchen, preserving fruits for the winter.

Russ touched his hat to her as she came up to him. 'Mrs Morgan.' He put his hand in his pocket and drew out a stubby knife with a curving blade. 'I borrowed this from the gardener at Newlands. Shall we begin?'

'I commend your foresight,' she said, the flutter of her nerves subsiding. 'By all means, let us make a start.'

They worked companionably and Molly was grateful for his help, the beau's height and long arms giving her more choice of greenery. He cut heavy bunches of scarlet rowan berries and long tendrils of ivy, before they moved on to a thick, late-flowering gorse, its vivid yellow flowers making a striking contrast to the dock, with its vibrant green leaves and red-brown seeds. They had almost finished when Molly became aware that the clouds were gathering and the threat of rain hung in the air. Russ filled her large basket until it was overflowing, then piled more ivy and dock leaves into her arms, saying he would carry the basket.

'Come on,' he said, glancing up at the lowering sky. 'We must hurry if we are not to be caught in a shower.'

They were in sight of the church when the first drops of rain began to fall and they ran the last few yards to the lychgate and up the path into the church, laughing and giggling like children. Molly dropped her burden on the empty table just inside the door, leaving space for Russ to put down the basket.

'Thank you,' she turned to him, still smiling. 'I could never have achieved so much without you.' She pulled off her gloves, the better to brush her damp curls from her face.

'You are missing most of them.' He pushed her hands away and she stood passively while he gently tucked the stray curls beneath her cap.

'There. That is better. Now, let me look at you.'

He turned her to face the great west window, his hands resting lightly on her shoulders. Until that moment she had felt comfortable, at ease, but suddenly it was impossible to move. He had his back to the light yet his dark eyes glowed, drawing her in. She wanted him. She recognised the feeling, but this was stronger, more overwhelming than anything she had ever known before. It would be so good to surrender, to give in, but she fought it, reminding herself of what she had to lose.

She tried to step away, only to find her retreat blocked by the solid planks of the box pew at her back.

'Please.' The word was little more than a croak. 'Please, stop it.'

'Stop what?' His breathing was not quite steady, but he kept his hands on her shoulders, held her gaze a prisoner with those dark, glinting eyes.

'S-stop flirting with me.'

'I am not flirting.'

His voice was low, deep, lulling her senses while his eyes were boring into her, dragging out her soul. In one last desperate bid to escape her own desire, she forced herself to twist away and turn her back on him.

'You *are*.' She fixed her hands on the edge of the pew, gripping the wood until her knuckles gleamed white. 'You must be. It is what rakes *do*. And you are undoubtedly a rake.'

'And you are a widow, Mrs Morgan. You are no innocent virgin. This is no flirtation, but neither am I forcing my attentions on you.'

She felt the weight of his hands again on her shoulders. He was standing close behind her, the heat of him radiating through the thin spencer and her muslin skirts. It was as much as she could do not to lean back against him and beg him to make love to her. His breath was warm on her cheek, his voice was low, seductive, and it wrapped itself around her like velvet. It would so easy to give in.

'You feel it, too, Molly. Admit it. You are trembling in your effort to resist.'

It was true. Her body was thrumming, taut as a bowstring. Desire tugged at her thighs and made her breasts ache. She remembered it well, that overwhelming sense of longing, but it faded as memories she had buried deep came back to haunt her. The agony of betrayal and the brutal, physical pain of being kicked and beaten until she could not even walk. She was seized by unreasoning fear.

'No, no! Let me go!'

Hearing the panic in her voice Russ released her and stepped away, frowning. Moments earlier she had been within an ace of falling into his arms, but now she was genuinely alarmed. She was scrubbing at her cheek with the back of her hand and he drew his handkerchief from his pocket.

'I beg your pardon,' he said quietly. 'Will you not tell me how I have upset you?'

She dashed another rogue tear from her cheek.

'I must go,' she muttered. 'I will finish this later.'

He turned to accompany her out of the church, half expecting her to wave him away, but she allowed him to walk with her to the lychgate, where they stopped and she held out the crumpled handkerchief.

'No, you keep it,' he said quietly. 'I give you my word I had not planned this, Molly. Truly I did not mean to frighten you. I would not have this affect our friendship.'

'Friends!' She gave a bitter laugh. 'We are not friends. We could never be friends!'

Russ watched her hurry away, head bowed against the downpour. He was startled to discover just how much her response had shaken him. He enjoyed spending time with Molly Morgan, they had grown very comfortable together and he had come to believe they were friends. But he could not deny the attraction, the sudden blaze of desire that had crackled between them as they stood together in the cool, silent church. Molly had felt it, too, he would stake his life on it, but she had shied away like a frightened animal and he had seen again that terror in her eyes.

Molly had disappeared from sight now, but still Russ stood sheltering at the lychgate. Part of him wanted to run after her and discover the cause of her fear, but something held him back. He did not want the responsibility. Women were trouble. His stepmother had taught him that at an early age. It was best not to get involved with the creatures. He had spent his adult life avoiding romantic attachments and he was not about to change that for a diminutive widow who strongly disapproved of him and his way of life.

'She is right,' he muttered, 'We cannot be friends and there's an end to it.'

And with that he settled his hat more firmly on his head and stepped out into the rain.

'Good heavens, we are invited to dine at Newlands this evening.'

'Surely not.'

Molly stared across the breakfast table at her brother, aware that her cheeks were heating up. Since her meeting with Russ yesterday, he had been constantly in her thoughts. She was distressed that such an enjoyable interlude had ended with her running away. Yet she had had no option. That moment in the church, the shocking attraction that had flowed between them, had threatened to overwhelm her. She had spent the time since then, including most of the night, berating herself for thinking she could flout the rules of propriety. She should have made sure she never went out of doors without a maid in attendance.

'Yes, yes,' said Edwin, his eyes fixed upon the letter. 'I confess it is most unexpected. When I saw Gerald a few days ago he made no mention of it. However, we have no other engagements tonight so I shall write back and accept. I am sure we will both enjoy a little company this evening, will we not? That is…' He looked up at last. 'Molly, did you speak? Have you made some other arrangement?'

Much as she wanted to, Molly could think of no reason why they should not go. And deep down inside she knew she wanted to see Russ. Surely there could be no harm in it, as long as they were not alone together. Indeed, unless she was to become a recluse, there was no way she could avoid meeting the beau while he remained at Newlands.

She summoned a smile. 'No, Edwin, we are both perfectly free this evening, although I, too, am a little surprised that they should invite us again at such short notice.'

However, when Lady Currick called to deliver a receipt for a saddle of mutton for Molly's cook, the mystery was soon solved.

'The ladies are going away,' Lady Currick informed Molly and Edwin, as she enjoyed a glass of wine with them. 'The Claydons and Mr and Mrs Sykes are accompanying Miss Kilburn and her companion to visit friends in Scarborough, so there will be no more dinners at Newlands until she returns.'

'Miss Kilburn is going away—for how long?'

Molly saw the dull flush on her brother's cheeks as he blurted out his question and she made a mental note to observe him and Agnes closely that evening. Lady Currick made no mention of the departure of two of the gentlemen and Molly was not equal to the task of enquiring, but she did wonder if Sir Gerald would remain at the house with only Mr Russington for company.

The question was answered almost as soon as they arrived at Newlands that evening. Molly clung to her brother's arm as they were shown into the drawing room, but the warmth of Miss Kilburn's welcome and the fact that Russ made no attempt to approach her calmed her initial nerves. She must do this. She must meet the beau as an acquaintance, nothing more.

They were the only guests and it was soon clear that Sir Gerald had not divulged the reason for the sudden departure of Aikers and Flemington.

'A prior engagement has called the gentlemen away and we, too, shall be departing soon,' remarked Mrs Sykes, sighing. 'I vow, Sir Gerald, I am surprised that you and Mr Russington will not come with us, rather than remain behind to rattle around in this house all on your own.'

'I expect we will spend most of our days out of doors,' returned Sir Gerald cheerfully. 'The park has been woefully neglected and overgrown, but there is plenty of sport to be had. The woodcock, for example, have been breeding very freely. I am planning a number of improvements to the estate, too, that need to be put into action.'

'I hope you aren't expecting Russington to advise you,' put in Lord Claydon, gently teasing.

'No, indeed,' replied Russ, smiling. 'I have excellent stewards on each of my properties, which leaves me with nothing to do but enjoy myself.'

There was general laughter at this and Molly wondered if she was the only one who heard the note of self-mockery in the beau's tone.

'I am sure it is not true,' remarked Edwin as the laughter died away.

'But it is, I assure you. My life is wholly given over to pleasure.'

'I pray you will not believe him, Edwin,' cried Sir Gerald, coming up. 'I rely upon his judgement in everything. Behind that languid and smiling exterior is a very sharp intellect.'

'I do not deny it,' drawled the beau. 'But that does not mean I waste my energies upon humdrum domestic matters. I have a very good man of business for that.'

'Aye, you do, and insist upon him giving you regular and detailed reports of all your lands and investments.' Sir Gerald clapped his friend on the shoulder and grinned at the assembled company. 'Russ would have everyone believe that he is a very frippery fellow, but you may take my word for it, it is all a hum.'

'Good heavens, Gerald, are you trying to put me to the blush?' Russ protested. He was smiling, but when he turned to look at Molly she saw that it did not reach his eyes. 'You will not deceive Mrs Morgan. She has had accurate reports of my reputation from the very best authority, is that not so, madam?'

Her chin went up. 'I believe one should judge a man on his actions rather than what is said of him.'

Edwin nodded his approval. 'Well said, my dear.'

He went off to talk to Agnes and Molly found herself momentarily alone. She tensed as Russ moved a little closer.

'Perhaps, ma'am, our host's *actions* in giving Aikers and Flemington their orders to quit have given you a better opinion of him than you have of me.'

'I do not think badly of you, Mr Russington.' After a glance to ensure no one could overhear them, Molly continued. 'We are agreed, sir, that you are a rake and I am a widow. *You* cannot help what you are and, as you pointed out yesterday, I am no innocent. I should have known better than to meet you without a chaperon.'

She gave a little nod and moved off. She was stronger now. Yesterday's weakness was gone and she would not submit to any man.

* * *

Russ made no attempt to speak to her again that evening and Molly did not know whether to be glad or sorry for it. Part of her was relieved that she was not having to fight down the undoubted attraction she felt for the man, but another part, an irresponsible, rebellious part, wanted to converse with him, to enjoy the verbal sparring that made her feel so very much alive. Thus, when she accompanied Edwin back to the vicarage late that night, she was aware of a feeling of discontent, as though some promised treat had not materialised. And as she blew out her bedside candle, she realised that with the ladies gone from Newlands, there would be even less opportunity to see Russ during the next few weeks.

'Oh, was ever life so trying!'

Molly was driving the gig and took advantage of the solitude to utter the words aloud. She was on her way home after her weekly visit to Prospect House and what she had learned there had left her seriously worried. One look at Fleur's radiant face was enough to tell Molly that her friend was in the first throes of a love affair. It had not taken Molly long to learn that Sir Gerald was an almost daily visitor to the farm and although he never came into the house itself, he and Fleur were in the habit of walking out each day. When Molly questioned Fleur about it, she merely laughed.

'You are making far too much of it.' Fleur's words were belied by the faint colour on her cheeks. 'Sir Gerald comes here to discuss farm management. He is intent upon improving Newlands and comes to talk to Moses, and very often he asks me questions, too, about the kitchen gardens and the best way to set up the accounts.' Her clear, innocent laugh rang out. 'Who would have believed I should ever have been so knowledgeable about household and farm matters that a gentleman would want my advice?'

Molly could believe it, only too well. With his sister away, Sir Gerald was making the most of his time to flirt with Fleur, only she was far too innocent to see it, and to every attempt of Molly's to warn her off, Fleur would only blush, and laugh, and say she had no intention of letting Sir Gerald compromise her.

'But she does not *know*,' declared Molly to the empty lane, making the pony trotting between the shafts twitch its ears nervously. 'She does not realise how irresistible a man can be. How he can take you in with his soft words and allurements.'

Nancy might say that Fleur was old enough to look after herself, but Molly had seen the soft glow in her eyes when she spoke of Sir Gerald Kilburn. She was falling in love and that could spell disaster. Molly would do anything in her power to protect her friend.

Russ lowered the spyglass and exhaled a long, steady breath, well satisfied with his early-morning observations. The freshening breeze on his cheek reminded him that the seasons were changing and the summer birds would soon be leaving the moors. He would not have many more opportunities like this and he must make the most of it.

The distant thud of hooves made him turn. He saw a rider approaching... Molly Morgan! He shook his head, telling himself he was being fanciful, because with the morning sun behind the figure he could only make out an outline. He did not even know if she could ride. He lifted his hand to block out the sun and there she was, cantering towards him on a sturdy bay cob. As she drew nearer the horse slowed to a trot, and he lowered his hand, waiting for her to come up to him. Now she was closer he could see the way her mannish riding jacket was moulded to her petite figure, the tiny waist accentuated even more by the billowing lavender skirts. She wore a curly-brimmed beaver hat over her dark hair, but the veil was turned back, flowing behind her like a gossamer pennant. He was glad he could see her face, for the air had whipped a becoming colour into her cheeks and her eyes sparkled with the exercise.

'Good day to you, Mrs Morgan.'

'I was looking for you.' His brows and his spirits rose at her words and she flushed, shaking her head. '*Not* for the pleasure of your company, Mr Russington.'

'Well, that has put me in my place.' He reached out and rubbed a hand over the pony's velvet nose. 'How may I help you?'

'I remembered you had made a habit of these early-morning walks and thought it the best time to talk to you. Alone.'

He gave a little bow, saying politely, 'I am at your disposal, madam.'

She hesitated for a heartbeat before kicking her foot free of the stirrup and jumping nimbly to the ground. He knew a moment's regret that she had not asked him to lift her down.

She said, 'Will you walk with me?'

Intrigued, he fell into step beside her. 'What of your pony?'

'Christopher will be happy to follow. He knows I have treats for him in my pocket.'

'*Christopher?*'

'Edwin called him that when he bought him for me. After the saint,' she added, a hint of laughter in her voice. 'because he is such a steady mount and will carry me anywhere.'

Russ glanced back at the cob, plodding along quietly behind them. 'By the look of him he is built more for endurance than speed.'

'He is,' she said, sighing. 'He cannot be persuaded to anything more than a gentle canter, but he has the most placid nature, nothing startles him.'

'I doubt if even cannon fire would move him,' he said frankly and was rewarded by hearing her low, full-throated laugh.

'I am sure you are right. His watchword is slow but steady! But I do not hunt and have few opportunities to ride, so there is no point in exchanging him for a faster mount that would only spend his time eating his head off in the stables. But I did not come here to talk about my horse.'

She fell silent. Glancing down at her, he saw the tiny crease in her brow and a downward tilt to her mouth. Her mood had grown serious and he was sorry for it, he liked her smile, the way she laughed. She did not do it often enough, he thought.

They had walked several more yards before the words came out in a rush.

'It is about Fleur. Mrs Dellafield. Sir Gerald has been showing her a great deal of attention.'

'Mrs Dellafield? I cannot recall meeting her.'

'She is housekeeper at Prospect House.'

'Ah. She was at the market, was she not? I have not seen her since. Unlike Kilburn's two departed guests, I have not been in the habit of visiting the house.'

'Well, your friend has,' she retorted. 'I understand he has become a regular caller there.'

'Has he?' Russ considered the matter. 'He has said nothing to me about it, but it is possible, I suppose. We do not spend the whole of every day in each other's pockets. It certainly explains his indignation when I told him of Aikers and Flemington's recent exploits.'

'And you said I was being cynical when I suggested he had an ulterior motive for sending them away.'

'I still think that. Kilburn is an honourable man. I have known him since we were at school together.'

'That is no recommendation!'

He exhaled in a long, exasperated hiss.

'Not all the tales you have heard of us are true, Mrs Morgan. Kilburn and I went to town together as young men. I admit we were rich, idle and ripe for a spree. We became part of a very fast set and we did kick up a dust in those early years. A couple of our number went beyond the bounds and were shockingly indiscreet about it, too. Kilburn and I condemned their actions and realised we had outgrown that particular group. We distanced ourselves, but it was too late, we were tainted by their scandals. Perhaps if we had withdrawn from town and lived as monks since those early years, or if we had married, we might have shaken off the reputation. But society has an insatiable appetite for gossip and eligible bachelors are always the subject of scandal and speculation.'

'But Prospect House cannot afford to be the subject of any such speculation. Your friend's attentions do Mrs Dellafield no good at all.'

'Hmm. Is she pretty?'

'Extremely pretty.'

'Then I cannot blame him for flirting with her.'

He heard her gasp of indignation, but she did not rip up at him. Instead she clasped her hands tightly together, as if suppressing her anger.

'He is inveigling himself into her affections,' she told him. 'He goes there supposedly because he wants to learn more about the farming methods.'

'It may well be true. He has certainly expressed that desire to me and it is common knowledge that Prospect Farm is one of the most productive in the area. Perhaps you are being too harsh upon Sir Gerald.'

'No.' She stopped and turned to look up at him. 'He could learn all he needs to know from Moses, who runs the farm, if that was his true intention.'

'And Mrs Dellafield could advise him to do so, if that was her wish.'

He spoke gently, but even so her eyes darkened with distress and a silent acknowledgement that he was right. She shook her head and began to walk again.

'She is besotted and cannot be made to see that he is trifling with her.'

Russ considered the matter. Gerald had certainly been rather preoccupied recently and the fact that he had said nothing about this liaison made him think it might be more serious than a mere flirtation.

He said abruptly. 'What do you know of Mrs Della-field? What is her birth?'

'She is a gentleman's daughter and perfectly respect-able, but like so many unfortunate women, she was obliged by circumstance to leave her home and seek refuge.'

'I take it she is not married?'

'No, but it is not unusual for housekeepers to use the

appellation. She is an innocent, Mr Russington, and I will not allow her to be hurt.'

'I take it you have spoken to the lady about your concerns?'

She nodded, her hands twisting themselves even tighter. 'She does not see the danger.'

'Perhaps there isn't any danger.' He caught her swift, incredulous glance and smiled. 'Despite what you think, madam, Sir Gerald is a gentleman. He would never force himself upon any woman.'

'Perhaps that is so, but he is a very engaging, extremely attractive man and he could break her heart without realising what he has done. Can you not talk to him, dissuade him from his pursuit of Fleur?'

'My dear Molly, why should he listen to me? If the lady is willing—perhaps he is merely passing the time of day with a pretty woman. What does your brother say of the matter?'

'Edwin says I should not interfere.' She bit her lip. 'But *you* could speak to Sir Gerald. He respects your judgement. I have heard him say so.'

'And in this instance my judgement is that your brother is right. Let the affair—if it is an affair—run its course.' He looked up. 'We have almost reached the track that will take me back to Newlands. Unless you wish to come with me, and talk to Kilburn yourself, then we must part here.'

She was silent and he could almost feel her anxiety. The colour had quite gone from her cheeks, and as they stepped on to the track, she spoke again.

'What will it take for you to keep your friend away from mine?' Her voice was low, but the meaning was quite clear. His eyes narrowed.

'Is that an offer, Mrs Morgan? Knowing my reputation, you should be wary of asking such a question.'

'Fleur is a virgin, an innocent. She has a great deal to lose if your friend seduces her.'

'And you have not?'

She shrugged. 'One night with you would not harm me quite so much. I would survive.'

One night. She was offering herself to him for one night. For a heartbeat he allowed himself to imagine having her in his bed. Undressing her. Making love to her. The sudden jolt of desire scorched him, but it was quickly cooled and washed away by a wave of fury. How dare she think he could be bought in such a way? Even more galling was the fact that he *cared* about her opinion!

Blinded by rage, he grabbed her horse's bridle and brought the creature round on to the path.

He said, his words biting, 'Your less-than-flattering proposal does you no credit, Mrs Morgan. You had best leave before I show you just how badly a rake can behave.'

'I—I beg your pardon.' Her face was crimson. 'I did not mean to offend you. I thought—'

'I know exactly what you thought. That Gerald and I would take any woman for sport. I do not know what sort of life you have had, madam, what sort of men you have known, but I can tell you now that we are not all savages.'

Without waiting for her approval he put his hands around her waist and threw her up on to the pony's back. It was roughly done and for a moment he thought she might topple off again, so he kept his hands on her, holding her firmly in the saddle until she had found her stirrup.

'Thank you,' she said icily. 'I have control now.'

'Good.' He stepped away. 'Then I suggest you go home, Mrs Morgan, and we will forget we ever had this conversation.'

He turned away and strode back towards Newlands. How dare she? How *dare* she think he would take her as payment of some debt? He had not yet met a woman who did not think she could use her body to get what she wanted. In his stepmother's case it was his family money and, not content with marrying his father, she had sought to gratify her lusts by seducing Russ, too. That had shown him just how grasping and avaricious women were. He had thought Molly Morgan was different, but no. She was the same as the rest.

But was she? The black rage abated slightly. She was by no means eager to throw herself into his arms. He thought back to that time in the church. She had panicked then at the mere idea that he might kiss her. And today, the thought of spending the night with him had been—he could not avoid the word—repugnant to her. His furious pace slowed. With the exception of her brother she did not appear to trust any of his sex. She was a widow— perhaps she had not enjoyed the marriage bed, but his instinct told him it was more than that. Someone, some *man*, had made her think they were all villains. Whoever it was had hurt her very badly.

He remembered holding Molly in the saddle, his hands almost spanning her tiny waist, and the thought of anyone hurting her made the bile rise in his gorge. Not that it was his problem. Molly Morgan was more than capable of looking after herself. And, it seemed, she had taken on the task of looking after the women of Prospect House, too.

'Well, I wish her well with that,' he muttered, lengthening his stride again. 'Let that occupy her time and keep her out of my way!'

Chapter Seven

Russ was still simmering with anger when he reached Newlands, and he made his way directly to his room to change. When he emerged some time later he learned that his host was still at breakfast, and he went downstairs to join him.

'So you *are* back!' Gerald was helping himself to more ham from a platter and waved his fork at Russ. 'I thought perhaps you had seen some particularly interesting species on the moors.'

'I did, but not the feathered kind.'

Russ dismissed his friend's enquiring look with a shake of his head and took his place at the table. A silent-footed servant appeared with a basket of warm bread rolls and he took two, suddenly realising how hungry he was. He wondered if Molly had yet broken her fast. She must have risen very early to ride out and find him. The decision could not have been the work of a moment. She must be very concerned for her friend.

He waited until the servants had left them alone and then said, at his most casual, 'Are you calling upon Mrs Dellafield today?'

'Ah.' Russ glanced up. Gerald was looking almost sheepish. 'How did you learn of it?'

'Did you think you could keep such a thing secret in a small town like this?' Russ countered.

'I have been meaning to tell you, when the time was right.' Gerald leaned forward, his eyes shining. 'She is an angel, Russ. Beautiful, innocent—'

'So I have been told.'

'No, no, it is true. She has confided in me. She was obliged to flee her home when her stepfather began to show an unnatural interest in her. Mrs Morgan is an old schoolfriend and took her in. Then, when Prospect House was set up, she became its housekeeper and has been there ever since, hiding from the world.' He sighed. 'Like Perrault's story of Sleeping Beauty in the wood.'

'It certainly sounds like a fairy tale.'

'I would have told you,' said Gerald, 'if circumstances had been different, I would have introduced you to her, but after Aikers and Flemington caused such a stir I did not want to suggest bringing another gentleman anywhere near the place.'

Russ reached for the coffee pot. 'How did it start?'

'You remember the day we were to ride to Knaresborough and my horse cast a shoe? It was such a fine day I decided to take a stroll on the far side of the valley—just exploring, you see—and found myself quite by chance beside the Prospect Farm orchards and that is where I first saw her. She looked such a picture that I could not help but stop and speak.' He laughed gently. 'She all but ran away from me, but I persuaded her to stay and talk. After that, well, I found myself riding that way quite often. I never go near the house but send a message, and if she is free, she comes out to meet me.' He frowned suddenly. 'It is no mere flirtation, Russ, if that is what you are thinking.'

'What else am I to think?'

Gerald smiled at that and Russ was startled to see the soft glow in his friend's eyes.

'She is like no other lady I have met before, but I assure you we just…talk. When she learned I really was interested in improving Newlands she was more than happy to discuss the running of the farm with me. She surprises me constantly. Her knowledge of the farm and its workings is almost as great as that man of theirs, Moses, who runs the place.'

'The devil she does!' Russ gave him a searching look. 'So you are not trifling with her.'

'Trifling! Good God, I should think not. But, it is a delicate situation. I need to be sure of my feelings and Fleur's before I introduce her to Agnes. I thought we were secure enough, for her friends at Prospect House would not say anything, I am sure. However, if tongues are beginning to wag—'

'They are not,' Russ cut in. 'I had it in confidence from a most discreet source. Nevertheless, I would urge caution, my friend. Many a man before you has been taken in by a pretty face.'

'If you think Fleur is trying to trap me into marriage then you are very far off,' retorted Gerald, bridling.

Russ put up his hands and quickly begged pardon.

'Very well,' said Gerald, only slightly mollified. 'And as it happens, I was planning to take the dogs out and go shooting today. My gamekeeper tells me there are woodcock in the West Park, if you wish to come.'

Russ agreed with alacrity and they both turned their attentions to their breakfast, harmony restored. Gerald's affection for Fleur Dellafield was sincere. Molly Morgan should take some comfort from that. Not that she would learn of it from him, since he had promised himself that he would not go near the infernal woman again if he could help it.

True to his namesake, Christopher carried Molly safely back to the vicarage, although her eyes were so misted with tears and her thoughts so awry that she had no true memory of the journey. How could she have been so crass as to offer herself to him like that! It was a blunder of monumental proportions. Molly ran up to her room, dismissing the maid as soon as she had thrown off her muddy habit and saying that she would lie down for a while.

She curled up on the bed, appalled at her behaviour. It had been building, this feeling that she must do something, ever since the baptism of Marjorie's baby. The sight of the child in its mother's arms had brought on such a wave of longing and regret that Molly had hardly been able to stand through the service. It brought back how much her own seduction had cost her and Molly was determined Fleur should not make the same mistakes. But to think that she might buy off Beau Russington with her favours was unforgivable. For all his reputation, she knew in her heart he was nothing like the men who had destroyed her life.

How would she be able to look him in the face when they next met? And they must meet, because Edwin and Agnes had become such friends that it was impossible that they would not be thrown into each other's company. At least with the ladies being absent Edwin would not expect her to visit Newlands and if she was to see

Russ in the town then they might ignore one another. That was the best she could hope for.

By afternoon the rain had set in, steady and relentless. The grey skies reflected Molly's low spirits and she moved from room to room, unable to settle to any task. Edwin was dining out and for want of any other occupation she ordered her own dinner to be served at five. The solitary meal did nothing to soothe Molly's nerves. She left the table more restless than ever and went upstairs to fetch her cloak. Her maid glanced out of the window.

'You ain't never going out in this, ma'am.'

'It is no more than a drizzle. I shall not melt.'

'No, but you will get soaked through,' Cissy retorted in a tone of long suffering. 'I suppose I had best get my cloak.'

'No, there is no need for you to get wet, too,' said Molly quickly. 'I am not going far, only to the church. My brother has mislaid his book of sermons, and I thought I might look for it. There will be no one abroad at this time and in this weather.'

'Not if they can help it,' muttered Cissy. 'Very well, ma'am. I'll build up the fire in your room for when you return. And put a hot brick in the oven, for you are bound to be chilled to the bone when you comes back and will catch your death if we don't take care.'

With these dismal words ringing in her ears Molly ran lightly down the stairs, flicking her hood into place as she stepped out of the house. The rain had turned the roads to mud and she kept her head down, trying to find the cleanest path, but by the time she reached the church her boots and her skirts were liberally splashed with dirt and her cloak felt heavy and cloying on her shoulders. If she did catch her death, as Cissy put it, then she would be well served, she thought miserably, her eyes dwelling on the table where she and Russ had left the plants they had collected. They had been so at ease together, collecting the ivy and green boughs for the church. Even now she could remember him standing close, enveloping her with his presence. Molly had not realised how much she had come to enjoy Russ's company until that moment when she had pushed him away and killed their burgeoning friendship.

'But if I had not... If he had kissed me...'

She dared not finish the sentence, dared not let her thoughts linger on what might have been. She knew now they could never be friends, but, oh, how she missed him. And they might at least have been acquaintances, able to exchange civil pleasantries, if only she had not tried to enlist his help in keeping Fleur safe from Sir Gerald.

She pulled her cloak a little tighter, but her shudder had little to do with the weather. It was shame and remorse, brought on by the memory of the disdain she had seen in his eyes. If only she could have that time over again! She should have asked him, begged him to help her. She might have appealed to his better nature, his honour as a gentleman. He might well have refused to help her, but at least he would not hold her in such contempt.

Molly sighed, her eyes wandering listlessly around the church. She had forgotten why she had come. Ah, yes, Edwin's little book of sermons. She made a half-hearted search, but it was now too dark to see very well and she knew she should go home. She carefully shut the door behind her, pulled her hood a little further over her head and hurried back to the road. She kept her eyes on the ground, trying to miss the worst of the puddles. A damp chill was settling on the back of her neck where the rain was seeping through her cloak and she thought she might have to admit to Cissy that it had been fool-hardy to come out in such weather.

Something made her look up and she stopped. Russ, hatless and with his hair plastered to his head, was stand-ing in the rain, blocking her way. She knew from the look in his eyes that this was no chance meeting, he was not going to let her pass. She swung about and began to hurry away, but the next moment he was beside her, gripping her arm.

'We must talk.'

'In this weather? Do not be absurd.'

'You are already wet through. Another few moments won't hurt.'

They had reached the junction with Hobbs Lane and he turned into it, taking Molly with him.

'If you want me to apologise,' she began, 'for what I said this morning, then I do. Wholeheartedly. I should never have said such a thing. Now I pray you will let me go.'

'Not yet. I want to talk to you.'

The high hedgerows and overhanging trees offered some shelter from the misty drizzle, but they increased the gloom and the sense of danger. Molly's heart was thundering, making it hard to breathe.

'There is nothing to talk about,' she told him, strug-gling against his iron hold. 'We cannot meet without upsetting one another.'

'Tell me,' he said. 'Tell me what happened to make you hate men so much.'

She tried to prise his fingers from her arm. 'Please. Please let me go.'

'No. I want to understand why you are like this. Your commitment to Prospect House, your abhorrence of men. Something occurred in your past and I want to know.' His grip tightened. 'Since this morning I have been imagining the worst.'

Molly stopped struggling. He would not be satisfied until she told him something.

'I fell in love,' she said simply. 'It is a familiar story, shockingly commonplace, in fact. I was just seventeen. He was a handsome Irish soldier, here with his regiment for the summer. He was very charming, told me he loved me and promised we would be married. I was quite prepared to follow the drum, but the militia left. He went with them and I—' She turned her head, gazing up the lane and blinking rapidly. 'I was left behind. I was too proud to make a fuss, to tell my family until he was gone and it was too late.'

The memory was still painful, but at that moment she would not have resisted if Russ had put his arms about her. She would have taken comfort from his sympathy, his strength. Instead, with a sigh that might have been compassion, he released her and the thought that he pitied her was like salt in an open wound. She dragged together her few final shreds of pride to keep her head up and her voice level. 'I was ruined. As many another foolish girl has been before. Now you know the truth.'

'A broken heart? Abandoned by your lover?' He shook his head. 'There is more you aren't telling me.'

'Is that not enough?'

'No!' He raked one hand through his hair. 'A failed

love affair is not enough to give you this…this *aversion* to men.'

'I do not have an aversion,' she protested. 'I am perfectly friendly with many of my neighbours in Compton Parva, and I love Edwin, very much.'

'These are men who pose no threat to you!' His eyes narrowed. 'Was your marriage unhappy?'

'That is none of your business. I shall not listen to you!'

When she turned to walk away he stepped in front of her, so close she found herself staring at the solid wall of his chest.

'Do not try to fob me off, Molly.'

She gave a little cry of frustration and beat her fists against him.

'You have no right to pester me like this.'

'I am determined to know,' he said, covering her hands and holding them still. 'If you will not tell me, I shall ask your brother.'

'He knows nothing about it!'

Her words had shocked him. His head went back, as if she had struck him.

'No one knows,' she whispered. 'It is in the past. Finished.'

'It is not finished,' he said slowly. 'It is eating away at you and it will ruin your life if you do not stop it. You are a young woman, Molly Morgan. Young enough to marry again, to fall in love again.'

'Never! I am done with all men.'

'I do not believe that.' His fingers tightened. 'Can you deny you feel something when I touch you? You are trembling now.'

'That is because I am angry.'

'Are you sure about that?' he said gently, 'You have a passionate nature, Molly. You can love again, if only you will let yourself. I know it.'

'Of course, you do.' Her rising panic manifested itself in scorn. 'You think yourself irresistible to any female!'

'No, no, I do not mean me. I mean a good man. A man of the cloth, perhaps. Someone who thinks as you do. But you will need to stop running.'

He put his fingers under her chin and eased her head up, holding her eyes with his own. They were full of gentleness and understanding. Molly's tongue flickered nervously over her lips. It would be so easy to throw herself against him, to take comfort and strength from him, just for a while. She knew it was wrong, it could not be, but even as she told herself she must not give in, the look in his dark eyes changed. She could not move, could not breathe. Her body was no longer her own. The hood slipped back as she tilted her face up, eyes half-closed, inviting a kiss that did not come. His mouth was tantalisingly close and she pushed up on to her toes to reach him.

At first touch, his lips were soft and cool against hers. There was a heartbeat's hesitation before he began to kiss her and then she was lost. She forgot about the rain on her face, the soft whisper of it in the hedgerow. She was aware only of Russ's mouth on hers, his arms around her, binding her to him. She whimpered, a soft sound in her throat, and he deepened the kiss, his tongue flickering, teasing, exploring and, tentatively, she responded. She had never been kissed like this before, so tenderly, so thoroughly. Desire blossomed in every inch of her body and her heart, silent for so many years, began to sing.

Molly gave a little sigh of regret when at last the kiss

ended. Russ kept his arms about her and she rested her head against his shoulder, gazing up in wonder at his face. He was looking down at her, a tiny crease in his brow, as if he was seeing her for the first time. Then he seemed to recollect himself and he gently released her.

'You see, I was right. There is passion in you, Molly Morgan.'

Molly stared at him. The light was fading and although she knew he was smiling she could not make out his features in the gloom. It was as if she was waking slowly from a dream. The feeling of well-being was slipping away and a chill was seeping through her damp clothes. She put a hand to her lips. They felt bruised, swollen and she had a sudden urge to weep, although she was not sure why.

Russ swallowed a sigh as he regarded the silent, dejected little figure in front of him. He hated seeing her thus, he wanted to drag her back into his arms and kiss away her unhappiness. His body was aroused and aching to do that and more. He wanted to set her up in luxury, shower her with gifts and spend the long nights in her arms, awaking the passion he had just glimpsed within her. But that was impossible. He reached out to pull her hood back over her head. 'I am the very last man who can give you lasting happiness. But, do you know? I envy him, whoever he may be.'

Still she said nothing and just gazed at him with stormy, troubled eyes. Then, without a word, she picked up her skirts, turned and fled.

Neither Russ nor Sir Gerald were present in church the following Sunday, for which Molly was very thankful. She had no idea how she was to face Russ after that kiss. Her insides twisted into knots every time she thought of it, which was almost constantly. The thick shell she had painstakingly built around herself was shattered, the desire she felt for Russ was as strong as anything she had ever felt for her first love. Stronger. She wanted him with an aching intensity that left her feeling weak, while the desolation that accompanied it tore at her. He could never be hers, he had told her so himself. He would not even beguile her with soft words and empty promises. The sight of Fleur, radiant and clearly very much in love, no longer filled Molly with the desire to save her friend—instead, she envied her. Molly sat through the service with her head bowed, not hearing the sermon but praying intently that this madness would soon pass.

Although Molly did not see Russ or Sir Gerald for the next few days, it was impossible not to hear about them. Lady Currick invited Molly and a number of other ladies to take tea with her, ostensibly to discuss charitable works in the parish, but once these matters had been dealt with the conversation turned to the latest gossip from Newlands.

'I have heard the two gentlemen are living there like savages now the ladies have departed,' said one of the matrons, her eyes wide and twinkling in her round face. 'The servants have all been turned off. Heaven knows what they are up to!'

'Nothing to excite your imagination,' replied Lady Currick dampeningly. 'Sir Gerald discovered the housekeeper is suffering very badly from rheumatism and he has sent her off to Harrogate for two weeks to take the waters. She is accompanied by her niece, who happens to be first housemaid.'

'Well, I have never heard the like!' declared the matron. 'Two weeks, for a servant.'

'Quite.' Lady Currick paused while the tea cups were refreshed. 'Sir Gerald knew it would be highly improper for the other female servants to be above stairs with no one to manage them, so he gave them all leave to go home until the housekeeper returns. Paid them, too! Well, of course, that set up a protest from the rest of the house staff, and the result was that Sir Gerald said they might *all* have a holiday, if they so wished. Of course, some of them had nowhere to go and preferred to remain, but the result is that there are barely half a dozen servants at Newlands now, all male, and they are doing everything that is required for their masters.'

There was a general cry of disbelief and Lady Currick could not suppress a little smile of superiority.

She said, 'I know it is true, because Currick went shooting with the gentlemen yesterday and stayed to dine at Newlands. That was when Sir Gerald was obliged to explain everything, because his valet was serving dinner for them. However, Currick had no fault to find with the dinner, nor the house, so it is to be supposed the gentlemen will go on quite comfortably until their servants return.'

Mrs Thomas, wife of the prosperous local mill owner, gave a loud tut of disapproval. 'Paying for the housekeeper to go to Harrogate for treatment is one thing. She is, after all, a very necessary member of the household, but to be giving the servants their wages and sending them off to do what they will—I am shocked, Lady Currick. Shocked. Such behaviour could lead to a general discontent amongst our servants. It sets a very bad example to the town.'

'It shows a generosity I had not expected of Sir Gerald,' put in Molly, feeling obliged to defend the gentleman.

'Well, I only hope he does not live to regret it,' muttered Mrs Thomas in ominous tones. 'And heaven knows what state the house will be in by the time the servants return!'

It was clear to Molly that the ladies of Compton Parva considered any past scandals attaching to Sir Gerald paled into insignificance against this latest outrage and she lost no time in relating the news to Edwin at dinner that evening. She was a little disappointed, but not surprised, to discover that he already knew of it.

'So Kilburn has done it, has he?' Edwin grinned. 'He asked me what I thought of the scheme when I rode over there on Monday last. I believe he and Russ were quite looking forward to living informally for a while, although I am sure they will be very glad to have their comforts restored after a fortnight.'

'I feel sorry for the staff who are left,' said Molly. 'They will all be working twice as hard.'

'I did mention that to Sir Gerald, but he said he would give them extra wages, so he did not think they would object overmuch. Trouble is,' mused Edwin, helping himself to more rice and mutton from the dishes on the table, 'this sort of thing can have unforeseen consequences. Servants with too much time to spare can get up to mischief. They may not even return at all. But it is something for Compton Parva to talk about, what?'

'With the harvest to be gathered in they should have

more than enough to occupy them. They should not be gossiping at all.'

'People must have some entertainment and talking about others provides endless amusement. You are too severe upon our neighbours, Molly.'

'Am I?' She fixed an anxious gaze upon her brother. 'Do you think they consider me too serious and disapproving? Do *you* think it?'

Edwin put down his fork. 'I think you have grown old before your time,' he said gently. 'You are only four-and-twenty, my dear. I worry sometimes that I have allowed you to take on too much here.'

'But I enjoy helping you, Edwin.'

'I know and I very much appreciate it.' He hesitated, as if choosing his next words with care. 'But what if I should marry?'

Molly laughed. 'My dear Edwin, if that should happen, then naturally I should move out. We agreed as much when I first came to live with you and it is even more necessary now. I would not expect your wife to share a house with such a managing female as I have become!'

Edwin laughed, too, plainly relieved, but his words only deepened Molly's unease. Her brother often talked of Agnes Kilburn and it was clear his attachment to her was serious. If they should marry, the links with Newlands would be strengthened. Unless Molly moved away from the area altogether, there would be no avoiding Sir Gerald and his friends.

There would be no avoiding Russ.

Compton Parva was taking advantage of a spell of hot, dry weather to bring in the harvest. Molly drove over to

Prospect House on Tuesday to help pack up the surplus produce from the farm, ready for market day. She was glad of the activity, for it helped to keep her mind from dwelling on Russ. She desperately wanted to see him again, but she must keep her distance from a man who had the power to make her lose all sense of judgement. A man who, by a touch, could reduce her to a quivering mass of need and longing.

The house was unusually quiet when she arrived. She was met by Marjorie, who took her into the morning room where her baby was sleeping peacefully in a crib.

'Everyone else is out of doors,' she told Molly. 'I have been sorting out things we might sell at market tomorrow.'

She indicated the table, which was covered with embroidered goods, including fine handkerchiefs and exquisite children's nightgowns. Molly spent an hour with her, admiring the baby and helping her to choose and price the various items to be sold, before making her way to the dairy, where Nancy was hard at work with the butter churn.

'In good time,' Nancy greeted her. 'All the others have gone to help in the fields, so I am left alone to deal with everything here.'

'I thought that might be the case,' said Molly, stripping off her gloves. 'What can I do?'

'If you could cut and wrap the butter I have already prepared, that would help, my love. Thank you.'

'I thought Fleur might be helping you,' remarked Molly, slipping into the clean linen apron Nancy handed to her.

'She is with Moses and the others at the farm. I said

with her fair complexion she would be better staying out of the sun, but she insisted.'

There was something in Nancy's tone that made Molly look at her.

'And do you think Sir Gerald will pass this way?'

'Undoubtedly.' Nancy gave the handle a couple more turns before opening the barrel and giving a satisfied nod. 'They manage to see one another nearly every day. I wish you would speak to her, Molly. I have tried, but she is in such a daze of happiness she will not listen to me. She has thrown her hat over the windmill and will return by Weeping Cross.'

Molly nodded, saying nothing. She was beginning to think the old saying applied to more than just Fleur.

'Molly—have you been here all day?' Fleur embraced her warmly, then broke away, smiling. 'Now I feel guilty for not coming back earlier, but there was so much to do at the farm.'

'There always is, at harvest time.' Molly took her arm. 'Come along into the morning room. I am about to prepare tea and I am sure you are ready for a little refreshment.'

'I am indeed,' agreed Fleur, laughing. 'Only give me a moment to take off my bonnet and wash my face and hands and I shall be with you.'

Fleur ran upstairs and Molly busied herself with making tea until she returned. She was still trying to decide how to introduce the topic of Sir Gerald without sounding as if she was lecturing when Fleur came into the morning room and asked if Nancy was joining them.

'No,' replied Molly, distracted. 'She is too busy in the kitchen today.'

'Just as well, since she is at outs with me over Sir Gerald. Has she told you?'

Molly said cautiously, 'She says you see him regularly.'

'I do.' There was no doubting the happiness shining from Fleur's eyes. 'You will not believe how much we have to discuss.' She laughed. 'We talk about farming and husbandry and crop yields. Can you believe it?'

'Yes, I can, if he wishes to ingratiate himself with you.'

Fleur blushed and shook her head. 'It is not like that, Molly. He will not come to the house because he says he is fearful for my reputation. We meet out of doors. Moses or one of the girls is always nearby. You look sceptical, my love, but he is most truly a gentleman. H-he has done nothing more scandalous than to kiss my hand! He says the farms at Newlands are in a pitiable state and he is determined to improve them. He has even sent his steward across to discuss our farming methods with Moses.'

'That I can understand, since we have been at pains to make Prospect Farm a success. But, Fleur, do you honestly believe he is only interested in the farm?'

'No, of course not. He has said he would like to bring his sister across to meet me, when she returns to Newlands. But you need not lecture me, Molly. I know full well I must not read too much into that.' Fleur sighed. 'I believe we are friends, you see. I know it cannot be anything more, but when Gerald eventually leaves Newlands, I shall have such happy memories.'

'And will that be enough?' asked Molly, aware of the ache she felt inside whenever she thought of Russ and that was after so very few encounters.

Fleur's smile slipped a little. 'It will have to be.'

Chapter Eight

Molly returned from Prospect House just as the sun was setting and was surprised to find Edwin waiting for her in the hall.

'Molly, love, you are later than I expected. Is all well at Prospect House? Marjorie, and her baby?'

'Yes, yes, everything is well, but there was so much to do—butter and cheese to be packed, eggs to be collected. Oh, a hundred little things. And with Marjorie looking after her new baby, they were glad of another pair of hands. However, Marjorie has been able to return to her sewing and is once more overseeing the other girls. They have produced some delightful work, including several pairs of gloves and embroidered slippers to sell tomorrow.' Weary as she was, she summoned up a laugh. 'I might even buy a pair for you, Edwin.'

His responding smile was distracted.

'Molly, my dear, do you remember I was talking of the unforeseen consequences of Sir Gerald's sending his staff away to enjoy themselves?'

'Of course. Edwin, what is it?'

Her immediate concern was dispelled when she saw

how his eyes were dancing. 'I think you had best come into the drawing room, my dear.'

Russ had been surprised when Gerald informed him that he had paid most of his staff to go away for a while, but he had no objection to living frugally for a few weeks. Indeed, it suited his mood very well and since Gerald refused to quit Newlands, a period of self-denial where he might feel sorry for himself was just what he wanted.

'It will not be so bad,' Gerald had told him. 'Remember when we first arrived in London and had only one manservant between us? The stables are still fully staffed, so what with riding, hunting and shooting, we shall be out of doors every day. And for the rest, your man and mine are both capable of turning out a good meal. Besides, there are some servants left below stairs. No, my friend, we shall go on very well.'

And so it seemed. They sat very comfortably in the kitchen in the evenings, drinking wine while the two valets cooked, and when they met the squire out shooting and invited him to take pot luck with them, they sat down to succulent beefsteaks with oyster sauce. Even Sir William had confessed it was very pleasant to be able to relax in one's stockinged feet occasionally.

The good weather held into their second week, allowing Russ and Gerald to ride out regularly, but no matter how hard he rode or how tired he might be, Russ was aware of a simmering disquiet and a wish to see Molly Morgan. She was on his mind constantly, and when, late one afternoon, he and Gerald returned from a long day's riding and they glimpsed a figure moving past the drawing-room window, his pulse leapt.

'Now, who the devil can that be?' muttered Gerald.

With no women servants in the house it must be a visitor and Russ thought, *hoped*, it might be Molly. He quickened his stride, preceding Gerald indoors and making his way directly to the drawing room. He threw open the door, but it was not Molly standing before the fire in the sprigged muslin gown. This visitor was much younger than Molly, and instead of a mass of unruly dark locks, she had honey-gold curls that cascaded down from a topknot and framed a lively countenance enhanced by a pair of mischievous brown eyes.

'So you are back at last,' she said in her pretty, musical voice. 'I thought you would *never* come!'

Russ heard the door close behind him and found Gerald standing at his side, an enquiring lift to his brows.

'Gerald' he said, fighting to keep his voice level, 'let me introduce you to Miss Serena Russington. My half-sister.'

She clutched her hands before her and fixed those large, imploring eyes upon her host. 'I hope you do not mind my calling unannounced, Sir Gerald, but I had no choice. I am quite, quite desperate!'

'Are you, by Jove?' Gerald looked at Russ. 'Perhaps I should leave you two alone.'

'No, no need for that,' said Russ, keeping his eyes on Serena. 'Perhaps, my girl, you will tell us just why you are here and where is your chaperon? And your carriage? I did not see one in the stables.'

'I am alone and I took the mail to Compton Magna and then a very kind farmer took me up and dropped me at your gates.' She drew a breath. 'I have run away.'

For the first time Russ became aware of the two bandboxes beside the sofa.

'The devil you have!' Before he could say more, Gerald announced that such a situation required some refreshment and he lounged out of the room. Russ looked at his half-sister with brooding suspicion. 'Do you mean to tell me you have travelled the length of England to reach me?'

'No, no, of course not.' She sank down into a chair. 'I left the Tonbridge seminary two months ago, because they said I was unteachable.' She threw him a look of mild reproach. 'You are joint trustee for my affairs, Russ, so Henry must have written and told you of it all.'

'Perhaps his letter went astray,' he suggested, cravenly putting the blame for his ignorance upon his brother.

'Fustian. You ignore him, as I do, as much as I can,' she replied frankly. 'Well, Henry collected me from Tonbridge and took me directly to Mrs Wetherby's academy, which is near Harrogate. And I have *tried* to be good and to settle in, Russ, but it is impossible. They are so very severe.'

'Possibly that is why my brother chose it.'

'That and the fact that it is so far north he knew it would be impossible for me to get home. It is like a convent, Russ. Everyone is so serious and the teachers are so strict with me, I am not enjoying it one little bit. They will not allow us to go out of the building unattended.'

'Clearly you have managed it, however.'

Her eyes twinkled. 'I knotted the bedsheets and climbed out the window at midnight! I had to get away, Russ. I am nearly seventeen and far too old for school now. I promise you, I was at my wits' end to know what to do. Then I saw the report in the society pages of the local paper, saying that Sir Gerald had purchased Newlands and was in residence there with a party of friends, including—now, how had they worded it?—*several prominent bachelors*! Well, knowing you are Sir Gerald's best friend *and* the most prominent bachelor in London, I guessed you would be here, so I caught the night mail, determined to throw myself on your mercy.' She smiled, but then gave a sigh. 'I did write to Henry and suggest I might live at home with him and Dorothea until I am presented, but his reply said that was not possible. It is Dorothea's doing, of course. She does not want me to live with the family.'

Russ thought this very likely. The last time he had seen his two nieces, they were promising to take after their mother—short, plump and affected. There was no doubt they would be very much cast into the shade by Serena with her glowing vivacity.

'What do you expect me to do about it?' he asked at last.

'Since you are also my guardian, you can write to the school and tell them I am not coming back. Then, I thought, perhaps, you might talk to Henry, explain how desperately unhappy I was. Perhaps he could find some lady for me to live with until my come out. I shall be very good, I promise you, if only I am not confined in a school with lots of silly, giggling girls.'

He laughed at that. 'I wish I might believe you, Serena.'

Gerald returned, carrying a tray full of decanters and glasses and, with his half-sister's permission, Russ explained the situation to him.

'I will write to Henry about it, I give you my word, Serena,' he concluded. 'But for now I see no option other than you to return to the school.'

She turned her soulful gaze upon Gerald as he handed her a very small glass of ratafia.

'You would not force me to go back to such a place, would you, Sir Gerald?'

'Well—' he glanced at Russ '—it might be necessary for you to return. Just for a short time, until other arrangements can be made.'

'May I not stay here?'

'Impossible,' said Russ immediately. 'It would be most improper. There are no other females in the house.'

'But you are my brother.'

'Half-brother,' he corrected her. 'And *my* reputation would do nothing to improve the situation!'

The dark eyes widened. 'Then what shall do? I made sure you would not turn me away, and it is almost night.' She heaved a sigh. 'P-perhaps you will escort me to the local inn.'

'Can't do that,' said Gerald, shaking his head. 'To-morrow is market day. All the local hostelries will be as full as they can hold. And not with the sort of people one would want mixing with one's sister.'

'That's true.' Russ pushed his fingers through his hair. 'I will have to take you back to Compton Magna. We should be able to find accommodation for you at the White Hart, and I will pay for a chambermaid to sleep in your room tonight.'

'But that is a good ten miles away,' cried Serena. 'You would not abandon me there, would you?'

'Of course not. I shall remain there, too.'

Serena gave a small sniff and he ground his teeth.

'What else do you expect me to do with you? I am aware it is not ideal, but it is the best I can think of, so late in the day.'

Sir Gerald cleared his throat. 'I think I know some-one who might help.' He glanced at Russ. 'I am sure the vicar and his sister would take Miss Russington in for the night.'

Serena wrinkled her nose. 'That sounds very dull, but I suppose for one night it would do no harm.'

Russ wanted to say no. He did not want to go cap in hand to Molly and ask for her help.

'Frayne would never turn away anyone in need,' Gerald went on. 'But if you *are* going, Russ, I should send for the gig now. Any later and they will be sitting down to dinner.'

Whatever Molly had been expecting, it was not this. Russ was in the drawing room, standing before the empty fireplace, and hanging on his arm was the most ravishing young lady she had ever seen. A searing pain, almost physical, ran through Molly, but before she could fully recognise it, her emotions were thrown into further turmoil when Edwin introduced the beauty as Russ's half-sister.

'Miss Russington arrived at Newlands, fully expecting Agnes to be there to receive her,' he explained.

Molly regarded the visitors in uncomprehending silence for some time after Edwin had finished. Russ cleared his throat.

'I understand what an imposition it is, Mrs Morgan, and if there was any other solution, I assure you I would not ask this of you.'

Molly's confusion was lifting. She knew full well that if there had been any choice, Russ would not have come here, but she could not deny that his sister's plight tugged at her heart. Whatever her differences with Beau Russington, his sister was not responsible and must be put at ease. She summoned all her inner strength to focus on her role as the vicar's sister.

'Oh, dear, how very unfortunate for you.' She smiled warmly at Serena. 'I assure you it is no trouble at all to have you stay here. If Edwin has not given instructions for the guest room to be prepared, then I shall do that immediately. And perhaps you would like to come up to my room? You may take off your pelisse and bonnet and we may both tidy ourselves before dinner.' She directed her polite society smile towards Russ. 'I hope you mean to stay and dine with us, too, Mr Russington?'

'If I may, yes. Thank you.'

Was it a trick of the candlelight, or did some of the darkness leave his eyes?

'Capital!' Edwin cast his beaming smile over them all and rubbed his hands together. 'Very well then, Molly, if you would like to take our guest upstairs, I will find a bottle of claret for Russ and I to enjoy while we wait for you!'

Serena was chattering away quite happily by the time they reached Molly's bedchamber. She had decided they must be on first-name terms and she lost no time telling Molly about her flight from the school. Molly did not comment, but she could quite understand that a strict regime would be very galling to such a lively girl on the verge of womanhood.

'It is very good of you to take me in,' said Serena, throwing her powder-blue pelisse and matching bonnet carelessly over a chair. 'Russ was quite at a loss to know what to do with me.'

'I am sure he was,' Molly murmured. 'But you say

he plans to drive you back to Harrogate in the morning. Will you not be tempted to run away again?'

'Oh, I am sure I shall, but he has promised me he will write to Henry—Lord Hambridge, our older brother,' she explained, seeing Molly's puzzled frown. 'It is Henry and his wife, Dorothea, who have had the ordering of my education. Russ has never bothered himself with me, but he is also my guardian, and I think it is time he stirred himself to do something, do not you?'

'Are you an orphan, then?' asked Molly, ignoring the question.

'Not exactly. Mama left when I was eight years old.'

'Oh, you poor child!'

Serena gave a little shrug. 'I barely knew her, so it made little difference. She only married Papa for his money. He quite doted on her, I believe, and was forever buying her presents. When Papa died, poor Henry found his inheritance sadly depleted. Mama ran off and married a rich Italian count almost as soon as she was widowed, so it is very likely that they were already lovers, do you not think?'

Molly was shocked at this matter-of-fact recital of Serena's history, but her murmurs of sympathy were waved aside.

'I am not supposed to know any of this, but between the servants' gossip, what Henry could be persuaded to tell me and the reports in the scandal sheets, I was able to discover almost everything.' She accepted Molly's invitation to sit down at the dressing table and brush her curls, but the revelations were clearly uppermost in her mind for she said as she stared at her reflection, 'Mama was very beautiful and I am said to be her image. I suppose that is why Russ was so reluctant to allow me to stay at Newlands tonight. He told me it was because his reputation is so bad, but I think he is afraid for *my* reputation. He thinks people will say I am too much like my mother.'

Molly was silent, imagining the hurt the children must have felt, to be abandoned whilst still grieving for their father. Serena reached out and caught her hands.

'Now I have made you unhappy,' she said. 'Please do not be sad for me, Molly. I do not feel it now, I assure you. And I am very glad that Russ brought me here, because I think we are going to be very good friends!'

Privately Molly thought that one would always feel such a loss, but she merely smiled and said that as soon as she had changed her gown they would go down and join the gentlemen.

'May I help you?' offered Serena. 'It will save you waiting for your maid and I am in the habit of helping the other girls at the academy to dress.' Her eyes twinkled. 'It is one of the better rules of the establishment, that no matter how wealthy the family, ladies should always know how to help themselves!'

Molly accepted this gesture of friendship. She was herself naturally reserved and since moving to Compton Parva had made no close friends, so it felt a little odd to have a young and lively companion in her room. Odd but not unpleasant, she thought, smiling to herself.

'Now, what are you going to wear?' Serena threw open the doors of the linen press.

Molly stepped up beside her and looked at gowns neatly piled on the shelves. For the first time she noticed how dreary they looked, dominated by shades of black, grey and lavender.

'My dear Molly, I thought you had been a widow for years.'

'Six years, to be precise.'

'And you are still wearing these dull colours?' Serena regarded her in wide-eyed awe. 'You must have loved your husband very much.'

'I have some colours,' said Molly, ignoring her remark. 'Look on the top shelf. There is my yellow dimity and a sage-green muslin.'

Serena's snort in response was derisory. 'The dimity is too faded to be of any use and even the muslin is almost grey—I have no doubt you look positively haggard in it! Do you have nothing else?'

'No. That is, there are a few gowns in the bottom drawer of the chest, but I have not worn them since...' Her voice faded.

Since my wedding.

Serena was already opening the drawer and pulling out gowns that had not seen the light of day since Molly had put them in there when she moved in, five years ago. Three colourful silk gowns purchased as bride clothes and rarely worn. Molly watched Serena spreading the gowns over the bed and she waited for the painful memories to flood in, but there was nothing more than a little sadness, which was soon dispelled by Serena's unflagging cheerfulness. Serena lifted an apricot silk and declared that was what Molly should wear to dinner.

'It is not in the latest style, but no one will care for that,' said Serena, shaking out the gown and holding it up against Molly. 'It compliments your colouring perfectly.'

Molly laughed, suddenly feeling much more frivolous and carefree. 'Very well, just for you I shall wear it! And perhaps my coral beads instead of the pearls.'

'Perfect,' Serena declared. 'After all, this is an informal dinner for friends and there are only the four of us. Now, if you will tell me where you keep the coral beads, I shall fetch them for you.'

Molly was throwing the apricot gown over her head as she answered, 'In the box that sits in the top drawer.'

Too late did she remember what else was in that drawer. She flew across, just as Serena was lifting out a man's handkerchief, laundered and pressed with the embroidered monogram clearly displayed.

'Yes, the box is there, in the corner,' she said, whipping the handkerchief from Serena's hand. 'Do not bother about this. It…it is an old kerchief of my brother's that I keep forgetting to give back to him.' With a laugh she buried it deep beneath the combs, pouches and other mementos and shut the drawer. Nothing more was said and Molly could only hope Serena had not recognised that it was Russ's initials embroidered on the linen square and not Edwin's.

Having assured Edwin that there was no need to send a note to Newlands, that Gerald would not be expecting him to return until after dinner, Russ settled down with his host to await the ladies. The wine was very good and the vicar cheerful company, but he could not be at ease until he saw Molly again. True, she had issued the invitation for him to stay for dinner, but after their last meeting was she really prepared to sit down at table with him? After what had been said—after what he had said to her—how could they converse naturally? He shifted in his chair. Confound it, there was something about the woman that brought out the worst in him!

'I am sure they will not be much longer,' said Edwin,

mistaking his sudden frown for impatience. 'I have no doubt that they are chattering away and have forgotten the time. But I am glad of it,' he continued, refilling their glasses. 'Molly takes life far too seriously. She was such a lively child. Fearless, headstrong, even, but she married very young, you see.'

He broke off, his cheerful countenance momentarily shadowed, but his smile returned as the door opened and the ladies came in, arm in arm.

Molly was laughing at something Serena had said and Russ felt the breath catch in his chest. He thought she had never looked better, the creamy tones of her skin enhanced by the warm colour of her silk gown, and for an instant he caught a flash of the spirited, carefree girl she must have once been. Then it was gone. Molly was still smiling, but she had withdrawn a little and he was sorry for it.

During dinner Russ put himself out to please, exerting all his charm as he attempted to draw Molly into the conversation. Serena's natural vivacity was an advantage, for there were no awkward silences to be filled and he thought, by the time the ladies withdrew, that Molly was looking a little more at ease. She even met his eyes for one brief, shyly smiling moment.

The ladies were waiting for them when they returned to the drawing room but Russ noticed immediately that Serena was looking tired. Hardly surprising, he thought wryly, if she had been awake since midnight. He politely declined Edwin's invitation to remain until the tea tray was brought in.

'My sister needs her sleep,' he said, rising. 'I shall return in the morning to take her back to Harrogate.'

'Will we travel in your curricle, brother?'

He shook his head. 'Much as I am sure you would like to cut a dash, Serena, the weather does not look promising and I have no intention of being crushed under the hood with you and your bandboxes! Kilburn has already offered to lend us his *berline*.'

He had expected Serena to pout at the use of this rather staid vehicle, but she gave him a beaming smile.

'That is very good, because it means there will be room for Molly to come with us.'

Molly's exclamation and her look of shock convinced Russ that she had not been a party to this idea.

'You must not be selfish, Serena. We have already imposed enough upon Mrs Morgan. We cannot expect her to give up the whole of tomorrow for you.'

His sister gave a loud and heartfelt sigh, worthy of Mrs Siddons.

'Just the thought of going back to that place fills me with dread.' She turned her soulful gaze upon Molly. 'Oh, pray, ma'am, do say you will come along to support me in my interview with Mrs Wetherby. She is sure to be very angry with me and my nerves will be in shreds before we have gone half the distance if I do not have you to sustain me.'

Russ's lips twitched at this masterly performance, but he said gravely. 'And is my presence not sustaining enough, Serena?'

'But you are not a woman,' she replied, with unarguable logic. 'Molly is the nearest thing I have for a friend in the whole world, and besides that, she is eminently respectable, which is sure to impress Mrs Wetherby much more than if I turn up with only my rakish brother for escort.'

Russ was at a loss how to answer this. Edwin had broken into a fit of coughing, no doubt to cover his laughter, but Molly was looking distressed and he could not bear that.

'I am not interested in impressing Mrs Wetherby,' he retorted. 'I have no doubt Henry and I pay the woman an extortionate sum for your place at her academy, so she will do as she is bid!'

'Yes, I am sure she will, while you are present, but once you are gone I shall be at her mercy and subject to a thousand petty tyrannies.'

Russ was unimpressed, but Edwin was clearly moved as Serena began to hunt for her handkerchief.

'Perhaps there is some truth in that, Russington,' he said. 'Take Molly with you. She is accustomed to dealing with such matters in the parish and she may well be able to smooth things over with this Mrs Wetherby. Well, my love, what do you say? *Have* you any engagements tomorrow that cannot be rearranged?'

'It is too much of an imposition,' Russ objected. 'Mrs Morgan is not even related to Serena.'

'With Mama living in Italy my only other female relative is Henry's wife, Dorothea, and she is hundreds of miles to the south.' Serena gave a little sniff. 'Not that she has ever liked me. I am quite, quite friendless.'

Molly watched, listened, knew it was a performance, of sorts, but still she did not hesitate.

She said, 'That is not true, Serena. Of course, I will accompany you, if you think it might help.'

Serena's woeful looks vanished immediately, replaced by a beaming smile. She flew across the room to embrace Molly, words of gratitude tumbling from her lips.

It was some moments before she could be persuaded to sit down, but then Molly was able to observe the gentlemen's reactions. Edwin nodded at her, sure she was doing the right thing, but Russ was staring at her with dark, troubled eyes.

'No, we cannot ask that of you, ma'am.'

'I do not see why not,' argued Serena. 'Molly has offered to come with me and, as Mr Frayne says, she has some experience in these matters, which you most certainly do not, brother.'

'I am perfectly capable of dealing with an elderly schoolmistress,' he retorted, bridling.

'I am sure you are, sir.'

Molly knew her cynical agreement would not help matters, but the words were out before she could stop them. There was more than a suggestion of clenched teeth as Russ went on.

'And it would hardly be fitting for Mrs Morgan to travel back alone with me in a closed carriage.'

'No, indeed, Mr Russington.' She met his angry glare with a glittering smile. 'You would be obliged to ride on the box!'

'Oh, I am sure Russ would have no objection to doing that,' remarked Edwin, blissfully unaware of the tension behind this interchange.

'Then it is settled,' declared Serena, getting up. She walked across to kiss her brother's cheek. 'Thank you, dear Russ, I promise you I shall be ready to travel at whatever hour you choose in the morning and so will Molly!'

Molly stretched her lips into a smile but said nothing, wondering how she would survive a whole day in the beau's company.

* * *

Sir Gerald's elegant *berline* came to a halt before the vicarage, the horses snorting and tossing their heads as if impatient to be moving again.

'Good heavens, what an impressive equipage,' declared Serena, peering out of the morning-room window. 'We shall be travelling in style today!'

'Then let us not keep the horses standing longer than necessary,' replied Molly, shepherding her charge to the door.

Russ was already coming up the path to meet them as they stepped out of the house. He handed Serena into the carriage, then held his hand out to Molly.

'It is very good of you to give up your day for my sister.' He lowered his voice, 'I am very grateful, when you have every reason to hate me.'

'I do not hate you,' she replied, not meeting his eyes.

He turned so that his back was to the carriage, his words for Molly alone.

'What, not even for that kiss?'

Even without looking at him, she knew he was smiling. She could imagine the teasing glint in his eyes and she felt the familiar fluttering inside. She said quietly, 'I believe I have given you even more reason to hate me, for what I said to you.'

'Then let us forget the past, if we may. I would like to think we could still be friends. Do you think that is possible?'

The weight on her spirits lifted, just a little. 'Perhaps.'

'Good. I am glad.' He stepped aside, allowing her to enter the carriage before jumping in.

They were away, the glossy black horses proving they were more than just a good-looking team as they bowled out of the town and away towards Harrogate. Molly had chosen to sit beside Serena, but now she wondered if that was wise, because she was facing Russ and her wayward eyes wanted to rest upon him, to take in the elegance of his blue coat and white waistcoat, the intricately tied cravat with a diamond winking from its folds, and if she allowed her gaze to drop then she could not avoid seeing his powerful thighs encased in tight-fitting pantaloons.

One glance had been enough to take everything in and it was imprinted in her mind, from the thick, glossy black curls on his head to the highly polished Hessians on his feet, he was every inch the fashionable gentleman. There was nothing for it but to keep silent and feign an interest in what was passing outside the window, although they had not yet left Compton Parva and she was familiar with every building.

Serena knew no such reserve. She declared that her brother was looking as fine as fivepence.

'And what do you think of Molly's walking dress?' she went on. 'I helped her decide upon it this morning because we need her to look as dull and respectable as possible, and I vow she looks so severe I am quite afraid of her.'

'I do not believe you are afraid of anyone,' Molly retorted.

'You are right.' Russ grinned. 'My sister may be a minx, but I have never doubted her spirit. And Serena is quite wrong about your gown, it does not look dull at all. That shade of charcoal grey suits you. I have never seen you look better.'

The unexpected remark drove the heat into Molly's cheeks, but Serena appeared delighted with it.

'Good heavens, do not listen to him, Molly. He will turn your head with his compliments.'

Molly laughed. 'I cut my eye teeth long ago and I am no longer susceptible to compliments from rakes such as your brother.' She clapped her hands to her mouth. 'Oh, dear, I beg your pardon. I should not have called you that.'

'Not in front of my little sister, perhaps, but friends should be able to say what they wish to one another, should they not?'

His smile reassured Molly, but she upbraided herself for speaking so freely and she lapsed into silence, resolving to guard her tongue in future when dealing with Beau Russington.

They rattled on, making good time, but Molly noticed that Serena grew quieter as they approached Harrogate.

'I recognise this part of the road.' Serena peered anxiously out of the window. 'We will soon be at the school.'

Russ reached across and touched her hand. 'Don't sound so worried, brat, I will not let her eat you.'

'No, of course, she won't, not with my handsome big brother to protect me,' replied Serena, clearly trying to throw off her nerves. 'And looking every inch a London gentleman.'

'I want to make a favourable impression upon Mrs Wetherby. That is very important, if we are to persuade the woman to take you back.'

His words crystallised the thoughts that had been whirling around in Molly's head for the past half hour. She would be making the return journey alone with Russ. True, it had been agreed that he would ride up top with the coachman, but would he? Would she be strong enough to insist upon it?

You must be strong, Molly. A lot more than your reputation will be at risk if you spend two hours alone in a closed carriage with him.

'We must do our best to persuade Mrs Wetherby to give you a second chance, Serena,' said Russ. 'I have no doubt Mrs Morgan will agree with me on that point.'

Thus addressed, Molly had no option but to look at him, but that was a mistake because he was smiling at her and all her resolutions melted away before the warm look in his eyes. Suddenly there was nothing she wanted more than to be alone with him. Serena's voice broke into her thoughts.

'She would have to be made of stone not to be impressed by you, Russ. Is that not so, Molly?' Serena giggled. 'But then, I have always thought of Mrs Wetherby as a gorgon.'

'A gorgon turns other people to stone,' said Molly, pushing her own concerns to one side. 'I hope very much that isn't the case today!'

The carriage was slowing to negotiate the narrow gateway to Mrs Wetherby's Academy for Young Ladies. Russ sat forward and studied the house with narrowed eyes.

'Well, we are here, Serena. We had best get this over.'

'I have no doubt she will scold me royally.'

'Then you must prepare yourself to be suitably chastened.' Almost before the carriage had stopped he jumped out and let down the steps. 'Come along, ladies.'

They were admitted by a maidservant and shown into a small waiting room while Mrs Wetherby was apprised of their arrival. Russ stood with his hands behind his back, looking out of the window and the two ladies perched on the edge of a very hard and underpadded sofa. The silence stretched on for several minutes, marked by the steady tick, tick of the longcase clock in the corner, before footsteps could be heard and the maid returned to announce that Mrs Wetherby would see them in her office. As they followed the maid out of the room Serena slipped her hand into Molly's.

'I am very glad you are here to help me face the gorgon,' she whispered.

Chapter Nine

'Well,' said Serena, settling herself comfortably on her seat. 'That was not at all what I expected, although I cannot say I am sorry.'

They were all three of them in the *berline* again and on their way back to Compton Parva. Russ leaned back against the squabs, his anger draining away. He had not expected to lose his temper. He had politely explained everything to Mrs Wetherby, who had given instructions for Serena's bandboxes to be returned to her room. She had then invited them all to sit down in her office to discuss the matter and Russ had thought the situation was well in hand. Serena had been suitably, nay, admirably repentant and had kept silent with her eyes lowered while the schoolmistress rang a peal over her.

It was not unexpected and Russ listened, if not with pleasure, then at least with equanimity to the woman's homily. After all, Serena had acted outrageously in running away from the school. He accepted the schoolmistress's recriminations and held his irritation in check, even when she turned her wrath upon him, condemning his morals and his lifestyle before reproaching both him and Lord Hambridge for allowing their young sister to become wild beyond control. Mrs Wetherby had been angry, impolite and even offensive, but still he had said nothing.

Serena was regarding him now with something bordering on awe.

'You demolished her in a most masterly fashion, brother. I thought she was going to burst into tears when you said she lacked both the good manners and the intelligence to teach young ladies of refinement. I wish you had not sent me off at that point to pack my things and order my trunks to be taken back to the carriage, for I should dearly love to have heard what else you said to the gorgon.'

'It was wrong of me to have said half so much,' he said curtly, 'but when she turned upon Molly in that fashion I could not remain silent.'

It was the sight of Molly, white-faced and trembling, that had broken the hold on his temper. She had merely suggested to Mrs Wetherby in her quiet, diffident way, that perhaps the school's excessive restrictions might be expected to rouse rebellion in a lively sixteen-year-old and that had drawn the woman's ire. She had launched a blistering attack upon Molly, culminating in thinly veiled aspersions upon the widow's status and respectability.

'No, I could see that put you in a rage,' said Serena, cheerfully. 'But I am very glad that it did, for you left her in no doubt that I shall not be returning to her horrid school.'

He scowled at her. '*You* may be glad, brat, but it has left me in the devil of a fix. I shall have to hire some respectable female to keep you company until I can take you to Henry and Dorothea.'

'Who will immediately look for another horrid school for me!'

'You cannot know that. They might keep you with them until your come-out in the spring.'

'Ha, Dorothea will not allow that. She has never liked me.'

'Nonsense.' Russ uttered the denial without much conviction.

'And although she has agreed to take me to London for my come-out,' Serena went on, eyes sparkling and her cheeks flaming with indignation, 'I have no doubt she will want to marry me off as soon as maybe, to the first man who comes along!'

'Now, on that point you are very far out, my girl, because Henry and I would not agree to it.'

'If I might make a suggestion?' Molly's quiet voice interrupted their heated altercation. Russ and Serena both turned to look at her. 'Edwin thought that something like this might arise. That is, that Mrs Wetherby might refuse to take Serena back into the school. He mentioned it to me last night and suggested that, perhaps, Serena might stay with us at the vicarage until Miss Kilburn returns to Newlands at the end of next week. That would give you time to write to your brother, Mr Russington, and make more permanent arrangements.'

'Oh, yes.' Serena clapped her hands. 'That would be an excellent solution.'

'No, it would not. We could not impose upon Mrs Morgan and her brother in that way.'

'I should be delighted to have Serena's company.'

'But you are very busy with your committees and your...charities.'

Molly's chin went up. 'I take it you are referring to Prospect House.'

'Of course.'

'Prospect House?' Serena's interest was caught. 'Oh, what is that?'

'A scheme of Mrs Morgan's. A home for females who have…er…fallen on hard times.'

'It is a refuge,' explained Molly, 'And although it was my idea, it could not succeed without the approval of the townspeople. There is also Prospect Farm, which the women run to support themselves.' She looked back at Russ. 'I went there yesterday and can easily miss my visit next week.'

'No, no, why should you do that?' cried Serena, looking from one to the other. 'It sounds fascinating. I could come with you. I should like to help.'

Russ was frowning, but Molly was thankful he did not speak. She knew Serena well enough by now to guess that a direct order for her to stay away would only pique the girl's interest in Prospect House. She must reply cheerfully and make little of it.

'No, no, that will not be necessary,' she said. 'There will be a few household tasks that require my attention, but I thought I might take a little holiday from parish matters while you are with me.'

'Oh, yes, indeed, what a capital idea. We could go riding and Russ can escort us.'

'Before you make plans that involve us all, Serena, please bear in mind that your presence here is unexpected and dashed inconvenient.'

Serena did not appear at all cast down by her brother's curt reprimand.

'I do bear it in mind and if you and Sir Gerald have

already made arrangements, then I do not expect you to change them for me. Although it does make me even more grateful to Molly and Mr Frayne, who are putting themselves to such inconvenience for a total stranger.'

'If you are trying to make me feel guilty, Serena, you won't do it,' Russ growled. 'My withers are not wrung in the slightest.'

Serena pouted and Molly said quickly, 'I am sure there will be plenty of opportunity for you to ride once Miss Kilburn returns to Newlands.' She added, with a laugh, 'And your brother will tell you that my pony is such a slug, you would be forever waiting for us to catch up.'

'Ah, well.' Serena sighed, then she tucked her arm in Molly's, saying cheerfully, 'I am sure you and I will find a host of other things to do. And I shall make an especial effort to behave!'

Russ gave a crack of laughter. 'Then heaven help you, Mrs Morgan!'

Although Molly said nothing to either Russ or Edwin, she was anxious about how she was going to keep such a lively young lady entertained for a week. However, she need not have worried. Serena threw herself into life at the vicarage with cheerful energy. She was as happy sorting the linen cupboard as she was accompanying Molly to the shops in Compton Parva or gathering fruit from the kitchen garden. She even volunteered to help Molly with the Sunday school, as she informed her brother after the morning service.

'...so you may be easy, Russ. Molly is keeping me very busy and out of mischief.'

'I am glad to hear it.'

'And you must not be cross with Molly, brother, but I

now know much more about Prospect House.' She waved a hand towards the line of veiled figures making their way out of the church. 'We met them on their way in, so Molly had no choice but to introduce me. They are all very agreeable and I mean to visit, although Molly explained about why they are living there and I quite see why they say it will not do for them to call upon *me*. But, Russ, Nancy—she is their cook, you know, even though she is a *lady* and the most delightful creature!—Nancy tells me that one of their number, Marjorie, is at home with her new baby, whom I long to see. And even more than that, they have a puppy, whom they are training to guard them all! And Molly has agreed to take me with her when she goes there on Tuesday.'

Molly added quickly, 'Only if your brother does not object.'

He shrugged. 'It was inevitable that Serena would hear more about the refuge from someone. Perhaps it is best that she has learned of it from you.'

'Then I may go, Russ?'

'Yes, as long as Mrs Morgan thinks you can be of use to her.'

Molly was relieved that he was not angry, but the glinting smile in his eyes brought the colour rising to her cheeks. She was annoyed at her own weakness and murmured an excuse to move away towards the little party preparing to walk back to Prospect House.

Nancy greeted her in typically blunt fashion. 'Do you think it was wise to take in Beau Russington's sister, Molly?'

'It was Edwin's suggestion.' Molly bit her lip. 'Besides, where else could she go?'

'Her brother might have hired a companion for her. Or

there are several mothers in Compton Parva with daughters of that age who might have obliged him.'

'But all that takes time, and as for other families, Serena knows none of them.' Molly smiled. 'Truly, I am enjoying her company.'

'She is very engaging, I grant you, but it is bound to bring you into company with her rakish brother, which cannot be what you want. Or is it?'

Under Nancy's scrutiny Molly felt her colour rising even more. She said slowly, 'I do not believe he is as black as he is painted.'

'Oh, good heavens. Do not tell me you are developing a tendress for the man!'

'Of course not.' She tried to laugh it off. 'I merely wish to be just.'

'Is that why you have stopped lecturing Fleur about her friendship with Sir Gerald?'

Molly followed Nancy's eyes to where the couple were standing a little way apart, deep in conversation. She sighed.

'Fleur says she knows nothing can come of it.'

'Perhaps not.'

Nancy's thoughtful gaze moved to Russ. Serena was still chattering to him, but his eyes were fixed on Molly, who held her breath. She was waiting for the inevitable comment, but Nancy surprised her.

'It is time I gathered up my flock and took them back to the house. Shall we see you as usual next week, Molly? Good. Until Tuesday, then.'

With that Nancy was gone, sweeping Fleur up as she passed. With something between a sigh and a smile Molly turned away. She beckoned to Serena, who parted from her brother and ran over to join her.

'The local children will be arriving soon for their Sunday lessons,' Molly told her. 'We must prepare the little room set aside for them. Mrs Birch, who usually runs the class, is gone to stay with her daughter, so your help is much appreciated today.'

'Well, I do hope I am being useful,' said Serena seriously. 'I had no idea there was so much to be done in a parish, what with organising relief for the poor, raising funds for the widows and orphans and paying charity visits. We have not had a spare moment!'

Molly smiled. She was deliberately working Serena hard, not only to keep her from boredom, but also to show her a little of the world outside her normal sphere. She would not allow Serena to go into houses where there was sickness, but they had taken baskets of food to several needy families and even called upon a newly bereaved widow with a parcel of mourning clothes, including two gowns that Serena had persuaded Molly to give away.

'You wear far too much black and can well afford to part with some of them,' Serena had told her. 'All those dark gowns make you look so *dull*, Molly, and I know full well that you are not in the least dull!'

Molly laughed at that. 'It is impossible to be so in your company!'

It was true. Molly was enjoying herself much more than she would have guessed. Russ called almost every day to enquire after his sister and sometimes stayed to take tea with them. On these occasions Molly's attempts to keep in the background were thwarted by Serena, who included her in every conversation. Russ was unfailingly polite, but Molly felt tongue-tied and shy in his company, knowing how drab and colourless she must seem compared to Serena's vivacity and youth.

That thought returned to Molly when she and Serena were in Hebden's the following day. Serena was making polite conversation with Lady Currick, to whom she had been introduced at All Souls on Sunday, and Molly moved across to take a closer look at the roll of deep red lustring lying at one end of the counter.

'Is it not beautiful?' commented Miss Hebden, coming over. 'I took delivery of it only this morning. Just look at the way it shines when you move it. 'Tis just the colour I imagine the finest rubies would be.'

'And it would look very well on Molly,' put in Serena. 'Do you not agree, Lady Currick? What a fine gown it would make for her!'

'It would indeed.' Lady Currick moved closer. 'And I have seen the perfect design for it in my latest ladies' magazine. An evening gown. Nothing too fancy, but suitable for dining and dancing. As soon as I get home I shall look it out for you, Molly.'

'And if you want the lustring, Mrs Morgan, you shall have it on account,' said Miss Hebden eagerly. 'I can have a length packed up and sent over to you in a trice.'

Serena clutched her arm. 'Oh, yes, do have it, Molly. I should so love to see you dressed in such a colour.'

'As would all her friends,' Lady Currick agreed.

Molly looked at the smiling faces around her and gave a nervous little laugh.

'I feel you are all conspiring in this.' She looked back at the material. 'It *is* lovely...'

'Then if Lady Currick will send me the illustration I will work out how much material you will need and send it all over by the end of the day, complete with ribbons, buttons and thread.' Miss Hebden beamed at her. 'How would that be, Mrs Morgan?'

'Perfect!' said Lady Currick. 'And you can take everything to that clever little seamstress at Prospect House to have it made up for you.'

'No, no, I must not. I need to think about this.'

'You do not,' Serena told her. 'Your friends have thought about it for you. All you have to do is to agree!'

Molly was still unsure the following day when she and Serena set out for Prospect House, the precious parcel resting at their feet.

'It is such an imposition,' she declared, neatly turning the gig on to the drive. 'Everyone here is so busy that I do not like to ask them for such a favour.'

'Well, you have already told me you will pay for the sewing, so it is not as if you want the gown made up for free,' Serena reasoned. 'And you do not need to ask, for I shall do it for you!'

Any plans Molly had for working that morning were thwarted as soon as Serena explained about the material. Fleur and Nancy immediately called for Marjorie to join them in the morning room, where Molly laughingly submitted to being measured, pinned and prodded while the ladies discussed how quickly the gown could be made up.

'My brother and Sir Gerald are coming to the vicarage for dinner on Thursday night,' Serena told them. 'It would be above anything great if Molly could wear her new gown.'

Molly's protests against such haste were silenced by Fleur.

· 'Of course, we shall do it,' she said. 'Both housemaids

can sew a fine seam now. I shall help, too, and Marjorie shall direct us all.'

'And you are not to be worrying about the baby,' added Marjorie, anticipating Molly's next argument. 'Once I have fed her, Nancy and Daisy can watch her for me.'

'But it is market day tomorrow.' Molly made one final bid to dissuade them. 'Who will take the goods to market if you are all working on my gown?'

Nancy put her hands on her hips and looked at her. 'Heavens, Molly Morgan, do you think we are capable of doing only one thing at a time? We shall manage, especially with you and Miss Serena here to help us today. Come along, ladies, let us get to work!'

'Well, are you glad we persuaded you?'

Serena gave Molly's skirts a final twitch and turned her to face the looking glass. The ruby-red silk glowed in the candlelight and hung in fine folds from the high waist with just enough fullness in the skirts for them to swing out slightly over her hips. Short, puffed sleeves were finished with Vandyke cuffs, which were mirrored by the decoration around the waistline and the hem.

Molly's fingers traced the swirling embroidered pattern on the bodice, then her hand moved up to her bare neck. The square bodice was cut very low, just as it had been in the illustration.

'Perhaps I should add a muslin fichu,' she murmured.

'There is not the least need,' declared Serena, with all the conviction of one who knew about these things. 'The neckline shows off your fine skin, Molly, and once you have added your pearls you will look very elegant indeed. Are you sure you will not wear the cap, too?'

Molly glanced at the matching hat they had made for

her, decorated with two curling feathers. She smiled. Did they think she was going to be attending grand balls and assemblies?

'Not tonight.'

'You are quite right,' agreed Serena. 'It would be de trop for a small dinner. Come along then, shall we go down?'

Russ did not need to look out of the window to follow the route his friend's carriage was taking that evening. He had come this way every day since Serena had been a guest at the vicarage and it was not only out of duty. He had wanted to see Molly. He was well aware she did her best to avoid him, but it did not matter that she kept in the background, not speaking unless it was necessary, he was aware of her with every fibre of his being. Not that anything could come of it. She had made it quite clear that she was afraid of him and he knew in his heart that he was not the man for her. She needed— deserved—someone who would live up to her high moral standards. Someone she could trust.

The carriage drew up at the gate and he followed Gerald to the door, reflecting that after tomorrow he would have no excuse to call again. Agnes would soon be back at Newlands and Serena would come there to stay, until he and his brother decided just what they were to do with her.

'Ah, gentlemen, come in, come in.'

Edwin Frayne came forward to greet them as they walked into the drawing room. Pleasantries were exchanged, but Russ's eyes went round the room, looking in vain for Molly.

'The girls are not yet come down,' said Edwin, ushering them towards the fire. 'They have been closeted together these two hours, prettying themselves for you! But that need not stop us enjoying a glass of wine together. Sit down, sirs, and I will serve you.'

The three gentlemen were well enough acquainted to talk freely on sporting matters until the sound of female voices from the hall heralded the arrival of the ladies. They all rose as the door opened. Serena and Molly came in together, but Russ lost sight of his sister, for it was Molly who held his attention.

He had never seen her look better. Her face was alight with laughter and the creamy whiteness of her skin was enhanced not only by her dark hair, but also by the deep red of her gown. The silk skirts whispered and flowed as she moved, the soft folds catching the candlelight and glowing jewel bright. Her hair was simply dressed with a few dusky curls framing her face and the rest piled high on her head, except for one glossy ringlet that rested on her shoulder. He imagined drawing her close and pulling out the pins to let those luxuriant dark locks tumble down her back. But it was not the red silk he wanted beneath his hands, it was her smooth naked skin.

'Well, brother, do you like Molly's new gown?'

Serena's voice brought the pleasant daydream crashing down. Not by the flicker of an eyelid would he allow his thoughts to show, but a polite smile was beyond him. All he could manage was a short reply, his voice devoid of emotion.

Molly had felt his eyes upon her when she came in, and she hoped he might say how well the colour suited her or approve the new way of dressing her hair.

'Mrs Morgan looks very well.'

'Very well? She looks perfectly splendid!' Sir Gerald came up to take her hand. 'Do come and sit down, ma'am. I was saying to your brother how kind it is of you to take pity upon us. I had not realised how dependent I had become upon luxury until I gave the staff their holiday.'

She responded, grateful for his jovial chatter, and accepted a glass of wine from Edwin, but she resolutely kept her eyes away from Russ.

'It could be worse,' she told herself, keeping her smile in place and pretending to listen to the conversation flowing around her. 'He might have offered you insincere compliments and paid you the sort of attentions you most abhor.'

But for all that she could not deny the stab of disappointment at his lack of interest.

Edwin was refilling the gentlemen's glasses and he said to Sir Gerald, 'Have you heard from Miss Kilburn?'

'Aye. I had a letter from her only today to say she is looking forward to returning to Newlands on Friday, which means that you, Serena, can come to us the following day. Mr and Mrs Sykes are returning, too, and Agnes tells me they have concocted some plan between them to hold a ball at Newlands, so it is to be hoped all our staff do return to us!'

'A ball!' cried Serena, 'Oh, that will be beyond anything.'

Russ put up a hand to quell his sister's raptures. 'It will not be for several weeks, Serena, you may no longer be with us.'

'Oh, you would not be so cruel as to send me away beforehand!'

'Since I have not heard back from Henry nothing is

yet settled.' His expression softened a little. 'And I suppose you would very likely run back here if I did send you away.'

'I should indeed! And, Sir Gerald, you will invite Molly and Edwin to the ball, won't you?'

'Of course, they are top of the list,' he replied. 'But we hope they will come to Newlands before that. Agnes expressly mentions you both in her letter and hopes you will be able to join us for dinner next week, on a day to suit you—no need to commit yourself now, Frayne, I know how busy you are with your parish matters. You may send back your reply with our coachman on Saturday, when he comes to collect Serena.'

'Oh, there is no need for that,' replied Edwin. 'We shall be only too pleased to deliver Miss Russington to you and we may confirm the engagement with Miss Kilburn in person.'

Russ laughed. 'I have no doubt you will be glad to see the back of my bothersome sister, eh, Frayne?'

'No, no, I wasn't...' Edwin trailed off, a telltale flush on his cheeks.

'Do not allow my *tiresome* brother to tease you, Mr Frayne,' Serena retorted. Putting her nose in the air, she pointedly turned away from Russ. 'And will all your servants be returned by then, Sir Gerald?'

'I sincerely hope so,' he declared. 'The housekeeper arrived back from Harrogate today and the rest should be here by the morning. Pleasant as it has been for Russ and me to have the place to ourselves, we shall be glad to have a full complement of staff again. And, of course, Miss Russington, I shall set them to work immediately to prepare a room for you.'

Serena thanked him prettily, adding, 'Although I shall be exceedingly sorry to leave Molly and Mr Frayne.'

'But it will be a relief to your brother,' remarked Molly, rising as the servant came in to announce dinner. 'Mr Russington will no longer be obliged to call here.'

There was no mistaking the sting in the words, but Russ had no opportunity to respond. Molly had taken Gerald's arm to go into dinner and he followed with Serena and Edwin, wondering what he might do to make amends. He had not intended to wound Molly, but his reaction to seeing her tonight had shocked him. When she had entered the room tonight, her eyes sparkling and a laugh trembling on her lips, his heart had soared, but then Serena had asked his opinion of the red gown and his only thought had been how quickly he could remove it. He had felt like a callow youth. Out of his depth, out of control.

For years now Russ had considered himself immune to female charms. There were few women for whom he had ever felt affection and he had been able to leave them with no more than a momentary pang of regret. He was damned if he knew what it was about little Molly Morgan, with her serious demeanour and her high morals, that had found the chink in his armour.

The answer came as he watched her presiding over her brother's dinner table. He liked her. He admired the quiet way she went about her duties as her brother's helper, her fierce dedication to protecting the women at Prospect House. Her honesty. He liked the little things about her, too. The way she pondered a serious question before answering, the way her face lit up when she laughed. In his opinion she should laugh a great deal more, which brought him full circle. He had hurt her tonight and he must make amends, if he could, before he left the vicarage that evening.

Russ curbed his impatience as Edwin refreshed the brandy glasses, but thankfully neither the vicar nor Sir Gerald were in roistering mood and it was less than an hour after dinner that they joined the ladies. Kilburn immediately crossed the room to where Serena was sitting at the piano and Russ watched them for a moment, aware of his duty as guardian, but Gerald was behaving very much as he did with his own sister.

Serena and Gerald were happily engaged at the pianoforte and the others settled down to listen to them. Molly moved to a seat beside the table in the corner, ostensibly to take advantage of the candlelight for her sewing, but Russ had seen her do this before, effacing herself in company, avoiding attention. Avoiding him.

With the fire blazing and curtains pulled against the autumn night it was cosily warm in the little drawing room and soon Edwin was dozing in his chair. Russ went across to Molly. She looked a little wary at his approach, but her first words were not unfriendly. She glanced towards the pianoforte.

'Your sister and Sir Gerald perform well together.'

'Yes. I am pleased to see Serena has learned something at the various establishments she has attended.'

'She is a very accomplished young woman,' Molly replied. 'She also has the knack of putting strangers at their ease. I have noticed it during the past week, when she has come about the town with me.'

He nodded. 'She may be a minx, but she is an engaging one. As her guardians, Henry and I will need all our wits to keep her out of scrapes. Until she has a husband to take over that role.'

'There will be no shortage of admirers for such a lively young heiress.'

She glanced across the room again and he said, anticipating her question, 'Serena is too young to be forming an attachment for a few years yet.'

'She is sixteen,' said Molly. 'She is not too young to fall in love.'

Russ knew she was talking of her own experience. He wanted to ask her if she still loved the villain who had stolen her dreams, but he was afraid to know the answer. She bent her head once more over her sewing.

'And what of Sir Gerald?' she murmured. 'Has he any thoughts of settling down?'

'Good heavens, no. He is far too old for Serena. They get on very well, I think, because he treats her very much as he does his own sister.'

Russ paused. Gerald's ease of manner made him think of his own fractured family. The comparison did not please him.

He said suddenly, 'Henry and I have seen very little of Serena. It would have been better, perhaps, if we had spent more time together. Henry was one-and-twenty, and already married, by the time our mother died. Father married again within a twelvemonth and barely a year after that Serena was born.' His jaw tightened. 'I remember all too clearly Father bringing home his new bride. He was besotted and only too happy to indulge his new wife. They pursued a life of pleasure, splitting their time between London and visits to friends.'

'And did you go with them?'

'No. I was at school and saw them but rarely. Henry

set up his own establishment, and when Serena was born she was left to the care of servants.'

'That must have been a lonely time for you and your sister,' murmured Molly.

'Yes.'

It was the first time Russ had admitted it. Molly was still setting her stitches, not looking at him, and sitting here beside her, within the cosy glow of the candles, he felt more at ease than he had done for years.

'I never thought about it at the time, but Henry had a hopeful family, Father had his new wife, I was not necessary to anyone's happiness. Serena, I thought of not at all. My godmother died and left me her fortune, which meant I did not need to consider any career, other than a life of idleness and dissipation.

'My father died suddenly when I was twenty, by which time my habits were fixed. I was living in town, with sufficient fortune to enjoy myself.' He fell silent, looking back over the years, before continuing quietly, 'That was when my stepmother approached me. Having run through my father's fortune, she hoped to seduce me into sharing mine with her. When I rejected her advances, she ran off with her Italian lover.'

Molly's sewing lay unheeded on her lap as she listened to Russ calmly relating his history, but this last revelation was too much, even though she had heard something of it from Serena.

'That is very sad,' she said quietly. 'How could any mother abandon her children?'

He shrugged. 'Her Italian count is very rich. Women will do anything for money.'

'Not all women, Russ.'

The words were out before she could stop them. He fixed his dark eyes on her, and she returned his look steadily, her heart going out to the wild and lonely young man he had been. She should not have spoken and should not have used his name, but it had been instinctive. Even now she wanted to reach out to him, to take his face in her hands and kiss away the years of hurt and pain.

The sudden crashing of chords and Serena's trilling laugh shattered the moment. Molly carefully fixed the needle into the material and folded up her sewing. What a conceited fool she was to think she might give comfort to Beau Russington, who had his pick of the most beautiful women in the land. He might talk to her as a friend, but he did not want her in his bed, his reaction earlier this evening had shown that all too clearly.

'I should ring for the tea tray.' She went to rise.

'Not yet.' He put out his hand to stop her. 'Gerald and Serena have embarked upon another duet. Why not let them finish that first?'

She sank back on her chair. His touch had sent a shower of burning arrows through her skin and she rubbed her arm as the lively strains of an English folk song filled the room. She searched around for something cheerful to say.

'Despite everything, your sister is a most delightful young lady. She has enchanted everyone in Compton Parva.'

'I am glad to hear you say that.' Russ shifted in his seat to watch the singers. 'She was barely eight years old when her mother left England, but Eleanor had no more time for her daughter than for her stepsons. Perhaps that was for the best. She would not have been an influence for good.' He turned back to Molly. 'I have to confess I can take no credit for the way she has turned out. I did not wish to involve myself in my half-sister's education, I left all that to Henry. She lived at Hambridge Hall with Henry and Dorothea in the short periods when she was not at school and he occasionally invited me to join them. A belated attempt to instil some family feeling into us, I suppose, but for the most part we went our own ways. However, I need to bestir myself a little now. My brother has a daughter, you see, who is to be presented in the spring. The last time I saw my niece she was not at all promising, so I suspect Dorothea is reluctant to have Serena live with them until her daughter is safely married off. I confess I am at a loss to know what to do with the chit!'

'She is a young woman,' Molly reminded him gently.

He sighed. 'Aye, you are right. It is clear that she has outgrown school. She needs a chaperon or a companion who can match her spirit and energy. Someone who can guide her and keep her safe without stifling her natural liveliness, but they must be of good birth and impeccable character.'

Neither of them had noticed that the music had ended and Serena was approaching with Sir Gerald.

'Are you talking about me, Russ?' she cried, dropping a hand on her brother's shoulder.

'Aye, I am wondering what the devil I am to do with you.'

'Perhaps you should take a wife,' Serena murmured, wickedly. 'Then I could live with you.'

Gerald laughed. 'I wish I might see Beau Russington leg-shackled to a woman of impeccable character!'

Molly saw Russ's brows rise, and he replied with a

touch of hauteur, 'My dear Kilburn, I could not settle for anything less.'

Feeling slightly sick, she flew off to ring for the tea tray. She did not want to hear any more.

A woman of impeccable character.

The words had taunted Molly throughout her sleepless night. She had as good as told Russ that she had had a lover before her marriage.

Yet he left Serena in your care.

Only because there was no one else.

She had tossed and turned, thumping her pillow, throwing off the covers, trying to find some rest and solace in the darkness, but her mind would not be quiet. By the time the sun came up she was resigned to the fact that Russ would never consider her for his wife. But she had never expected that he would, and until recently she had never even thought of marrying again. She had been quite content with her life in Compton Parva.

Hadn't she?

Molly stopped brushing her hair and stared at her reflection. Russ had stirred up feelings and regrets she had thought long dead and she was not sure if she was most pleased or sorry for it.

Chapter Ten

'Steady, boy. Easy, Flash.'

Russ eased his horse back from the headlong gallop that had seen them flying across the moor. He cursed himself for being so foolhardy. That last stumble might have seen him take a tumble or, worse, Flash might have broken a leg. And however careless of his own life Russ might be, he should not risk his faithful mount.

He came to a halt on the highest point of the promontory that forced the road in the valley bottom into a curving arc around it. The sun was still shining over the high ground, but below the land was already in shadow and a few lights twinkled in distant Compton Parva, nestled at the western end of the valley. He would wager that at least one of those lights came from the lamp outside the vicarage, shining out to welcome all souls, however damaged.

A movement caught his eye—a solitary vehicle had come into view from the east. He could see it was a gig making its way at a smart pace towards the town. The driver was a woman and although Russ could not be sure at this distance, he thought it might well be Molly on her way back from Prospect House.

Molly. Why was it that at their every meeting, he acted like a crass fool? Last night he had been brusque to the point of rudeness when Serena had asked his opinion of Molly's new gown. Then, just when he thought he had mended those fences, Serena, the minx, had said he should marry. That had caught him off guard, because at that very moment he had been thinking that Molly might well make the perfect wife. As if that was not enough, Gerald, damn him, had chosen that moment to tease him and he had answered angrily and without thinking. He wished now he had cut out his tongue before speaking. It was only after the words had left his mouth that he recalled what Molly had told him about being seduced by a rascally soldier. He had never thought any the worse of her for that, but he was sure she would consider herself disgraced.

He closed his eyes and shook his head in disbelief that he, the celebrated Beau Russington, famed for his polished address, should behave like a doltish school-boy over a woman. The fact was that he had never *cared* about a woman before. He had thought them all self-seeking fortune hunters, like his stepmother. Selfish beings, selling their favours to the highest bidder. It had been made abundantly plain to him from an early age that no matter how badly he behaved, any one of the beauties that graced the town could be his for a sum. But the price for the virginal debutantes who filled the London salons was marriage and that was a price he was not prepared to pay.

Until now. He rubbed a hand across his face. Molly Morgan had already suffered in her young life and she deserved a better husband than a jaded rake with a dubious past. Opening his eyes, Russ glanced down, expecting to see that the gig had rounded the bend by now, but the road to the west was deserted. He followed it back until he saw the vehicle had stopped just short of the bend. He pulled out his spyglass and through the deepening gloom he could see that the vehicle was resting at an ugly angle. His heart jolted in alarm until he saw that Molly was on her feet and standing beside it. Without hesitating he touched his heels to his horse's flanks.

'Come up, Flash. It would appear the lady is in distress.'

The lurching jolt as the wheel cracked and splintered sent Molly tumbling out of the gig. She was winded, but not hurt, and scrambled to her feet. The mare was standing between the shafts, trembling violently, but she, too, appeared unhurt. The gig's wheel, however, was smashed beyond repair. There was no possibility of moving on.

Molly tried to unfasten the harness, but found her fingers would not work properly. She was shaking and decided she would need to sit down and recover a little before she tried to do anything. A convenient milestone provided a seat, which was much more welcome than its message, that she was still three miles from Compton Parva.

She glanced up and down the road, but it was deserted and likely to remain so, since it was growing dark and there was no moon tonight to aid travellers. If only she had not hit that stone. If only she had not stayed so late at Prospect House. Her meeting with Fleur had lasted longer than usual, then she had spent a good half hour talking to Daisy about her good fortune.

And it *was* good fortune, she thought now, to be offered the post as Sir Gerald's housekeeper. Fleur had explained about Miss Kilburn visiting Prospect House and telling her how the old housekeeper had returned from Harrogate with her rheumatism no better for taking the waters, and how Agnes and her brother had agreed that she should be given a pension and allowed to retire to a tied house on the estate.

'And then, dear Molly, Agnes offered Daisy the post of housekeeper, with a place for Billy in the stables. Is that not wonderful news?' Fleur had ended, a soft glow of happiness shining in her eyes, 'Agnes did not say so, but I think Sir Gerald must be behind this, do not you? I cannot recall having told anyone else that we have been training Daisy for just such a position.'

As the main patron of Prospect House, Molly had felt it incumbent upon her to talk to Daisy and assure herself that she was willing to take the position. Ten minutes in Daisy's company was long enough to convince her. There could be no doubting it, nor Billy's joy at being employed as a stablehand. Molly began to wonder if she had misjudged Sir Gerald. Perhaps his attachment to Fleur was more serious than she had first thought. She wanted to believe it, for Fleur's sake, but could he be trusted, any more than his friend? Russ had flirted with her, even kissed her, but last night he had left her in no doubt that she could never meet his exacting standards.

And yet he had confided in her, told her how shamefully his stepmother had behaved. Molly felt a tiny flicker of hope, although she was afraid to acknowledge it. Did that not argue a level of intimacy that went beyond friendship? She was still pondering the matter when she heard someone trotting along the road. Even in the semigloom she knew it was Russ, even before he spoke. It was as if she had once more conjured him by the sheer power of thought.

'Mrs Morgan, are you hurt?'

'A little bruised, perhaps, but nothing serious.' She came forward, waving one hand towards the gig. 'I am going to walk back to town, but first I n-need to unharness T-Tabby.'

She could not keep the quiver from her voice. Russ jumped down and quickly led her back to the milestone.

'Sit down again and I will do it.'

She resumed her seat and looked down at her hands. They were still shaking and for the first time she noticed the mud and grass stains on her pelisse. No doubt her hair was an unsightly tangle, too. She wondered idly when she had become so concerned about such things. She glanced up at Russ, knowing he was the reason. Becoming acquainted with Beau Russington had made her much more conscious of her appearance. Much more dissatisfied with it, if she was to be honest.

Molly watched him as he ran his hands gently over the mare, murmuring softly to reassure her while he checked for injury. There was little hope that such a connoisseur of women would spare her more than a glance when he could have his pick of the most beautiful women in society. And no hope at all that he might form any serious attachment. Although he might find it diverting to indulge her in a little flirtation, a few stolen kisses.

If they were alone and she was sufficiently encouraging he might go further. He might lie with her on some grassy bank and make love to her. He had kissed her once. He might be tempted to do so again. *She* might tempt him to do so. A pleasurable shiver ran through Molly at such an outrageous thought, rapidly succeeded by panic as cruel memories intruded. She looked up and down the deserted road and glanced uneasily behind her at the dense woodland. Oh, why had she not brought her maid or a groom? She had thought herself quite safe, driving in the gig.

'There now, all done, we can get on.'

Russ gently led the mare from the shafts. A low whistle brought his own horse closer and Russ caught up the reins. He waited for a moment, observing the two animals, then gave a satisfied nod.

'These two will walk together, I think, and without the carriage, we will be able to take the packhorse trail across the hill, that will save a good mile.' He turned towards Molly. 'If you will take my arm, I shall escort you home.'

Molly was surprised how shaky her legs were as she stood up. Dropping the reins, Russ reached out to grab her as she stumbled. She was already feeling foolish for her wicked thoughts and now she was mortified to display such weakness. She glanced up to see that he was smiling down at her and her cheeks grew painfully hot.

'My dear Molly, you cannot walk all the way back to Compton Parva.'

All her good sense had disappeared. She was quite unequal to protesting at his form of address and could only watch in silence as he pulled the big hunter closer and jumped nimbly into the saddle.

'Come along.' He held out his hand. 'Put your foot on my boot and I will pull you up.'

Worse and worse. She wanted to weep with vexation and her own feebleness. Instead she silently followed his instructions and moments later she was sitting across the saddle in front of him, almost cradled in his arms.

'You are perfectly safe,' he told her, his breath fluttering through her untidy curls and playing havoc with her already-disordered nerves. 'I shall not let you fall.'

She kept her eyes lowered. She had no fear of slipping off the horse, but sitting across a gentleman's lap, and in particular *this* gentleman's lap, was not making it easy to relax. Then, when they began to move, she had no choice but to lean against Russ and allow her body to move with the big horse's gait. She settled herself more comfortably and it was impossible not to rest her cheek against his shoulder. She closed her eyes, breathing in the smell of him, the wool of his coat, the well-laundered linen of his shirt and neckcloth, the spicy scent of citrus and musk that mingled with the fresh sweat on his skin. It was very male. Frightening and exciting. Intoxicating.

Two miles. Russ gazed up at the darkening sky, where the first stars were making their appearance. It was not long enough, even at this slow pace. He wanted to ride for ever through this twilight world with Molly in his arms, feeling her soft body resting against him, trusting him to protect her. That last thought made him feel like a giant, the hero from some Greek myth or perhaps a chivalrous knight from the pages of a medieval romance.

He smiled but without humour. There was nothing noble about his life. He had followed a selfish, hedonistic existence, careless of anyone or anything. Even now, when he should have been thinking only of escorting Molly to the safety of her home, he felt the temptation growing, the desire to make love to her, to awaken the passion he knew lay just beneath the surface. But it must not be. She was a respectable pillar of this community and a liaison with him would destroy everything she had worked for.

He fought against the attraction, forcing aside his desires while he silently raged against the injustice of it all. However, he could not suppress a low growl of frustration and she stirred, one dainty hand coming up to rest against his chest.

'Did you speak, sir?'

'We shall not be back before dark,' he replied, prevaricating.

'It is of little consequence. In a situation such as this I think my reputation will survive.'

'It is not your reputation that concerns me.'

'N-no?' Her hand moved up, the fingers clutching at the lapel of his coat. 'Then what, sir?'

He knew he should keep his eyes on the road. He knew that to look down at her would be his undoing, but he could not resist. She was gazing up at him, the starlight reflecting in her eyes. The breath caught in his throat.

'I am afraid,' he muttered, bringing his horse to a stand, 'I am very much afraid I will not be able to help myself.' She was leaning back against his arm and he tensed the muscles, pulling her closer. 'I might... I might do this.'

She gazed up at him, unprotesting, as he lowered his head. Her lips parted beneath his and at the same time her hand on his lapel tugged him closer. He was lost. Her body melted against him as he took her firmly in his arms and deepened the kiss. She responded and, when her tongue tangled with his, little arrows of desire fired his blood. Time had stopped, nothing mattered but Molly, her delicious softness in his arms, the taste of her on his lips. He slid one hand to her breast and she whimpered with pleasure. It was only when Flash shifted restlessly that he came to his senses. He broke off the kiss, dragging in a long, shuddering breath.

Molly eased herself upright as the horse began to walk on again. She was dazed, her body still trembling with the powerful shock of that kiss. She had not wanted it to end and she knew Russ felt the same, because she was practically sitting on his lap and, even through the layers of material between them, his arousal was evident. A shiver of exhilaration ran through her. Did he want more than that one stolen kiss? Was he about to offer her carte blanche? The excitement pooled deep inside and a delicious lightness began to curl up through her. She wanted him. She could not deny it. She wanted to throw caution to the winds and ride away with him into an unknown future.

The last time she had felt anything like this she had been a girl of seventeen, in the heady throes of first love. The feelings and sensations might be familiar, but now they were so much hotter and stronger than anything she had experienced before. How could this be? Had she not learned anything in the past seven years? He would not offer her marriage. She was a lost soul as far as he was concerned, certainly not the woman of impeccable character he demanded for his bride. But all her arguments were fruitless. All she knew was that she wanted him. Desperately. She put a hand up to her mouth, stunned at her own wantonness.

'I beg your pardon,' he said, misreading her distress.

She shook her head, swallowed and tried to make light of it.

'I cannot say you did not warn me,' she said. 'Let us call it your reward for rescuing me.'

'No hysterics, no outrage?' He gave a shaky laugh. 'Ah, darling Molly, you are very calm when you must be aware how much I would like to carry you off this minute!'

Darling Molly!

The hand that had been covering her mouth dropped to her breast, as if to stop her pounding heart from breaking through. Her whole being ached for him and she was ready to agree to anything, *anything* he might suggest.

'I cannot do it,' he said. 'You bravely told me about your past, so I know what a struggle it has been for you to build your reputation here. I cannot destroy all those years of work for a few hours' pleasure.'

Is that how he thought of her, a quick, brief coupling before he moved on? Molly was not at all sure what she had been hoping for, but his words fell on her like cold water, shocking her back to the reality of the situation. For a brief, heady period she had allowed her body to rule her head. She could not deny the deep pleasure of his kiss, but she knew—*she knew*—it would only lead to disappointment. She had not only her own experience to draw on, but also that of the girls and women living at Prospect House.

Those who had given into men's blandishments lost their maidenhood, their good name and almost all chance of living a respectable life. A hasty marriage had saved her from ruin once and she had been about to sacrifice everything and give in to her desires. She should be thankful that Russ refused to take advantage of her. She *was* thankful. But it did not stop her feeling angry, an anger made all the hotter by the bitter and irrational disappointment that she was not desirable enough to tempt him. She drew on every ounce of pride to formulate an answer.

'I am very glad we have clarified that point, sir,' she said with icy politeness. 'We may now be easy when we meet and know exactly where we stand with one another. We are almost at the vicarage. If you let me down here, there will be no need for anyone to know you brought me home.'

'Molly, are you angry with me? Surely you did not *want* me to—'

'Too late, someone is already coming out to meet us... It is Edwin. He must have been looking out for me.'

She waved to her brother, holding on to her brittle cheerfulness as he ran up to them.

'Molly, thank God you are back. I was about to come looking for you! Tell me at once what has happened. An accident?'

'Yes, yes, but nothing serious. Do help me down, Edwin, then we need not trouble Mr Russington to dismount.'

'Of course, but what happened?' Edwin demanded as he reached up for her.

'The gig wheel smashed on a stone,' Russ explained briefly. 'Your sister was thrown out. Thankfully she suffered no hurt. I brought her home and the horse. The gig is a couple of miles out of town, but it is slewed on to the grass verge and not blocking the highway. It should be safe enough until morning.'

'Thank goodness it was not more serious,' said Edwin, putting an arm around Molly. 'Although even in this light I can see you are distressed, my love. Let us get you inside. And, Russ, you must come in, too. Come and take a glass of wine with me, sir.'

'Thank you, but no. Allow me to take your carriage horse to the stable, but then I must get back.'

To Molly's relief, Edwin did not press him to stay, but he reiterated his thanks as Russ trotted away to the yard.

'Well, well, Molly. This is the second time Russington has come to your rescue. Who would have thought a notorious rake could behave so chivalrously?'

'Who indeed?' said Molly and promptly burst into tears.

Edwin ushered Molly indoors, clearly worried by her lachrymose behaviour, but she did not realise just how alarmed he was until the following day, when she received two sets of callers. Agnes Kilburn and Serena were shown into the morning room, where Molly had been sitting for an hour with her embroidery lying untouched on her lap. Serena bounced in, explaining that Edwin had called at Newlands that morning.

'He told us all about your accident yesterday. He *said* he had come to thank Russ for bringing you home,' she chattered on, untying the strings of her bonnet and casting it aside. 'But he would have done that last night, would he not? *I* think his real reason for calling was to see Agnes. He is so smitten that he cannot keep away!'

Molly invited a blushing Agnes to come and sit beside her and admonished Serena with a look.

'There really was no need for you to make a special journey to see me,' she said. 'It was the veriest spill and I was not at all hurt, I assure you.'

'But Edwin told us you had spent the evening crying, which he says you never do,' argued Serena. 'I thought my brother might be the cause. Was he uncivil to you?'

'No, of course not.' Molly tried to sound indignant, but Serena was not deceived.

'You are blushing, Molly Morgan! Did he flirt with you—did he try to kiss you?'

'That is enough, Serena!' Agnes chided her. 'Horrid girl, I shall take you back to Newlands this minute if you do not behave yourself.'

'But I want to *know*,' protested Serena, not a whit abashed.

'There is nothing to know,' replied Molly. 'Mr Russington came upon me standing beside the broken gig and—and brought me home.'

'But Edwin says he carried you before him on his horse. In his arms!'

'I was too shaken to walk, so he took me up.' Molly put up her hand. 'And no, Serena, he did not try to flirt with me.' She added, trying not to sigh, 'Far from it.'

Agnes gave her a searching look, but at that moment the door opened and more visitors walked in. Molly jumped up to greet them.

'Why, Fleur, Nancy, I had no idea you intended to come to town today.'

'How could we stay away?' cried Fleur, flying across the room to take Molly's outstretched hands. 'As soon as we heard of your mishap we had to come and see you.'

There was a pause while greetings were exchanged and Molly was persuaded to sit back down on the sofa between Agnes and Fleur. It was some moments before she could ask how they had learned the news.

'From Sir Gerald, of course,' said Nancy. 'He told Fleur Edwin was most anxious about you.'

'All this fuss over a little tumble,' exclaimed Molly. 'I assure you all I am perfectly well.'

'No, she is not,' put in Serena. 'She is in love with my brother.'

This declaration brought an indignant protest from Molly and a reprimand from Agnes, but Nancy laughed.

'So we have another pair of lovers. Oh, pray do not look at me like that, Fleur. You and Sir Gerald have been smelling of April and May for weeks now and Molly herself told me that Edwin will use any excuse to visit Newlands. Anyone would think it was spring in Compton Parva, rather than autumn.'

'Nancy, you are jumping to conclusions,' muttered Fleur, her cheeks crimson. 'What will Miss Kilburn think...?'

'Miss Kilburn has already guessed it,' replied Agnes, smiling. 'Why else would Gerald be so eager for me to make your acquaintance? But as for Mr Frayne's attentions to me—' it was her turn to blush '—nothing has been said, there is no understanding between us.'

'Only that you cannot keep your eyes from one another when you are in the same room,' remarked Serena gleefully.

Despite her blushes, Agnes drew herself up and said with gentle dignity, 'We did not come here to talk about me. It is Molly who concerns us.'

'And I assure you there is no need,' Molly replied, her own colour much heightened. 'The idea that I am...am in love with Mr Russington is laughable. He...he would never give a thought to me.'

Fleur tutted softly. 'You do not know that.'

'Yes, I do.' Molly forgot to play her part and this time the sigh escaped her. 'He told me so himself.' She realised her words had caused a flutter of indignation in her audience and added hurriedly, 'Pray do not think I mind, he was merely trying to reassure me that I was perfectly safe, travelling alone with him.'

'Then it shows he was concerned for you,' said Fleur.

'It shows a sad lack of tact,' countered Nancy. 'One would expect a hardened flirt to have more address.'

'He clearly does not think me worth the effort.'

'And he never will while you are wearing those old gowns.' Nancy eyed Molly's sober grey silk with disfavour. 'You should have more bright colours, like the red lustring.'

Fleur took her hands. 'It really is time for you to leave off your mourning, Molly,' she said gently. 'You are still a young woman and may yet find another husband.'

Molly shuddered and crossed her arms. 'I do not *want* another husband.'

'A lover, then,' said Nancy.

Agnes gave a little cry of alarm. 'I am not sure we should be discussing this here.'

'If you are afraid for my sensibilities, pray do not be,' put in Serena cheerfully. 'After all, it is my brother who is responsible for all this, so I think I must have some part in it. And if you were to ask me,' she went on, 'I do not think he is indifferent to Molly. He told me he likes her very well.'

Molly blinked rapidly. 'There is a great difference between like and love.'

'I hope you are not going to go into a decline,' said Fleur, giving her a searching look.

'No, of course, she is not,' Nancy retorted. 'She is going to show she does not give the snap of her fingers for any man.'

That made Molly smile. 'I thought I had been doing that for the past six years.'

'No, you have been hiding behind your widow's weeds,' Nancy told her. 'It is time now to throw them off.'

'No, no, I cannot. I would not feel right. I am the vicar's sister. I have my place to maintain.' Molly's voice died away as she wondered how soon she would have to relinquish that position to his wife.

'A change of clothes will not make you any less capable, my love,' said Fleur, squeezing her arm. 'I remember when we were at school together you loved bright colours and you looked so well in them.'

'And she will do so again,' said Nancy. 'Now, do not argue, Molly. We are your friends, and we are determined on this change for you.'

'Yes, and our ball takes place in three weeks, which will be the perfect time to show off the transformation,' said Agnes, her eyes dancing.

'Perfect!' Serena clapped her hands. 'We shall turn you from a dull little caterpillar into a gorgeous butterfly. And we shall show my foolish brother just what he is missing!'

'You are a fool, Russington. You are torturing yourself unnecessarily. Go back to London and forget Molly Morgan.'

It was not the first time Russ had looked into the mirror and offered himself advice, but he had never yet taken it. He pushed the diamond pin firmly into the folds of his cravat and stood back to admire the effect. He looked every inch the fashionable gentleman, perhaps a little too fashionable for a country ball. The snowy linen was almost startling in the candlelight and showed how tanned his face had become during his stay at Newlands. Hardly surprising, since he and Gerald spent most of their days out of doors. His black curls had been brushed until they glowed, the coat of blue superfine fitted without a crease over his shoulders and, combined with the immaculate white waistcoat, pale breeches and brilliant black leather dancing pumps, it was an ensemble that drew admiring glances in the smartest London salons. It certainly impressed the good people of Compton Parva, but then, thought Russ, a faint, self-deprecating smile curling his lip, they would expect nothing less of Beau Russington, the darling of fashionable society.

He turned away from the mirror, his ears picking up the sounds from below of the orchestra tuning up. The dancing would begin soon. He would have to hurry if he was not to be late. Not that it would matter very much, a smiling apology and a few words would smooth things over with Agnes, he was sure. His mind returned to Molly. It was strange how all his charm and polished address disappeared when he was in her company. She was not impressed by him and he did not wish her to be. He just wished she liked him a little more.

Like. He considered the word as he ran lightly down the stairs. She was attracted to him, but he was a rake and she strongly disapproved of rakes, even when they rescued maidens in distress. Admittedly he should not have kissed her, but she had taken that very well, and it was only when they reached the vicarage that she had become agitated, even angry with him, and since then she had shown very clearly that she wanted nothing more to do with him.

In the three weeks since he had carried her home on horseback she had studiously avoided his company, crying off from a dinner party and darting away if she spotted him in the town. If any other woman had shown such an aversion to his company, he would have laughed and put her out of his mind, but he could not do that with Molly. She filled his thoughts during the day and kept him awake at night. Confound it, he should be grateful to her for her efforts. It was best that they did not meet, but knowing she would be at the ball tonight filled him with a mix of apprehension and anticipation, the like of which he had not known since his boyhood.

The reception rooms were already crowded with chattering guests when he entered. His hostess was standing a little way from the door with Serena and Edwin Frayne and, judging by the way Agnes was blushing and the vicar's beaming smile, it was clear that Miss Kilburn's recent absence had in no way lessened the attraction between them. Across the room, Gerald caught his eye and winked. Russ walked over to join him.

'I think my sister has made a conquest,' he murmured, sweeping a glass of wine from a passing waiter and handing it to Russ. 'I confess after the tragic loss of her fiancé, I thought she would end up an old maid, but I am very hopeful now. Frayne would be just the man for her.' He laughed suddenly. 'Who would have thought it? Perhaps there is something in the air of Compton Parva that makes love blossom.'

There was a glint in his friend's eyes that made Russ think he was about to refer to Molly, so he said quickly, 'I believe your sister invited Mrs Dellafield. Is she here?'

'Molly convinced Agnes that there was no hope of the invitation being accepted, so she decided not to embarrass the lady by sending one.' Gerald's reply was offhand, and his eyes were constantly moving about the room. 'Ah, more guests are arriving. I had best go and meet them. And talking of Mrs Morgan, I'd be obliged if you would take a glass of wine to her and make sure she is enjoying herself.'

Russ shot his friend a suspicious look, but Gerald met it with a bland smile before walking off. Surely Gerald did not suspect Russ was developing a tendress for the widow? He had been at pains not to give himself away, but then so, too, was Gerald very reticent when it came to talking about Fleur Dellafield. Russ hoped that meant his friend's interest was waning. He recalled Molly's foolhardy attempt to protect her friend and he could not be sure she would not try something even more rash. Russ looked around the room. Despite her diminutive figure Molly Morgan should be easy to spot, there were very few ladies wearing blacks or greys tonight. Unless, of course, she was wearing that dark red gown.

Then he saw her and he was transfixed.

Molly was enjoying herself and could only be grateful to her friends for their persistence. As she listened politely to Sir William expounding on the virtues of the new closed stove he had purchased for Currick Hall, she reflected upon everyone's kindness to her. She had met with nothing but praise at her appearance this evening. Even one of her elderly neighbours had indulged her in a little flirtation, but in such a gentle, kindly way that she had not felt at all alarmed by it. In fact, it had, along with a second glass of champagne, given a much-needed boost to her confidence.

She had not wanted to be *transformed*, as Serena put it. Indeed, she had argued against it, but her friends had convinced her that a change of style was the best way to answer Russ's snub and show him she cared not a jot for his opinion. So she had allowed Nancy to cut her hair to make the most of her natural curls and Serena, Agnes and Fleur had spent happy hours in her bedchamber, removing all but a few of her mourning clothes. She had not allowed them to throw out anything, but the alacrity with which Cissy packed the garments into a trunk for storage in the attics told Molly that her friends were not alone in their opinion that it was time for a change.

News of her transformation had quickly reached all her neighbours, and shortly after her friends' visit, various packages had begun to arrive. A parcel of coloured ostrich feathers and assorted ribbons that Miss Hebden said had been lying unsold at the back of her store, Mrs Thomas sent over a length of emerald-green velvet and Agnes brought her a bolt of blue satin that she declared she would never use.

Marjorie had immediately fashioned the velvet into an elegant pelisse and matching bonnet and the sapphire-blue satin had been made up into the beautiful evening gown that Molly was now wearing. It was trimmed at the bodice, sleeves and hem with silver net that shimmered in the candlelight whenever she moved and a chaplet of silver foil was wound twice around her hair and glinted between her dark, glossy curls.

Molly glanced down at the blue satin slippers that peeped out from beneath her gown. Lady Currick had brought them to the vicarage earlier that day and when Molly had demurred she had pressed them upon her, saying earnestly, 'Do please take them, Mrs Morgan. I bought them thinking they would do for Nell, but she will not be wearing such strong colours at her come-out, and she has such dainty feet. You are the only lady I know who could wear them!'

Everyone had been so kind, so generous, and to think she had been tempted to throw it all away, to sacrifice her good name and give up her place in this town, just because a man had kissed her.

'I really do think the committee should consider a Rumford stove for Prospect House,' Sir William declared. 'What say you, Mrs Morgan, will you support me if I suggest it?'

His lady tapped his arm with her fan. 'My dear man, we are at a ball! This is not the place to discuss such matters. Tell Molly instead how fine she is looking.'

Sir William looked so taken aback that Molly felt the laughter bubbling up.

'No, no, I assure you I want no compliments, ma'am, and Sir William knows I am always delighted to talk about Prospect House.'

Someone had come up beside her and she looked up, still laughing. It was Russ, looking so handsome that her heart leapt. There was no time to pretend indifference, the laughter slid into what she hoped was a polite smile, but she could not drag her gaze from his face. He was holding out a glass to her.

'Our host thought you might like some champagne.'

'Why, thank you.'

She took a sip from the glass and peeped up at him. There was no doubting the admiration in his eyes and she felt a little kick of satisfaction. She wanted him to experience a moment's regret for what he had rejected. He looked as if he would speak, but Lady Currick came in first.

'Well, Mr Russington, what do you think of our little friend? Is she not looking very well tonight?'

'Never better,' he replied. 'I hope you will be dancing this evening, Mrs Morgan.'

He had not taken his eyes off Molly, but for once she did not blush and look away. She gave him an arch smile.

'I might be persuaded to do so.'

Sir William gave a crack of laughter. 'There you are, Russington. Go to it and *persuade* the lady.'

Molly waited while Russ made her a little bow. 'They are striking up for the first dance now, madam, if you would do me the honour?'

'Ah, how unfortunate, Mr Russington,' she said gently. 'You see, I am already engaged.'

Only by the slightest change in his countenance did he show his surprise, but she was looking out for it.

'Ah, I see. Perhaps later, then?'

'Perhaps.' She glanced past him at Mr Sykes, who had come up to them.

'Well, Mrs Morgan, shall we take our places?'

With a wide smile Molly handed Russ her champagne glass and went off with her partner.

Molly felt the exhilaration fizzing through her blood. Perhaps it was naughty of her to tease Russ, but such an opportunity might not arise again. It was very likely that he would now shrug those broad shoulders and forget all about her. If he did, then she had lost nothing, but it had soothed her pride to be able to refuse him. She was engaged for the next three dances, the final one with Sir Gerald and as he led her off the floor he asked her if she was enjoying herself.

'Oh, immensely,' she told him. 'I am very grateful to

your sister. She secured partners for me even before I came into the room tonight. Everyone has been so kind, including yourself, Sir Gerald.'

'It is no hardship to be kind to a pretty woman, ma'am, and you are looking particularly well this evening.' He glanced across the room. 'And if I am not mistaken Russ is waiting to pounce on us. Agnes told me you were punishing him for some slight.'

'She did?' Molly blushed. 'It was not so very serious. I assure you.'

'I am glad to hear it. She said I was not to let him near you until after supper, but he is my friend and I cannot help feeling sorry for the fellow.' He looked down at Molly, placing his free hand over her fingers as they lay on his arm. 'So, ma'am, shall I tell him you are engaged to me, or do you think he has waited long enough?'

Could she do this? Molly had been laughing and joking all evening, even flirting in a gentle, harmless way, but could she do the same with a man whose very nearness turned her into a trembling mass of longing? She put up her chin. That was all in the past. She had far too much to lose to let herself be seduced by any man, but a little flirtation in the safety of the ballroom, what harm could that do?

'Oh, I think I should take pity on Mr Russington, sir, do not you?'

Chapter Eleven

Russ kept smiling as Gerald brought Molly over to him. His jaw tightened as he watched them talking together, Gerald leaning in a little closer and giving her hand a comforting pat. Something very like jealousy ripped through him. He was too experienced to let it show, however. He greeted their arrival with all his usual urbanity and this time Molly accepted his invitation to dance.

'Here she is, then,' declared Gerald, 'but 'tis with reluctance that I relinquish my fair partner to you, Russ. Look after her!'

He lounged away and Russ led Molly off to take their places in the next set.

'I feared I should not be able to dance with you tonight, madam.'

'Then you should have come in earlier.' She added, 'There are any number of ladies without partners tonight, so I hope you have not been standing at the side, watching me.'

'By no means. I have danced with Agnes and Mrs Sykes. And Lady Currick's daughter, Helen.'

'How delightful for them and it is especially useful for

Nell,' she told him. 'She needs a little practice at dealing with roués before her come-out.'

She met his frowning glance with a look of pure innocence. Nettled, he changed the subject.

'I have the strangest feeling you have been avoiding me, Mrs Morgan.'

'Now, why should I do that, Mr Russington?'

'Something to do with our last meeting perhaps.'

She laughed. 'That would be a sad recompense for your rescuing me that night.'

'But you have already rewarded me for that service,' he reminded her. She blushed adorably at that and he glanced about to make sure they could not be overheard before he continued. 'At the time you appeared angry that I did not want more than that one kiss.'

Her eyes widened. 'You said you did not wish to ruin me. Why should I be angry about that?'

They were silent as they performed their part in the dance, stepping up and away, gracefully circling as they progressed through the set.

'Perhaps you *wanted* me to ruin you,' he murmured, when at last they came back together.

To his surprise, she did not react angrily to his suggestion. Perfectly calm, she appeared to consider it while they waited for their next turn.

'I should be very foolish to want that, Mr Russington.' They were moving again and as she put her hand into his, she added softly, 'So much better to meet you on occasions like this, when I can enjoy your considerable charms without the least danger of yielding to them.'

By heaven, she had learned the art of dalliance very quickly! Russ was glad when the dance parted them again, relieved to have some time to think about this new Molly Morgan. It was not only her clothes that had changed, but her whole demeanour. He had seen signs of it occasionally in the past, when she had been at her most relaxed, but this evening was different. She was positively goading him.

And he was enjoying it.

Russ had to stifle a laugh. She had acknowledged the attraction between them, agreed nothing could come of it, but instead of keeping her distance she was determined to meet him head on. A dangerous policy, but he was more than willing to oblige her. After all, as she said, they were safe enough in company.

No danger?

Molly might be able to deceive everyone else this evening, but she could not lie to herself. Every smile, every word she shared with Russ was intoxicating, but all the time she had to keep reminding herself that it was not real. The banter, the coy looks, the teasing smiles were all part of a game and she was playing it with a master. He knew to a nicety how to engage with her, when to challenge, when to tease or praise her and Molly was pleased to discover that she could hold her own with him.

She allowed Russ to take her into supper, but insisted they sit with their hosts. Edwin was already at the table, deep in conversation with Agnes, and since Gerald soon went off to talk to his guests, any hope Molly had entertained of being spared the full force of Russ's attraction was dashed.

He was the perfect companion, moving the candles so they did not glare in her eyes, selecting the choicest morsels for her plate and bringing the tray of sweetmeats within her reach. She was outwardly calm, but it was an effort with Russ sitting beside her, his sleeve brushing her arm, his thigh only inches away. When he beckoned a waiter to bring them more wine she covered her glass, knowing that she must keep her wits about her.

'Lemonade, then,' Russ suggested, nodding to the waiter to attend to it. 'The evening is young yet, and you will need some refreshment.' He leaned closer. 'I am set upon a second dance with you tonight.'

Her hand hovered over the sweetmeat dish. 'You may well be disappointed.'

'Oh?' She observed with satisfaction the way his hand tightened around his wine glass. 'Are all the remaining dances taken?'

She picked out a small sugar bonbon. 'And if I told you they were?'

'I should be obliged to dispose of one of your partners.'

The quiet menace in his voice startled Molly and she dropped the sweetmeat.

'It…it is as well then that that is not the case.'

His hold on the wine glass eased.

'It is very well,' he said, smiling at her. He picked up the bonbon and popped it into her mouth. 'Very well indeed.'

Molly was aware that anyone watching them at supper could have been in no doubt that Russ was flirting with her and now they were standing up together for a boisterous country dance which demanded she hold his hands as they skipped and twirled about the room. After a good supper and a generous supply of wine, everyone was much more relaxed and the ballroom was full of laughter and chatter that all but drowned out the music. It was very hot, too, even though the long windows had been thrown wide. By the time the music ended, Molly knew that this second dance with Russ was a mistake. She had enjoyed it too much, the control she had kept over herself all evening had vanished and her wayward body wanted him as much as ever.

She was fully aware of the danger when she allowed him to escort her out on to the terrace and she offered no resistance as he gently pulled her into the deep shadows and kissed her. On the contrary, she clung to him, pressing her body against his as she returned the kiss with a passion she had not known she possessed. It frightened her, a little, but by the time they broke apart she had made her decision. She put a hand up to his face.

'Russ, I want you to take me to your bed.'

Russ closed his eyes. How many times had he dreamed she would say those words to him? If she had done so when they first met he would have complied willingly, but not now. Now he cared too much for her. It would not just be her reputation that would be destroyed if he went further. She was not some rich society widow who could retire to her country estates for a few months until the scandal had died down. If Molly lost her good name, she would lose her standing in Compton Parva. She would no longer be able to help her brother or to promote the charitable causes so close to her heart, including Prospect House.

'Molly, do not tempt me.' His arms tightened around her. 'You are a widow and I have awakened feelings that you thought long dead. You need a husband, Molly, a good man who will love you as you deserve.'

She drew in a long breath. 'My body is crying out for *you*, Russ.' She pushed herself away, trying to read his face in the shadows. 'Do you deny that you want me?'

'No, of course, I do not deny it.' He looked up at the sky and sighed. 'I have no constancy, Molly. I have had many mistresses, but my interest rarely lasts more than a month. Such fleeting lust would destroy you. You deserve a steady, faithful husband, not someone like me. You know what I am.'

'Yes.' She buried her face in his shoulder. 'You are a rake. You have a reputation as a lover and…and I am ready to endure—'

'What is this?' He took her arms and held her away from him, frowning. 'Endure? Molly, I am talking of pleasure, not pain.'

She averted her face and said quietly, 'I believe men experience these things differently.'

'You are wrong. The women I have taken to bed enjoyed it every bit as much as I.'

'Perhaps I am made differently.'

He said savagely, 'I do not believe that.' He put one hand beneath her chin, compelling her to look up at him. 'If you have not enjoyed lovemaking, then the man was at fault, Molly, not you.'

He felt a wave of anger growing against whoever it was who had hurt her so badly.

She sighed. 'I thought you wanted me.'

'I do.' Russ closed his eyes. She must never know how much he wanted her! He said gently, 'I do, Molly, but I would not take another man's prize.'

'Prize!' With a cry she tore herself away from him. 'I am no *prize*,' she said bitterly. 'I am just a…a *thing*, to be used and—and broken for a man's pleasure.'

His anger boiled over into a red rage that manifested in a growl.

'Aye, you told me! You were seduced by some blackguard who took your innocence and abandoned you—'

She had her back to him, but he saw her hand come up as if to silence him.

'I was not talking of that,' she whispered, dragging out her handkerchief to wipe her eyes. 'It was far, far worse than that.'

Russ stopped himself from reaching out for her. He should say something soothing, let it pass. Tomorrow he could leave Compton Parva and go back to London, to his old, carefree life and she would remain only a faint, pleasant memory. But looking at the small, dejected figure in front of him, he knew it was already too late. He put his hands on her shoulders and guided her towards the far end of the terrace, away from the open windows.

'Tell me,' he said, sitting down on a stone bench and pulling her down beside him. 'Tell me what happened.'

For a while there was only the muted sounds from the ballroom and the occasional call of a night bird to break the silence. Then he heard her sigh.

'Niall was a rogue,' she said slowly, dragging her handkerchief between her fingers. 'A handsome, Irish rogue with a smooth tongue and a roving eye. I was seventeen and so in love that I desperately wanted to please him. I will not lie, I wanted it, too. I wanted to give myself to him, wholly. But when it happened it was rushed and painful and…disappointing. It was only the once, then he was gone, my Irish soldier. He left before he even knew he had got me with child.

'My parents were horrified when they discovered my situation. They found me a husband, or more accurately, they *bought* me a husband. Morgan was a yeoman farmer, not a gentleman, but then, I suppose they were thankful to find anyone to marry me. I insisted Morgan should be told about the baby. He swore it would make no difference to the way he felt about me. That he loved me. Love!' She shuddered. 'I experienced no love at his hands. He t-took me for his pleasure. It was brutish and punishing. To him I was an undeserving slattern who should be grateful that he had married me and saved my good name. It was worse when he had been drinking, because if he could not... If he could not p-perform, he would beat me. I always tried to stay on my feet, because—' her hands crept over her stomach and her voice was barely a thread '—it was a kick that killed the baby. My baby.'

Silently Russ took her in his arms, and she turned her face into his shoulder, weeping. There was nothing he could say to make it better, so he rested his cheek against her head and held her. At last the tears subsided. When she struggled to sit up he released her, but she did not object when he kept one arm about her shoulders. She wiped her eyes and began to speak again.

'Morgan never knew what he had done. He died in a drunken brawl the night after that last beating. I was very near my time and everyone thought it was the shock of Morgan's death that made the baby come early, but I knew the truth. I could not bear to go back to my parents, they had already made it clear they considered that losing the baby was a...a judgement upon me for my sins. As soon as I was well enough I sold the farm and came north to live with Edwin. I used Morgan's money to set up Prospect House and tried to forget my old life. The bruises have healed, but I have never been able to throw off the repulsion of being married to such a man.'

She fell silent and he gave voice to the question that had been nagging at him.

'And yet you offered yourself to me, to save your friend?'

She gave a little shrug. 'Having endured a man's attentions in bed before, I thought I could do so again, if I must.' She hung her head. 'I thought I *could* do so, if it was with you.'

With a sigh he pulled her into his arms. 'How could you even think of making such a sacrifice?'

She turned her face into his chest, muffling her response. 'I have made a mull of everything. I am such a fool.'

'Yes, you are fool,' he agreed, resting his cheek against her hair again. Even in the chill of an autumn evening she smelled of summer flowers. 'But a very adorable one.'

'It is kind of you to say so,' she said. 'And very generous, but I think I should go now.'

She pushed herself out of his arms, but he held on to her hand. 'Are you engaged for any other dances this evening?'

'No, but—'

'Then come with me. By my reckoning we have at least two hours.'

'For what?'

He smiled. 'Come with me.'

He led her down the steps and around the house to a side door. It opened on to one of the servants' halls and, as he had hoped, it was deserted. They climbed the stairs, guided by the lighted lanterns that hung at intervals from the bare walls. He uttered up a silent prayer when they reached his bedchamber without seeing anyone. Once they were inside he turned the key in the lock. Molly's fingers tightened nervously around his.

'My man is the soul of discretion,' he explained, 'but I do not want anyone to disturb us.'

He took a taper to the small fire burning in the hearth. Soon the room was bathed in the soft, golden glow of candles. He turned. Molly had not moved from where he had left her, by the door. He shrugged himself out of his evening coat and threw it over a chair, then he held out his hands to her.

'Will you trust me not to hurt you?'

Slowly she walked towards him and gave him her hands. He drew her into his arms and kissed her gently. She was tense, nervous and he made no move to deepen the kiss until she relaxed against him. He would not rush her, she was as nervous as a colt, but slowly she began to respond. Her arms slipped around his neck and her tongue tangled with his, stirring his blood. Without breaking the kiss he lifted her and carried her across to the bed.

She drew away from him in alarm as he laid her on the covers and he murmured again, 'Trust me.'

Even in the shadows of the bed's canopy he could see her eyes were wide and anxious. He waited, making no move to join her until she reached for him. Russ measured his length against hers, cupping her face and gently kissing her lips before placing soft, butterfly kisses across her cheek and over her jaw. Her head went back, inviting him to trail his lips along the length of her throat. He paused to give particular attention to the little dip between the collarbones and she sighed. His hand cupped her breast and she pushed against his fingers. Even through the silk and silver net, he could feel the nub harden as he caressed her. With practised ease he slipped his hand inside the bodice. She flinched and he paused, raising his head to gaze down at her.

'You only have to tell me and I will stop,' he whispered. 'I will do nothing against your will. You have my word.'

The look in her eyes and her tremulous smile made his soul soar and he bent his head to kiss her again, long and deeply, while his fingers caressed the cushioned roundness of her breast. Then he shifted his position, eased the breast from its silky wrapping and took the hardened peak in his mouth while his fingers moved across to work their magic on its twin. She began to stir restlessly, her hands moving over his shoulders, plucking at his shirt. He raised his head and shifted until he was kneeling beside her. His breath caught at the sight of her breasts, unconfined and wantonly displayed, but he must not be distracted from his purpose. Gently he gathered her skirts, uncovering the dainty ankles and silk stockings, fastened at the knee with lacy garters. He shifted again, positioning himself between her legs and bending to kiss her mouth once more.

This time when he raised his head she reached for him, gripping his shirt to pull him back for more, but he resisted. Gently easing her hands away, he slid down the bed and began to kiss her leg, just above the knee. She tensed, but made no protest, so he continued to caress her, his lips moving upwards across the soft inner thigh.

Molly closed her eyes and gave herself up to the sensations that were flooding through her. Her very bones felt like liquid, soft and pliant. Russ's gentle hands had taken control of her body, easing her apart so that his mouth, his tongue could smooth over the tender skin of her thigh, moving ever closer towards her aching core. She whimpered, but she did not pull away, instead she was arching, inviting him.

He shifted again, his hands slid beneath her hips and held her firm while his mouth finally reached the hinge of her thighs and his tongue licked and flickered with unerring precision. She felt the pressure building, rippling through her, and she tried to move away from the sweet, delicious torture but she was his prisoner. A very willing prisoner, was her last coherent thought as her body convulsed in white-hot spasms of unbearable ecstasy. She was flying, higher, higher, until her world splintered and she cried out in sheer joy as her body shuddered and she felt herself falling, tumbling from heaven into oblivion.

Russ was cradling her in his arms as consciousness returned. She raised a hand to touch his cheek.

'Thank you,' she whispered.

'It is for you, Molly. To show you how wonderful it can be.'

Her scent was on his lips as he kissed her. His hand slipped once more to her breast and she felt her body waking again beneath his touch. She gave herself up to the pleasure of it as he used his hands and his mouth to bring her again and again to the edge of climax and beyond. Until she collapsed against him, sated and exhausted.

She allowed herself a few moments' recovery, then her hand slid over his chest and down towards the buttoned flap of his breeches. His body reacted to her touch, but he caught her fingers.

'There is no need,' he murmured, his breath warm against her cheek. 'Tonight is about your pleasure, Molly.'

'And it would please me to satisfy you,' she replied, moving closer and unfastening the flap. He was already hard and aroused as her fingers pushed aside the cloth to release his erection. He had been denying himself while he attended to her needs, but now she returned the favour eagerly, revelling in her power over him as she kissed, caressed and stroked him until he caught her hands, pushing down as he reached his own satisfying release.

They lay together, wrapped in each other's arms, their bodies resting from the onslaught, but at last Russ stirred.

'I would like to keep you with me all night, but we must return. There is such a crush in the ballroom that I doubt our absence has been noted, but just in case, we must get you into the ladies' retiring room, and I will return via the terrace.' He sat up. 'We must protect your reputation.'

He helped her from the bed, and straightened his clothes while she shook out her skirts.

'Ah, yes, my reputation.'

He watched as she went across to the looking glass, checking that her bodice was once more decorously arranged and tidying her curls.

'I have no wish to ruin you, Molly.'

'I am aware of that.'

When she turned back to him it seemed the most natural thing in the world to open his arms to her and equally natural for her to walk into them. She rested her head on his shoulder and he heard her sigh.

'I am most truly grateful to you for this, Russ. It has been wonderful. A revelation. But you may be easy. I shall not pursue you to do this again.'

Her words, so matter-of-fact, so understanding, hit him like a body blow. He had known from the start it must only be for one night but now he discovered that he did not want to let her go. He wanted her in his bed, to make love to her night after night. To consummate their union. But Molly Morgan would never consent to be his mistress and he would never ask it of her. The only solution would be marriage.

No! Russ shied away from the thought in panic. He was a confirmed bachelor. What he had seen of marriage had given him an aversion to that state. His stepmother and his sister-in-law were both grasping, selfish women, hell-bent on sucking a man dry of his fortune and his energies. He knew Molly was nothing like that, but her goodness frightened him even more. He had never loved anyone in his life and he doubted if he could remain faithful.

He said now, 'You need a good man for your husband, Molly. A man who will treat you as you deserve, one who loves you. What you do not need is a hardened libertine who will be bored with you within a month.'

She moved out of his arms and looked at him, perplexed.

'I never expected you to love me Russ,' she said. 'Neither did I expect you to marry me.'

'How could I?' He barely heard her, for he was desperately trying to convince himself as much as Molly that marriage was out of the question. 'I am not made for domestic felicity, Molly, nor do I want a clinging wife. And you, with your provincial morals and good deeds, would be the very worst partner for me. It would destroy you, my dear, and I do not want to do that.'

Molly listened with increasing dismay. Did he not believe her? Perhaps he thought she was trying to shame him into making her an offer, but nothing could be further from the truth. What they had just shared had been quite, quite wonderful and she was angry that he should now sully it with this unwarranted attack. Her head came up.

'You have made yourself very clear, sir. Now, let me be equally so. I never came here looking for a husband and I agree that your rakehell ways would never be acceptable to someone with my...my *provincial morals*. I am only sorry that you believe I would even contemplate such a union.' She gave her skirts one final shake and walked towards the door. 'My only concern now is to return to the ballroom without causing a scandal!'

Molly gained the safety of the retiring room without being seen by any of Newlands's servants or guests. She could only hope that the attendant there would put her flushed cheeks and tousled appearance down to the lively dancing. She stayed there as long as she dared before making her way into the ballroom. Another country dance was in progress and the room buzzed with happy chatter, voices raised to make themselves heard above the music. Molly looked around. Serena was dancing, but Edwin was standing with Agnes and Sir Gerald at the side of the room. Molly made her way over to them, more than a little afraid they would ask her to explain her absence. Edwin saw her approaching and held his hand out to her.

'Molly, do come and join us. I looked for you earlier, for I wanted you to be the first to know, but somehow things got a little out of hand.' He flushed and looked a little conscious. 'Almost everyone here seems to know it now—have you heard? Agnes has agreed to be my wife!'

Molly did not need to feign her delight. She kissed Agnes and then Edwin before turning to Sir Gerald to express the hope that he was happy at the news.

'Overjoyed, ma'am,' he replied, his open, cheerful countenance suffused in a beaming smile. 'Agnes mentioned it to me shortly after supper and from that moment word spread like wildfire. By the time the musicians struck up for the *boulanger*, everyone seemed to know of it!'

'And to approve, thankfully,' added Edwin. 'Lady Currick is already talking of a party, to celebrate our betrothal.'

'At the King's Head,' put in Agnes, 'so that everyone in the town may come and celebrate it.' She touched Molly's arm. 'I know this is very sudden, Molly. Are you sure you do not object?'

'Not at all,' she said, smiling. 'You are made for one another and you, Agnes, will be the perfect vicar's wife, I am sure.'

'I am so glad you approve,' said Agnes, slipping her arm through Molly's. 'And you will live with us,' she continued. 'Edwin and I are agreed that you should continue to make your home at the vicarage.'

'That is very kind, but I intend to set up my own establishment.' Molly added, with perfect sincerity, 'I have been feeling restless for some time now, so perhaps I shall begin by going away for a short holiday.'

Somewhere far away, where she might reflect on all that had happened and dispel the nagging ache that had settled itself around her heart.

'Yes, but not until after the wedding,' said Edwin quickly. 'You will be needed to help with all the arrangements.'

Gerald laughed. 'I said as much to Russ just now. He was all for leaving Newlands in the next few days, but I told him I expect him to support me, especially at the betrothal party which Lady Currick hopes to arrange for a week tomorrow. There is no way I shall allow him to abandon me before that!'

There was no escaping talk of the forthcoming nuptials for the rest of the evening or the following week. Molly could only be glad no one had noticed that she and Russ had been absent from the ballroom for more than an hour. Her head told her that she must now put that whole incident behind her, but her heart refused to obey. She wanted Russ more than ever and it was impossible to avoid him in the town, or at Newlands, where Edwin and Molly dined three times in almost as many days. It was a struggle to keep her eyes from following Russ as he moved across a room, or to converse with him calmly, when her whole body cried out for his touch. Her only consolation was his announcement that he had urgent business in London and must leave Compton Parva as soon as the betrothal party was over.

Word of the engagement had even reached Prospect House, as Molly discovered when she met Fleur and Nancy after the Sunday service at All Souls.

'And what a good thing it is we persuaded Gerald

not to invite me,' said Fleur, glancing around to make sure there was no one near enough to overhear. 'I understand a report on the ball and the announcement was sent to the *Herald* and they will doubtless send it on to the London papers. Miss Hebden told me the *Herald* always gives a full list of guests at any such occasion. Just imagine how it would have been if I had gone and if Papa had read of it.'

'If, if,' exclaimed Nancy impatiently. 'You didn't go and there's an end to it. Instead of worrying about what might have been, you should be telling Molly your own news.'

'Sir Gerald has proposed?' Molly asked quickly.

'Shh.' Fleur was blushing furiously. 'Yes, he has. He had spoken of it a week ago, but I told him I could not accept his offer without his sister's blessing. Then Agnes announced her engagement and he was emboldened to discuss it with her yesterday, and he rode over directly to tell me that she has no objections, so now we are to be married. But it is still a secret, Molly. Apart from Nancy, you are the only one who knows of it at present, and I would be obliged if you did not make it generally known, if you please, but—oh, Molly, was ever anything so wonderful?'

No, thought Molly, stifling a sharp stab of self-pity. She did not begrudge her brother and her friends their happiness, but it threw into sharp relief her own predicament and the growing realisation that she had lost her heart to a rake.

Molly did not see Sir Gerald again until market day, when she returned to the vicarage just as he was leaving. She greeted him with a smile and asked him if he had come upon his sister's business, or his own.

'So Fleur has told you,' he declared, relief in his voice. 'I hope we have your blessing?'

'Of course. Does this mean we will be arranging a double wedding?'

His face clouded. 'I should like that, but Fleur lives in fear of her father. She knows he is still searching and is afraid if the *banns* are read for three weeks he will find her before we can be married. That is one of the reasons we are not making any announcement, in case the scandal sheets should get wind of it. I have been discussing the matter with Edwin and we are agreed that a licence would be the very thing. He has told me he is meeting with the bishop at Nidderton very soon and has promised to discuss it with him then.'

'I suppose you have told Mr Russington?' said Molly, trying to sound casual.

He paused. 'As a matter of fact I haven't. Russ has been more than a little discouraging about the whole affair. When he learned I was serious, he even suggested Fleur might only be interested in my money! That quite upset me, I can tell you, and we haven't mentioned the matter since. But to be truthful, the fewer people who know of it the better. You know what servants are like and in a small place like Compton Parva once word gets out...'

'Yes, I do know.' So Russ *had* tried to dissuade his friend from pursuing Fleur. Molly felt more than a little guilty for asking him to do so. She tried not to think of the inducement she had offered him, nor his indignant refusal. She said now, 'But he is your close friend, Sir Gerald. You should tell him.'

'I will, of course, but he has been so out of temper this past week he has bitten my head off for the slightest thing! No, once Edwin has spoken to the bishop, then I shall ask Russ to be my groomsman and also to go with me to make the application.' A rueful twinkle came into his eyes. 'Given his reputation and my own, I think perhaps I am wise to have your brother speak to the bishop for me, don't you think?'

'I do, but Edwin told me that his business will keep him away for a week, at least,' said Molly. 'How will you bear the wait?'

Gerald caught her hands. 'Bless you for your concern, Molly. Your brother has promised to write as soon as it is agreed, then we may be easy. Not that there will be an unseemly rush to the altar,' he added, looking as stern as was possible for such an easy-going gentleman. 'I will have no hint of scandal attached to Fleur. I am in no way ashamed of my future bride and mean to reinstate her into her proper place in society. I swear to you, Molly, that Fleur's well-being is and always will be paramount to me.'

With that he went off, leaving Molly convinced that her friend could not be anything but happy with such a caring husband.

No one observing Russ's calm and smiling demeanour on Friday evening would have known that he would rather have been anywhere than at the King's Head. He stood with the Newlands party and watched as Agnes and Edwin received the congratulations of each new arrival.

'This is such a happy time,' declared Serena, who was standing beside him. She gave a little laugh and took his arm. 'I do hope there will be another announcement shortly, Russ.'

Russ glanced down sharply. 'What makes you say that?'

Her limpid look was innocence itself. 'Just the way two people have been behaving recently.'

She certainly could not mean Molly and himself, for they had barely spoken two words together all evening. He allowed his eyes to shift to where Molly was standing beside her brother. She was wearing another new creation, this time of plum-red satin over a white petticoat.

'Molly looks very well tonight, do you not think?' murmured Serena, following his gaze. 'She has changed a great deal since I first met her. Very much like a butterfly, in all her new finery.'

Russ did not reply. The vicar and his fiancée were taking to the floor for the first dance and he wondered if he might ask Molly to stand up with him, but before he could move, Gerald had stepped up and Molly was taking his hand and smiling up at him, her cheeks gently flushed. Not for the first time in recent weeks Russ felt a stab of jealousy towards his oldest friend.

Serena squeezed his arm. 'Since quite the prettiest lady in the room is engaged, you had best stand up with me,' she told him.

Hiding his frustration beneath a smile, Russ led his sister out to join one of the sets. The dance seemed interminably long and when it ended he spotted Molly crossing the room to talk to Sir William and Lady Currick, who had just arrived with their daughter.

When Serena begged him to take her over to speak to Nell Currick, he was only too pleased to oblige, but as they came up, Sir William carried Molly off to join the next set. Robbed of a second chance to dance with Molly, Russ excused himself quickly before Serena could suggest he stand up with Nell or her mother. He moved away to the side of the room, where he stood, watching the dancing and trying hard not to scowl. Hell and damnation, he was behaving like a mooncalf, something he had vowed he would never do over any woman. Molly, meanwhile, appeared to be enjoying herself immensely. Serena was right. Dressed in her bright new gowns she was indeed the prettiest woman in the room. Damn her.

Molly wished she might stop smiling but she knew Russ was watching her and she was determined not to give him any clue that she was unhappy. When her dance with Sir William ended, she thought Russ might ask her to dance with him, but instead she saw him leading out Agnes Kilburn. Molly would have liked to sit out the next dance, but pride would not allow her to refuse when Mr Sykes asked her to stand up with him.

There was a break in the dancing after that and Molly accompanied Mr and Mrs Sykes to the refreshment room. She was helping herself to a glass of lemonade when she heard the familiar deep voice at her shoulder.

'You are quite the belle of the ball this evening, Mrs Morgan.'

She turned to Russ and made a little curtsy.

'La, thank you, sir. I shall take that as a compliment.'

'You have certainly been too busy to dance with me, have you not?'

His eyes were glinting and the slight upward curve to

his lips caused her insides to flutter. The temptation was to smile back at him, maybe even hint that she was not engaged for any more dances, but Molly was not ready to make her peace with him yet. She must show him that she was immune to his charms.

'It is gratifying to be in such demand as a dance partner,' she said airily. 'I do not know when I have enjoyed dancing more.'

'And will you honour me with your hand for one of the next dances, madam?'

She widened her eyes. 'Oh, heavens, I cannot make any promises, Mr Russington. I do not know yet who may ask me to stand up with them.'

'Would you not prefer to dance with me?'

He moved closer, unnerving her, and she said sharply, 'I have no preferences, Mr Russington.'

'No? Surely all this new finery is aimed at finding a husband.'

He was rattled. Molly knew she should be pleased, it gave her the upper hand, but instead she felt only a sick kind of misery that they had lost the easy-going camaraderie she had come to enjoy.

'I have no wish for a husband,' she told him, her voice low and angry. 'And if I did, it would be a man of integrity, a man I could trust and who would make me comfortable. Certainly not a *rake.*'

She closed her lips firmly before any more rash words could escape. She had spoken to wound him and his silence and the muscle working in his cheek showed she might just have done it. At the very least she had made him angry.

'This is plain-speaking indeed, madam.'

'I find it best to speak honestly, sir, so there can be no

misunderstanding. But our situation makes it necessary for us to be civil to one another, Mr Russington.' She kept her smile in place as she met his eyes with a defiant look. 'I hope we can continue to do that.'

'Do you?'

'But of course.' She gave a tinkling laugh, light and brittle as glass. 'I would not have our friends and family think there is anything amiss between us.'

He smiled then, a cold, courteous smile that did not reach his eyes.

'Nor I, madam. I think our family and friends can rest assured there is *nothing* between us.'

With a stiff little bow he walked away and not a moment too soon, for Molly felt her resolve crumbling and she turned away, blinking back tears. Serena and the others should be proud of her. She had shown the great Beau Russington that she did not care the snap of her fingers for him. Now all she wanted to do was to crawl away into a dark corner and cry.

After that things went from bad to worse. She was standing with Mr and Mrs Thomas when she saw Russ approaching her and in a fit of pique worthy of a schoolgirl, she put her nose in the air and turned her back upon him.

Foolish woman. Cutting off your nose to spite your face!

Ashamed of her own behaviour, she excused herself from dancing with anyone else and made her way towards the door, eager to be alone.

'Molly, are you quite well?'

Serena was at her side and looking anxiously at her.

'I need a little air, that is all.'

'You cannot go out alone,' said Serena, taking her arm.

'I am not going very far,' said Molly, desperate for solitude. 'And no one will see me if I remain on the balcony.

'But you might be taken ill. I shall come with you.'

Unequal to the fight, Molly allowed Serena to accompany her out of the assembly rooms. The outer doors led on to the balcony and from there a flight of stairs ran down to the yard so that patrons might enter and leave the rooms without passing through the inn itself. Molly stepped out into the cool air, thankful for the shadows thrown up from the lanterns that illuminated the yard below them.

Serena wrinkled her nose. 'Are you sure you want to stay out here? All I can smell is the stables.'

'But it is cooler.'

'True. Are you not enjoying yourself, Molly?'

'I think I am a little tired,' she replied. 'I am not accustomed to dancing so much.'

Serena chuckled. 'Our plan to transform you has worked beautifully. And Russ has been watching you all evening.'

'I do not want him to watch me,' Molly retorted, feeling that tears were very close. 'I merely want him to go away.'

Serena turned towards her and took her hands. 'Is that truly what you want, Molly? I thought you loved my brother.'

Swallowing hard, Molly averted her gaze, staring down into the yard. 'Of…of course not. He is not at all the sort of man to suit me.'

With my provincial morals and good deeds.

'Well, that is a shame,' sighed Serena, 'because I think you are just the sort of woman Russ needs.'

If only that were true, thought Molly sadly.

Below her, a dusty travelling chaise clattered over the cobbles and the yard burst into life. Ostlers ran to the horses and the landlord came bustling out to open the carriage door, bowing low as an elderly man climbed out. There was something vaguely familiar about the portly, bewigged figure and instead of turning away to answer Serena she moved a little closer to the rail. The old man's strident voice carried clearly up to her.

'My name is Dellafield. I sent ahead to bespeak a room for the night.'

'Dellafield,' said Serena, beside her. 'Isn't that the name of the housekeeper at—'

Molly grabbed her wrist and pulled her back into the shadows.

'Serena,' she hissed, 'promise me you will not say a word about this.'

'If you wish, but—'

'Promise!'

'Yes, yes, of course.'

Molly nodded, her mind racing. 'Let us go back inside. And, Serena, remember, I rely upon you not to say a word to anyone!'

They returned to the ballroom to find the music had stopped and Sir William Currick was standing on a chair, congratulating Miss Kilburn and Mr Frayne upon their engagement. All eyes were on the speaker and Molly made her way through the crowd until she was beside Sir Gerald. She plucked at his sleeve and drew him to the side of the room, where she quickly explained what she had overheard.

'So Fleur's father has found her,' he exclaimed.

'Not necessarily,' Molly said slowly. 'It's more likely he saw my name or Edwin's on the list of guests at your ball. The Dellafields were our neighbours in Hertfordshire, and Fleur and I were at school together. Having tried all other avenues, perhaps he hopes Fleur and I may have kept in touch.'

'Even if you do not tell him it is only a matter of time before he learns about Prospect House.' Gerald was thinking quickly, one fist thudding into his palm. 'I must delay no longer—once Fleur is my wife, I shall be able to protect her. Come, Molly, let us find your brother. Fleur and I will go with him to see the bishop tomorrow.'

But Edwin had by this time replaced Sir William on the chair and was making a speech of thanks. They were obliged to wait until he had finished before they could pull him to one side and explain what had happened.

'I shall send word to Prospect House this very night,' said Gerald, 'and we will accompany you to Nidderton in the morning. Once we have the licence we can be married there and then Fleur will be safe.'

Edwin put out his hands. 'I wish that were possible, Gerald, but my meeting is tomorrow morning. If I am not to be late, then I must be leaving Compton Parva before dawn and on horseback. I delayed my departure so I might attend this party with Agnes, you see.'

'Then we will follow on in the carriage at daybreak,' Gerald stated. 'You will come with us, will you not, Molly? I will not have any hint of impropriety attending Fleur. Not only do we have to drive in a closed carriage all the way to Nidderton, but we will be obliged to spend at least one night there before I can make her my wife.' He took her hands. 'Pray say you will do it,

Molly. You are Fleur's oldest friend. I know she will want you with her.'

'Yes, I will come,' she replied. 'To tell the truth I shall be glad to be out of town when Fleur's father comes calling!'

Across the room, Russ watched as Gerald kissed Molly's hands, one after the other, saw her obvious pleasure at the gesture. A man of integrity. A man she could trust. Damnation, had she set her cap at him? Had Gerald been dangling after her all along and using Fleur Dellafield as a smokescreen? He turned away, feeling as if he had been punched in the gut. He could no longer think clearly and the sooner this damned evening was over the better.

Edwin touched Molly's arm. 'My dear, I have sent for the carriage. I think it is time I was leaving. I have a very early start in the morning.'

'Of course. I will collect my wrap and come with you.'

'No, no, there is no need for that. Lady Currick or one of the other ladies will see you home. There will be at least two more dances. I pray you will stay and enjoy yourself.'

'I have had all the enjoyment I shall get this evening,' she said, trying and failing to make light of it.

Thankfully her brother was too preoccupied to notice. He glanced back across the room. 'I think Gerald, too, would like to be going home and preparing for the morrow, but he knows it's best to stay. He does not want to rouse any suspicions.' He touched her arm. 'I persuaded him he must tell Agnes about this before he leaves in the morning, but he is adamant that no one else should know of his plans at the present time, Molly, so we must be careful.'

Molly wondered if Russ would disapprove of what amounted to an elopement. Would he disapprove of her for helping them? Her eyes grew hot and she blinked rapidly. Not that it would make any difference now, since their friendship was quite at an end.

They had reached the yard when the landlord came running out of the taproom.

'Mr Frayne, there is a gentleman arrived, sir, and he was asking about yourself and Mrs Morgan. I think he wishes to call upon you tomorrow—since you are here, would you like to see him now, before you leave?'

Edwin helped Molly into the carriage before answering the landlord.

'I think not. My sister is far too fatigued for that. But we don't wish to offend the fellow, so you had best not mention that we were here tonight. He can call at the vicarage tomorrow—but tell him not to call too early, mind you!' He jumped in after Molly and muttered as the door closed upon them, 'Hopefully by the time he comes, we will both be away from home.'

Russ strode out across the moors, hoping the fresh early-morning air would clear his head. He had risen before dawn and slipped out of the house as soon as there was light to see his way. He had spent a restless night, the images of Gerald and Molly haunting his dreams. Molly dancing with Gerald, laughing with him. Talking with him. Allowing him to kiss her hands.

Surely there was nothing in it, yet Gerald had been oddly distracted on the journey back from the King's Head and, unusually, he had not shared his thoughts with Russ. They had not clashed over a woman since their schooldays and Russ hoped that his suspicions were unfounded, but there was no doubt that Molly had been very friendly towards Gerald last night. Whereas towards him—his thoughts veered off. He had only himself to blame if she was angry with him. He had taken her to his room, pleasured her—yes, *pleasured* her, he reminded himself—but then he had explained why it could go no further. Why he was not the man for her.

He whipped his stick across the dying heather. Confound it, he had spoken no more than the truth. He was trying to save her from the hurt and disappointment of losing her heart to a rake.

He stopped. Had she lost her heart already? Was she—*could* she be in love with him?

The idea was enticing. He wanted it to be true and he could almost believe it was. Molly was no flirt, but she had kissed him, trusted him. He began to walk again, more slowly this time. Above him the clear grey sky was slowly changing to blue as the first bars of sunlight appeared on the horizon, and the golden rays seemed to pierce his soul. He had already acknowledged that Molly was not greedy and grasping like his stepmother. Now he was forced to recognise his own feelings. He loved her. Deeply. But was it possible he could be a faithful husband?

No. A ridiculous fancy. Most likely due to lack of food—after all, he had been walking for more than an hour and had eaten nothing since last night. He turned to make his way back to Newlands, but the idea of marriage had taken hold and he could not shake it off. It might already be too late. Perhaps Gerald had stolen the march on him and was going to offer for Molly today. After all, it was no secret that Edwin was going away, so she would be alone. Russ recalled now when he had pressed Gerald to tell him what was the matter, all his friend would do was laugh and say he would explain everything once tomorrow was over. The leaden weight was now dragging at his heart. Did Molly think Gerald a man of integrity, a man who would make her comfortable?

'But she does not love him!'

The words burst from him. He would stake his life that they were true, yet he feared she might accept an offer from Gerald. After all, Russ had awakened the passion in Molly, had told her she would find happiness with another man. Why should that man not be Kilburn? Suddenly the thought of losing Molly hit Russ like a physical blow. He veered away from the house and almost ran to the stables. He must go and see her, tell her what a crass fool he had been and put his future, his happiness, in her hands.

He was surprised to find the stable yard already bustling with activity. The Kilburns' barouche was being wheeled out of the carriage house and while Russ waited for his horse to be saddled he asked the head groom who had ordered the carriage.

'Miss Kilburn, sir. She and the other ladies are driving into Compton Parva this morning.' The fellow allowed a grin to split his weather-beaten features. 'I believe they're going shopping again, sir.'

Russ realised he had been holding his breath. So Gerald had not ordered the barouche and a quick glance in the stables showed that his friend's grey hack was still in its stall. He scrambled up on to his horse and gathered up the reins. He had the chance to get to Molly first and put right the damage he had done.

Once they had clattered out of the yard, Russ gave Flash his head and galloped through the park to the gates, but he steadied the big horse once they reached the road. Impatient as he was to see Molly he did not wish to arrive looking flustered.

The morning sun was warm on his back as he trotted into the town and, as he knocked on the vicarage door, his spirits were high.

They sank moments later with the news that Mrs Morgan had gone out. The manservant was very polite, but refused to divulge his mistress's direction. Even when Russ asked him directly if she had gone to Prospect House, the fellow remained tight-lipped.

'And when do you expect her back?'

'I'm afraid I cannot say, sir.'

'Come, man, surely you know when your mistress will return.'

The man coloured, but stood his ground. 'My mistress has given me no instructions to divulge such information, sir.'

Russ wondered if she had seen his approach and had given orders to deny her. As the door closed he stepped back and looked up at the first-floor windows, but they were blank. Not even the twitch of a curtain to suggest anyone was watching him. Yet the feeling persisted that the manservant was hiding something and he wondered whether Gerald would be admitted if, or when, he called. Russ decided he would not leave town just yet. There was a small coffee house just across the road from the vicarage and he strolled over. There were not many customers and he positioned himself at a table near the window, from where he had a good view of the vicarage door. If nothing else, it would give him an opportunity to break his fast.

Two hours later the only caller at the vicarage had been an elderly gentleman, who had also been turned away, and Russ left the coffee shop, cursing himself for being so foolishly jealous of his best friend. He walked back to the King's Head, where he had left his horse, but as he passed the door and headed for the yard a tap boy came running out to beg him to step inside and join Miss Kilburn and her party, who were taking coffee in a private parlour. Russ guessed the ladies had finished their shopping trip. He would be expected to escort them back to Newlands and in truth he did not object, so he turned back and entered the inn. Hopefully conversing with Agnes, Serena and Mrs Sykes might take his mind off Molly.

The ladies greeted him cheerfully and bade him sit at the table with them. While they waited for fresh coffee to be brought in, Russ evaded questions about what had brought him to the town so early.

'When you did not join us for breakfast we assumed you were out with Gerald,' remarked Serena, as the servants withdrew again.

'Oh?' Russ looked up. 'Where has he gone?'

'He left word that he is visiting friends,' explained Agnes, pouring coffee for everyone.

'Strange that he should say nothing about this last night,' remarked Russ.

Agnes waved a dismissive hand. 'Perhaps he only had word from them when we returned from the King's Head.'

'Russ, you will never guess what we heard when we arrived in Compton Parva this morning,' declared Serena, her eyes wide. 'Miss Hebden told us that Molly was seen getting into a carriage early this morning. The whole town is buzzing with it.'

'Then the whole town should be ashamed of themselves,' retorted Agnes, directing a frown at Serena. 'Most likely Molly was going to Prospect House.'

'Then why did she not take the gig?' argued Serena. She turned to Russ, her eyes wide. 'But what if she has run off with someone? Did you know that Gerald left at dawn and in a closed carriage? What if they were running off together?'

'Serena!' Agnes was laughing and shaking her head, declaring that she was talking nonsense.

'So Gerald is not at Newlands?' Russ tried to subdue his growing suspicion.

'No,' said Agnes, avoiding his eye. 'He left word that we were not to expect him to return before tomorrow evening at the earliest. Oh, dear, this coffee pot is empty. Ring the bell, Serena, if you please, and we will order more.'

Russ schooled his countenance to indifference and kept silent while they waited for the servant to refresh the coffee pot. He would not believe there was any intrigue between Gerald and Molly. It was one thing to think Gerald might go to the vicarage and propose, but he was quite sure Molly would never agree to an elopement. Besides, she was of age and had no need to run away. No, it was a ridiculous idea and once the servant had withdrawn Russ asked cheerfully what other news the ladies had gleaned in the town that morning.

'Why, nothing,' replied Agnes, smiling at him. 'Do

you think we are such sad creatures that we only live for gossip?'

'Well, there was the altercation Serena and I overheard between the landlord and one of his guests as we came in today,' declared Mrs Sykes. 'The gentleman was complaining that the landlord had misled him and he was asking all and sundry about Mrs D—'

'Oh, la, but that is nothing to do with us,' exclaimed Serena, rudely talking over the older lady. 'We should be more concerned about Gerald. Russ, I think he has *eloped* with Molly.'

He said sharply, 'Do not be so foolish, Serena. I beg you will not utter such damaging nonsense again.'

'Oh, I shall not say it to anyone else,' Serena replied sunnily.

'You will not say anything more at all!' he growled.

'Only I could not but notice that Gerald and Molly were on such good terms last night,' she continued, quite ignoring her brother. 'But I suppose that is not surprising, for Molly was looking exceptionally well, did you not think, Russ? She is quite transformed these past few weeks. Or had you not noticed?'

'Pray do not tease your brother, Serena,' Agnes begged, her cup clattering in its saucer.

'And why not? It is clear that he loves Molly Morgan.'

'Mercy me!' Mrs Sykes began to fan herself rapidly.

Russ barked, 'Serena, that is enough!'

But his minx of a sister merely turned her frank gaze upon him and demanded that he deny it, if it was not true.

'And Molly is quite as much in love with you,' she continued, reaching for another piece of cake.

He ground his teeth. 'If…*if* that were so, she would hardly be running off with Kilburn.'

Serena studied the cake for a moment before taking a tiny bite. 'Well, after the way you behaved last night I think she might well run off with *anyone*, just to teach you a lesson. And I cannot but think it a mistake. They will both be very miserable, don't you agree?'

A stillness had fallen over the room. Russ clenched his fists, trying to steady his breathing and to think calmly.

'No,' he said at last. 'Molly is not the sort to elope with anyone. I know her too well to think she would countenance such impropriety.' He caught the look that passed between Agnes and Serena and was instantly on the alert. 'Well, what is it?'

'Gerald told his man he was heading for Nidderton,' said Agnes.

'Is that not where Mr Frayne is meeting the bishop?' murmured Serena. 'And bishops can issue licences for a speedy marriage.' She looked at Russ as he pushed his chair back, the legs scraping across the boards. 'You are going after them.'

'Yes.' He snatched up his hat. 'I do not think for a moment there is any truth in your outrageous supposition, but I need to be sure.'

'Splendid. And when you get back, brother mine, you may thank me properly.'

He was at the door, but at these words he stopped. 'When I get back, sister,' he said with menace, 'I shall arrange for you to be sent to a nunnery, you interfering baggage!'

The private parlour at the Bear was comfortable enough. A cheerful fire blazed in the hearth, but even with the shutters closed the sounds from the market square intruded. However, everyone was too grateful to have found accommodation to complain. Edwin had joined Molly, Fleur and Gerald for the evening, assuring them that he had seen quite enough of his ecclesiastical colleagues during the day and was happy not to dine with them. However, when the covers were removed, he declined Gerald's invitation to join him in a glass of brandy.

'I know it is not late, but it is time I returned to my own lodgings. Do not forget I have been up since before dawn.'

'So, too, have we,' said Molly, smothering a yawn. 'It has been a long day.'

'But a successful one,' put in Gerald. He reached out and caught Fleur's hand. 'We are both extremely grateful. To Molly, for agreeing to come with us, and to you, Edwin, for promoting our cause with your bishop.' He patted his pocket. 'I have the licence safe and tomorrow I shall make Fleur my wife.'

'And I shall have great pleasure in marrying you,' declared Edwin, rising. 'Now, if you will excuse me, I had best leave before I fall asleep at the table.'

Molly walked with him to the door, returning to find Gerald alone in the private parlour, sipping at his brandy.

'Fleur has gone out to, um, pluck a rose,' he said, using the familiar euphemism to indicate Fleur had gone out to the privy. 'She is afraid she will not sleep tonight, and I suggested she take a glass of something before we all retire.' He waved towards the bottles on the table. 'You see our host has provided some light wine, as well as the brandy. Will you join us?'

'With pleasure, Sir Gerald, although I do not foresee any difficulty in sleeping.'

'Nor I, but—' He broke off, frowning at the sounds

of an altercation in the passageway. 'What the devil is going on?'

They both jumped to their feet as the door burst open and Russ came in, his greatcoat flapping open and a thunderous scowl on his face. He closed the door upon the still-protesting landlord and stood with his back against it, ignoring Gerald and glaring at Molly, who instinctively retreated behind the table.

'Aye, madam,' he barked, throwing his hat and gloves on to a chair, 'you may well cower away from me!'

'I say, old friend,' Gerald protested, 'there is no reason to be so angry with Molly.'

'Oh, isn't there?' Molly took another step away at his icy tones. 'She deceived me.'

'Because we did not tell you what was happening? That was my fault,' said Gerald. 'I swore her to secrecy'

'And why would you do that?' Russ rounded on his friend. 'Did you think I would call you out?' His lip curled. 'I would not waste my time. You are welcome to marry the jade.'

'No, no, Russ, you have it all wrong,' cried Molly, but her words went unheeded as Gerald moved forward, his face darkening.

'You go too far, Russington.'

'I haven't gone far enough yet!'

Molly watched in alarm as the two men squared up to one another. She flew around the table and pushed herself between them.

'You cannot start a fight here!' she said angrily, one hand on each chest. 'Pray be sensible. You are friends.'

'Not any longer!' snapped Russ. He took Molly by the shoulders and firmly put her to one side. 'Out of the way, strumpet, and let me at him!'

For a brief moment chaos reigned. Molly grabbed his arm and Gerald protested as Russ tried to shake her off, but they all froze as a loud shriek rent the air.

'What is going on here?'

In the sudden silence Russ looked towards the door, where Fleur was standing with her hands on her pale cheeks.

'What the devil!' he exclaimed as she ran across the room and into Gerald's arms. Not that he really needed to ask. He looked back at Gerald. 'So you are not marrying Molly.'

'Molly?' Gerald blinked at him over Fleur's golden head. 'No, of course, I am not. She is here as chaperon. Fleur and I are to be married tomorrow, by licence.'

'Ah, of course.' Russ nodded slowly. 'I understand now. I owe you all an apology.'

He looked around for Molly. She had backed away and was now glaring at him.

'How *dare* you?' Her voice was shaking with anger. 'How dare you force your way in here and insult everyone in that brutish manner? You will go, this minute.'

'Not before you give me a chance to explain.'

'I have heard quite enough from you,' she threw at him. 'A jade, am I? A strumpet! You had best leave, before I summon the landlord to *throw* you out!'

'My love.' Fleur pushed herself out of Gerald's arms. 'I need a little air. Will you take me outside, please?'

'What, now?' asked Gerald, a note of surprise in his voice. Russ was looking at Molly, but from the tail of his eye he saw Gerald jump, as if he had been pinched. 'Oh, aye, yes. Of course.'

'No!' exclaimed Molly. 'Fleur, you cannot leave me alone with this...this *monster*!'

Ignoring her protests, Gerald whisked Fleur out of the room and closed the door firmly behind them. Russ knew they were giving him a chance to make his peace with Molly, but was it too late? She was still glaring at him, her arms folded as if to shield herself from attack.

He took a deep breath. 'I beg your pardon. Coming in here, what I said to you—it was very wrong of me.'

Silence. He tried again.

'I did not intend—that is, when Serena suggested you had run off with Kilburn I didn't believe her. I knew there had to be another explanation.'

'Ha! If that was so, why would you come chasing all the way to Nidderton?'

'Because I had to be sure. I could not bear the thought of your marrying Kilburn.'

'You were the one who said I must find myself a husband.'

She threw the words at him and he flinched.

'Yes, I know, but...I was wrong.'

'Oh? You think I am unworthy of a gentleman.'

'No!'

'You called me a jade.'

'I apologised for that.'

'And a...a strumpet.' Her voice positively shook with rage.

'I have said it was wrong of me. But I was angry. I have spent the whole day searching the town for you. I have called at every inn and hotel and tavern, trying to find you.'

'Why on earth would you do that?'

* * *

Molly's heart was pounding against her ribs so hard it hurt. Russ, too, appeared to be breathing heavily. He would not look at her, but was scowling at the floor.

She moved a step closer. 'Why, Russ?'

'Because I love you!'

It was as if the words were wrenched from him. He raised his head and looked at her.

'I could not let you marry Kilburn without telling you how I felt.'

She put one hand on a chair back to steady herself. It was what she wanted to hear, what she had dreamed of, but her anger still simmered and she was not about to throw herself into his arms.

'And what difference did you think that would make, if I *had* been about to marry Sir Gerald?' she asked him, her voice was dripping with scorn. 'Did you think I would cry off and marry you, because you are more fashionable than your friend, or perhaps because your fortune is ten times larger?'

'No! I know you too well to think you would be influenced by either of those things. I thought you cared for me.' He exhaled. 'I thought you loved me.'

'And yet you believed I might marry your friend?' She shook her head. 'For a man with such a reputation as a lover, Charles Russington, you are woefully ignorant of women.'

'Of women like you, yes.'

'I am not so very different.'

'Oh, but you are.' He gave her a rueful smile. 'You are good and kind and strong. A reformer. A woman of principal. Not at all the sort to attract me, and yet, from the first moment we met, I was lost. When I am near you, I cannot think properly. The polished address that I am supposed to possess all disappears. I admit it, I behave like a moonstruck schoolboy. I cannot help it, Molly, I have fallen helplessly, hopelessly in love with you.'

He had been moving closer as he spoke, his eyes holding Molly's, begging her to believe him. He went down on one knee before her.

'Nothing else matters to me but your happiness, Molly. I have never felt like this before, as if my very existence depends upon one person. Upon *you*. I want you in my life, Molly Morgan. I want you with me, at my side, as my wife, my friend. More than that, I want to be in *your* life, to help you with your charities if you will let me. I want to learn from your goodness.

'I cannot tell you how it will end, my love, but I give you my word I will try with all my heart to be a good husband to you, to love and cherish you for the rest of your days.' He reached out to take her hands. 'What do you say, dearest? It is a big risk, I know, but will you trust me to take care of you? Will you honour me with your heart and your hand?'

'Oh, Russ.' His face swam before her eyes. 'Oh, Russ, *how* I love you!'

She tugged at his hands and the next instant he was on his feet and pulling her into his arms.

'Say it,' he muttered, covering her face with kisses. 'Put me out of my misery, darling Molly, and say you will marry me.'

Darling Molly.

Her heart took flight at that and she answered him breathlessly. 'Yes, yes, I will marry you.'

With a growl of triumph, he captured her lips again,

kissing her so soundly that her very bones turned to water. When Russ ended the kiss she sighed and leaned against him, eyes closed, and it was not until she heard a soft, apologetic cough that she realised they were not alone.

Gerald and Fleur had come in and were looking at them with unfeigned delight.

'So you have made it up,' remarked Gerald, grinning.

'Yes,' said Russ, keeping is arms tight around Molly. 'Do you think the bishop would grant us a licence, too?'

'Undoubtedly. Frayne told us the fellow was pleased to be bringing one reprobate back into the fold, so I am sure he will be delighted to make it two.'

'Well, my love?' Russ looked down at Molly, who was still resting her head against his shoulder. 'Shall we be married in Nidderton? Perhaps Fleur and Gerald would delay their return to Newlands long enough to attend us.'

'I would like that,' she said softly. She added, blushing, 'Very much.'

Gerald clapped his hands. 'Then it is settled. Did I not tell you there was something in the air here? And, Russ, now you are here you can be my groomsman, tomorrow, If you will.'

'With all my heart, my friend.'

'Capital!' Gerald opened the door. 'Now, where's that rascally landlord? He must fetch us more glasses and we will celebrate!'

An hour later, after several toasts by the gentlemen and not a few tears shed by the ladies, Fleur announced she was going to bed. Molly would have accompanied her, but she waved her back to her seat.

'You have not yet finished your wine,' she said. 'I am sure Gerald will escort me to my room.

'With pleasure, my love. I am ready for my bed now, too. We have a busy day ahead.' He kissed Molly's cheek, then clasped Russ's hand. 'Goodnight, my friend. Fleur and I are delighted you will be with us for our wedding tomorrow and the news that you and Molly are to be married has made our happiness complete.'

With a final wave he took Fleur's arm and they went out, leaving Molly and Russ alone.

'Where are you staying?' she asked him.

'I left Flash at the Fox and Goose while I searched for you. I should be able to get lodging there for the night.'

'But it is late and you cannot be *sure* of getting a room.'

Molly kept her eyes lowered while the silence dragged on for a full minute.

'No,' he said slowly. 'They may be full by now.'

She studied her wine, turning the glass round and round in her hands.

'Fleur and I have separate rooms,' she murmured. 'You could share mine.'

She wondered if she had shocked him and looked up anxiously.

'Is that what you want, Molly?' He was watching her, a mixture of hope and concern in his dark eyes.

She rose and held out her hand to him. 'It is what I have wanted, ever since that night at Newlands.'

There was plenty of noise from the taproom but thankfully the stairs and corridors were deserted as Molly led Russ into her room. Pausing only to turn the key in the lock, he took her in his arms and kissed her.

'Are you sure about this, Molly?'

'Very sure.' Smiling, she cupped his face. 'I do not want to wait another moment for you.'

She drew him down to her, pressing her lips against his as her fingers slid into his hair and tangled with the silky curls. His tongue danced into her mouth, flickering, teasing, and she pressed herself against him as her body responded. Between kisses they began to undress one another, their fingers scrabbling with strings and buttons until they fell together, naked, on to the bed.

She gave a little mewl of pleasure as he put his mouth to one breast, while his fingers played with the other. She shifted restlessly as the lightness rippled through her body, but she resisted the pull of desire and concentrated on Russ's pleasure, kissing and stroking his hard, aroused body until she knew he was also at the tipping point, then she straddled him, taking him inside her, gasping at the delight of it and revelling at her power as he groaned beneath her. She bent forward to kiss him and he gasped as her breasts skimmed his chest. In one swift movement he caught her in his arms and rolled her over, taking control, never breaking the kiss.

He began to push into her, slowly and steadily, every movement a caress that took her closer to the pinnacle. Her response was instinctive, tensing around him, lifting her hips, feeling the heat building. When she would have cried out he stopped her mouth with a kiss, his tongue thrusting deep, and she felt her body melting beneath the onslaught until she was almost fainting with delight. He carried her higher, the ripples building into a flood. She was flying, soaring, almost delirious with the pleasure of it all. Russ gasped out her name and their bodies shuddered and bucked against one another. She felt the dam burst within her and clung on tightly as the final spasm took her over the edge and consciousness splintered. She and Russ collapsed together, sated, exhausted and cradled in each other's arms.

Gently, Russ drew the covers over them to keep off the chill air, and as he wrapped himself around her, Molly felt a glow of contentment. She snuggled against him and closed her eyes. The past was done now. She could look forward to the future.

Epilogue

One year later

The church of All Souls was full. Fleur and Gerald had already moved to the font with their baby girl, waiting for Edwin to begin the baptism. Molly felt her happiness growing as she gazed around her at all the familiar faces.

Agnes was sitting closer to the pulpit, as befitted the vicar's wife, and Molly was relieved to see that she was glowing with health as she approached the final stages of her pregnancy. Then there were her friends from Prospect House, filling their allotted pews, and in front of them were the servants from Newlands. Molly had watched in delight as Daisy Matthews, in her role as housekeeper, had proudly led them in, including her son, Billy, almost swaggering in his new livery as Sir Gerald's tiger.

Beside her, Russ lowered his head to murmur in her ear, 'Lady Kilburn is looking radiant today.'

Molly's gaze moved back to Fleur.

'Of course,' she whispered. 'She is very happy in her marriage.'

'And you, Molly—' his deep velvet voice sent the familiar ripple of pleasure through her '—are *you* happy?'

She glanced down at the sleeping baby in her arms. Their son, about to be christened as Charles Edwin Gerald Russington.

'Oh, yes. I could not be happier.'

She gazed up at him, her eyes shining with love, and Russ's heart swelled. He was overwhelmed with the pride and joy he felt for his family. He had never dreamt he would settle for life in a small town so far from London, but he was no longer a lost soul. Everything he wanted, everything he needed was here in Compton Parva.

He had come home.

Putting one arm protectively about Molly, he smiled down at her.

'Come along, then, my darling wife. Let us join Fleur and Gerald at the font and allow your brother to do his duty.'

* * * * *

BEAUTY AND THE
BROODING LORD

To L.F., my lovely editor.

Your patience, help and guidance have been invaluable.

Chapter One

London—1816

Serena stepped out on to the terrace. It was a warm night and the earlier rain had passed, leaving only a few small clouds scudding across the sky. She hesitated, her heart beating rapidly. She knew she was risking her reputation, but how could she know if Sir Timothy was the man for her unless they kissed? She ran lightly down the steps at the end of the terrace, where a path led away from the house to a leafy arch set between high hedges. A slight breeze ruffled her skirts and she gave a little shiver as she stepped through the arch. Surely there could be no danger in one little embrace?

The rose garden looked very different from when she had been here a few days ago with her brother and sister-in-law, Lord and Lady Hambridge. Henry had been keen to see the paintings Lord Grindlesham was selling and, while the gentlemen went off to the gallery, his wife had shown Serena and Dorothea the gardens. Now, in the moonlight the paths gleamed pale silver and the roses themselves ranged from near black to pale blue-grey. But if the flowers had lost their colour, their scent was enhanced and Serena breathed in the heady fragrance as she made her way along the path, but when she reached the turn in the path she was aware of something else besides rose scent in the night air. A faint hint of tobacco.

Ahead she saw an arbour surrounded by climbing roses and her heart gave a little skip. There, in the shadows, was the unmistakable figure of a man. His upper body was hidden, but his crossed legs in their light-coloured knee breeches and white silk stockings were plainly visible in the gloom. Serena had expected to find her swain pacing up and down, impatient for her to arrive, but here he was, sitting at his ease. She quashed the faint ripple of disappointment and hurried up to him, smiling.

'Forgive me, I was delayed. I—' She broke off with a gasp as she peered into the shadows. '*You* are not Sir Timothy.'

'No, I am not.'

The reply was an irritable growl. The figure rose from the seat and Serena took a hasty step backwards. She realised now that he was nothing like Sir Timothy Forsbrook. This man was much larger, for a start, although his upper body was so broad that he did not look overly tall. Where Sir Timothy's glossy black locks were carefully styled about his head, the stranger's hair was lighter and too long to be fashionable. And as he stepped out of the arbour she thought he was not at all handsome. In the moonlight his craggy face appeared harsh, as if he was scowling at her.

He towered over her and she took another step away.

'Excuse me—' She would have walked on but his next words stopped her.

'There was a fellow here, but he has gone.'

'Gone?'

'Aye. He had the impudence to suggest I should vacate the seat, so I kicked him out.'

She swallowed. 'Literally?'

His great shoulders lifted in a shrug. 'No. Mere jostling. He retreated rather than have my fist spoil his face.'

She sucked in a long, indignant breath. 'That is disgraceful behaviour. Quite boorish.'

'I suppose you would have preferred me to give way. But why should I? I came out here to enjoy a cigarillo in peace. You two will have to find some other place for your lovemaking.'

His voice dripped scorn. Serena's face burned with mortification.

'How dare you! It is nothing like that.'

'No?'

Knowing she was in the wrong did nothing for Serena's temper. She drew herself up and said angrily, 'You are odiously rude!'

'If it's soft words you want I suggest you go and find your lover.'

'Oh, I shall go,' she told him in a shaking voice,' and he is *not* my lover.'

He grinned, his teeth gleaming white in the moonlight. 'No need to be coy on my account, madam.'

Serena gasped. 'Oooh, you…you…'

He folded his arms and looked down at her. 'Yes?'

For a moment she glared at him, her hands closing into fists as she tried to control her rage. It would be

most undignified to rip up at him. Resisting the urge
to stamp her foot, she turned and swept off, muttering
angrily under her breath all the insults she would like
to hurl at the odious creature.

Serena hurried back to the ballroom. It was half-
empty, most of the guests having gone in to supper.
Those who remained were talking in little groups and
she prayed no one had noticed her entry, for her agitation must be evident. She slipped away to the small
room set aside for the ladies, where she had earlier left
her cloak and outdoor shoes. The looking glass showed
that her cheeks were still flushed and her brown eyes
sparkled with anger. She made a pretence of tidying
her hair, although in truth her honey-gold curls were
remarkably in place.

Really, she thought indignantly, it was most frus-
trating. All she wanted to do was to find an interesting husband, one who would not bore her silly within
a week, like the exceedingly correct suitors her half-
brothers insisted upon presenting to her. These respectable gentlemen were to be her dancing partners for the
whole evening, which was the reason Henry and Dorothea had thought it safe to go off to the card room and
allow Serena out of their sight. But a short break in the
dancing had given Serena the opportunity to slip out
and meet one whom she knew to be a rake and who was
therefore *much* more interesting.

Serena remained in the retiring room until her indignation had died away, then she shook out her skirts, put
up her head and sailed downstairs to the supper room
where she found her brother and sister-in-law enjoying
a cold collation in the far corner. Nearer at hand, Eliz-

abeth Downing and her brother were part of a lively group gathered about one of the larger tables. Elizabeth waved and Serena walked over. Immediately Jack Downing sprang up and pulled out a chair for her, then he proceeded to hover solicitously until Serena had been provided with a plate of delicacies and a glass of wine.

After the incident in the rose garden such attention was balm to Serena's spirits. Mr Downing was a serious young man whom she had previously apostrophised as stuffy, but at least he was not *rude*. She now thanked him prettily and allowed him to engage her in conversation until the musicians could be heard tuning up again and everyone began to drift back to the ballroom.

The dancing recommenced and Serena looked around for Sir Timothy. Imagining his ignominious departure from the rose garden, she was not surprised to learn that he had gone home, but she felt no sympathy for him. She wished he had come to blows with the rude stranger and knocked him down rather than walking off and leaving her to endure a most unpleasant encounter. However, when she recalled the size of the stranger, she doubted Sir Timothy would have got the better of him.

The evening was proving to be exceedingly tedious and after a couple of dances Serena excused herself and went in search of her sister-in-law.

'What, you wish to leave, before the dancing is ended?' Lady Hambridge gave the loud, irritating laugh that announced she had enjoyed too much wine this evening. She shook her head at Serena and said playfully, 'This is most unlike you, Serena! No, no, we cannot go yet, for you are engaged to stand up with Lord Afton. I should be failing in my duty if I were to take you away before he has danced with you.'

Viscount Afton was the highest-ranking bachelor at this evening's ball. Serena thought him dull, pompous and old enough to be her grandfather, but it would do no good to say as much to her sister-in-law, so when the time came she pinned on a smile and went off to dance the quadrille. As the dance ended she spotted a familiar figure at the side of the room. She touched Lord Afton's arm.

'Tell me, my lord, do you know that gentleman, the large man talking to Lord Grindlesham?'

'What's that, m'dear?' The Viscount looked about him and gave a disdainful grunt. 'Do you mean that great bear of a man? That's Lord Quinn. Damned unpleasant fellow. No one likes him.'

She was pleased that Lord Afton shared her opinion of the stranger from the rose garden, but curious, too.

'If that is the case, why is he invited?'

'Rich as Croesus,' he replied shortly. 'He don't often show his face in town, but Grindlesham is selling off his art collection and that will be the reason he is come. Rufus Quinn is considered to be something of a connoisseur, I believe.' He huffed. 'Well, he can afford to indulge himself.'

There was a bitter note in the viscount's tone, but since it was well known that Lord Afton had little fortune, it did not surprise Serena. As he led her back to join Dorothea and Henry, she took the opportunity to study Lord Quinn from a safe distance. In the blaze of candlelight, it was clear to see that he was no arbiter of fashion. His coat of dark blue superfine fitted well enough across his impressive shoulders, but no servant was needed to ease him into it and the simple arrangement of his neckcloth would not rouse envy in the breast of any aspiring dandy. His brown hair was not brushed into artful disorder; it was positively untidy. His face was rugged, his nose not quite straight and his brow fierce. He looked impatient and she already knew his manners were abominable. All in all, Serena decided, he was a man not worthy of her attention.

At last the evening was over and Serena accompanied her brother and sister-in-law to the hall. It was crowded and noisy, and the servants announcing whose carriage was at the door were obliged to bellow over the chatter of the guests. There was much pushing and shoving and Henry guided his ladies to one side, away from the throng.

'It's like a dashed cattle market,' he muttered. 'Whatever persuaded Grindlesham to invite so many? And that reminds me.' He turned a frowning gaze upon Serena. 'I saw you talking to Forsbrook earlier. Who introduced you to him?'

Serena spread her hands. 'I really cannot recall, but it is impossible to avoid such introductions in town.'

'I suppose you are right,' he agreed grudgingly, 'but he's a dashed Lothario and you'd be advised to stay away from him.'

'Indeed, you would,' added Dorothea. 'He has the most unsavoury reputation.'

'What of it?' Serena countered. 'Most gentlemen in London have an unsavoury reputation. Even Russ, before his marriage.'

Henry scowled. 'That was different. Forsbrook is an out-and-out libertine. Russ was never that.'

'The pity of it is that such men are so attractive to a large number of our sex,' declared Dorothea repressively.

'Well, they would have to be,' reasoned Serena. 'One can only conclude that they are experts at making love to a woman.'

Henry spluttered and Dorothea said in a scandalised voice, 'Serena, *hush*. You cannot say such a thing—it is most unladylike.'

Serena begged pardon and closed her lips upon any more unwise utterances. Clearly it would not do to admit that she thought she might like to marry just such a man. She had been out for two years and was still unmarried. Oh, she had had offers, but all the men Henry and Russ considered eligible were so very *dull*. In fact, Serena was finding life in town rather dull, too.

It had not been so bad when she had been staying with Russ, for although he was ten years her senior both he and his wife were lively and quick-witted. But Russ had taken Molly to the north to await the birth of their second child and Serena was now living in Bruton Street with Henry, who was her guardian and eldest half-brother. Having married off their own daughter very successfully two years ago, he and Dorothea were keen to find a respectable husband for Serena.

She understood perfectly the reason for this. The Russington family history was tainted by scandal and they were anxious to avoid adding to it. Good birth was considered essential, a title an advantage, but respectability was prized higher than a fortune and Serena was kept well away from any gentleman whose reputation was less than spotless, with the result that she had not yet met any man whose company she enjoyed for more than a very short time. Naturally, she wanted her husband to be handsome, but she also wanted a man of wit and intelligence. An educated man with a sense of humour, with whom she might enjoy lively conversation.

Finally, she wanted him to be skilled at pleasuring a woman. Not that she knew a great deal about what went on in the marriage bed, because young ladies were not supposed to be interested in such things. What she *had* learned was all very confusing. If Dorothea was to be believed, it was a wife's duty to accept her husband's attentions with fortitude, whereas Molly had told her that the union, when a husband and wife truly loved one another, could be beyond wonderful. It seemed that love was the answer, but none of the suitors presented to Serena had roused the faintest flicker of interest. She had therefore decided she must take a hand in her own destiny. Russ had been considered a rake before he had married his beloved Molly and Serena thought such a man would suit her very well.

Therefore, whenever she could escape Henry and Dorothea's watchful eyes at any ball, breakfast or assembly, she sought out the rakes and gentlemen of more dubious reputation. The problem was that it was so difficult to be alone with any gentleman in town. Her flirtation with the dashing Lord Fyfield, for example, had been going well until they were spotted by one of Dorothea's bosom friends in Green Park and Serena had to account very quickly for being alone with a gentleman. Word of the assignation had soon reached Bruton Street and Henry had lost no time in putting an end to Lord Fyfield's attentions before he had even kissed her.

It was all most unsatisfactory and Serena's spirit rebelled against being so confined. She wanted to marry, but not one of the milk-and-water sops that her family put forward. No, she wanted a man who could hold her interest. One who knew how to make love to a woman. Was that too much to ask? Her musing ended when a servant announced Lord Hambridge's carriage.

'At last,' said Henry. 'Come along, my dears, let us get home.'

Serena followed as he pushed his way towards the door with a word here and there to clear the path. A large, commanding figure stood in their way. Serena could only see his back but she immediately recognised Lord Quinn's tousled head. A word from Henry and he stood aside, but there was no smile, no word of apology. His rugged face was stony and although his gaze moved over Serena, she had the impression that he was looking through her. However, she did note that those eyes, which had laughed at her so insolently in the rose garden, were a warm brown, the colour of fresh hazelnuts.

Serena decided she would strike Sir Timothy from her list of prospective husbands, but at the Downings' party the following day, he sought her out and told her he had come with the sole intention of apologising for his absence from the Grindleshams' rose garden. He begged for the opportunity to make it up to her and Serena decided she would at least listen to what he had in mind for her entertainment. After all, he was extremely fashionable and very handsome, with his black curls and Grecian profile, and there was no denying that he had about him a dangerously rakish air. She decided to give him another chance.

His proposal that he should escort her to Vauxhall when it opened for the Season was too tempting to resist. He painted an alluring picture of the two of them, cloaked and masked, wandering through the gardens and marvelling at the mechanical exhibits such as the famous waterfall.

The clandestine escapade appealed to Serena's adventurous soul and she dismissed the tiny voice inside that urged caution. She must allow Sir Timothy to kiss her, just once, for how else was she to know if she would like him as a husband? And from all she had heard there was no better setting for a romantic interlude than Vauxhall, with its shadowy arbours and dark avenues hung with coloured lights.

Serena knew it was one thing to allow a hopeful young man to steal a kiss in a shadowy alcove of a private ball—which she had done once or twice—quite another to go off alone with a gentleman to Vauxhall, but Elizabeth had already told her that she and her family were going to the gardens that night and if it went horribly wrong, if she found she did not like being kissed, or Sir Timothy should become importunate, she would seek them out and beg their protection. That would be humiliating and once Henry knew about it he would probably banish her to the country for the rest of the Season, but one must be prepared to risk all in the search for a husband. All she needed now was to work out a way to slip out of her brother's house without raising any suspicions.

Her plans came to fruition two days later, at breakfast, when the butler brought in the post and delivered a letter to Serena. Dorothea looked up.

'What have you there—is it a love letter from one of your beaux, perhaps?'

Dorothea's arch tone grated, for Serena knew quite well that correspondence between herself and any gentleman who was not related to her would be highly improper. However, she replied calmly and with perfect honesty, 'It is from Mrs Downing. She invites me to join her party at Vauxhall tomorrow evening.'

'Vauxhall?' Henry looked up from the perusal of his own post. 'It is not at all the place for young ladies, especially tomorrow, for it is May Day, when all sorts of common folk will be out celebrating. I have no doubt that the disreputable among them will be masked, too.'

'Mrs Downing sees no harm in it,' replied Serena. 'Mr Jack Downing will be with them, too.' She glanced at her sister-in-law, upon whom the young man's name acted like a talisman.

'Henry, my dear, I do not see there can be any harm in it, if she is with the Downings. And I believe Madame Saqui is performing. I confess I should very much like to see her myself. I am told that last Season she ended her display by running along the tightrope with fireworks exploding all around her.' Dorothea picked up her coffee cup. 'Perhaps we should go as well, I doubt we would be able to obtain a supper box at this late notice, but we might enjoy the spectacle.'

Serena held her breath. Her own plans for tomorrow evening would have to be drastically changed if Dorothea and Henry decided to go to Vauxhall.

'To go all that way and not be able to sit comfortably for supper?' Henry's mouth turned down. 'Bad enough that we should be mixing with heaven knows what class of person, but if we cannot sup in our own box it would be insupportable. Besides, I am already promised to dine tomorrow at White's.'

'I could report back to you upon Madame Saqui's performance,' Serena suggested. 'Then you may decide if it is worth the effort for another time.'

Henry turned an approving gaze upon his half-sister. 'An excellent idea, Serena. I am sure, if this rope dancer is any good, you will wish to see her again.'

She gave him a dazzling smile. 'Indeed I shall, Henry. And perhaps you will order the carriage to take me to the Downings' house tomorrow evening. Since they live *en route*, I do not wish to inconvenience them by making them come out of their way to collect me.'

With the matter thus settled, Serena breathed a sigh of relief. So far, everything was going to plan. Her hints last night to Elizabeth had resulted in the Downings' timely invitation, which had aroused no suspicions. Now she must carefully pen a note to be delivered tomorrow evening, regretfully crying off because of a malaise. She sipped her coffee. A malaise called Sir Timothy Forsbrook. She did not like deceiving her friends, but it must be done, if she was to find lasting happiness.

Serena dressed with care the following evening, choosing a high-waisted evening gown of lemon satin with an overdress of white gauze. As befitted a de-mure young lady she tucked a fine white fichu into the low neck of her gown. Lemon satin slippers, white kid gloves and a white crape fan completed her ensemble and over everything she wore a cashmere shawl, its wide border embroidered with acanthus leaves. Sir Tim-othy had promised to provide a domino and mask for her, because for Serena to carry such items would only invite comment from her brother or his wife.

Darkness was already falling when the Hambridge carriage pulled up at the Downings' house in Wardour Street. Serena stepped down and airily told the coachman there was no need to wait. She stood on the pavement, making a show of fussing with her reticule until the coach was out of sight, then she turned and ran quickly back to the chaise waiting further along the street. Sir Timothy jumped down as she approached.

'You have come!'

'Of course, did you doubt it?' She laughed as he handed her into the chaise. 'I sent my letter of apology to the Downings this morning. They will have set off for Vauxhall a good half-hour since.'

'So, no one knows where you are. My clever, adorable angel.' Sir Timothy tried to take her in his arms, but she held him off.

'Not yet, someone might recognise us!'

He released her and threw himself back against the padded seat. 'Little chance of that in this poor light. But there is no hurry.' He lifted her fingers to his lips. 'We have all night. Tell me instead what you have been doing since we last met. I want to know every little detail.'

It was already growing dark by the time Rufus Quinn left London. The meeting at the Royal Society had gone on longer than he had anticipated, but he could not pass up the opportunity to talk with the celebrated astronomer Miss Caroline Herschel, who rarely came to London. After that he had taken advantage of the moonlight to drive home, rather than spend another night in town. He had no time for society, everyone was too set up in their own importance. If people weren't vying for superiority they were all wishing to line their pockets at someone else's expense. Quinn hated it, and had only allowed himself to be dragged to the Grindleshams' ball because he wanted the Titian. In the event, Quinn had merely told Grindlesham to name his price and the painting had been his. He had wasted an evening watching the overdressed popinjays cavorting around a ballroom when he could have been at home enjoying a glass of his excellent claret and reading a good book.

Even when he had slipped away to enjoy a cigarillo he had been interrupted by an insufferable cockscomb who had wanted him to make himself scarce. Quinn had soon sent him about his business, but damme if the fellow had not gone off with never a thought for his mistress! A smile tugged at his lips as he remembered her reaction when she arrived. Spirited little thing, though, the way she had stood up to him. No tears or vapours. Reminded him of his Barbara, God rest her soul. His good humour faded, but he shook off the threatening black mood, blaming it on fatigue.

By nursing his team, Quinn usually managed the journey into Hertfordshire without a break, but tonight he felt unaccountably tired. Another yawn broke from him. Confound it, he would have to stop if he was not to fall asleep over the reins. He gave a grunt of satisfaction when he reached Hitchin and spotted the Swan ahead of him, light spilling from its windows. He guided his team into the cobbled yard, where torches flared and ostlers came running out to attend him. The landlord appeared, wiping his hands on his apron.

'Evening, my lord, trouble with your team?'

'Nothing like that, Jennings, but I need a short rest.'

He saw the landlord look past him and anticipated his next question. 'I left my tiger in town. Clem follows on tomorrow in the carriage with Shere, my valet. They have a rather valuable cargo.'

'Been buying pictures again, my lord?' The landlord gave him a fatherly grin. 'I think what you're wanting now is a bite to eat and a tankard of home-brewed, sir, to see you on your way.'

'Aye, you are right. Lead on, Jennings. Find me a table and somewhere quiet to sit, if you will.'

'No difficulty there, sir. It's fair quiet here tonight, it being May Day. The night mail's due in later, but there's never time for the passengers to get out. No, the only other customers I'm expecting tonight is a honeymoon couple, travelling from London.' Jennings winked and tapped his nose. 'A servant rode ahead to say they wouldn't be here 'til late and that they'd take a cold supper in their room.'

It was gone midnight when Quinn walked out of the inn, refreshed and ready for the final stage of his journey. It was very quiet and the yard was empty save for the ostler looking after his curricle and pair. As he crossed the yard Quinn heard a faint cry.

The ostler looked up towards the gallery and grinned. 'Sounds like someone's having a good time, m'lord.'

Quinn grunted. It was no business of his. He merely wanted his own bed. He stopped to pull his gloves on and give the greys a critical glance. They were rested well enough and should carry him home in well under the hour. He was just about to step into the curricle when a shrill scream rent the air. It was cut off almost immediately, but there was no mistaking the terror in the voice.

Quinn did not hesitate. He raced up the stairs. A disturbance could be heard from the first door he reached, but it was locked. Quinn launched himself at the door, which gave way with a splintering crash. The inrush of air caused the candles on the table to flicker, but he took in the scene in one glance. The meal laid out on the table was almost untouched, but the two chairs were overturned and a drift of white gauze lay on the floor, like a wraith.

A man scrambled off the bed and hurled himself at Quinn, fists flying, but one blow to the jaw sent him crashing to the floor. Quinn stood over him, hands clenched, but his opponent was unconscious.

A whisper of silk made him look towards the bed as a figure scrabbled away and huddled in the corner of the room. In the gloom he could make out nothing but a mass of fair hair and a pale gown, and the fact that the woman was shaking uncontrollably.

He untangled a wrap from one of the chairs, a large cashmere shawl, heavy and expensive. This was no drab from the stews picked up for a night's gratification. He shook it out and approached the woman, who was fumbling to pull together the torn pieces of her bodice.

'Here, let me put this around you.' She did not respond, but neither did she shrink away as he threw the shawl about her shoulders. Gently, he led her out of the shadows. 'Are you hurt?'

'N-no, not really. I...he...' Her voice failed and he caught her as she swayed.

'You need not worry about him any longer,' he said. 'Come, I will take you out of here.'

He escorted her from the room, keeping one arm around her, lest she stumble. The landlord met them at the bottom of the stairs.

'The lads said there was some trouble, my lord.'

'The lady is, er, distressed.'

'Ah.' Jennings nodded wisely. 'Had a falling out with her husband, has she?'

'Is that what he told you?' Quinn was surprised to hear the woman speak. The voice, coming from behind the tangled curtain of hair, was quiet but firm. She put a hand to her head. 'He is not my husband.'

The landlord regarded her with disapproval and Quinn's arm tightened protectively around the dainty figure.

'I came upon the lady defending her honour.' His tone dared Jennings to dispute the fact that she was a respectable female. The landlord met his eyes, considering, then shook his head.

'She needs a woman to look after her, my lord, and since the wife died...' He spread his hands in a helpless gesture. 'I'll find a chaise to take her home...'

Quinn glanced down at the hunched figure beside him. She was calm enough now, but he doubted she would endure the long drive back to town.

'Is there a maid you could send with her?'

'Nay, my lord. As I told you, they'm all out, it being May Day.'

'Then I will take her to Melham Court and put her in the care of my housekeeper.' Quinn guided her to the curricle and lifted her, unresisting, on to the seat. As he took his place beside her he glanced up at the gallery. 'Her companion is unconscious at present, but when he wakes—'

'Don't you worry about that, my lord. We will deal with him. I don't hold with such goings on in my establishment.'

'And. Jennings…' Quinn gathered up the reins '…the lady was never here.'

The landlord nodded. 'My lads'll do as I tell 'em.'

With that Quinn whipped up his team and the curricle bowled out into the night.

Chapter Two

Quinn drove steadily, but as the curricle rounded the first bend he felt the figure beside him sway and he quickly put an arm about her shoulders.

'Easy now. I don't want you falling out on to the road.'

'No, of course not.' She sounded very calm and made no move to shake him off. 'I do not feel quite myself.'

'That is understandable.' He frowned. There was something familiar about her voice, but he couldn't quite place it.

'No, what I mean is, my head is swimming. He made me drink the wine. He was trying to get me drunk.'

'Did he succeed?'

'Not quite.' There was a long pause. 'You must think me very foolish.'

'I do. But you are not the first.'

'I should have known better. Molly—my sister-in-law—is patroness of Prospect House, a refuge for women who have, who have been...' A shudder ran through her. 'I have met some of them and learned their history, but I thought it could never happen to me. I thought I knew better.'

She was talking quite naturally, as if they were old friends, but Quinn guessed that was the shock. It would not last. Reaction would set in at some point and he must be ready for that. For now, talking was a way to distract her from her ordeal.

'It is common among the young,' he remarked, 'to think they are awake upon every suit.'

'Where are you taking me?'

'To Melham Court. My housekeeper will look after you. I am Quinn, by the way.'

'I know. You were pointed out to me at the Grindleshams' ball.'

So that was it! He felt a stab of shock. The hair, the voice—he could place her now, the outraged beauty from the rose garden. Well, however wilful she might be, it was clear she had got herself into a situation far beyond her control.

She said now, 'I was told you are the rudest man in London.'

'Which was your own opinion, when we met in the garden.'

'Ah, yes. Do you wish me to apologise?'

'No. I admit it, I *was* rude to you.' He glanced down at her. 'You have the advantage of me. I do not know your name.'

'S-Serena Russington. I am Lord Hambridge's ward. But I pray you will not blame him for my present predicament.'

'I don't. I have no doubt you told him some tarradiddle so you could slip away this evening.'

She tensed, and said coldly, 'I think you should release me. It is most improper for you to have your arm about me like this.'

'Improper, perhaps, but necessary. In the dark you will not be prepared for the twists and turns of the road. My team, however, are very familiar with this route and need little guidance from me.'

'You can drive one-handed?' Her indignation died away as quickly as it had come. 'I am impressed. Not that you wish to impress me, do you, Lord Quinn? You think me a sad romp.'

'No, I merely think you foolish.' The stiff little body beside him drooped a little and he softened his tone. 'Perhaps you should tell me how you came to be at the Swan this evening. And who was your companion?'

He thought at first she would not reply. Then she began to speak, her voice low and tightly controlled.

'The man was Sir Timothy Forsbrook. He said he would take me to Vauxhall Gardens, but instead he was going to carry me off to Scotland. I did not realise the deceit until we were out of London.' She added bitterly, 'He tricked me finely! He *said* that he thought I wanted to elope with him, so he had arranged it all. Elope!' She shuddered. 'I am sure I gave him no such indication!'

'Yet you agreed to go to Vauxhall with him.'

Silence, then, 'Yes.'

'And would I be correct in assuming your dowry is...substantial?'

'Of course. I know *now* that is why he ran off with me, but he d-did not admit it at first. When I told him I did not wish to elope he begged pardon and said he had quite misunderstood and we would go back just as soon as we had changed horses. When we reached the Swan, I wanted to remain in the carriage, but the night mail followed us into the yard and he said I would be sure to attract attention. He…he had bespoken a room where I might rest in private.'

'And you believed him?' He could not keep the incredulity out of his voice.

'He had given me no cause then to think he would not respect my wishes. He was so polite, so remorseful that I truly believed he was in earnest, that he really was protecting my honour. Instead he…he t-tried to…'

She began to shake, quite violently, and his arm tightened.

'Enough. I can guess the rest.'

With relief he saw they were approaching the gatehouse of Melham Court and he slowed the greys. The bridge and archway leading into the courtyard were narrow, but at least there were no tight corners to negotiate one-handed. He brought the team to a stand before the door and a servant ran out to take their heads. Serena was still trembling. Quinn picked her up and carried her into the house. It was the work of a moment, but he was aware of two things. She weighed almost nothing in his arms and she smelled of summer meadows.

If Dunnock thought it unusual for his master to arrive with a strange woman in his arms, he was too wise a butler to show it. Quinn made directly for the drawing room, requesting that the housekeeper should attend him.

It was his custom whenever he was returning to Melham to send word ahead in order that the principal rooms could be prepared, so he was not surprised to find a good blaze in the hearth. He lowered Serena gently into a chair beside the fire and she huddled into her shawl, leaning towards the flames. She barely seemed to notice him.

His housekeeper came bustling in and he explained without preamble.

'I found Miss Russington at the Swan. She is very distressed and I need you to take care of her, Mrs Talbot. She will need a hot brick for her bed.' He glanced down at the dishevelled figure hunched over the fire. 'And a bath.'

'Aye, of course, my lord. I always make sure there is hot water when you are due back, but 'tis only enough for one. And...' She stopped, consternation in every line of her kindly face.

'Yes?'

'Everything is set up in your dressing room, my lord. I can easily have the hip bath removed to the guest room, but there is no fire burning there and it will take a time to get it warm.'

'Bathe her in my rooms, then, while you have the guest room prepared. And be sure to have a bed made up in there for one of the maids. She must not be left alone—do you understand me? I will remain here until you have finished.'

'Very good, my lord.' The housekeeper turned to Serena. 'Come along then, my dear, let us get you into a warm bath and you will soon feel better. And perhaps we'll find you a little soup afterwards, what do you say to that?'

Serena made no response, but she allowed Mrs Talbot to help her out of the room. Quinn threw himself into the vacated chair. All this was a damned nuisance, but what else could he do? A hired coach would have taken several hours to get her back to town and, aside from the perils of making such a journey alone and at night, there was no telling what distress she would be in by the time she reached her home. He was not prepared to have that on his conscience.

It would not do for him to remain here, though. As soon as the women had finished with his dressing room he would pack himself a bag and remove to Prior's Holt. Tony Beckford and his wife were still in London, but the staff there knew him well and would not deny him, even at this late hour. He closed his eyes, too tired to consider anything more right now.

An hour later Mrs Talbot's tactful cough roused Quinn from his sleep.

He sat up in the chair, saying irritably, 'What is it now?'

'I beg your pardon, my lord, but 'tis the young lady. She is still in the bath. I've built up the fires in the guest room—and in your bedroom, too, my lord—but the bathwater is turning cold now. I've looked out one of my dressing gowns for her, too, but she won't budge. I'm afraid she will catch a chill if we don't get her dry soon.'

'For heaven's sake, woman, can't you get her out of the water?'

'Every time anyone goes near her she screams fit to bust.' The housekeeper wrung her hands. 'She keeps scrubbing away at herself, sir, and muttering. I'm sure I don't know what to do for the best.'

Smothering an oath Quinn pushed himself to his feet. 'Very well, let me see her.'

The steamy warmth of the dressing room hit Quinn as soon as he entered. Serena was sitting in the hip bath but facing away from him, the smooth skin of her neck and shoulders golden in the candlelight. Someone had pinned up her fair curls to keep them dry and she was rubbing at her arms with the sponge. A young maid was in attendance, watching Serena with an almost frightened intensity. A screen was set up to protect the bather from the draughty window and thrown over it was a large towel and a bundle of white cotton that he assumed was Mrs Talbot's dressing gown.

The housekeeper picked up the towel, saying cheerily, 'Now then, miss, time we wrapped you in this nice warm sheet.'

'I am not yet clean.' Serena rubbed even harder at her arms.

'You'll take the skin off if you scrub yourself any more, miss. Come along.'

Serena lashed out, shrieking, and Mrs Talbot backed away, turning an anguished face to Quinn. He took the towel from her.

'Leave us, both of you.'

The maid scuttled out, followed more slowly by the housekeeper, and Quinn moved around until he was facing Serena. There was a livid bruise on one cheek and she had rubbed her arms until they were red, but he saw marks on her neck and arms that had not been caused by the constant scouring. He wished now that he had spent longer punishing Forsbrook rather than knocking him out with a single blow. Serena ignored him and continued to rub the sponge over her body. He knelt beside her.

'Miss Russington, Serena, you must get out and dry yourself.'

'No, no, not until I have washed it away. I c-can still feel his h-hands on me.'

Quinn gently touched her cheek. 'Did he do this?'

She pulled her head away but did not answer him. Instead she gripped the sponge even tighter as she scrubbed at her skin.

'What did he do to you, Serena? Tell me,' he commanded.

She stilled, although she did not look at him. A shudder rippled through her.

'He k-kissed me. When I told him to stop he—he laughed and t-tore my gown. Then he grabbed me.' She put her hands over her breasts.

'Did he do anything else? Serena?'

He spoke sharply, demanding a response and she gave a tiny shake of her head.

'He—he tried, but I scratched and bit him. That was when he hit me. Then he t-tried to ch-choke me.'

Her hands crept to her throat and Quinn felt his anger growing. He fought it down.

He said calmly, 'You showed great courage, Serena, but you must be brave again now. We must get you dry or you will be very ill and all your fighting will be in vain. You do not want that to happen, do you?' He had her attention now. Her dark eyes were fixed on him. He rose and held out one hand. 'Come.'

He held her gaze, willing her to obey. Slowly she took his proffered hand and rose from the water. He had the impression of a womanly form, all soft curves and creamy skin, but he kept his eyes on her face. She was on the verge of hysteria and the slightest error on his part could overset her. As she stepped out of the hip bath he wrapped her in the towel. She did not move but looked up at him with eyes so full of trust that the constriction around his chest was like an iron band.

Panic shot through him. She was relying upon him to act honourably and just for a moment he doubted his ability to do so.

She stood motionless while Quinn dried her body, steeling himself not to linger over those luscious curves. When he had finished he dragged the wrap from the screen.

'Put this on. It belongs to Mrs Talbot, so it will be far too large, but it will keep you warm.' Briskly he helped her into the dressing gown and knotted the belt. He tried not to think about her tiny waist or how easily his hands could span it.

'There, now you are—' He had been about to say *respectable* but that was wholly inappropriate. And untrue. Even in the voluminous robe, her cheeks flushed and wisps of errant curls framing her face, she was undeniably tempting and desirable. He cleared his throat and stepped back, ready to turn away.

'Th-thank you.' Her face crumpled. 'Everyone has been most kind.'

She gave a wrenching sob and Quinn could not help himself. He gathered her into his arms, where she remained rigid and tense against him.

'It is all right, Serena. You are safe now.'

He cursed the inadequacy of the words, but she leaned into him while hard, noisy sobs tore through her. He continued to hold her, but the room was cooling rapidly, so he swept her up and carried her through the adjoining door into his bedchamber. She clung to him as he used one foot to push the large armchair closer to the fire, then sat down with Serena across his lap. The sobs had turned to tears and she was weeping unrestrainedly, but at least with the warmth of his body on one side and a good fire on the other, she should not become chilled. She huddled against him, clutching at his coat. The curls piled upon her head were tickling his chin and he reached up to pull out the pins. Her hair fell down her back in a thick curtain of rippling gold that shimmered in the firelight.

At last the weeping stopped. She gave a sigh, muffled because her face was still hidden in his shoulder.

'I beg your pardon,' she muttered. 'I *never* cry.'

'You have had a trying day.' His lips twitched at the understatement. He shifted slightly so that he could reach into his pocket. 'Here. I would rather you blew your nose on this than my coat.'

She gave a watery chuckle as she took the handkerchief.

'That's better,' he told her. 'Now, can you walk, or shall I carry you to your room?'

Immediately she clung to him.

'Not yet.' Her voice was breathless with fear. 'Please, may we stay here for a little longer? I do not want to be alone just yet.'

Quinn sat back in the chair, stifling an impatient sigh. 'Another five minutes then.'

He settled her more comfortably on his lap and arranged the wrap over her bare feet. Very pretty little feet, he noted.

'You must think me a…a blasted nuisance,' she murmured.

'I do.' He smiled at the unladylike term.

'I was t-trying to find a husband, you see.'

He glanced down at the golden head and the profile with its straight little nose and dainty chin. Her eyes were closed, the long lashes fanning out on to her bruised cheek. Her mouth, what he could see of it, was drooping slightly at present, but it looked eminently kissable.

'I do not see that you needed to go to such dangerous lengths for that. There must be hundreds of eligible suitors lining up to offer for you.'

Her hand tightened on his lapel and she snuggled closer. 'That is just it. The eligible ones are not at all interesting.' She said drowsily, 'And much as I want to run my own establishment I *cannot* bring myself to marry a man who bores me.'

'You would rather have one who abuses you?'

He could not keep the anger from his voice, but she did not respond and when he looked down he saw she was sleeping. Quinn put his head back and closed his eyes. He would take her to her room and get Mrs Talbot to put her to bed, but not yet. He had to admit there was something rather pleasant about the way she was nestled against him.

Quinn had no idea how long he slept, but when he opened his eyes the first rays of the dawn sun were shining through the window and glinting on the golden head resting on his shoulder. He groaned.

'Oh, Lord.'

Chapter Three

Serena's eyelids fluttered as she awoke from a deep slumber. She lay still for a moment, allowing the usual morning noises to soothe her, but something was not quite right. The birdsong outside her window was not mixed with the rumble of carriages and her bed—it was comfortable, yes, but the pillow was fatter and the freshly laundered sheets smelled of lavender. Her nightgown, too, did not feel like her usual soft linen and it was so large that it was tangled around her.

She sat up quickly, much to the alarm of the little maid who was tidying a truckle bed in the corner. The girl jumped up and regarded Serena with anxious eyes.

'Oh, mistress, I beg your pardon. Did I wake you?'

Serena gave a slight shake of the head and pulled the voluminous cotton wrap closer about her. There were dark terrors prowling at the edge of her memory but she could not face them just yet. The hangings around her bed had not been drawn and she looked slowly around the room. It was unfamiliar, but comfortably furnished and full of morning sunshine.

'Where am I?'

The question was more to herself than the maid, but the girl bobbed a curtsy.

'Melham Court, m'm. Lord Quinn's Hertfordshire residence.'

Quinn. He had rescued her from... No. She would not think of that. She would think of Lord Quinn, the way he had coaxed her from the bath. The way he had held her. She put a hand to her head. Was it only last night that he had brought her here? She must have spoken aloud, for the little maid bobbed another curtsy.

'Yes, m'm. Shall I call Mrs Talbot?'

'No, no, pray do not disturb her. But I should like something to drink.' Serena smiled at the young maid. 'Could you fetch me something warm. Hot chocolate, perhaps, or coffee?'

'Of course, m'm. I'll do that straight away. But Mrs Talbot did say I was to inform her, as soon as you was awake.'

The maid hurried off and Serena drew up her knees, clasping her arms about them as she finally turned her mind to the events that had brought her here. She touched her neck. Her windpipe felt bruised and it hurt when she swallowed. The shock and fear she had felt at Sir Timothy's attempted seduction was still there, but on top of that she felt remorse and humiliation. She had been foolish in the extreme. Arrogant, too, to think she could play such games without risk.

How worried Henry and Dorothea must be. She glanced at the bell-pull and considered requesting a note should be sent to them immediately, but decided against it. She would be back with them in a few hours, she was sure. Lord Quinn would arrange it.

She rested her chin on her knees and considered her

host. Her rescuer. It was curious that she should have such confidence in a stranger. She had felt nothing but revulsion when Sir Timothy had put his hands on her. She remembered trying to wash away the feel of his touch from her skin, yet she had allowed Quinn to see her completely naked. She had not flinched as he had dried her and dressed her in this ridiculously large wrap. And when she wept he had cradled her in his arms. For such a big man he had been surprisingly gentle and she had clung to him, feeling safe and secure enough to curl up on his lap and fall asleep.

No man had ever held her thus before, not even Papa. In truth, Serena barely remembered her father. Neither could she remember much about her mother. Mama was a shadowy figure, nothing more than swirl of fashionable silks and a trace of perfume who had disappeared from her life completely when Papa had died. Serena had grown up in the care of nannies until she was old enough to be sent to school and after that she only met her half-brothers on rare occasions. She had grown up resilient, self-sufficient and independent. But very much alone.

There was a murmur of voices outside the door and the maid came in, carrying a tray laden with coffee, bread and butter. She was followed by the housekeeper, Mrs Talbot, who had a foaming cloud of lemon and white over her arm. She greeted Serena with a cheerful smile.

'Good morning to you, Miss Russington. I trust you slept well? We have done what we can to clean and repair your clothing. 'tis not perfect, but I think, with your shawl about you, it will do to get you home.'

Home! Serena glanced at the window. The angle of

the sun showed it was much later than she had first thought.

'Oh, heavens, yes.' She waved away the breakfast tray. 'There is no time to lose. I must get up immediately. I did not realise I had slept so long.'

'All in good time, miss.' Gently but firmly, the older lady ushered Serena back into bed and smoothed the bedclothes so that the maid could put the tray down before her. 'Lord Quinn instructed that you should be left to sleep as long as you wished this morning.'

'That is all very well, but—'

The housekeeper put up her hands. 'Lord Quinn insists you break your fast before you go downstairs. And his lordship likes his orders to be obeyed.'

Serena sank back against the pillows. She did not feel up to a battle of wills with anyone, let alone a man to whom she owed so much. Obediently she drank her coffee while Mrs Talbot directed the maid in her duties, tidying the room and building up the fire, before sending her away to wash her hands and fetch up hot water.

'When Meggy comes back she will help you to dress,' she told Serena, when the coffee was drunk and the last crumb eaten. 'Then you are to go down to the library.' She picked up the tray and headed for the door. 'Lord Quinn is waiting there for you.'

Some half-hour later Serena asked Meggy to show her the way to the library. A glance in the looking glass on the dressing table told her the bruise on her cheek was now blue-black, but there was nothing she could do to hide it. However, it was not painful and Serena did her best to ignore it. Mrs Talbot had washed her muslin fichu and Serena crossed it over the bodice of her gown and tied it at the back, so no one would see the repairs, but there were shadowy marks on the petticoats, evidence of her struggle with Sir Timothy. As she descended the stairs, the whisper of her satin skirts taunted her. It was easy enough to replace a gown, but her lost reputation was an altogether different matter.

She had been oblivious to her surroundings last night and had no idea what Melham Court looked like from the outside, but from what she could see inside, it was clearly an old building and everything suggested it was well maintained. The wainscoting and the staircase, with its intricately carved balusters, were polished to a high shine and there was not a speck of dust on the windowsills. Fine paintings covered the walls and exquisite porcelain was displayed on side tables. Serena was in no mood to dwell on her surroundings, but there was an indefinable feeling of calm comfort about the house. Meggy left her in the staircase hall, where a waiting footman escorted her through the great hall, with its lofty vaulted roof, to the library.

Serena's step faltered as the servant opened the door and it was with a definite straightening of the back that she stepped across the threshold. Lord Quinn was standing in the window embrasure, scrutinising a large framed canvas propped against one side of the bay. He did not appear to notice her entry and she walked across the room until she, too, could see the picture. It was a woman, half-naked, sitting on a velvet-covered couch and looking into a mirror held aloft by two red-haired cherubs. The painting glowed with colour, especially the golden sheen of the woman's hair and the deep red velvet drapes that covered the lower half of her body.

She said, 'Is that a Titian?'

'Yes. *Venus with a Mirror.*'

'By the master, or a copy by his students? I believe there are several versions in existence.' He looked at her in surprise and she explained, 'My half-brother made a tour of Italy during the Peace of Amiens. He came back full of admiration for the old masters and talked of them to anyone who would listen.'

Serena stopped. She often encouraged Henry to tell her about art, especially when he summoned her to his study to criticise some aspect of her behaviour. She thought wryly that the situation now was not so very different. Lord Quinn had turned his attention back to the painting.

'Experts are agreed this is by the master.' He beckoned her to come closer. 'Look at the brush strokes. He has given her a most natural complexion and the velvet is so fine one can almost see each thread.'

His enthusiasm was infectious and it distracted her from other, more disturbing thoughts, a dark, shadowy terror she did not want to face. She took another step towards the picture. 'I like the way we see her reflection in the mirror.'

'But look at her eyes,' he said. 'She is not actually looking in the mirror; her gaze is towards someone out of the frame. Her lover perhaps?'

He turned to her for an answer as if it was the most natural thing in the world. Serena felt a blush stealing into her cheeks. She was an unmarried lady, she should not discuss such things with a stranger. His look changed, as if he realised how inappropriate was their conversation and he turned away with something between a cough and a growl.

'I beg your pardon. I should not be talking about

Titian when there are far more important matters to discuss.'

There were indeed. Her spirits sank and she waited to be rebuked for her folly.

'That bruise on your face, for example. Does it hurt?'

She blinked. 'No...that is, only if I touch it.'

He nodded, then turned and walked across to the desk. 'You must be wishing you were at home.'

No. I wish I could run away and hide from the world.

'Of course.'

'I took the liberty of writing to Lord and Lady Hambridge, to assure them that you are safe.' He picked up a letter. 'I sent it at first light and this has just arrived, express. They are on their way to fetch you.'

'Thank you, my lord. You are too kind.' She looked at her hands, twisting themselves together as if trying to wipe away the shame of it all. 'Kinder than I have any right to expect.'

Her voice wobbled and she bowed her head to hide her tears.

'Enough of that, madam. You were served an ill turn by a rogue. *He* is to blame, not you. You behaved foolishly, to be sure, but you have escaped quite lightly, in the circumstances.' She kept her head down and dashed a tear from her cheek. She heard a couple of hasty steps and he was before her, holding out his handkerchief. 'Come now, dry your eyes. Lord and Lady Hambridge will not be much more than an hour. What would you like to do until then?'

Serena wiped away the tears and took a couple of deep breaths. 'I had best return to my room.'

As she handed the handkerchief back to him he caught her fingers and she looked up quickly. His hazel eyes were fixed upon her and she felt the full force of his penetrating gaze.

'If I were a doctor I would prescribe fresh air to put a little colour back into your cheeks.' His brows snapped together. 'There is no need to look like that, Miss Russington. I have no designs upon your virtue, but I would have you look less like a corpse when your brother comes to fetch you.'

His rough manner had its affect. For the first time since this whole sorry business had begun she felt like smiling, if only a little.

'Very well, my lord. I shall take a turn in the gardens. If you will excuse me...'

'Oh, no,' he said. 'The place is a rabbit warren. I will not risk losing you.'

'I must not take any more of your time,' she protested.

'Not at all. I should like to show you the gardens. Now run upstairs and fetch your shawl.'

Quinn escorted his guest out of doors, resigning himself to an hour's tedium. He could have appointed a servant to accompany her, if he was so worried about the woman's well-being, but something had made him speak, and once the words were out there was no going back. He led her out into the cobbled courtyard around which the old house was built. The west front with its central, castellated gatehouse was of sturdy stone, while the other three walls were all half or fully timbered, the upper stories jutted out and a haphazard collection of leaded windows overlooked the yard.

'The building predates the Tudor monarchs, I think?' she said, looking around.

'Yes. It is medieval in origin but there have been alterations, over the centuries.' He pointed out the most notable features. 'Look up there. That room on the first floor was originally the solar, but it was rebuilt later and you can see Henry VIII's emblems carved on the timbers. And over there, the open arcade running along the eastern side is one of the finest of its kind.'

'And the clock face in the gatehouse tower, is that new?'

'Yes. I installed that a few years ago, when we carried out repairs.'

He was reluctant to say too much for fear of boring her, but Serena appeared to be genuinely interested. She asked pertinent questions and he found himself telling her what he knew of the house's history.

'It was built for a wealthy farmer and passed into my own family only two generations back. My ancestors never cared for it,' he told her. 'There are few guest chambers and the reception rooms are small. The house does not lend itself to entertaining.'

'Oh, but surely there is room to dance in the great hall,' she replied. 'It would be a wonderful setting for a ball and guests could always be accommodated at the local inns, could they not?'

'I did not move here to be sociable, Miss Russington.'

She lapsed into silence and he cursed himself for snapping at her. He sensed she had withdrawn from him, even though her fingers still rested on his sleeve. He led her out through the arch saying, as they crossed the bridge, 'There is a moat, too. You may not have noticed it when we drove in last night.'

Damnation, another blunder, to remind her how she came to be here! Nothing for it but to continue.

'The stables, gardens and outhouses are spread over the adjoining land, but the moat surrounds the house and has always defined its limits.'

'Perfect, if you do not wish to be sociable.'

He glanced down quickly, not sure he had heard aright. She was looking around her, but he detected a very slight upward tilt to her mouth. So, she had not quite lost her spirit. The thought cheered him.

'My lord, someone is approaching!' Her hand tightened on his arm and he looked up.

'Devil take it, 'tis Crawshaw, the vicar. And he has seen us.'

Serena watched the stocky figure in cleric's robes hurry towards them, one hand holding his shallow-crowned hat firmly on his head. She pulled her fan from her reticule, spreading it wide as the vicar greeted them.

'Lord Quinn. Well met, sir, well met indeed. I was hoping for a word.'

He stopped before them, beaming and looking from Quinn to Serena, clearly waiting to be presented. Surely even someone as famously rude as Lord Quinn must comply. She kept the fan high, almost hiding her face. Better that Mr Crawshaw should think her shy than he should see that tell-tale bruise.

'Miss Russington is waiting for her guardian to collect her,' explained Lord Quinn, once introductions had been performed. 'We expect him any moment.'

'Then I shall not keep you,' replied the vicar. 'I merely wanted to discuss the repairs to the bell tower. Have you seen the church, ma'am? It is a fine example of the perpendicular Gothic. You must allow Lord Quinn to show it to you before you leave.'

Serena murmured something polite and Quinn dismissed Mr Crawshaw with a promise that he would make a generous donation to the restoration fund.

'Nothing could have been more unfortunate,' he muttered under his breath, when the vicar had gone on his way. 'I beg your pardon, Miss Russington. I hope I have given him the impression that you have only spent the morning here.'

'Is he likely to speak of me?'

'I hope not, but I thought it best to keep to the truth as far as possible.'

'Of course. To be caught out in a lie would be the worst of all worlds,' she replied. 'Let us pray he is too intent upon repairing his bell tower.'

Quinn gave a bark of laughter. 'After what I said to him, I have no doubt he will expect me to pay for the whole.'

'Would you have done that if I had not been here?' She sighed. 'Your silence gives me my answer. I do not know how I am to repay you for all your kindness, my lord.'

'I do not want any recompense, madam, merely to see you safely returned to your guardian.'

'Perhaps I should go indoors until then, lest there are more visitors.'

'If you wish.' He hesitated. 'But the sun is still shining and you have not yet seen the gardens.'

Hell and damnation, Quinn, what are you doing?

He should take her back, leave her with Mrs Talbot until Hambridge arrived. After all, he had put himself out more than enough for the woman already. But when she indicated that she would like to continue their walk, he was not displeased. The day suddenly became a little brighter.

* * *

It was like a dream, thought Serena. To be walking with a stranger, calmly discussing flowers. She felt oddly detached from everything. Until she had climbed into Sir Timothy's carriage yesterday, she had thought herself very much in control of her own life, but she realised now that had been an illusion. Her half-brothers and their wives had always been there to protect her. Even when she had slipped away to flirt with some gentleman, their proximity had given her a modicum of protection.

Putting herself in Sir Timothy's power had changed all that. She had been in real danger. He had intended to rape her, then force her into marriage to gain control of her fortune. She had fought him desperately, prepared to die rather than give in, and the bruises around her throat convinced her that her defiance might well have ended with her death.

Quinn had rescued her, but her life was still in ruins. Dorothea and Henry would insist she went into the country. If the whole affair could be hushed up then after a suitable period she might be allowed to return to society, but she knew she would never be as confident, happy and carefree as she had been one day ago. Things had changed. *She* had changed. No matter how brightly the sun shone everything was dulled by the grey cloud that enveloped her and weighed heavily upon her spirits.

'You are not attending, Miss Russington.'

Lord Quinn's gruff tones brought Serena out of her reverie and she quickly begged pardon.

'I asked what you thought of these roses from China. They bloom every spring, even this year, despite the atrocious weather.'

'Oh. Yes. They are very beautiful.' She glanced up, needing to be truthful. 'I was thinking of my future.'

'No doubt you think it destroyed for ever,' he said. 'Do not believe it. You are feeling very sorry for yourself at present but you will forget this unfortunate episode, in time.'

'I do not think so.' She pulled her arm free to rearrange her shawl.

'Believe me, you will recover. Why should you not, when you have all the advantages of birth, fortune and a family to support you?'

'I never thought myself in any danger until yesterday. Until Sir Timothy b-began to maul me.' Her fingers crept to her throat. 'I thought I was going to die. I shall never forget that.'

'Perhaps not, but you must not let it blight your life.'

His cool assurance annoyed her.

'How dare you tell me what I must or must not do? What do you know about me, about how I feel?' She gave an angry sob, saying wildly, 'There is nothing left for me now. Nothing.'

'Stop that!' He caught her shoulders, pulling her round to face him and giving her a little shake. 'You are what,' he demanded, 'eighteen, nineteen?'

She turned her head away, presenting the undamaged side of her face to him.

'Much older than that.' She sniffed. 'I am almost one-and-twenty.'

'Very well then. You have years of happiness before you, if you wish it, and with such advantages as many can only dream of. How dare you think your life is over, merely because some ignominious creature tried to se-

duce you? He did not succeed and you are alive, Serena.
Alive. You should be grateful for that.'

He has lost someone.

She looked up into his eyes and saw the pain behind
his anger. Her self-pity faded. She wanted to apologise,
to ask him about his past, but even as the words were
forming he released her and turned away.

'It is time we returned to the house.' He drew her
hand back through his arm. 'Your family will be here
soon. It is better that they do not find us wandering
out of doors.'

Serena was sitting in the drawing room with Mrs
Talbot when Henry and Dorothea arrived. The latticed
windows of the panelled room looked out across the
gardens, so she did not hear the coach on the drive,
but at the sound of voices in the great hall she rose and
faced the door.

'Where is she?' Dorothea's shrill voice echoed
through the house and an instant later she was in the
room, hurrying towards Serena. 'Oh, good heavens,
look at your face!'

'It is only a bruise, Dorothea. I have suffered no other
hurt, I promise you.'

'Then you have escaped more lightly than you deserve! What on earth possessed you to go off like that?
We have been positively *frantic* with worry!'

'Now, now, my dear, do not scold her. We must be
thankful that Serena is safe and well.' Henry followed
his wife into the room, less anger and more concern
in his face.

Dorothea took Serena's hands and gave her a searching
look. 'You are sure there is no *irrevocable* harm done?'

'None, Dorothea, you have my word.' Serena glanced at Mrs Talbot, who was moving towards the door.

'If you will excuse me, Miss Russington, I am sure Lord and Lady Hambridge would like a little wine and cake after their journey.'

As the door closed behind the housekeeper, Dorothea rounded on Serena.

'Foolish, *thoughtless* girl, to deceive us in this way! When you did not come home last night I naturally thought I had mistaken the matter and you were staying with the Downings. Then this morning, when Elizabeth and her brother came to ask if you had recovered, I was quite thrown into a panic.' Dorothea sank down on the sofa, pulling out her handkerchief. 'I was so overset there was no keeping from them that you were not at home. The shame of it! It will be months before we will be able to hold our heads up again.'

Henry patted her shoulder. 'There, there, my dear, pray do not distress yourself.' He looked at Serena and took up the tale. 'If it had not been for the fact that you had quite clearly engineered this whole escapade, Serena, we would have called in the Runners immediately. As it is, Lord Quinn's note arrived shortly after the Downings had quit the house.'

'It was very bad of me, Henry, I apologise.'

'Apologies are no good,' snapped Dorothea. 'Your credit with the Downings is quite gone. Oh, they have promised they will not say a word, but I do not doubt they are laughing up their sleeves at us, convinced you made a secret assignation.'

'I did, Dorothea, but everything went horribly wrong.' Serena hung her head. 'I arranged to go to Vauxhall with Sir Timothy Forsbrook.'

'Forsbrook!' cried Henry. 'Then what are you doing at Melham Court?'

They were interrupted by a soft knock on the door and their host came in.

'I could not help overhearing your question, Hambridge,' he said, with all his customary bluntness. 'Perhaps you will allow me to answer for your sister. She is not yet fully recovered from her ordeal.' Gently, he took Serena's arm and guided her back to her chair. 'Forsbrook abducted Miss Russington and brought her to the Swan, just outside Hitchin, where I came upon him, forcing his attentions upon her.'

'The devil he was!' Henry sank down beside his wife.

'I understand his plan was to make sure of her before carrying on to the border, where he would make her his wife.'

'For her fortune, no doubt!' put in Dorothea.

Quinn bowed. 'Precisely, ma'am. When Miss Russington realised his intention, she bravely fought him off, but it left her understandably distressed. There being no suitable female at the Swan, I brought Miss Russington to Melham Court and placed her in the care of my housekeeper.'

The way Quinn relayed the story it all sounded so sensible and straightforward, thought Serena. And perfectly respectable. There was no reason he should tell them that he had helped her, naked, from the bath. That she had spent the night in his arms.

A second knock heralded the return of Mrs Talbot with refreshments. Serena took advantage of the distraction to glance up at Quinn. His smile was brief but reassuring.

When they were alone again, Henry said, 'We are in your debt, my lord, for your assistance to our sister.'

'Although I have to say she brought it on herself,' Dorothea said, 'scheming to go off alone with a man. I have warned her, time and again, what would come of her headstrong ways!'

Quinn shook his head. 'Whatever Miss Russington's behaviour, madam, it is Forsbrook who acted wrongly.'

'I should call him out,' muttered Henry, frowning, 'But I fear that would only make matters worse.'

'I agree,' said Quinn. 'The object now must be to protect Miss Russington's reputation.'

'If it can be done,' said Dorothea, shooting a resentful glance at Serena. 'You know how these things get about.'

Henry was more optimistic. 'Forsbrook will not want it known that his abduction failed. But you mean the Downings, I suppose, my dear, since they are the only other people who know of this. They have agreed to say nothing and I am sure they will keep their word. After all, what do they really know, save that Serena did not go to Vauxhall with them? No, the main thing now is to get Serena back to Bruton Street with all speed. I am sure Lord Quinn will understand if we do not tarry.'

'Of course. The sooner you remove Miss Russington from this house the better.'

Serena had grown used to Quinn's manner, but she saw Henry blink at these terse words and Dorothea positively bridled.

Serena said quickly, 'Then let us not take up any more of Lord Quinn's time. If you have finished your wine, Brother, we will be gone.'

* * *

'Well,' exclaimed Henry, as the carriage rattled out of the courtyard, 'I had heard it said that Rufus Quinn had no social graces and now I have seen it for myself. Why, he virtually threw us out of the house.'

'You said yourself we should not tarry,' Serena reminded him, but she could not help feeling disappointed. Quinn had left it to Henry to escort her to the carriage.

'That may be so, but the fellow was positively curt,' retorted Henry, settling himself back into a corner. 'Heaven knows he must have some good qualities, Serena, but you have to admit he has no manners.'

'Yes, for all his wealth he is odiously rude,' Dorothea agreed. She glanced out of the window, 'And I had expected Melham Court to be much grander. Why, I should be ashamed to receive visitors in such a small house.'

'I do not think Lord Quinn wishes to be sociable,' murmured Serena.

Henry snorted. 'Well, thank goodness he spends so little time in town, because I confess I should find it difficult to be civil to such a man!'

Chapter Four

Serena kept to her room for a full week and even after that she was reluctant to leave the house. Gradually the bruises and the horror of the abduction faded, but her spirits remained low. She had no defence against Dorothea's constant reminders of how badly she had behaved. Even a note from Elizabeth Downing, wishing her well, could not raise her mood. Henry cheerfully assured her that she could go out and about again as if nothing had happened.

'Trust me,' he told her, 'Lord Byron's flight to the Continent and the salacious rumours that have been circulating about him have cast your little scrape into the shade. And now there's speculation that poor Brummell is quite done up. And don't forget Princess Charlotte's recent wedding. The gossipmongers are far too busy to concern themselves with you, Sister.'

Dorothea, who had been listening, gave a little snort of derision. 'You believe that if you will, Henry, but I think such optimism is misplaced.'

It was. Late one afternoon, barely ten days after the thwarted abduction, Serena heard the ominous words that

Lord Hambridge wished to see her in his study. Henry and his wife were deep in conversation when she entered and looked so anxious that she stopped by the door.

'Is something wrong?'

'It is indeed,' exclaimed Dorothea. 'You are undone.'

'Undone?' Serena moved to a chair and perched herself on the edge of it. 'I don't understand.'

'I was taking tea with Lady Grindlesham two days ago when more visitors came in,' Dorothea told her. 'Among them Mr Walsham. He had just returned to London after going north to attend his father's funeral.' She added pointedly, 'He was one of the suitors you rejected, Serena.'

'Yes, I remember. A horrid little man. What of it?'

Dorothea tapped her foot on the floor and glared at her husband, who said solemnly, 'Walsham was on the night mail on May Day. It stopped at the Swan. *He saw you there*, Serena, going up the stairs with a man. He is now making it very clear to everyone that he is exceedingly relieved you rejected his offer.'

Dorothea jumped up and began to pace the room. 'You know what a gossip Walsham is,' she said. 'And a vicious tongue, too. Of course, I told him he must be mistaken, that it could not have been you, but the damage is done. I have just come back from Bond Street, where more than one acquaintance stopped me to ask after you. Lady Mattishall even asked me outright if you had eloped!'

'Oh, dear,' said Serena faintly.

'It is time you were seen out and about,' Henry told her. 'You must drive out with Dorothea, then at least we may stop the rumours that you have run off. And there is one stroke of luck,' he continued. 'Walsham was unable to name the fellow at the Swan. If I had dined at home rather than going to White's that night, we might have said I was escorting you. As it is, we must continue to deny that it was you at Hitchin that night.'

'Which the Downings will not believe,' cut in his wife, still pacing.

'Elizabeth assured me in her letter that they have not said anything,' added Serena.

'Which is quite true,' Henry agreed. 'And in time the rumours will be forgotten.'

'In time!' Dorothea shook her head. 'Serena is very nearly one-and-twenty. By next Season she will be considered an old maid. I vow I am ready to give up on her!'

'Perhaps you should. I know I have disgraced myself, and I am very sorry for it.'

'Well, one thing is plain now, madam.' Dorothea stopped her perambulations and glared at Serena. 'There is no possibility of your marrying well!'

Henry protested mildly, 'Come, come, my dear. Serena still has a considerable fortune. *Someone* will have her.'

Serena winced. 'I will not marry a man merely to save my reputation,' she said. 'I am already resigned to remaining single.'

Dorothea's eyes narrowed. 'Pray do not think we will allow you to set up your own establishment. What would people say about us then?'

'They would most likely say I was an eccentric. And they would pity you most sincerely.'

'It is not to be thought of,' declared Henry. 'Once you come into your own money at five-and-twenty it will be a different matter, but at the moment you are far too young to consider such a thing.'

'Perhaps I could go and live with Russ and Molly at Compton Parva.'

Henry shook his head. 'It will not do. You are known there and I have no doubt they will have heard all about this little episode, even in such an out-of-the-way place. I have written to Russ, assuring him it is all nonsense and that there is no need for him to come to town.'

'No indeed,' agreed Dorothea. 'His concern must be for his wife. I believe the birth was a difficult one and she is not yet recovered. They will not be able to look after Serena.'

Serena's chin went up. 'I do not expect anyone to look after me. I merely need somewhere to live.'

'To hide, more like.'

'Call it that, if you wish, Dorothea.' Serena rose. 'I will drive out with you in the carriage, so that people may see I am in town, but please do not ask me to accompany you to any balls or parties. I do not feel ready to meet anyone just yet. Perhaps you could say I am recuperating,' she suggested. 'That would give you an excuse to ship me off to the country.'

'It would, my dear, if that is really what you want, but let us discuss it again later. Off you go now and change your gown for dinner. We will say no more about it tonight.' Henry waited until Serena had left the room, then he said slowly, 'I do not like it, Dorothea. She has lost her spirit.'

'That can only be a good thing. The girl was growing far too wild.'

'I grant you she was always a little hot to hand, but this new meekness—I cannot be easy. Perhaps we should call the doctor.'

'What, and have him quack her with expensive and

unnecessary medicines? No, leave her be, Henry. I have long considered that she thinks far too highly of herself. This incident with Forsbrook has brought her down to earth. I have no doubt she will recover and, in the meantime, we should seek out a husband for her. With her fortune it should not be impossible to find an acceptable match, despite this scandal.'

'I agree. There are several fellows who would take her, I am sure.'

'Then we should see to it, while she is so biddable.'

Henry shook his head. 'I don't know, Dorothea— would it be right to persuade her to tie the knot when she is not herself? When her spirits return she might regret it.'

His wife cast him an impatient glance. 'That will be her husband's problem, not ours.'

Quinn scooped up the small pile of letters from his desk and glanced at each one. Nothing from Bruton Street.

'Confound it, what do you expect?' he growled to himself as he threw the letters back down.

It was nearly two weeks since Hambridge had carried Serena away from Melham Court, but the fellow was unlikely to write and thank him for his part in rescuing his ward and it would be highly improper for Serena to do so. Discretion was the watchword and it would be foolhardy for any mention of the matter to be committed to paper.

He reached for a pen and began to trim the nib. He should forget all about it. After all, he wanted no thanks for what he had done. But the image of Serena haunted his dreams. Not the cowering figure he had come upon at the Swan, but Serena as he had seen her in the gardens of Grindlesham House, head up, eyes sparkling with indignation. The same eyes that had gazed upon him so trustingly as he coaxed her from her bath.

His hands stilled at the memory. He had subdued the thought at the time, but she had reminded him of a painting he had seen as a very young man: another Titian Venus, but this time the goddess was rising from the sea. Shy, vulnerable and utterly enchanting.

Quinn shifted in his chair. Enough of this. He had no interest in Serena Russington. She had foolishly put herself in danger and he had acted as any gentleman would, nothing more. The Hambridges would look after her and quell any gossip, so there was no point in Quinn worrying about the chit. But he was damned if he could forget her!

He heard voices in the hall and the study door opened.

'Tony!' Quinn jumped up and came around the desk, holding out his hand to his friend. 'I thought you were staying in town for another month at least.'

'That had been my intention. Lottie remains in town—she has engagements that she cannot break, but I confess my curiosity got the better of me.' Sir Anthony Beckford gestured towards his buckskins and glossy Hessians. 'I am on my way now to Prior's Holt, but thought I would stop off and try some of the claret you were boasting of.'

'By all means. Come along to the drawing room and I will have Dunnock fetch some.'

In very little time they were sitting comfortably, a decanter on the small table between them and a glass of ruby-red wine in hand.

Quinn watched in amusement as his friend made a

show of sniffing the wine and taking a sip before nodding appreciatively.

'Excellent. This came in through Bristol, you say? I
must put my man on to it.'

'Send him to Averys and they will see to it.' Quinn
shot a glance at his friend. 'But you did not come here
merely to taste my wine. What is it that has whetted
your curiosity?'

'Why you, my friend.' Tony lifted his glass to the
light and twisted the stem between his fingers. 'I came
to discover for myself if you have taken a mistress.'

The calm atmosphere of the drawing room became
suddenly tense. Quinn schooled his expression into one
of amusement.

'What an absurd idea. You know I am not in the petticoat line.'

'That is what I thought, but the rumours in town
made me wonder.'

Quinn put down his glass. The way his hand had
been tightening around it he was afraid he might snap
the stem.

'Then perhaps you would be good enough to tell me
just what it is that you have heard.'

'I was at White's a couple of nights back and
Walsham came in. You may not know him. Something
of a mushroom, but with connections enough to give
him entrée into most places in town. He strolls up to
Hambridge and asks after his sister. Now, in general
such a remark would pass unnoticed, but a sudden hush
fell over the room, and Hambridge looked so put out
there was no ignoring it.' Tony settled himself more
comfortably in his chair. 'Walsham did not leave it
there, however. He pulls out his snuff box and says, in

the coolest way imaginable, "Your good lady told me I was mistaken in thinking Miss Russington was at the Swan and it must be so, because Jack Downing says she cried off from Vauxhall that very same evening, pleading ill health. I trust it is not serious, no one's seen her for well over a week." Well, by this time Hambridge is frowning like a thundercloud. He jumped to his feet, exclaiming that he had no patience with all the tattling busybodies who try to make mischief out of nothing. Then he stalked off. Quite out of character, I thought. He is generally such a dull dog.'

'And this is all?' Quinn refilled their glasses. 'My dear Tony, I am surprised at you, to be taking note of such a trifle.'

'And I should not have thought any more about it, had I not gone to Tattersall's yesterday. You will recall there was a very pretty Arab mare I had my eye on, but that is by the by. I ran into Sir Timothy Forsbrook there, you see. He was selling his greys and mighty cut up about it, too. Blamed it all on a woman who had dashed his hopes. He was in his cups and happy to tell anyone who would listen how the mysterious *Miss R.* had persuaded him to run away with her on May Day, only to abandon him at Hitchin for a much richer prize.' Tony's shoulders lifted a fraction. 'The *richer prize* was not named, of course, but I remembered you had travelled to Melham Court that evening, and would have passed the Swan.' He paused. 'It made me wonder—'

'Hell and damnation!'

At Quinn's violent exclamation Tony's casual manner deserted him and he sat bolt upright.

'Never say that there is any truth in this, Quinn!'

'No. Yes!' Quinn jumped to his feet. 'Has anyone else connected me with this affair?'

'Not yet, although at the clubs last night they were already beginning to link Forsbrook's juicy tale to Walsham's gossip. 'tis commonly believed now that the lady is Serena Russington, Hambridge's ward.'

Cursing softly, Quinn went over to the window. He said over his shoulder, 'I stopped at the Swan on my way home. Forsbrook was there and I...er...removed Miss Russington from his company. She was unharmed, save for a few bruises, but it was already gone midnight so I was obliged to bring her here.' *No need to go into detail, Quinn.* 'I put her into Mrs Talbot's care until the Hambridges could collect her the next day. As for her persuading Forsbrook to elope, I believe it was quite the reverse. He tricked her into accompanying him.'

'Then why hasn't Hambridge called him out?'

'He thought it would cause the sort of scandal he was anxious to avoid.' Quinn's jaw tightened. 'I agreed with him, at the time. I thought Forsbrook would be too embarrassed by what had happened to blab about it. Now I see we were wrong.' He turned back and looked at his friend. 'Well there, at least, I will be able to act!'

'The devil you will. Confound it, Quinn, you are so rarely in town your mere presence there sets the *ton* by the ears. If you come back to call the fellow out, I won't be the only one to remember you live within a stone's throw of Hitchin. No, no, you keep well out of it, my friend. No need to become involved.'

'I am already involved,' Quinn reminded him, a trifle grimly. 'And the devil of it is that Crawshaw met her here, the following morning.'

'The vicar! That's a dashed nuisance.'

'Aye. I had no choice but to introduce him. So far he hasn't said anything, but...' Quinn let the words hang and a brooding silence fell over the room.

At last Tony gave a sigh. 'Well, Crawshaw is a good fellow and not one to gossip. I suppose your servants know the whole?'

'How could they not? I can rely upon Dunnock and Mrs Talbot to be discreet, but some of the younger ones may let it slip.'

'And since most of 'em are related to my own staff, everyone at Prior's Holt knows of your visitor by now. Not to worry. I'll have a word, stop it spreading further if I can. Of course, it would be better coming from Lottie, as mistress of the house, but she's still in town. I'll write to her, tell her to do what she can to squash any rumours she hears.'

'You are both very good, but I fear it may be too late for that.'

'Well, there is no need to involve yourself further,' said Tony with finality. 'You know as well as I that once gossip starts it must run its course, and if Hambridge is wise he will remove his sister from town until this has all died down.' He rose. 'Now, I had best be getting on to Prior's Holt or they will not have time to find me a decent dinner.'

'If that is the case then you can come back here and take pot luck with me,' said Quinn, accompanying him out of the house.

Once his friend had driven away Quinn returned to his study, but the letters he had planned to deal with that morning remained unopened. Instead he sat in his chair for a full half-hour, staring into space and thinking over all Tony had told him.

* * *

'Smile, Serena. And sit up straight. Remember this is for your benefit.'

Dorothea's hissed whisper was cut short as she turned to greet Lady Drycroft, whose carriage had drawn up alongside their own. It was the third day running that Dorothea had taken Serena out at the fashionable hour and the May sunshine had encouraged even greater crowds than usual to throng Hyde Park. Progress around the gravelled drives was little faster than a walk.

It was a nightmare, thought Serena. To be smiling, calmly exchanging greetings, when all she wanted was to hide from the world. It was her own fault, she had compromised herself by running off with a man and Dorothea and Henry were doing their best to mend matters. All that was expected of Serena was that she appear in public and act as if nothing had happened.

Two weeks ago, she would not have doubted her ability to ride the storm. But she was not the same confident lady who had set out to meet Sir Timothy Forsbrook. She had lost her self-assurance and no longer felt any interest in what was happening to her. However, it was easier to try to please Dorothea than oppose her, so she smiled and replied politely to the barbed comments of the spiteful. At the same time she discounted her friends' kind words, knowing she had brought this fate upon herself. Her face ached with smiling. All she really wanted to do was to take to her bed. To go to sleep and never wake up.

They returned to Bruton Street an hour later and entered the house just as Henry was crossing the hall. He waited while they discarded their bonnets and spencers, then ushered them into the drawing room.

'How was your drive around the Ring today?'

'Humiliating,' replied Dorothea. 'We received only the coolest of nods from several matrons, including Lady Mattishall. The Duchess of Bonsall cut us altogether! No one believes Serena has been ill. I have had to suffer innumerable sly remarks.'

'They will come to believe it, if you persevere. They *have* to believe it,' Henry added, his teeth clenched. He shrugged off his anxiety and said more cheerfully, 'Now that Serena is out and about again this little setback will soon be forgotten.'

'Little setback?' Dorothea retorted. 'Have you not noticed how few invitations we have received recently?' She waved towards the mantelpiece, which was usually crowded with cards. 'And even when I do go out, I am teased about it constantly.'

Serena thought that if Dorothea had not been so cool to those she considered inferior, then society might have been a little more sympathetic, but she said nothing. It did not seem worth the effort.

'Well, we must bear it for a few more weeks,' Henry replied. 'Then you can leave town for the summer. What say you to hiring a house at Worthing? You and Serena can travel ahead and I will join you as soon as Parliament rises.'

'Worthing! What is the good of that, when everyone of note will be in Brighton?'

'That is just the point, Dorothea,' Henry explained patiently. 'By the time you meet your acquaintances again, other scandals will have arisen to eclipse Serena's disgrace. Poor Brummell, for one, the wolves are already circling his door. And who knows,' he added hopefully, 'you might by then have found a husband for her.'

'You forget, Henry, I do not want a husband.'

Serena's quiet words brought a cry of exasperation from Dorothea.

'You see,' she cried, turning to her husband. 'You see what I have to put up with? If ever there was such an ungrateful wretch. Oh, go up to your room, girl, and change for dinner. Henry, where are you going?'

'I am also going up to change, my dear,' said her long-suffering husband. 'I am engaged to dine at White's tonight, so you and Serena must excuse me.'

Serena quietly followed Henry out of the room, wishing that she, too, could escape what promised to be a depressing meal in the company of her sister-in-law.

'Well, now, Miss Serena, 'tis a beautiful morning.'

Serena winced at Polly's cheerful greeting. She heard the rattle of crockery and dragged herself up in bed so that her maid could place the tray across her lap.

'Will you be joining my lady for breakfast today, ma'am?'

Polly had asked the same question every morning since Serena had returned from Melham Court and Serena's reply never varied.

'Not today, Polly. A cup of tea will suffice.'

The maid's eyes moved to the plate of bread and butter lying on the tray, but she had given up trying to persuade her mistress to eat anything in the mornings. She left Serena to drink her tea while she bustled about the room, collecting together the clean chemise, stockings and gown that her mistress would wear that day.

'Lady Hambridge is expecting visitors this morning, Miss Serena, and she has asked that you wear the powder-blue muslin.'

'Visitors?'

'Miss Althea—Lady Newbold, I *should* say, miss. She is bringing Master Arthur to visit his grandmama.'

'Oh, Lord.'

Serena closed her eyes. Althea was Henry and Dorothea's only child. She was the same age as Serena but had already been married for two years and provided her husband with a lusty heir. Dorothea was understandably proud of her daughter's achievements, as she constantly reminded Serena. There was no doubt that Althea would want to hear every horrid detail of this latest scrape, while Serena would be expected to play the doting aunt to little Arthur who, in her opinion, was developing into a bad-tempered child.

She gave a little sigh. 'Pray give my apologies and say I have the headache.'

'I will, miss,' said Polly, shaking out the blue muslin. 'But not if you are going to mope around in your room all day. We'll get you dressed and you can stroll in the gardens.' The maid met Serena's questioning eyes with a determined look in her own. 'Are we agreed, miss?'

The sun shone down on Serena's bare head and the bright day lifted her spirits sufficiently for her to think Polly had been right to press her into going out of doors. She allowed her shawl to slip off her shoulders so she could feel the sun's comforting warmth on her skin. The black cloud that enveloped her spirits was still there, but it had thinned a little.

The crunch of footsteps on the gravel path behind her made her turn.

'Lord Quinn!' Her pulse quickened. Embarrassment, she thought, given the circumstances of their previous meeting.

He came towards her, his large frame blocking the sun. 'The butler told me you were taking the air.'

'And my sister?' She looked past him, expecting to see Dorothea hurrying along behind.

'Lady Hambridge has a guest, so I said not to bother her. I would find you myself.'

Serena imagined the servants falling back before him, if not cowed by his sheer size, then dominated by the force of his personality.

'Are you come to town to buy more artwork, my lord?'

'No, I came to see how you go on.'

He stopped, towering over her, the brim of his hat shadowing his face. He looked serious, which was an advantage, since it saved her the trouble of smiling.

'As you see, sir.'

'You are very pale. I had expected you to have fully recovered your looks by now.'

'You say what everyone else is thinking, my lord. Which is why I am in the garden today.'

'Then let us walk.'

'The path is not wide enough.'

'It is if you take my arm.'

Serena hesitated, then slipped her hand on to his sleeve and they strolled on.

'This is a very small garden, compared to your own grounds at Melham Court.'

'It is sufficient to give you an airing,' he replied. 'You have been indoors too long and have lost your bloom.' She winced and he said quickly, 'Forgive me, I am not in the habit of making pretty speeches.'

A wry smile flickered within her. 'I am becoming accustomed to it, my lord. It does not offend me.'

'It doesn't?' He stopped and looked down at her. 'My friends tell me I can be brutal.'

There was a shadow of concern in his hazel eyes. It disconcerted her and she looked away.

'You tell the truth. I appreciate that.'

They had completed a full circuit of the walled garden before Lord Quinn spoke again.

'I believe there has been some talk.'

'Yes. I was recognised, at the inn. My brother has denied it, of course, but to little effect.'

'And your keeping to the house has not helped.'

'No.' She touched her cheek. 'But it was agreed I should not be seen abroad until the bruises had died down.'

'Were they very painful?'

'No more than I deserve.'

The words were a whisper, but he heard them.

'Forsbrook is the villain here, Serena, not you.' He drew a breath, as if reining in his anger, and laid his free hand over her fingers, where they rested on his arm. 'You will come about, my dear.'

The change in tone brought a sudden constriction to her throat. She fought it down and with it the desire to tell him that she did not want to *come about*.

She said, 'My brother and his wife are doing their best to make sure of it. I have started going out in the carriage. They think it is very necessary that I am seen.' She bit her lip. 'You may not know, Sir Timothy set it about that the plan to elope was mine.'

'Yes, I had heard,' he growled. 'Hambridge has denied it, of course.'

'Yes, and I hear that Sir Timothy has left town now.'

'I know.' She looked up quickly and he added, 'I, er, persuaded him.'

Serena caught the dangerous note in his voice and decided it would not be wise to ask the means of his persuasion.

'That was kind of you, but the damage is done, I fear.' Serena thought of Dorothea, sitting with her daughter in the drawing room. She said lightly, 'My reputation is ruined. My sister-in-law says no one will marry me now.'

'I will, Serena. I will marry you.'

Chapter Five

There, he had said it. Quinn felt the little hand on his sleeve tremble.

'It…it is not your place to offer for me,' she said, her voice constricted. 'None of this is your fault. You should not be punished for another's wickedness.'

'You have a very low opinion of yourself, my dear, if you think it would be a punishment to marry you.'

'Pray do not joke with me, my lord.'

'I do not. I say nothing but the truth.'

She shook her head. 'I thank you for your kind offer, Lord Quinn, but I cannot accept.'

'Why not?'

'Because you have no reason to marry me.'

A hiss of exasperation escaped him. 'Serena, you spent the night in my house.'

'It was an act of kindness. You rescued me.'

'That is beside the point. I took you to Melham Court. Mrs Talbot prepared a bed for you, but my entire household is aware you were in my room until dawn. My neighbour was in town and heard the gossip about what occurred at Hitchin and he is already drawing his own conclusions. It is only a matter of time before it becomes public knowledge.'

She waved distractedly. 'But you do not *want* to marry me!'

He caught her hands and turned her to face him. 'I am one-and-thirty and I must marry one day. It may as well be you as anyone.'

A laugh escaped her. 'When you put it so prettily, my lord, how can I refuse?'

'Precisely.' He smiled. 'I think we shall deal very well together, Serena. You are not unintelligent, you will not expect us to live in each other's pockets and there is plenty to keep you occupied. I have several properties, some are let, but there is more than one that requires a mistress. Of course, if you would rather not trouble yourself with such things there are housekeepers—'

'No, no, my lord, I like to be busy and would happily run your houses. That is, if I should accept your offer.'

'Then what say you, Serena—will you be my wife?' He saw the troubled look in her eyes and turned away, fixing his attention on a bee hovering around a nearby rose bush. He cleared his throat. 'If you are worried about the...er...other duties of a wife, I give you my word I will not force myself upon you. We will have separate bedchambers, and I shall respect your wishes on that aspect of our marriage. I shall not touch you without your consent. Until you ask it of me.'

The image flashed into his mind of Serena rising from the bath, her hair curling wildly from the steam and the water running from her naked body. Could he do this? Could he share a house with this woman and not take her to his bed? Easily, he told himself. This was a marriage of expedience, to save his reputation as much as Serena's. The affections of neither party were engaged.

So why did he feel such disappointment at her next words?

'I am very grateful of the honour you do me, Lord Quinn, but I cannot accept your offer.' She withdrew her hands from his clasp. 'It is not right that you should suffer for the rest of your life on account of my folly.'

'Suffer? Madam, I do not consider marriage to you a cause of misery. I should count myself honoured to have secured your hand.' She looked up, her dark, liquid eyes shadowed with doubt. He said, 'I am not the marrying kind, Serena, but I *am* a target for the tricks and stratagems of every matchmaking mother in town. I have even been pursued into Hertfordshire, upon occasion. I soon learned that being civil has little effect on determined parents or their daughters.'

'So you became the rudest man in town,' she murmured, a faint smile replacing the frown in her eyes.

'Oh, I was already that,' he told her. 'I do not suffer fools gladly and my manner of plain speaking is not to everyone's taste, but many females are willing to overlook that, to secure a rich husband. There is a novel out at present which is very popular—you may have read it. It begins by asserting that every single man of large fortune must be in want of a wife.'

'Yes, I know it. But it is love that triumphs in the end. You may yet fall in love, my lord.'

'No, I assure you that will not happen.' Quinn paused. 'I was engaged, once, but the lady died.'

'I am very sorry.'

He waved a hand, as if to deflect her sympathy. 'It was a long time ago. The past is gone. We cannot change it.'

'No, but it can haunt us.' She twisted her hands together. 'Perhaps you remember my mother...no?' She gave a little smile. 'Then it is only right you know, so you may reconsider offering for me. She caused quite a scandal some dozen years ago when she ran off and married a rich Italian. My father had not been dead many months.' She gave a little shrug. 'I barely remember her. The thing is...' She paused again. 'I have been told that I am very like her, in looks. And now that I have created a scandal, they will say I am like her in other ways, too.'

'I do not believe that.'

She flushed. 'No, I do not *think* it is true.'

'Then let us waste no more time on it.' He waved an impatient hand. 'Consider this, instead. In marrying me you would gain the protection of my name.'

'And *you* would have protection from unscrupulous husband-hunters.'

'Exactly, madam. So, Serena, what is your answer?'

Quinn thought he should leave, give her time to consider the matter. He was about to suggest as much when a maid came hurrying towards them.

'Miss Russington, the mistress has asked that you come to the drawing room. Immediately.'

Serena looked at Polly, who shifted uncomfortably from one foot to the other.

'I beg your pardon, ma'am.' She cast a nervous look towards Lord Quinn. 'I told her ladyship that you was in the gardens and she said I was to fetch you at once, no excuses.' Polly dragged in a deep breath, as if steeling herself to continue. 'She said, ma'am, that if you're well enough to walk in the gardens then you're well enough to join her and Lady Newbold, and to look after Master Arthur.'

'And who the devil might these people be?' demanded Lord Quinn.

Serena explained. 'Lady Newbold is my niece, Lady Hambridge's daughter. Arthur is her son, a grossly indulged infant who cries all the time. Possibly because he is overfed,' she added thoughtfully. 'Dorothea will want me to amuse him so she and Althea can talk uninterrupted.'

'Very much like a spinster aunt with nothing better to do,' Quinn muttered.

He had voiced her own thoughts and Serena could not quite stifle a sigh.

'Perhaps you should let me accompany you,' he suggested. 'We could inform Lady Hambridge and her daughter that the situation has changed.' He was regarding her steadily. 'Well, madam, what do you say. Will you accept my hand in marriage?'

Polly gave a little squeak but Serena ignored it. Could she do this? Could she marry a man she barely knew? She considered the alternative. Months, possibly years of enduring Dorothea's constant jibes. She and Henry did not really want Serena in their house. Russ and Molly had their own family now. No one needed her. No one wanted her.

She took a breath. 'Yes, Lord Quinn. Yes, I will marry you.'

'Well, I must say, Sister, I never expected to see you settled so well!'

Henry was beaming down at her, but Serena felt none

of his delight. It was her wedding day, but the sense of detachment, of sleepwalking through each day, had intensified during the past two weeks. It was as if she was merely an observer, watching a story played out before her. It was not that Serena was unhappy, rather that nothing seemed to touch her.

Dorothea's shock when Lord Quinn had announced he and Serena were to be married had soon turned to rapture. There had been a brief battle of wills when it was announced they were to be married by special licence in Bruton Street; Lady Hambridge had wanted a big wedding, perhaps in Hanover Square, where they might invite the world to see that Serena was not ruined at all but, on the contrary, making a splendid alliance. However, Dorothea was no match for Lord Quinn, who told her bluntly that the ceremony would be a private one.

'It will take place here, madam. Or, if you prefer, at Melham Court, with no one but yourselves and my neighbour. Make your choice.'

Dorothea had bridled at that, but Henry had quietly pointed out that, as Serena's guardian, he felt obliged to stand the expense of her wedding. This hit the right note with his spouse, for the considering look she threw at Serena said clearly that she was in favour of spending as little as possible upon her ungrateful sister-in-law.

Serena herself was silent throughout this interchange. Quinn had asked her earlier, and in private, if she wished her wedding to be a grand affair and she had been emphatic in her denial. She could summon no enthusiasm at all for her forthcoming nuptials. She allowed Dorothea to decide upon her bridal clothes and made no demur when she was informed that, apart from her brother and sister-in-law, the only witnesses to the ceremony would be Lord and Lady Newbold, and Quinn's neighbours, the Beckfords.

When Quinn had suggested she should invite a friend to support her, Serena had declined. She had lost touch with her friends from the various schools she had attended and since then Miss Downing had become her closest friend. In normal circumstances she would have wanted Elizabeth present, but Serena was too ashamed of the way she had deceived the Downings to invite them. So now here she was on her wedding day, in the drawing room of Bruton Street with only a handful of guests around her and feeling more alone than ever.

Quinn appeared at her side. 'You are very pale. Serena. Are you feeling faint? Would you like to sit down?'

'Tush, man, of course she does not wish to sit!' replied Henry. 'Serena never faints. She has more energy than the rest of us put together.'

'Then you must excuse a new husband for being over-protective.' Quinn took her hand and pulled it on to his arm, holding it there in a warm clasp. 'If you will excuse us, Hambridge.'

He led her away, muttering under his breath. 'Damned, insensitive fellow. Does he not know you at all?'

Surprise pierced the grey cloak of indifference wrapped about Serena.

Not as well as you, apparently, my lord.

She said, mildly, 'He and Dorothea have their own concerns. Pray do not be too critical of them. They have always done their duty by me.'

'And your other brother has not even made the effort to attend.'

'Now there you are being unjust,' she protested, roused briefly from her lethargy. 'I explained to you that Russ has a new daughter. I wrote to him, expressly forbidding him to leave Molly and the baby at such a time.'

She did not add that it had been necessary to hint at a whirlwind romance between herself and Quinn, to stop Russ posting south.

'I confess I should have liked them here,' she murmured.

'Then we shall call on them as soon as they are receiving visitors.'

'Thank you, my lord, you are very kind.'

He turned to face her. 'I am nothing of the sort. It is my duty now to attend to your comfort, Serena.'

Again, she felt a little kick of pleasure that he should think well of her, when she was so undeserving. She glanced up to find him regarding her, a faint smile in his eyes.

'The spirited lady who upbraided me in the Grindleshams' rose garden would expect nothing less of her husband.'

A stronger sensation jolted her, making her pulse race and the nerve ends tingle throughout her body.

She shook her head, her cheeks burning. 'How can you even refer to that meeting, knowing how foolishly, how *shamefully* I behaved? The creature I was then is quite, quite dead, my lord.'

'Oh, I hope not.' Her eyes flew to his face. Had she heard him correctly? He flicked her cheek with a careless finger. 'Never mind that now. I see my neighbours are eager to congratulate us. Come along.'

He led her towards Sir Anthony and Lady Beckford,

who were smiling and nodding at them from the far side of the room. Serena had only been introduced to them that morning, but now Sir Anthony reached out for her hands and lifted one then the other to his lips.

'Lady Quinn, may I offer you my congratulations?'

'Nonsense, it is Quinn who is to be congratulated upon winning himself such a lovely bride.' Lady Beckford bustled her husband out of the way and kissed Serena's cheek. 'You cannot know how delighted I am to have you as a neighbour, my dear. I hope we will be welcoming you to Prior's Holt very soon.'

'Thank you, my lady.'

'No, no, we shall not stand on ceremony—you must call me Lottie and I shall call you Serena, if I may? I am sure we shall spend many a happy hour closeted together and complaining about our husbands!'

Sir Anthony protested at that, trying to look severe and telling his wife to behave, but Lottie was irrepressible. She slid one arm about Serena.

'One always needs a close friend with whom one can grumble without it being taken seriously. Tony, Quinn and his lady must dine with us as soon as possible after the honeymoon. Where are you taking her, Quinn? Now the horrid war is over will you go abroad—Italy, perhaps?' She paused and looked from Serena to Quinn and back again. 'You *are* going away, are you not?'

'Lottie, pray do not be so inquisitive.' Tony frowned at his wife. 'It is none of our business.'

'It is no secret,' said Quinn. 'We spend tonight at Melham Court and tomorrow we set off to tour my estates. Serena must decide which, if any, she wishes to use.'

'But I thought most of them are let,' said Lottie.

'They are, but that is a minor problem, if Serena takes a fancy to one of them.'

Tears stung the back of Serena's eyes at Quinn's concern for her wishes.

Dorothea came up, smiling graciously at everyone. 'Serena, my dear, we have prepared a wedding breakfast for our guests, if you and Lord Quinn would like to lead the way to the dining room?'

He held out his arm. 'Well, madam wife, shall we go in?'

Quinn tasted nothing of the light repast laid out for him. Serena, too, he noticed only picked at her food in silence. Thank heaven Tony and Lottie were present to make polite conversation with their hosts and the Newbolds.

Lady Hambridge might have been denied her grand ceremony, but when the time came for Quinn and his bride to leave, she insisted they wait while the servants were marshalled to line the hall for their departure. All the guests spilled out on to the flagway to see them off and Dorothea even went so far as to embrace Serena.

'I hope you realise your good fortune, madam. Lord Quinn has saved you from shame and disgrace. I pray he will not live to regret it.'

Her words were softly spoken but Quinn heard them. He saw the flush on Serena's cheek and a flash of irritation ran through him. What a dragon the woman was, to say such a thing to a bride on her wedding day! For Serena's sake he took polite leave of her family but exchanged warmer farewells with Lottie and Tony before handing his bride into the waiting chaise. As the door closed upon them and they rattled away along the

street, he sat back with a sigh. Then he turned his head
to look at his new wife, sitting quietly beside him, hands
folded in her lap.

'Well, Serena?'

She gave him a little smile. 'I am very grateful to
you, my lord.'

His brows snapped together. 'Confound it, madam, I
do not *want* your gratitude.' She flinched, distress shadowing her dark eyes, and he cursed his harsh tongue and
hasty temper. He said more gently, 'I beg your pardon,
I was not always such a brute, but I have lived alone
for too long and have forgotten my manners. They will
improve, you have my word upon it.'

She was looking down at her hands and he noticed
how tightly they were clenched together.

'I only hope you will not regret marrying me, sir.'

*Damn Lady Hambridge for putting that thought in
her head!*

'We agreed this marriage was to the advantage of
both of us, did we not, madam?'

'Yes, but—'

He put his fingers to her lips. 'Hush now. We shall
deal extremely well together, my dear, trust me.'

Serena's heart skipped a beat. The gesture was gentle, even affectionate, and he was smiling at her, his
hazel eyes warm.

'I do.' She said again, more strongly, 'I do trust you,
my lord.'

'Good.'

His fingers slid from her lips and he cupped her
cheek. It was an intimate gesture and for an instant she
wanted to press against his palm and absorb some of

his strength. Her eyelids drooped as something stirred, deep inside: pleasure, anticipation. Desire. She wanted to chase the fleeting sensation, explore and enjoy it, but all too soon it was gone, replaced by a dark and undefined feeling of terror.

Her eyes flew open. Suddenly the air within the carriage was charged with menace. She was back in the candlelit bedroom at the Swan, with Sir Timothy bearing down on her, his hands around her neck. Serena could not help herself, she recoiled, shuddering. Immediately Quinn's hand dropped. He turned away from her to look out of the window, pointing at an inn sign as it flashed into view.

'Ah. We are passing Old Mother Red Cap's. So we are not yet at Highgate. Plenty of time to sleep, if you wish. It has been a busy morning.'

Quinn's tone was conversational and Serena's panic subsided. He settled back in his corner and closed his eyes and she drew in a deep, steadying breath. He had told her he would not force his attentions upon her and he was keeping his word. She felt a sudden rush of gratitude. Rufus Quinn might be known as the rudest man in London, but to her he had shown nothing but kindness.

The steady rocking of the carriage was soothing, but Serena was too on edge to sleep. However, she no longer dreaded their arrival at Melham Court. There would inevitably be some gossip, for the servants knew of her previous visit, but for the first time she thought that with Quinn's support it would not be so very bad.

In another example of his thoughtfulness, he had ordered the coachman to avoid Hitchin. The new route was slightly longer and the road a little rougher, but

Serena was glad they would not pass the Swan and revive those terrifying memories.

She was not sure if Quinn was really sleeping, but he kept to his corner with his eyes closed until they were on the final approach to Melham Court, when he sat up and stretched.

'The house should be in sight by now,' he told her, glancing out of the window. He gave a little bark of laughter. 'And my people have gone out of their way to welcome you. Look.'

Leaning forward, Serena peered through the glass as the carriage bowled around the last, sweeping curve and she saw that the bridge and the arch of the gatehouse had been decorated with flowers and gaily coloured ribbons which fluttered in the breeze.

The team did not check as they rattled across the bridge and through the arch into the courtyard, where the servants were all waiting to greet them. Serena spotted Meggy, the serving girl who had looked after her on her first visit, and also Polly, who was now her full-time maid. Henry had agreed to Polly leaving his employ and she had travelled to Melham Court earlier that morning, along with Serena's baggage.

Unlike the staff of Hambridge House, who had lined the hall in solemn silence to see them off, Lord Quinn's servants were milling around the courtyard, laughing and cheering as the carriage came to a halt. More ribbons and flowers adorned the courtyard, hanging from the upper windows and forming a decorative arch around the open door, where the housekeeper and butler were waiting. Quinn jumped down and turned back to give Serena his hand.

'Welcome to your new home, Lady Quinn.'

Serena had made up her mind that, however hard it might be, she would look cheerful upon her arrival at Melham Court, but in the event it was no effort at all. The delight of the servants was infectious and, with her hand tucked snugly into the crook of Quinn's arm, she went with him into the house. The butler and Mrs Talbot fell back before them and there was no doubting that their smiles and words of welcome were genuine.

The newlyweds were ushered into the drawing room where Mrs Talbot bustled about them, pointing out the cakes and wine on a side table for their delectation and asking in the same breath if Lady Quinn would like to rest before taking refreshments.

Serena smiled. 'My lord's carriage is so comfortable I am not at all fatigued, I assure you. A little wine would be very welcome, I think.'

She untied the strings of her cloak and immediately Quinn was behind her, lifting it from her shoulders. He handed it to Mrs Talbot to take away before going across to the table to pour two glasses of wine.

'You were anxious about your reception here, I believe.' He handed her a glass. 'I hope this relieves your mind. Believe me, it is none of my doing.'

'I *am* reassured, thank you.' She took a sip of the wine. It was rich and fruity, and would no doubt make her light-headed if she drank too much of it. She put it down on the mantelshelf. 'I hope the welcome will be as warm at all your houses.'

'At the first of them it will be, I am sure of it, because we travel to my hunting lodge in Leicestershire. As to the properties which are let, Johnson, my steward, has written to request that we may call, but I have made it clear we will be staying at local hostelries. In the main they are very good and we shall not be uncomfortable.' He emptied his glass and went back to the table to put it down. 'I told Johnson to bespeak separate bedchambers for us at every stop. And here, too, you have your own rooms.'

Quinn's broad back was towards her and Serena had no indication of his mood. The thought that he was happy with the arrangement, that he did not want her, was strangely dispiriting, even though the idea of consummating their marriage filled her with a blind panic.

She said carefully, 'If that is your wish, my lord.'

'No, but it is yours, I believe.'

His blunt honesty disarmed her and she hung her head. She was staring at the floor when his feet appeared within her view. He put his fingers beneath her chin and tilted it up until she was looking into his face. She felt dwarfed by his presence. He towered over her, blocking her view of everything save his broad shoulders in their covering of superfine broadcloth.

He was so close that she could see the exquisite tailoring of his coat and appreciate the fine linen of his shirt and neckcloth. She thought she could even detect the fresh smell of clean linen and a hint of spicy soap on his skin. When she had first seen him this morning his brown hair had been brushed back, but now it hung over his brow, too long to be fashionable but giving his rugged features a boyish look.

'I told you I should not press you,' he said, holding her gaze. 'You shall come to me when *you* are ready and not before.'

She gave a tremulous smile and did not move as he slowly lowered his head towards her. She froze, waiting for the black, blinding terror, but it did not come. His fingers pushed her chin a little higher and, nervously, she ran her tongue over her lips. His head was too close now for her eyes to focus and she closed them. She felt his mouth brush hers, fleeting and light as a butterfly. It was over in an instant, but the sensations that shot through her body startled her. A white heat that made her want to grab him and drag his mouth back to hers. To lose herself in his kiss.

Slowly her eyes opened. Quinn had raised his head but he was watching her, his gaze more intense, as if he was looking into her soul. When he removed his hand from her chin she felt unsteady, as if she was standing on the edge of a cliff, ready to topple. Quickly she took a step back.

'I… I should change for dinner.' Another step, but instead of feeling safer as she moved away she felt the panic growing. She fluttered a hand. 'N-no need to ring for the housekeeper, I will find her, or someone…'

And with that she turned and fled.

Quinn did not move until she was gone. Then he raised one fist and placed the back of it against his mouth. He could still taste her sweetness, still feel the soft cushion of her lips against his. She had not shuddered. Had not pulled away from him.

'Well,' he said to the empty room. 'That's progress, I suppose.'

It was late July before Quinn brought Serena back to Hertfordshire. Within days of their return, Charlotte Beckford sent them an invitation to dine at Prior's Holt.

'I hope you do not object that you are the only guests,' said Lottie, when she welcomed them into the elegant drawing room. 'After such a long time traipsing around the country I thought you might like a quiet little dinner.'

'Yes, thank you.' Serena perched on the edge of a sofa. 'We dined with several of Quinn's tenants during our travels, but it was all rather formal. They were very much aware that he is their landlord.'

'And did you visit *all* your estates, even Northumberland?' asked Tony. 'That must have been a gruelling schedule.'

'No.' Quinn carried two glasses of wine over to the sofa and took a seat beside Serena. 'We only went as far north as Leicester before going to Devon, then on to Sussex, where we took the opportunity to stop a few nights in Worthing.'

'Worthing!' Tony exclaimed. 'What in heaven's name took you there?'

'You forget, my dear,' said Lottie, a laugh trembling in her voice. 'The Hambridges were going to Worthing directly after the wedding and with Redlands being only ten miles away, it would have looked odd if they had *not* called in.'

'Aye, it would,' Quinn agreed. 'They are there with the Newbolds.'

Serena did not miss the horrified look that passed between Tony and his wife.

'And, you stayed with them?'

Quinn shook his head. 'I had already contacted an old friend who was delighted to put us up. I do not think my wife was too unhappy with the arrangement.'

He glanced at Serena, his eyes warm with amusement, and she could not but smile in response. The days spent in Sussex had been the most interesting and enjoyable of the whole tour. Redlands, Quinn's Sussex property, was a grand Palladian mansion, much used for entertaining by Quinn's parents, but he had leased it to a rich nabob who had returned from India with a large fortune and ambitions to match. Ten minutes in his tenant's company had shown Serena why Quinn had advised they refuse the invitation to stay at the house and instead they had been the guests of Dr Young and his wife, Eliza.

It was not long before Serena realised that her husband's friend was the celebrated polymath, Thomas Young. The doctor was quite delighted when Serena told him she knew of his work on decipherment of Egyptian hieroglyphs, and more specifically the Rosetta Stone, and when the gentlemen joined the ladies in the drawing room each evening their discussions ranged widely, from medicine, physics and Egyptology to Dr Young's thoughts on tuning musical instruments and his abhorrence of slavery.

'A visit to Henry and Dorothea was unavoidable, since we were in the area,' Serena said now, 'but I was very glad we were not obliged to stay with them.'

'Aye,' added Quinn, with feeling. 'One dinner in their company was quite sufficient. However, Serena assures me her other brother, Russ, is a very different character. He and his family live in the north. Yorkshire, I believe. We will visit them on our way to the Northumberland house. I want to show Serena the coalmines.'

'Coal!' Lottie pulled a face.

'They are very lucrative, even if they are not beautiful,' remarked Tony, laughing at his wife's look of distaste. 'However, visiting properties ranging from Devon to Leicestershire and Sussex in six weeks is no mean feat. You must be completely fatigued, Lady Quinn.'

That had been the point of it, thought Serena. Travelling the breadth of the country, driving about each of the estates, meeting tenants, talking to stewards and local villagers. There had been no time or energy for dalliance. Her husband had been attentive and friendly, dinners had been companionable enough, but every night Serena left Quinn alone with his brandy and retired to her room. Mostly she fell into a deep, dreamless sleep of exhaustion, but some nights her slumbers were disturbed by dark, terrifying nightmares: Sir Timothy ripping her clothes, pressing hot, brandy-fumed kisses upon her, dragging her back from the window when she shrieked for someone to help her.

'Scream if you wish,' he had jeered, throwing her down on the bed. 'Do you think anyone can hear you? Do you think anyone *cares*?'

'And what did you think of the other houses, Lady Quinn?' Serena jumped as Lady Beckford addressed her. 'Are you going to turn out any of the tenants?'

'Lottie!'

'What have I said?' She raised her brows at her husband. 'Is that not what Quinn told us he would do, if Serena wanted to live in one of them?'

Quinn laughed. 'I did, but you need not fear for my tenants just yet. We have the hunting lodge in Leicestershire and my wife tells me she is not enamoured of any of the other properties.'

'They are all very fine,' put in Serena, 'but most are very large. I prefer Melham Court and I agree with

Quinn—it is better that the properties are occupied rather than standing empty for most of the year.'

'Well I for one am very relieved to hear it,' Lottie told her. 'I think we are going to be very good friends, Serena!'

Chapter Six

Lottie repeated this sentiment when the two ladies retired to the drawing room after dinner.

'Tony will be glad not to lose Quinn's company. They have been friends for ever, you know, and went to the same school. It might even be said they grew up together.'

'Oh?' Serena was puzzled. 'I thought Quinn's family preferred houses where they might entertain in style.'

'They did.' Lottie sat down on the sofa and patted the seat, inviting Serena to join her. 'However, they left Quinn in Hertfordshire for most of the year, until he was old enough to go to school.'

'Ah, poor boy!'

'Quite.' Lottie's cheerful face showed uncharacteristic disapproval. 'Fortunately, Tony's family is an ancient one and Lord and Lady Quinn considered him a suitable companion, so Quinn spent a great deal of his time here at Prior's Holt.'

Serena shifted in her seat. 'Perhaps you should not be telling me this, if your husband told you in confidence.'

'No, no, my family lived nearby, you see, and most

of it is common knowledge locally. But if you would rather not hear any more—'

'On the contrary,' Serena assured her. 'I would like to know as much as possible. Everything. It might help me to be a better wife.' She flushed. 'You are aware that the circumstances of our marriage are somewhat… unusual.'

Lottie gave her a speaking look and reached across to squeeze her hand.

She continued, 'Quinn received a great deal more affection here than from his own parents. It came as no surprise when he offered for Tony's sister.'

'Ah.' Quinn's words came back to Serena. 'She died, I believe?'

'Yes. Poor Barbara. Such a lively girl. She was barely a year younger than Quinn and they were inseparable. They wanted to marry once she reached eighteen but Quinn's parents refused to countenance a match. They had selected a viscount's daughter for his bride. Quinn stood firm, though. He and Barbara were engaged as soon as he reached his majority.' She spread her hands and gave a loud sigh. 'Barbara went off to town to purchase her bride clothes and contracted a fever while she was there. She was dead within the month. Poor Quinn—he loved her so much. He has hated London ever since and rarely goes into society.'

Lottie paused and Serena could think of nothing to say to fill the silence. She knew what it was like to be brought up by nannies and tutors, and her heart went out to the lonely child Quinn had been. And then how devastating to lose the love of his life so cruelly.

'But that is all changed now.' Lottie gave herself a little shake, throwing off the melancholy thoughts.

'We always hoped Quinn would find someone else to make him happy.'

'You mistake,' stammered Serena. 'It is n-not a love match.'

'Not yet, but you are so beautiful I have no doubt he will soon fall in love with you,' replied Lottie comfortably. 'Tell me, is there any indication that you might be in an *interesting state*? Oh, now I have made you blush! Pray forgive me, Serena. I should not be asking such questions, should I? Tony is always chiding me for being far too forward.'

'No, no, I am not offended, but, no, I am n-not with child...'

Lottie reached out and caught her hands. 'Do not worry, my dear, there is plenty of time. Your marriage is very young yet.'

Serena murmured her agreement and sought for a way to turn the conversation away from her marriage.

'Do you have children, Lady Beckford?'

'Call me Lottie, my dear, I pray you.' She smiled, but a shadow passed across her face. 'Alas, no. I suffered an illness in the early years of our marriage, you see, which has left my heart weak. We have consulted the best doctors in the land but they are all agreed that it would be unwise for me to bear a child.'

'Oh, I am sorry.'

'Do not be. Tony and I came to terms with the fact long ago and have a very happy life, I assure you.' She gave Serena a quick, mischievous look. 'And I hope you will make us godparents to your own children, that we may spoil them quite shamelessly!'

Serena wondered what Lottie would say if she knew that the marriage was not even consummated, but she summoned up a laugh, determined her new friend should not suspect there was anything amiss. However, it was with relief that she heard the door open and the gentlemen came in, putting an end to further confidences.

Quinn followed his host into the drawing room and his eyes went immediately to Serena. He thought how good it was to hear her laugh, but when he drew closer he saw that the merriment did not reach her eyes and he was surprised how much that disturbed him. How much he wanted to make her happy.

He gave her a small, reassuring smile and lowered himself into a chair near the empty fireplace, where he could watch her. There was no doubt she was beautiful, with her golden curls, chocolate-coloured eyes and her serene smile, but she had a distant, detached air and he was haunted by the memory of the first time he had seen her, full of energy, her eyes sparking fire at him.

'What say you, Quinn?' Tony's voice jolted him back to the present.

'I beg your pardon, what was that?'

'You know we always hold a ball every summer, but this year Lottie deliberately delayed until you returned, because she wants to introduce your new bride to the neighbourhood. It will not be a very large affair, mainly local families, although we have invited some of our friends from town, those who have not gone off to Brighton for the summer.'

From across the room Lottie wagged her finger at Quinn. 'You have refused my invitations thus far, my lord, but you cannot do so this time.'

'Indeed, I cannot. If my wife wishes to attend then we shall do so.' He looked a question at Serena.

'Of course. We are delighted to accept.'

Was he the only one to notice the lack of enthusiasm in her response? She wanted company no more than he. In that, at least, they were in accord.

The drive back to Melham Court was accomplished in silence. It was impossible to pierce the darkness, but Serena was aware of Quinn's abstraction. Prior's Holt was the home of his lost love. Did visiting there remind him of Barbara? She could not ask him such a question, but she longed to reach out for his hand, to comfort him and take comfort in return. Instead they remained in their separate corners for the journey.

'It has been a tiring evening,' Quinn remarked as he handed her out of the carriage. 'Shall I escort you directly to your room?'

'Yes, thank you.' As they made their way up the stairs she asked him a question that had been teasing her. 'Would you rather we did not go to Lady Beckford's ball?'

'By no means. You know I am not fond of such events, but I think it is necessary that we go to this, do not you?'

'Why yes, I do.' She risked a tiny smile. 'I have no doubt your neighbours will be agog to see your new bride.'

'They will indeed.' They had reached the door of her chamber and he stopped. 'We shall at some point be obliged to hold something similar here, but this will relieve you of the necessity of planning anything of that nature just yet.'

'Oh?' Her head came up. 'Do you think I could not do it?'

'I am sure you could, but I would like you to take your time to settle into your new home.'

He raised her hand to his lips, murmured goodnight and walked away, leaving Serena to enter her chamber where she found Polly dozing in a chair.

'Oh, lawks, my lady, I beg your pardon. I tried so hard to stay awake.'

She waved away the maid's apologies. 'I see no reason why you should not rest while you wait for me.'

Polly bustled around, helping her into her nightgown, and Serena allowed her thoughts to wander. She was disappointed at the little spurt of anger that had caused her to challenge Quinn like that, for she had resolved to maintain an attitude of quiet obedience towards her husband. After all, he had rescued her from a shameful escapade and deserved nothing less than a conformable wife, as Dorothea had pointed out to her constantly in the days leading up to the wedding.

'It was your wilfulness that brought you to this pass, Serena. You must curb that headstrong nature of yours. No man wants to be married to a termagant!'

'Would you like me to stay and brush out your curls, ma'am?'

'Thank you, Polly, but I can do that. Off you go to bed now.'

When the maid had gone, Serena sat at her dressing table and pulled the brush slowly through her hair. Day and night her sister-in-law's words ran through her head, a never-ending litany. Since the wedding she had tried to be a model wife and Quinn appeared quite content.

Certainly, he had made no physical demands upon her. Apart from that one kiss, on their wedding day.

It was seared in her memory, the feel of his lips on hers, the sudden scorching desire that had shocked her to the core. She had run away from him then and he had made no effort to detain her, or to kiss her again. He was unfailingly polite and considerate, but it appeared that Quinn did not want her, termagant or no.

A week later they were back at Prior's Holt for the Beckfords' ball. It was their first formal engagement and a little shiver ran down Serena's back as the liveried servant announced them. Lord and Lady Quinn. There was no going back now.

Quinn put his hand over her fingers, where they rested on his arm.

'Nervous?'

She glanced up at him. She had prepared carefully for the evening, choosing to wear once more the gown she had worn on her wedding day. The cream muslin was decorated at the neck, sleeves and hem with delicately embroidered apricot flowers and a tracery of leaves, all enhanced by silver thread work. She had allowed Polly to nestle matching roses among her curls and had put on the diamond ear drops and necklace that Quinn had given her as a wedding gift. In looks at least she hoped she would not disappoint.

'I trust I shall not let you down, my lord.'

He squeezed her hand. 'You could never do that, Serena.'

She straightened her shoulders and raised her head. She had little interest in what anyone thought of her, but this was Quinn's neighbourhood and she wanted to make a good impression, for his sake.

Lottie came forward to greet them, Tony only a step behind. Serena was enveloped in a warm, scented embrace before her hostess carried her away, bent upon introducing the new bride to as many people as possible before the dancing began.

'I am so glad you did not come fashionably late,' she said, linking arms with Serena. 'The dancing will not commence for an hour yet, so we have plenty of time for introductions. You will be acquainted with most of our guests from town, I am sure. Indeed, one is a close friend of yours, I believe. But our near neighbours are all impatient to meet you.'

'Should we not wait for my husband?' asked Serena, hanging back.

Lottie gave a little laugh. 'You must not worry about Quinn. He is the most unsociable man I know and would not enjoy doing the pretty. Much better to leave him with Tony. Now, let me see, who shall be first? Let us begin with Sir Grinwald and Lady Brook, the local magistrate and his wife...'

Time passed in a whirl of new names and faces for Serena. She was aware that behind the polite greetings and questions, Lottie's guests were all very curious. As Sir Grinwald put it, most improperly, they wanted to know what had made the old dog put his head in the parson's mousetrap at last. For the first time she was grateful that Dorothea had insisted she should be well versed in the social graces. Now that training came to her aid. She smiled and talked, responding to compliments and turning off sly questions about married life with an elegant riposte.

Everyone was charming, but Serena was not fooled. Quinn's immediate neighbours were genuinely welcoming, but she detected a coolness in those who mixed more in London society. They had heard the rumours and were reserving judgement upon the new Lady Quinn.

There was only one awkward moment. Lottie was glancing about her, wondering who next should be presented to the new bride, when Serena spotted Mrs Downing across the room, accompanied by her son and daughter. Shock held her motionless, then she recalled Lottie's words about the guests here tonight: *one is a close friend of yours.* She meant Elizabeth, of course.

How wrong Lottie was to think they could still be friends, thought Serena, wretchedly. She was not aware of holding her breath, until Lottie tugged her arm and led her off to introduce her to an elderly couple who were near neighbours. It was only then she realised how relieved she was that she need not face the Downings. Not yet.

'Well, it is going very well,' announced Lottie at last. 'Now let us go through to the ballroom, for that scraping of fiddles tells me the musicians are ready to strike up. To whom shall we allow the honour of the first dance with you, I wonder?'

'No one.' Quinn appeared, his large frame blocking their way. 'You have done quite enough for now, Lottie. I have come to claim my bride for the first two dances.'

His manner brooked no argument and with no more than a half-hearted pout, their hostess stood aside.

'Very well, my lord, I suppose you may do so, if you wish.'

'I do wish it.' He held out his hand to Serena. 'Come along, madam.'

Lottie's eyes widened at his peremptory tone and she shot one final, mischievous glance at Serena before walking away.

'Was I impolite?' he muttered, as he escorted Serena on to the dance floor.

'Exceedingly,' she responded. 'But I am very glad you came for me. My head is spinning from so many introductions. It will be a relief to dance with you.'

'You may quickly change your mind on that,' he warned her. 'I am sadly out of practice.'

But when the dance started Serena discovered that her husband was an excellent dancer. For such a big man he was very light on his feet and moved through the dance with the lithe grace of a wild animal. Not a bear at all, she thought. A big cat. Powerful. Agile. Dangerous.

As he clasped her hand for the promenade she missed her step and immediately his hold tightened, steadying her. She looked up to convey her thanks, but all thought of gratitude faded under the blaze of possession she saw in his eyes. For an instant the heaviness that constantly overlaid her spirits was pierced, like sunshine breaking through rainclouds.

The carefree girl she had been would have revelled in that look. The old Serena would have agreed to accompany him on any adventure, stand shoulder to shoulder with him to face any danger. No. She dragged her eyes away. That wilful creature was no more. She would be a good wife who would cause him no trouble.

Who would have thought a dance could be so pleasurable? As Quinn turned, circled and promenaded with

Serena he knew he had never enjoyed a dance more. True, his partner was extremely beautiful and at least half the men in the room envied him his place with her, but that did not matter. If they had been alone in the ballroom he would have been just as happy. He felt an overriding urge to protect her and when she stumbled he was ready, his grip sure, supporting her. Even such a small service gave him a rush of pleasure, heightened by the grateful look she threw at him. It was a fleeting glance and disappointment stabbed him when she looked away.

The two dances were over all too soon and even as they left the floor Lottie was waiting for them, Serena's next partner at her side. At least it was Atherton, Quinn thought grimly. Fifty, if he was a day, and happily married. Quinn made his way to the card room, knowing that if he remained in the ballroom he would be obliged to dance, and how could he give his attention to his partner while Serena was dancing with another man?

However, he soon discovered that even cards could not hold his attention. The music was audible from the card room and when he heard a new tune he wondered who was now dancing with Serena. Was it another elderly neighbour, or some young buck intent upon flirtation?

'Come along, my lord, we are waiting for you.'

The jovial voice of a fellow player cut through Quinn's thoughts and he selected his discard. It was quickly swept up by his neighbour, who gave a triumphant cry and displayed his winning hand. Quinn felt a touch on his shoulder and looked round to find Tony beside him.

'Not like you to make such an error.'

'No.' Quinn threw in his hand and rose from the table. 'I am playing abominably tonight. Let us return to the ballroom. I want to see how my wife does.'

'Serena is doing very well, my friend, trust me.'

'I should still like to see for myself.'

'No doubt you intend to stand, brooding, at the side of the room and watch her like a lovesick moonling?' Tony laughed. 'Lottie would never allow that.'

'Is it any wonder I never attend these dashed events?' muttered Quinn, scowling.

Tony grinned. 'You will have to accustom yourself to this sort of thing, now you are married. Unless you are prepared to dance with one or other of the ladies present, you had best come to the library with me, out of the way.' When Quinn hesitated he added quietly, 'You may safely leave Lottie to look after your wife, old friend.'

They went across the hall to the study, where a decanter and glasses stood on the desk.

'This is my bolthole,' explained Tony. 'I always find time to slip away here for a while. Of course, I must not be absent for too long or I shall incur Lottie's wrath, but one is rarely missed for the odd half-hour. Sit down and I will bring you a glass of wine. I had it fetched from Averys in Bristol, as you suggested. I believe it was worth the longer journey.'

Two wing chairs flanked the empty hearth. Quinn lowered himself into one and for a while silence reigned.

'So, my friend, what is your opinion of married life?'

Quinn studied his glass. 'It is not uncomfortable. Serena and I find we have much in common.'

'I am glad to hear it. And when do you go to town?'

'We do not.'

'Oh? You are still recovering perhaps from your

jauntering all over the country. But once you are rested you will be hiring a house in town, I am sure.'

'We have no plans to visit London.' Quinn glanced up. 'That surprises you? I do not see why it should. Neither Serena nor I wish for society. You are aware of the circumstances of our marriage, the rumours and gossip. I would not ask my wife to face that.'

Tony hesitated, 'It might be better to face it now than have people say your wife is in hiding.'

Quinn frowned. 'They would not dare.'

'Not in your presence, certainly, but there are rumours about why you married her.' Tony coughed. 'Some might think you are ashamed of your bride.'

'Ashamed! No, indeed, quite the contrary. Serena is not only beautiful but intelligent, too, and well educated.' He sat forward, grinning. 'If you could have seen her at Worthing, Tony, when we were staying with the Youngs. She is well read and has an enquiring mind. She knows enough about Egyptology to put some pertinent questions to Thomas. He was most impressed and has invited us to attend his next lectures.'

'That will mean going to London.'

'Yes, but we will not stay more than a night or two, as I have done in the past. We need not go into society.'

'You would turn Serena into a recluse like yourself.' Tony's countenance was unusually solemn. 'We were not acquainted with Serena when she was Miss Russington, but one saw her everywhere and could not fail to notice her. Oh, it was nothing detrimental, my friend, so you need not show hackle! She had a reputation as a cheerful, spirited young lady who could be relied upon to bring life to the dullest party. Lottie tells me her admirers swore she could light up a room.'

'Could she?' Quinn thought of the first time he had seen Serena, fire in her eyes and an angry flush upon her cheek. Had that fire been extinguished, or was it merely damped down?

'Her family kept her pretty well hedged about, of course,' Tony continued. 'But that is understandable, given her history.'

'They stifled her,' said Quinn. 'If Hambridge and his wife had not tried to clip her wings she would not have felt it necessary to give them the slip.'

'But that is just it, my friend. She may not have intended any harm, but there is no denying she did go off unescorted.'

'Marriage should have reinstated her.'

'I'm afraid not.' Tony fixed his eyes on Quinn. 'It has only given credence to Forsbrook's claim that she left him when a more attractive proposition presented itself.'

Quinn jumped to his feet, cursing roundly. He strode up and down the room, his brow furrowed.

'I had hoped that particular story had been forgotten.'

'It might have been, if Forsbrook wasn't back in town and presenting himself as the injured party. The thing is,' Tony went on slowly, 'there are some who say that Serena is following in her mother's footsteps.'

'The devil they are! Then I must deal with Forsbrook once and for all!'

'Call him out? That would only add fuel to the fire.'

Quinn stopped pacing and ran a hand over his face. 'Then what do you suggest I do to protect my wife?'

'It strikes me that you have two options. You could keep Serena from town and make a pleasant enough life for yourself in the provinces.'

'As you said earlier, turn her into a recluse, like myself.' Quinn met his friend's eyes steadily. 'And the second option?'

'Take her to London, face down the gossips. Serena has been used to town life—parties, concerts, the theatre, debating societies—you, too, once enjoyed those things.' He grinned suddenly. 'Not so much the parties, perhaps, where you were surrounded by flatterers and matchmaking mamas, but the rest of it.' Tony pushed himself out of his chair and stood before Quinn, one hand resting on his shoulder. 'You have shut yourself away since Barbara died. Society is not all bad, my friend. Perhaps it is time you started living again.' He glanced at the ormolu clock on the mantelshelf as it chimed the half-hour. 'Our guests will be going into supper shortly. We should join our wives.'

Since when had dancing become a chore? Serena kept her smile in place as she went down the dance with her latest partner. Sir Grinwald was not only the local magistrate but also one of Quinn's closest neighbours. He was a kindly gentleman and she could not blame him if she was not enjoying herself. She could not blame any of her partners. It was just that she did not *feel* anything tonight.

No, she corrected herself, that was not quite true. She had felt something when she danced with Quinn. A certain *frisson*, a little thrill of excitement.

The sort of thing I was seeking in a husband.

The thought brought a little flush of remorse to her cheeks as she recalled how reckless she had been. But no more. In future she would be the very model of decorum. The music ended and Sir Grinwald led her off the floor to where his wife was waiting.

'I must find Lady Beckford,' said Serena. 'She seems determined that I should dance all evening.'

'And why not?' declared Lady Brook, beaming at her. 'You young things have so much energy.'

Serena merely smiled. Such kind people would be hurt if they knew how little she wanted to be here. She turned away, her smile faltering as she found herself face to face with Miss Elizabeth Downing.

Chapter Seven

'Please, do not run away.' Elizabeth touched her arm. 'I was looking for you, to find out how you go on. I have been worried about you.'

Serena hung her head. 'How can you, after the way I tricked you and your family?'

'We are friends.' Elizabeth stepped closer, saying quietly, 'And as a friend, tell me, if you will, and truthfully. Did you mean to elope with Sir Timothy that night?'

'No.' Serena sighed. 'I agreed to go with him to Vauxhall, but instead—'

'I thought as much,' said Elizabeth, relief warming her voice. 'I have heard his scandalous hints but I did not think even you would take such a step.'

Even you!

Serena closed her eyes as a wave of mortification washed over her. 'Oh, Lizzie, can you ever forgive me?'

'It is already done. Mama, too, is anxious to speak to you.' Elizabeth took her arm. 'Come along, she is waiting for us across the room.'

'Oh, no, I cannot face her.'

'Of course you can.'

Elizabeth tightened her grip. Mrs Downing was standing with a group of fashionable matrons and as the girls approached she turned to greet them, holding out her hands to Serena and drawing her forward to kiss her cheek. There was no mistaking the looks of surprise that passed between the other ladies as they witnessed such obvious affection. Mrs Downing cut short Serena's whispered apologies and drew the girls away from the interested stares of her companions.

'Enough of that now, my dear,' she said, squeezing Serena's arm. 'I was put out at first, but a little reflection convinced me it was a girlish prank that went horribly wrong.'

'It was,' muttered Serena, shuddering.

'But it is all over now,' Mrs Downing continued. 'You have come out of it remarkably well, when all is said and done. I, for one, am very pleased for you.'

'Thank you, ma'am.' Serena looked about her. 'And your son, is he here this evening?' She swallowed. 'Is he very angry with me?'

'Oh, yes, he's here somewhere,' replied Elizabeth cheerfully. 'He was outraged at first, of course, but he has got over that.'

'He is far too staid for you, my dear,' replied Jack's fond mama. 'I never thought it a good match.'

Serena blinked. 'But Dorothea said it was your dearest wish.'

'It might well have been Lady Hambridge's dearest wish,' retorted Mrs Downing drily. 'I am sure she was only too eager to see you settled. Well, she should be delighted that you have married so well.'

Serena thought of the letter she had received that morning from her sister-in-law.

'Dorothea is mortified by all the gossip. She and my brother have extended their stay at Worthing.'

A shadow of annoyance crossed Mrs Downing's kindly face. 'She would have done better to remain in town and deny it, especially now. Running away only gives credence to the rumours. Really, the woman is most—' Mrs Downing closed her lips firmly upon whatever utterance she had been about to make.

Serena sighed. 'You cannot deny I have given her a great deal of trouble, ma'am.'

Mrs Downing patted her hands. 'You are not the first young lady to be taken in by a rake, my dear. You acted recklessly, but that is all in the past now. You may believe that your true friends will support you.' She looked past Serena and smiled. 'There you are, my lord. Pray accept our felicitations upon your marriage.'

Serena looked up to find Quinn at her side.

'Thank you.' He nodded, unsmiling, before addressing her. 'I have come to take you to supper. Lady Beckford has reserved seats for us at her table. If you will excuse us, ma'am?'

'By all means,' replied Mrs Downing graciously. 'And you will be very welcome in Wardour Street, when you bring your bride to town. I hope we may expect to see you there soon, my lord?'

'As to that, we have not yet made any plans,' replied Quinn, pulling Serena's hand on to his arm. As he led her away he muttered, 'It is very warm here tonight, even with the doors leading to the terrace opened wide, and August has only just begun. London will be white-hot, but I will take you there if you wish it.'

The possibility of meeting Sir Timothy made her

shudder, but Serena knew a good wife deferred to her husband in all things.

She said in a colourless voice, 'I have no preference either way, my lord. It is for you to decide.'

Tony's words in the library came back to Quinn. Was this the same woman who could be relied upon to bring life to any party? Now she walked beside him, eyes lowered, a picture of meek obedience. The light had gone out of Serena.

Sitting between Quinn and their host at supper did much to restore Serena's spirits and afterwards Sir Anthony demanded the honour of standing up with her when dancing recommenced. Quinn would have followed, but he was waylaid by one of his neighbours who wanted the opportunity to discuss a shared boundary. He gave Serena a brief, wry smile and turned aside, leaving Tony to escort Serena to the ballroom.

As they emerged from the supper room a stocky, sober-looking young man stepped in front of them.

'Ah, Downing,' Tony greeted him jovially. 'Come to beg me to give up my partner, is that it?'

Jack Downing made a very proper bow. 'It is indeed, sir. If Lady Quinn will do me the honour?'

'With pleasure.' Serena smiled, glad to accept this olive branch. 'If Sir Anthony does not object?'

'Well, of course I object to giving you up, but you will be wanting to dance with your old friend, I've no doubt.' Laughing, Tony strolled off, leaving Serena to take Jack's arm.

Throughout the dance she tried to converse, but by the time they made their bows and parted she was weary of the effort. Really, why had he asked her to dance if he was intent upon being morose and silent? She wondered if he was jealous, but she quickly dismissed the idea. Jack Downing had considered her an eligible match, but his feelings had never been engaged, she was sure of it, and from the little Elizabeth had said, the scandal had cured him of any slight fancy he might have had for her.

Quinn watched his wife going down the dance, pleased that the rift with the Downings was mended. He had heard that Jack Downing was one of Serena's admirers and that Lady Hambridge had been in favour of the match, but to his mind it would never have worked. The fellow looked like a dull dog, too starched up to appeal to Serena.

And is a surly recluse any more appealing?

Thrusting aside the unwelcome thought, Quinn turned away. He headed for Tony's study again, but even there he could not settle and after a while he went back to watch the dancing. Serena was now partnered by another neighbour, but her pleasure seemed muted, her smile a little strained. He would not be surprised if she was fatigued by the noise and the heat. Perhaps she was ready to leave. He resolved to ask her as soon as the dance ended.

The crowded, candlelit room was very warm and the air would be fresher out of doors. Quinn stepped outside and moved away from the house to look at the gardens, bathed in moonlight. He had spent many happy days here, as a boy and a young man, enjoying the company of Anthony and his sister. For once the memories of Barbara did not tear at him and he could face them with affection. Perhaps, at last, he could put his grief behind him and appreciate the time they had had together. Perhaps he could move on.

A group of guests strolled out on to the terrace, their chatter preceding them. They were strangers, presumably Tony and Lottie's acquaintances from town. No matter, there was plenty of room. The terrace ran the length of the house and it was an easy matter for Quinn to ignore them, until a voice caught his attention.

'Oh, yes. I have known her since her come-out. You are surprised, I suppose, that I have not cut her acquaintance, considering her scandalous behaviour.'

Quinn frowned. The speaker had his back to him, too busy addressing the little crowd gathered about him to notice anyone else on the terrace, but at that moment he turned slightly and Quinn recognised Jack Downing. Someone spoke, too low for Quinn to make out the words, and Downing laughed.

'So true. A lady can never be too careful of her reputation. I consider myself fortunate to have escaped her wiles. But she has changed.' The sneering tone was even more pronounced. 'She is but a shadow of her former self. She has lost her sparkle, her youth is completely cut up.' An exaggerated sigh was followed by a short, derisive laugh. 'Not so long ago, Serena Russington was considered a veritable diamond in society, but now… now she is no more than a drab country housewife.'

Two steps took Quinn to the group. He caught Downing's arm and swung him around. The look of shock on the younger man's face was almost comical, although Quinn was in too much of a rage to think so.

'L-Lord Quinn, I—'

Quinn cut him short.

'Do you think it gentlemanly to disparage a lady?' he snarled, dragging Downing away from the group.

'I intended n-no harm,' Downing stammered as Quinn towered over him, menace in every line of his body. 'I beg your pardon!'

The music had ended and the group on the terrace was hushed save for a frightened squeak from one of the ladies as they watched Downing retreat. Quinn followed, blinded by rage.

'Pardon be damned,' he ground out. 'I'll teach you to—'

'Quinn!' Tony grabbed his arm as he was about to launch himself at the snivelling figure in front of him. 'Damn it, man, come away. You cannot start a brawl in my house!'

Quinn tried to shake him off. 'Can I not?'

'For heaven's sake, man, the fellow has apologised.'

'Indeed, indeed, I have, sir,' gabbled Downing. 'It was ungentlemanly conduct, I admit it. If you wish for satisfaction, my lord—'

'Of course he doesn't,' Beckford snapped.

'Oh, yes, I do! Confound it, Tony, let me go!'

His friend's response was to cling tighter while he addressed Downing.

'Get out of here, for heaven's sake. Leave my house forthwith and be grateful that you do so with your skin intact!'

Downing hesitated, then he gave a stiff little bow and strode off, his friends following him. The red mist was receding and Quinn let out a ragged breath.

'You may release me now, Tony. I shall not go after the wretch.'

'I take it he said something about your wife.'

'Aye.'

Quinn's anger had reduced to a simmer, with a dull ache of regret that he had allowed himself to be roused to such a fury. After all, what had the fellow said that was not true? His wife was retiring to the point of non-existence. It was not Serena's true self, he was damned sure of it. But he was even less sure he wanted a wife who was wilful, headstrong and high-spirited. Marriage had already overturned his quiet life. He rubbed a hand over his eyes.

'What the hell have I done?'

Tony squeezed his arm. 'Nothing that cannot be mended, I hope,' he said, misunderstanding. 'That young pup will think twice before insulting a lady again. Come along. Let us go inside.'

Serena was at her dressing table, submitting patiently to Polly's administrations upon her hair. Part of her wanted to crawl back into bed, but that was impossible. Ever since their return to Melham Court, the neighbours had been calling upon the new bride and Serena allowed herself to be dressed each morning in a new gown, ready to welcome all visitors. She had no doubt that there would be even more callers today, following last night's ball at Prior's Holt.

They would be sure to ask if Lady Quinn had enjoyed herself. At least there she might tell the truth. Dancing had improved her spirits and there had been no shortage of partners. Even Jack Downing had danced with her, although the family had left early and she had not had a chance to take her leave of them.

And then there was Quinn. He had seemed distracted when she sought him out at the end of the evening and barely spoke to her in the carriage. She had wanted to ask if she had offended him, but instead she remarked how much she had enjoyed the evening and expressed the hope that he, too, had found some pleasure in the society.

'It was interesting,' he had replied, his tone discouraging further conversation.

Nor had he made any effort to detain her when they arrived at the house and Serena had retired to her solitary bed. As she had done every night of her marriage.

That information was not something she could share with anyone, she thought, swallowing a sigh. But at least there was a glimmer of light. The nightmares had all but stopped.

'There, madam. We are done.' The maid put down the hairbrush and comb.

'Thank you, Polly.'

Serena rose and made her way to the door. She did not pause as she passed the long glass, knowing what her reflection would show. A plain muslin gown made high to the neck, the prim image enhanced by the lace cap pinned over her curls. The very model of wifely decorum.

Quinn pushed away his plate. He had no appetite for breakfast, having spent a restless night wondering if marrying Serena had been a disastrous mistake, and not only for himself. Serena was an extraordinary woman. Had marriage to him turned her into something less than ordinary?

A drab, country housewife.

Jack Downing's words had gnawed away at Quinn all through the dark night and he had been relieved when dawn came and he could leave his bed. But even an early morning gallop had not helped. He could not outrun his thoughts and had returned to breakfast as restless and discontented as ever.

Serena came in and he greeted her with a gruff good morning. She looked pale and a little unhappy, which only added to the guilty irritation brewing within him. He watched her cross to the table, her eyes downcast. The plum-coloured muslin did not suit her. It made her skin look grey, while the matching cap concealed the crowning glory that was her hair. He closed his lips tightly against the angry words that rose to his tongue. Is this what she thought a wife should look like? Or was it the result of Forsbrook's attack? Was she trying to keep him at bay with her dowdy appearance?

Suddenly it was all too much. He was incapable of making polite conversation over the teacups and had to get out before he said something to hurt her. His chair scraped back and with a muttered 'excuse me' he strode away.

Serena watched in dismay as Quinn hurled himself out of the room and after a brief, inward struggle she went after him. She had to run, but she was in time to see him disappear into the library, closing the door behind him with a definite snap. Without stopping to think she followed him into the room.

He was standing at a window, staring out. Serena closed the door and stood with her back pressed against it, one hand on the handle, ready for flight.

'My lord, is something amiss?'

'Go away, Serena.'

She was accustomed by now to his gruff tone. Instead of obeying him she walked closer.

'Perhaps I could help.'

'Yes, you can.' He swung about, scowling at her. 'You can go and change out of that damned ugly gown. It does you no favours. In fact, with the exception of the gown you wore last night, you have worn nothing remotely flattering since we married!'

She reeled back as if he had struck her. 'They are perfectly suitable. Dorothea would not have chosen them else...'

'Do you mean to tell me Lady Hambridge had the ordering of your wedding trousseau? Ha! That explains a great deal.'

'She said I should be appropriately dressed.'

'Did she? Those gowns are only appropriate for a matron in her dotage,' he said brutally.

Serena pulled her head up. 'Dorothea wanted me to look respectable.'

'Respectable—you look positively nun-like!' He took her shoulders and gave her a little shake. 'I want you to dress for what you are, Serena, a beautiful young woman. These clothes are more suited to a fifty-year-old.' His eyes moved to her hair. 'And as for that monstrosity—'

Before she could protest he tore off the cap, pulling with it the pins that had so artfully confined her curls, and she felt the heavy, silken weight tumble about her shoulders. A blaze of fury ripped through Serena. Her breast heaved and she glared at him, but as their eyes locked another sensation cut through her rage. Something altogether more dangerous. Desire.

She realised now that it had been curling within her since last evening, growing, spreading into every pore, every nerve-end. Now, at last, the barriers between them were down. She wanted him to reach out and pull her into his arms. She was almost quivering with longing, even though her limbs would not move. Invisible bonds were wrapped about her, keeping her still and mute.

Kiss me. Kiss me now!

Hope flared when his eyes darkened. There was naked lust in his glance and her heart began to thud so hard against her ribs he must surely hear it. She waited, breathless, for him to close the gap between them, to drag her into an embrace, yet even as he reached out for her she could not help herself. She flinched.

The effect was like a dowsing in ice-cold water. His hand dropped and he stepped back, dragging his eyes away from her.

'Forgive me,' he said, his voice ragged. 'That was not worthy of a gentleman.'

He turned on his heel and walked away, leaving Serena to stare after him, not sure whether she most wanted to laugh or cry with frustration.

Chapter Eight

Quinn brought the axe down, splitting the log cleanly in half. He picked up another and placed it on the block. His muscles screamed at him to stop but he couldn't. He had to keep working, to keep at bay the burning desire. It had almost consumed him this morning, when he had pulled off that damned mobcap and Serena's hair had tumbled free, a sunlit waterfall rippling down over her shoulders. She had been incandescent then, angry, raging, but gloriously alive. He had wanted to carry her off to his bed and make love to her, slowly, thoroughly, and then to watch her sleeping with that golden cloud of hair spread over the pillow.

Confound it, put such things from your mind or you will go mad!

He had given Serena his word that he would keep his distance, but every time he saw her it became more difficult. At first, his overriding thought had been to protect her, but now she was recovering and the glimpses of her fiery spirit were testing his self-control to the limit. Her passionate nature called to him, like some kindred spirit. He longed to meet fire with fire, but even the slightest hint of desire brought back her fear. Witness how she had recoiled from him in the library.

Perhaps she was wise to dress like a nun, to remind him that he must not touch her. He swung the axe again and again. The pile of firewood was growing, but when he glanced at the newly split logs even they reminded him of Serena's fair hair, gleaming in the sun. He wanted her, but he was damned if he knew how to proceed.

'Good morning, my lady. 'tis a sunny day for a change. Last night's rain has cleared the air and not before time.'

Serena slowly sat up in her bed and reached for the cup her maid had placed on the bedside table. Despite Polly's cheerful words, she felt only discontent as she gazed out of the window at the clear blue sky.

It was seven days since the Beckfords' ball. Six since Quinn had torn the cap from her head and at the same time ripped all pretence from her soul. In the past week neither of them had mentioned that incident, save one oblique reference when Quinn told her he was no judge of female attire and had no wish to dictate to her.

He had said, 'You must wear whatsoever you deem fitting for your station. Whatever makes you comfortable.'

Serena had thanked him politely, but although she continued to wear the dresses Dorothea had purchased for her, she never again donned any of the caps. Quinn was perfectly correct about the gowns and she bitterly regretted allowing her sister-in-law to dictate to her, but she was loath to go to the considerable expense of replacing them, when Quinn had as good as told her that he had no interest in what she wore.

She gazed now at the pale pink muslin that Polly had fetched from the linen press. She remembered Dorothea trying to force the same colour upon her during her first Season. She had protested violently on that occasion and, fortunately, Russ and Molly had supported her, allowing her to wear the brighter, jewel-like colours she preferred. The discontent turned into irritation and she waved a hand at the maid.

'Take that dress away and dispose of it, Polly. Bring me something else to wear.'

'Yes, m'm.'

It was a tiny act of rebellion, but Serena felt a little better for it.

Half an hour later she made her way to the breakfast room, checking in the doorway when she saw Quinn was sitting at the table. For the past week he had been out of the house by the time she came downstairs.

'Oh—good morning, my lord. I did not expect to see you.'

'I wanted to speak to you.' He rose and pulled out a chair for her. When she was seated he remained behind her. 'That gown is another of Lady Hambridge's choosing, I suppose.'

'It is, my lord.' She managed to speak coolly, although her spine tingled, knowing he was so close.

'Olive green and plain as a Quaker. Designed to blend into the shadows.' When she did not reply he went on, 'Is that a style and a colour you would choose for yourself?' He gave a little bark of laughter. 'Your silence tells me it is not. I have given you *carte blanche* to spend what you like on clothes, Serena.'

He had returned to his seat opposite and she flushed slightly, not meeting his eyes. 'I know, my lord. You are very good and I shall do so, in time.'

She risked one swift glance from under her lashes, bracing herself for his reply. He looked as if he would speak but thought better of it. Instead he reached for the coffee pot and filled her cup.

'What are you doing today?'

'I must speak to Mrs Talbot, and to Cook about tonight's dinner.'

'And are you free once you have seen them?'

'Lady Brook promised to call this morning.'

'Good lord, is she visiting you again today? The knocker has not stopped this past se'ennight.'

Serena's tension eased at the familiar, brusque tone. They were on safer ground now. She knew that despite his grumbling, Quinn was not displeased his neighbours were so attentive.

'Since the ball.' She nodded. 'It is very gratifying.'

'I dare say. What is Lady Brook's excuse today?'

'When I saw her yesterday she promised me a receipt for making apple tart the French way. She swears it is superior to any other method.'

Quinn stared at her across the breakfast table. 'Good God. Are you so at a loss for entertainment that you must resort to *baking*?'

'By no means. I shall accept gratefully and pass it on to Cook.'

'I am glad to hear it.' He refilled his own coffee cup. 'Are you very bored here, Serena?'

She looked up, startled. 'N-no, not at all. My days

are always full. I go through the menus with Cook and discuss household matters with Mrs Talbot. Then there are flowers to cut for the house—'

'Those are your household duties,' he interrupted her. 'What do you do for *pleasure*?'

She felt a little flutter of unease and said carefully, 'There are morning calls to be paid and received.'

'Yes, when you discuss the best way to cook apples. How stimulating!'

His tone was scathing and she bridled. 'And you enjoy the benefits of such conversations when you sit down to your dinner!'

His eyes widened in surprise, but there was something more gleaming in them. Something that set her pulse racing. She quickly looked away.

'I do indeed. I beg your pardon.' His tone was perfectly polite, amused, even, but she dared not look at him again. Instead she finished her bread and butter and pushed aside her plate.

'Are you done?'

'Yes.'

His lip curled. 'That is barely enough to keep a bird alive.'

'It is all I want.'

'Very well. Then run upstairs and fetch your shawl. I wish to show you something. Outside.'

'Now? I have arranged to see Mrs Talbot.'

'Send word that you will see her later.'

She could not help it. She stiffened at his autocratic tone, her brows rising. Quinn met her affronted gaze with narrowed eyes, then with a slight nod he threw down his napkin and stood, saying with exaggerated civility, 'Perhaps, my lady, you would be so good as to oblige me in this. I would very much appreciate your company.'

The change in manner brought the heat to her cheeks. 'Of course, my lord.'

'Good.' He walked to the door and held it open for her. 'I shall wait for you in the hall.'

Silently she left the table and walked to the door. As she passed him she glanced up. There was the glimmer of a smile in his eyes and her lips curved up a little in response. Really, she thought, he might be quite charming if he put his mind to it. The idea persisted only as long as it took her to cross the hall, for as she ascended the stairs he called after her.

'Five minutes. And do not keep me waiting!'

Slightly more than five minutes later Serena made her way back to the hall. Perhaps it was the sunshine streaming through the house, but the lethargy that had made her limbs feel so heavy and slow these past few weeks had eased and she ran lightly down the stairs, one hand on the rail the other clutching a thin silk shawl she hoped would be sufficient to keep off any light breeze.

As she descended the last flight she saw Quinn. He was staring out of the open door, his hands clasped behind his back. Not for the first time she thought how well he looked in country dress, his legs encased in buckskins and glossy top boots. A dark brown frock coat was stretched across his broad shoulders and the light flooding in through the open door brought out a tawny glint in his mane of light brown hair, reminding her of the big cats she had seen at the Exeter Exchange. But those animals had been caged, safely behind bars.

Quinn, on the other hand was here, just feet away from her.

And he is your husband.

Serena slowed as she reached the last few stairs, trying to understand the welter of emotions flooding through her. She wanted to flee, although she knew not where. At that moment Quinn turned towards her and the world steadied when he met her eyes. She trusted him to take care of her.

'Well, my lord, I am here.' She summoned up a smile as she crossed the hall.

'Yes.'

He took the shawl from her and draped it about her shoulders as they made their way out of the house. In the enclosed courtyard the summer sun was hot and bright and Serena stopped, blinking.

'Where are we going, sir, is it far?'

'No. Only to the stables.'

He pulled her fingers on to his arm and they set off again, not through the gatehouse as she had expected, but via a small enclosed passage opposite, where a solid oak door led to a small footbridge across the moat and directly into the new stable block.

'My grandfather had this entrance added to the house when he rebuilt the stables some fifty years ago. It made it quicker for the servants to summon his carriage.'

Serena nodded. Her old self would have explored every nook and cranny of her new home as soon as possible. Instead she had allowed Mrs Talbot to show her around Melham Court, going only to those rooms the housekeeper considered it necessary for the lady of the house to visit. Now she felt the first stirrings of curiosity to see more.

The stables were far more modern than the main house but equally well maintained. Not a weed was to be seen in the yard, where the cobbles were being swept by a couple of young stable hands under the watchful eye of Bourne, the head groom. The boys did not stop their work but Bourne gave a respectful nod in their direction.

'Morning, m'lord. M'lady.'

Serena acknowledged his greeting, then looked up at her companion.

'I have not been here before,' she remarked. 'I should very much like to look around, if I may?'

'Of course, I will show you.' Quinn turned to Bourne, who was waiting expectantly. 'We shall be back in, say, ten minutes.'

'Very good, m'lord.'

Quinn took Serena through the nearest double doors, into the carriage house. From there they progressed through the harness room and on via a feed store to the looseboxes and stalls. There were several men and boys in the stables, grooming the horses, mucking out the stalls or cleaning the carriages. Quinn presented every one of them to Serena as they made their way through the building.

'I am impressed,' she told him, when they had reached the end of the tour. 'You appear to know everyone and everything that goes on here.'

'A good master takes an interest in his staff. I look after them and they work hard for me.' He gave a short laugh. 'I admit I have rarely seen so many of them working at any one time. I suspect they were eager for a glimpse of their new mistress.'

'It was remiss of me not to come before.'

'Nonsense. My parents rarely came to the stables. I doubt my mother even knew the way here.'

He said no more, but Serena marvelled that he should have grown up to be such a considerate master if his parents were so indifferent. They had reached the loose boxes, in one of which was a powerful black horse.

'My favourite hack, Neptune.' Quinn introduced him. 'French-bred. He's an ugly brute, but strong. He can carry me all morning without tiring.'

Serena reached up one hand to scratch the long, bony nose. 'It must be difficult to find a mount that is up to your weight.'

He grunted. 'Luckily I don't aspire to cut a figure in Hyde Park.'

'Nor I.'

'But you do ride?' he asked her, a slight frown in his eyes. 'You and Lottie were talking of it at supper the other evening.'

'Why yes, but not in town,' she replied. 'That is, I was used to do so when I was living with Molly and Russ, but Henry prefers his carriage and Dorothea does not ride at all. They would not countenance my going out without them, even in the most respectable party.'

She could not keep the note of regret from her voice and felt slightly aggrieved when she saw that Quinn's brow had cleared. Perhaps he, like Dorothea, considered riding to be an unladylike activity.

She said, a little coldly, 'Thank you for taking the time to show me over your stables, my lord, but perhaps you would like to tell me why you wanted me to accompany you?'

'I should indeed.' He took her arm. 'Come along.'

The sunlight was blinding as they stepped into the

yard and Serena was momentarily dazzled, but as her vision cleared she saw that Bourne was walking a dapple-grey horse around the yard.

'There. The mare is what I wanted to show you.'

'She is a beauty,' said Serena, as Bourne brought the horse closer. 'Is she a new addition to your stable?'

'My tiger fetched her yesterday. She answers to the name of Crystal. Irish-bred and used to a lady's saddle.'

It took a moment for his words to register with Serena.

'You…you mean she is for *me*?'

'If you want her. Perhaps I should have discussed it with you first, but when Bourne told me yesterday morning that Lord Hackleby was selling off his horses I rode over to Pirton to see if there was anything in his stable suitable for a lady. If I had had more notice you might have come with me, but you had already arranged to call upon the Brooks.'

The groom brought the mare to a stand before them. Serena slowly put out her hand and ran it along the glossy neck, murmuring quietly to the animal.

'Hackleby bought her for his late wife, who was an enthusiastic rider,' Quinn told her. 'He says the mare is very well mannered, if handled properly. He also said she is fast and strong, can go for miles and will jump anything. Since Lady Hackleby died last winter the horse has been exercised by a groom. Clem put her through her paces and thinks she is a little out of condition, but with regular use would soon return to form. We have the lady's saddle, too, which I hope will fit you well enough until we can have one made for you.' He cleared his throat. 'Of course, if you would rather choose your own mount, we need not keep her.'

'No, no, she is perfect for me. She sounds as if she

has spirit, too, which is just what I like.' She glanced up at him. 'How did you know?'

'I did not expect anything less of you.'

She could not resist returning his smile.

'Not that I can take all the credit for it,' he continued. 'I wrote to Hambridge some weeks ago, asking him what sort of horse would suit you. His reply was that I should find you something steady. An old animal, perhaps. One that could be relied upon not to bolt with you.'

'A slug, in fact!' she replied tartly.

'Exactly.' His lips twitched. 'However, he also informed me that you had always been quite heedless of your own safety and had regularly flouted his advice regarding which of his horses were suitable for you. From that I gathered that a safe, steady mount was the last thing you would want.'

Serena's heart swelled. She knew an impulse to throw her arms about Quinn—well, as far as they would go around him. Such a display would shock the servants and might well give Quinn a disgust of her. Instead she tucked her arm into his.

'How can I ever thank you, my lord?'

Quinn nodded to Bourne to take the mare away and turned to escort Serena back to the house.

'By riding out with me as soon as Lady Brook has gone today. That is, if you have a riding habit?'

'I do, somewhere. It will be in one of the trunks we brought from Bruton Street. I am afraid it is not in the latest style.' She hesitated, then said haltingly, 'Dorothea did not include a new habit in my wedding *trousseau*.'

'No doubt she disapproves of ladies riding.'

Serena chuckled. 'She does.'

'It is of a piece with her taste in gowns.' He bent a

searching look upon her. 'Tell me truthfully, my dear, do you like *any* of the clothes she bought for you?'

She sobered and looked away. 'It was a difficult time. Dorothea acted as she thought best.'

Quinn held back a snort of derision and refrained from giving his opinion of Serena's sister-in-law.

He said decisively, 'I shall ask Lottie to recommend her favourite modistes and we will have them come here to fit you out with more suitable gowns.'

'The ones I have are perfectly suitable, my lord.'

'Aye, for an ageing dowager,' he retorted, then stopped. 'They are not the style you would have chosen for yourself, are they?' he asked again and put his hands on her shoulders, 'Tell me truthfully, Serena.'

'No.' She looked away, but he could see the distress in her face. 'But my judgement is not to be trusted. Not for the world would I want to disgrace you, my lord.'

Something contracted, hard as iron, around his heart. Without thinking he drew her into his arms. Immediately she stiffened. It was like holding a block of wood, was his first thought, quickly followed by the realisation that it was terror holding her motionless. Carefully he released her, knowing one wrong word and she would run from him. He pulled her hand back on to his arm and continued to walk.

'You could never disgrace me, Serena.'

He was looking straight ahead, but from the corner of his eye he saw her hand come up and dash away a tear.

When they reached the house, Serena excused herself and went up to her room to divest herself of her shawl and tidy her hair. Her head was still full of Dorothea's shrill tones, telling her how fortunate she was and how little she deserved it, but deep, deep inside was a faint glimmer of happiness.

She sat through Lady Brook's visit with outward calm, all the time wondering if Polly had managed to find her old riding habit. She had not needed it at all this year so perhaps it was gone. That thought pierced the blanket of indifference that was wrapped about Serena and she realised with something of a shock how much she wanted to ride the beautiful dapple-grey Quinn had bought for her. Something bubbled up inside. Something she had not felt for months. Joyful anticipation.

Quinn paced the hall. Lady Brook had left the house twenty minutes ago and Dunnock had informed him that my lady had gone directly upstairs to change. How long would that take her? he wondered. Fashionable ladies were notorious for taking an age over their *toilette*. Perhaps he had been over-eager in sending word to the stables. Then he heard a soft, melodious voice behind him.

'I trust I have not kept you waiting, my lord.'

He turned and the breath caught in his throat. Serena had paused, halfway down the stairs, one daintily gloved hand on the rail, the other holding her leather crop and the gathered skirts. A single glance told him that although the riding habit was not new, it was the work of a master. The soft wool jacket fitted snugly, the masculine tailoring and military frogging only serving to accentuate her womanly curves. Beneath her chin was a snowy cravat, tied with a simple knot. Her golden curls were tamed by a matching and very mannish beaver hat with a small brim.

The ensemble was both fetching and eye-catching. The bold colour suited her, too. It was the colour of young, rain-washed evergreens and it enhanced the creamy tones of her skin. It was the sort of outfit worn by a confident young woman, one who did not give a jot what the world thought of her. The woman Serena had once been. Now he read uncertainty in her brown eyes and smiled to reassure her.

'Not at all—you are in good time,' he said. 'I have ordered the horses to be brought to the door and they are not yet here.'

'Oh, good. I would not have had them standing in this sun.' She sounded relieved and was more forthcoming than he had ever known her. 'Polly found my habit you see. Fortunately, it still fits, even if it is a little sun-bleached in places. That is what comes of wearing it out of doors in all weathers, I suppose.'

She chattered away as she descended the last few stairs but Quinn was not attending, distracted by her dainty feet, encased in half-boots of soft kid. Strange, how arousing the glimpse of a shapely ankle could be.

'I hope you do not think it too shabby for our outing, my lord.'

'Hmm?' Her soft voice caught his attention. She was regarding him anxiously and he profoundly hoped his face gave no indication of his wandering thoughts. He cleared his throat. 'No, no, you look quite delightful,' he told her, further alarming himself with such a candid reply. He swung round towards the open door, his ears picking up the sound of hooves on the gravel. 'Shall we go?'

Serena's cheeks flamed. Silently she accompanied Quinn out to the drive, where Bourne was waiting with the dapple-grey and Quinn's diminutive tiger was holding on to Neptune. At the sight of his master, the powerful black horse threw up his head, almost lifting Clem from his feet and causing that worthy to remonstrate vociferously, chastising the animal in colourful language that made Serena stifle a giggle. It dispelled much of the awkwardness she had felt at Quinn's unexpected compliment.

'That's enough, Clem,' barked Quinn, but there was no mistaking the quiver of laughter in his voice. 'You had best walk Neptune around again while I attend to my lady.'

Serena looked at the mare and felt a ripple of excitement. This was no docile hack, but a large, spirited animal that would need all her skill to master. The meekness and deference she considered so necessary in her role as Quinn's wife had no place here.

With Bourne holding the mare's head, Quinn threw Serena up into the saddle and remained close until she was securely seated. She did her best to ignore the strong hands that brushed her skirts as he checked the girth and the stirrup, but she felt strangely bereft when he pronounced himself satisfied and stepped away. She buried the thought. She must give her attention to controlling the mare.

'Thank you, my lord.' She gathered up the reins and nodded to the groom. 'You may release her now, Bourne, I have her.'

'Are you sure, my lady? She's very fresh. And 'tis a while since she's had a lady on 'er back.'

'And it is a while since I have been on a horse,' replied Serena, smiling. 'We shall soon grow accustomed to one another. Let her go.'

Free of the groom's hand on her halter, the mare

threw up her head, but Serena was ready. She turned the animal, murmuring soothingly as Crystal pranced and sidled.

'There,' she said, finally coming to a stand again and running one hand along the glossy neck, 'We understand one another already, do we not?' Quinn was still standing, watching her. She read the approval in his face and her confidence grew even more. 'Well, my lord, will you mount up now? I should like to see just what this lady can do.'

The sound of hooves on the cobbles echoed around the courtyard as Quinn led the way out through the arch. They crossed the bridge and turned on to the path leading into the park. The lad waiting to open the gate for them gave a cheeky grin as he tugged his forelock and Serena could not but smile at him. The day was bright, the sun was warm on her back and suddenly, *suddenly* it was good to be alive. How long had it been since she felt like this?

'Well,' said Quinn. 'Shall we put your mare through her paces?'

She turned her smiling face towards him. 'By all means, my lord!'

Quinn touched his heels to Neptune's sides, marvelling at the change in his wife. Gone was the anxious, hesitant creature who had descended the stairs in her faded habit. Serena on horseback positively glowed with life and assurance. They cantered together through the park, heading for the dense woods that covered the rising ground in the distance. Quinn kept a steady pace, frequently glancing across at his companion. She looked completely at her ease. Very much like her name, he thought. Serene.

He drew rein, bringing Neptune to a walk. 'You ride very well. Is the saddle comfortable for you?'

'Perfectly, thank you, my lord.' She looked about her. 'From the height of the gate and the walls, I suppose this was once a deer park.'

'Yes, we still have red and fallow deer but they prefer the higher ground to the north. In Queen Elizabeth's time the park was double the size, but some of the land was sold off about a century ago and it was remodelled. That was when the avenues of beech, sycamore and lime were planted. They make good rides.' He pointed. 'That avenue leads to an ancient viewing tower, where visitors to Melham could watch the hunt. You can just see the top of it.'

She followed his outstretched finger with a steady, considering stare and he said, 'We could gallop there, if you wish.'

The look she threw at him was full of laughter and mischief. 'You have read my mind, my lord!'

She touched her heel to the mare's flank and set off, her skirts billowing around her.

'Whoa, Neptune.' He held the black in check, enjoying the view of Serena galloping away along the wide avenue. 'By God, she is a bruising rider.'

It needed no more than a word from Quinn for Neptune to leap forward in pursuit. For all his horse's strength, he wondered briefly if he had allowed Serena too much of a start. However, by the time they crested the rising ground Neptune had drawn level and they raced neck and neck towards the stone tower. It reared up before them, massive as a cliff face.

'Pull up,' shouted Quinn as they thundered towards it. 'Pull up, for God's sake!'

For one searing moment he thought Crystal had bolted and would crash into the tower, then he heard Serena laugh and at the very last moment she swung the mare away. The avenue had once extended past the tower to the very edge of Melham land, but it had been allowed to fall into disuse, and no more than a hundred yards beyond the tower was a mass of unkempt bushes and trees.

Quinn brought Neptune to a plunging halt and watched as Serena slowed the mare and brought her back towards him. He was torn between admiration of her skill and blazing anger at her reckless behaviour. She was smiling, her cheeks glowing from the exercise and her eyes sparkling. She had never looked so beautiful.

By heaven, if this is the real Serena then she will lead me a merry dance.

He said with a calm he was far from feeling, 'A trifle foolhardy, don't you think, to ride like that on a horse you do not know, over unknown ground?'

She looked a little conscience-stricken, but her eyes were still shining, which pleased him.

'I beg your pardon. I had not realised just how much I missed riding.' She glanced up at the tower. 'What a grand edifice. Can we go inside?'

'Of course.'

He jumped down and tied Neptune's reins to a bush. When he turned back, Serena had already dismounted and was following suit with the mare. He was disappointed that she had not waited for him to help her down. He would have liked the excuse to hold her in his arms.

* * *

Serena took her time fastening Crystal's reins to a branch. The heady exhilaration was fading and she was regretting her recklessness. Not that Quinn was angry with her, quite the opposite, but even now she felt the panic rising when she recalled the glow of admiration in his eyes. It was so confusing, because she really did want him to admire her, to *desire* her. When he smiled at her she wanted nothing more than to melt into his embrace and yet she could not overcome the black, chilling terror at the thought of being in any man's arms.

She wished she had not dismounted, for now he would have to help her up into the saddle again and that would mean standing close to him, breathing in his scent, the mix of soap and leather and spices that was so strangely intoxicating. She was afraid she might do something rash, like throw her arms about his neck and beg him to kiss her.

Such an action was fraught with danger. She could not be certain that he would want to kiss her and if he did, she might recoil, as she had done before. That would make him angry or, even worse, leave him wounded and unhappy. Then there was Dorothea's assertion that such forward behaviour in a wife would disgust any decent man and Serena had no doubt her husband was a good man.

Quinn was standing by the tower's bleached oak door. 'Well, shall we go in?'

'Is it not locked?' she asked, walking over to him.

'Of course, although it is doubtful if anyone would ever stray this far into the park.' He reached up to a small crevice between two of the stone blocks and pulled out a large iron key. 'So now you are one of the privileged few who know the secret.'

The smile that accompanied his words caused a sudden fluttering inside Serena, as if someone had opened a sack full of butterflies. She dragged her eyes away from his mouth and fixed them on the oak door, but even the sight of him turning the key in the lock made her tremble as she imagined those same fingers on her bare skin.

The door opened and she gave a nervous laugh. 'I expected it to creak, like something from a Gothic novel.'

'The tower is well maintained.'

He stood back to let her precede him into the gloom. The only light came from the open door and a small window set high up in the walls. 'This area was only ever used for storage. The main chamber is above us.' He glanced down at her. 'You are shivering. Are you afraid?'

She could not speak of it, the sudden terrifying memory that had assailed her. Cruel hands around her throat and blackness so deep it made her tremble. She said instead, 'It is very dark, after the bright sunshine.'

'Let me guide you, I will go first.'

He took her hand and drew her towards the stone steps built against the far wall. The terror faded as quickly as it had come. There was something comforting about the way Quinn's huge, warm hand enclosed her fingers. He would protect her from anything and anyone who threatened harm.

But he cannot protect you from yourself, Serena.

The steps opened directly into the main chamber, which boasted windows on all four sides. A large fireplace was built across one corner, with another set of stairs in the opposite corner, leading upwards.

'On inclement days, guests could watch the hunt from here,' Quinn told her.

He was still holding her hand and she was far too aware of him. She was torn between wanting to cling tighter and running for her life.

'It is a lovely, light room,' she said at last. She gently freed her fingers and walked from one window to the next. 'And the views are spectacular. One cannot quite see over the rise to Melham but there are wonderful views over the park.' Turning back, she looked about the room, anywhere rather than at Quinn. 'If it was furnished with a table and chairs, and a thick carpet over the flags, one might dine here very comfortably. A small party, of course, just a few friends. Or it would make a wonderful retreat from the world,' she went on, her imagination taking flight. 'Somewhere one might read in peace and solitude. Or sketch, perhaps.'

Her thoughts ran on. What a wonderful place this would be for a young boy to act out his adventures. His own little kingdom. A castle, perhaps, or a ship at sea.

'I suppose you are right,' said Quinn, coming to stand beside her. 'I never spent much time in here.'

She turned towards him. 'Did you ever play here? It would make a fine lair.'

'When I was a child this place was forbidden. I only remember being chased away from it. I suppose the adults were afraid we might come upon them indulging in an illicit liaison.'

'Your parents' guests?'

'Not only guests,' he said bitterly. 'My parents used

it, too, on the rare occasions they were here. Although not together. Never together.'

The bleakness in his eyes was chilling. She wanted to reach out to him, to kiss away the pain, but what right had she? He might turn away. He might reject her.

For all that she could not resist laying a hand gently on his arm. 'May we go up to the roof?'

Her words seemed to bring Quinn back from a dark place. She watched as he almost physically shrugged off his memories.

He did not take her hand this time and she followed him up the stairs to where another solid oak door opened outwards on to a flagged walkway. The wind gusted around them, but Serena barely noticed it as she slowly made her way around the parapet, drinking in the view. From here she could see the church and the village. Closer, just visible over the hill on the southern side, was the stone and timber square of Melham Court with its red-tiled roof and the tall brick chimneys reaching towards the sky. In the other direction, the woods stretched away into the distance, a thick bubbling blanket in a dozen shades of green.

'Look.' Quinn put one hand on her shoulder, the other stretching out towards a grassy knoll. 'Red deer.'

A small herd were grazing peacefully, watched over by a lordly stag.

Serena gave a small sigh. 'How privileged we are, to be able to stand here and see such beauty.'

'Indeed.'

There was something in the way he spoke the word, his voice slow and deep, that set Serena's body tingling. His hand still rested lightly on her shoulder and she held her breath, imagining his fingers tightening their hold, turning her about so that he might kiss her.

Her stomach swooped at the thought. She wanted it to happen. She wanted it so badly she was tempted to turn and drag his head down towards her. She fought against it. Her forward behaviour had already brought her to the point of ruin once and she was terrified that it would repel Quinn. She must keep quite still and savour the intimacy of standing thus, with her husband. The effort proved too much. She shivered and Quinn's hand dropped.

'Is it too cold for you? We should go inside.'

'No, I am not cold.' The moment had gone, disappearing like smoke. She sighed. 'But perhaps we should be getting back.'

The scene on the rooftop replayed itself over and over in Quinn's head as they made their way from the tower. He was enjoying showing Serena his world—her world now, too. When she had remarked on the view he had wanted to take her in his arms and tell her that she enhanced its beauty but he had hesitated. Soft words and compliments were not his style. And besides, she did not want his advances. Even his hand on her shoulder had made her shudder. Now she was standing beside him as he locked the door and replaced the key in its hiding place. She looked sad and he wanted desperately to make her smile again.

As they walked back to the horses he said, 'It is time we made use of the tower. I shall have the chimney swept and then you shall furnish it. There is plenty of spare furniture in the house, ask Mrs Talbot to show you. But if nothing suits then you must buy more.'

'How would you wish it furnished?'

'That is for you to decide. It can be your own private tower, where you may retire whenever you wish to be alone. Read, draw, whatever you wish to do. No one shall intrude upon you there.'

'Th-thank you.'

He threw her up into the saddle and when she was secure he untied the reins and handed them to her.

'Melham Court is your home now, Serena. I want you to be happy here. The tower shall be your retreat from the world.'

With that he turned to mount Neptune. There. He had said it. He had given her permission to shut herself away from the world. From him.

They rode directly to the stable yard, where the grooms were waiting to run to the horses' heads. Once again Serena dismounted before Quinn could help her, but she did not refuse his arm for the short walk back to the house.

'Thank you for buying Crystal, Quinn. She is perfect. I enjoyed our ride together.'

'And I.' He glanced back at the clock as they entered the main courtyard. 'I had not realised it was so late. There is barely an hour until dinner.'

'That should be sufficient,' she told him. 'I gave orders before we left that we would need hot water upon our return. I am learning to be a good housewife, you see, my lord.'

Her shy smile lifted his spirits as he led her into the hall. He thought she would make directly for the stairs, but she stopped.

'I have been thinking about the tower,' she said, stripping off her gloves. 'With your permission, sir,

I would like it to be a little parlour, with comfortable chairs where we may sit, if we wish, but I should also like to add a dining table. We might dine alone, or invite friends to join us. Perhaps in the summer, when we might go up on to the roof after dinner and watch the sun setting. The views are too special to be kept for us alone. I should like to share them. To share the happiness they bring.'

Where we may sit!

A glow of pleasure warmed Quinn's heart at her words, but he said carefully, 'An admirable idea, my dear, but are you sure that is what you wish?'

'It is.' She glanced up at him. 'I should like to replace the memories you have of the tower with happier ones, my lord.'

And with that she turned and hurried away, leaving Quinn to stare after her.

Chapter Nine

'Well, madam, if you don't like any of these, what *will* you wear tonight?'

Serena looked at the gowns spread over the bed. She was still glowing from the glorious afternoon spent riding with Quinn, although the happiness was fading a little now. Quinn was right about her wardrobe. Dorothea had called her dresses decorous. The old Serena would have said they were uniformly *dull*.

How had it come to this? she wondered. Her sister-in-law had disposed of all her lovely gowns and turned her into a dowd. Anger roiled inside her. At Dorothea, a little, but mainly at herself for allowing it.

'Do we have any of my old gowns, Polly, besides my riding habit?'

'No, ma'am. Lady Hambridge took them all away, saying you would not be needing them.'

Sighing, Serena returned to the selection of gowns in front of her and picked out the charcoal grey with its cream embroidery. It was severe but at least it did not make her look sallow. And she might leave off the bertha, the cape-like lace collar and ruff that covered the low neckline.

'And on your hair, madam? Will it be the matching cap?' Polly added, coaxingly, 'The lace edging is very fine.'

'It is indeed,' agreed Serena. 'I remember Dorothea telling me how expensive it was.'

Polly looked relieved. 'Well then, madam, will you wear it?'

Quinn came downstairs in good time for dinner. In fact, he knew he was early, for the long case clock in the great hall had only just begun to chime the hour. The ride that afternoon had sharpened his appetite and he hoped Serena would not keep him waiting. Not that she had ever done so yet, he thought, a reluctant smile tugging at his lips. She was not one of those fashionable beauties who lost track of time while sitting at their dressing table.

The smile grew as he entered the drawing room to see his wife was already there, gazing out of the window at the gardens, which were bathed in evening sunlight on the far side of the moat. She had her back to him but he was struck by the pleasing image she presented. Her curls were swept up on her head, enhancing the graceful line of her neck above the dark gown. Desire stirred and it positively leapt when she turned around and he saw the tantalising amount of satin-smooth skin exposed by the low décolletage. His gaze lingered on the creamy swell of her breasts. By heaven, he had not expected to lust after his own wife.

Quinn dragged his eyes away. Serena was a wife in name only and would remain so until she chose to change that.

He kept his eyes firmly on her face as she came towards him, but it did nothing to lessen the attraction. The afternoon's exertion had brought more colour to her cheeks. There was even the suggestion of a sparkle in her eyes.

'Good evening, my lord. I have chosen the least nun-like of my gowns. I hope you do not disapprove?'

His eyes narrowed. Was she *teasing* him? That explained the sparkle.

'Only the colour, my dear. It is quite funereal. Mayhap Lady Hambridge anticipated you would drive me to an early grave.'

She laughed at that. 'Mayhap she did. Dunnock tells me dinner can be served as soon as we wish, so shall we go in? We have only ourselves to please, after all.'

'By all means.' He gave her a searching look as he offered her his arm. 'Are you a mind-reader, too, Serena? Did you know I am decidedly sharp-set this evening?'

She shook her head, flushing. 'By no means, but I confess that I am very hungry, too.'

They sat down to dinner very much in harmony, and the accord lasted throughout the evening. Conversation had always flowed easily between them but this evening it was even more pleasurable. Quinn did not linger over his brandy, preferring his wife's company, but when he returned to the drawing room he found her a trifle preoccupied.

He knew what it was, of course. He had seen the nervous shadow flicker across her eyes when he looked at her. She knew he desired her but, confound it, had he not given his word he would not rush her? He wanted to remind her, but was afraid it would destroy the easy camaraderie they had been enjoying. So instead they talked of horses and riding, of his plans for the estate and tomorrow's dinner with Tony and Charlotte.

He said, trying for a light-hearted note, 'We must soon invite more than just the Beckfords to our table.'

'It will be expected, my lord, now you have a wife.'

There it was again. The faintest tremor on that last word. He glanced at the clock.

'It is nearing eleven. You must be fatigued after so much time out of doors today.'

Serena longed to tell him she was not at all tired. She wanted to say how much she enjoyed his company, to stay and converse with him into the early hours, and then to have him invite her to his bed. But Quinn was already rising from his seat, clearly anxious for her to go. Earlier she thought she had seen admiration in his eyes and perhaps a hint of desire, too. But not enough.

'Yes of course.' She rose and shook out her skirts while Quinn opened the door for her. 'Goodnight, my lord.'

He caught her hand as she went to pass him, obliging her to stop. He lifted her fingers to his lips, the veriest touch, but it sent fiery darts racing through her blood. Her eyes flew to his face.

He smiled. 'Goodnight, Serena. Sleep well.'

She hurried up the stairs. Sleep! How could she *sleep* when he had roused in her an indefinable yearning for she knew not what? When she reached the landing she slowed. She was not being honest. She knew exactly what she wanted. She wanted Quinn to sweep her off her feet and take her to bed. Just the thought of it set her spine tingling. But he had told her he would not force himself upon her. When they consummated their marriage, it would be her decision. Did that mean going to his room?

A shimmer of anxiety ran through her. Such wanton behaviour would go against everything she had been told a husband wanted in a wife. The argument went back and forth in her mind as she made her way to her bedchamber. Dorothea had been at pains to tell her how a wife should behave, but until that fateful night at Hitchin Serena had always scorned her sister-in-law's advice. Why, then, was she inclined to believe her now?

The answer was clear: she had no confidence in her own judgement. She was prepared to believe her sister-in-law knew best, just as she had been willing for her to dictate what clothes she should wear. Serena stopped at her door, her fingers clasped about the handle. Quinn did not approve Dorothea's choice of clothes. He had told her as much and now, as the heavy gloom of depression was beginning to lift from her spirits, she could see how wrong they were for her. How was Quinn to know what she wanted, unless she told him?

It was midnight and Quinn could not sleep. After tossing and turning until his bed was hot and uncomfortable, he sat up and reached for the tinderbox. The restlessness had been growing all day and riding out with Serena had only enhanced it. Instead of sleeping, all he could see in his mind's eye was Serena galloping through the avenue. Serena smiling up at him, her countenance flushed and alive with the pleasure of the ride. Serena at dinner, her golden curls piled high and that creamy skin glowing in the candlelight.

Once the candle was burning steadily, he sat for a moment, head bowed and his fingers clutching at his hair. He tried to breathe deeply, but the air felt thick and heavy in his lungs. Throwing aside the covers he jumped out of bed and walked, naked, to the window. He threw up the sash. The night was still, silent, but at least air flowed in, cooling his heated skin. A sliver of moon was reflected in the water of the moat and, together with the pinpricks of starlight, threw a blue-grey light over the surrounding land.

It was a view Quinn loved, but tonight he saw nothing, his thoughts turned inward, to the desire that burned so fiercely within him. It was not his custom to dredge up memories of Barbara but he did so now, trying to recall if he had felt this way about her. They had been young and very much in love, but indulging in anything more than a chaste kiss had been unthinkable. Ironic, then, that now he was married and even a kiss was out of the question.

His sharp ears picked up a noise outside his door. He eased the window closed, listening. There it was again, a definite padding of feet in the corridor. Frowning, he scooped up his dressing gown and shrugged himself into it. Who on earth was abroad in the house at this time of night? He would stake his life that it was not Shere. The valet's step was firm and steady. What he could hear was definitely stealthy. Furtive. Intruders, perhaps. He moved quietly towards the door, but now there was nothing but silence. He held his breath as his ears strained for the faintest sound. Then he heard it. The creak of the floorboard directly outside his room.

For a third time, Serena hesitated in the dark corridor. When had she become so indecisive? She must either carry out her plan or scurry back to her room and admit she was a coward. Screwing up her courage, she stepped up to Quinn's door, only to recoil as it flew open and Quinn's black shape filled the opening.

'Serena!'

Her hand was still clenched, ready to knock, and he caught it in his own. There was no going back now. He drew her into the bedchamber, a room the same size as her own, but whereas Serena's chamber was decorated in soft shades of yellow, the master bedroom was much darker and furnished with heavy mahogany pieces. A single candle burned, enough light to see the garish pattern on his silk banyan. He had loosely knotted the belt to hold it in place, but her heart, already thudding, jumped erratically when her eyes wandered to the alarming amount of bare chest on display.

'Why are you here?'

Her throat was too dry to speak. It was impossible to drag her eyes away from the muscled contours of his breast and the smattering of fine hairs that shadowed it.

'Serena?'

His finger beneath her chin obliged her to look up. He was smiling at her and she desperately wanted to smile back, but her nerves were too stretched. But she must speak. She must say something.

'I, um, I wanted to see you.'

'I am flattered.'

His hand dropped but his eyes were still upon her, warm and reassuring. If she kept looking at him, if she did not think about the black frame of the bed looming in the shadows behind him, the threatening darkness might not terrify her. She ran her tongue nervously across her dry lips.

'I am your w-wife, Quinn. It is time we...' The thunder of her heart was so loud she could not concentrate. 'We...'

Gently, he drew her closer, his huge frame blocking out the light. She turned her face up to him, wanting his kiss, wanting to feel safe. She would close her eyes and surrender to the desire that was slowly unfurling deep inside her. He lowered his head and her eyelids fluttered as his lips brushed hers. It was gentle, the merest touch, but the jolt of awareness took her by surprise and she jumped.

Immediately Quinn released her. Behind him she saw the huge bed, it loomed over them, throwing deep shadows on to the ceiling. The blackness of the canopy drew her eyes and held her gaze. She was transported back to the inn, trapped, powerless. Suffocating.

Don't let me go, Quinn. Hold me. Hold me!

The words screamed in her head, but she could not give voice to them and, worst of all, when she did manage to shift her eyes back to him, Quinn was looking at her in bewilderment. If only she could speak, explain, but fear held her mute and mixed with the dreadful terror that filled her head was Dorothea's voice, dripping with scorn.

He is too good for you. You do not deserve him. You will only disappoint him.

'Serena. What is it?'

Quinn put out his hand and she quickly stepped back.

'I c-cannot.' Her hands clutched at her wrap, pulling it tight beneath her chin. 'I thought I could, but... forgive me.'

And with a sob, she fled.

* * *

The morning sun streamed into Serena's bedchamber. She was sitting at her dressing table, staring at her wan face in the glass. After what had happened last night, how could she face Quinn? She had already asked Polly to bring her breakfast upstairs, to delay leaving her room, but the bread and butter remained untouched on the tray. Perhaps she should go back to bed and have Polly say that she was not well. A coward's way out, she knew, but it would buy her a little more time.

There was a light knock at the door and she turned as Quinn entered. Her heart sank. Would he dismiss Polly and demand an explanation for what had occurred last night? Instead he met her nervous gaze with a smile.

'Good morning, madam. It is such a glorious day that I thought we might ride out.' He spoke cheerfully and she wondered if last night had been nothing but a dream, but only for a moment. Quinn glanced towards Polly. 'Fetch my lady's riding habit, if you please.'

As the maid hurried off into the dressing room, Serena turned back to her glass and picked up the hairbrush.

'I am not sure I have the time to ride this morning,' she said, trying to keep the rising panic from her voice. 'I must see Cook. Surely you have not forgotten the Beckfords are dining with us again?'

'No, I have not forgotten. Nor have I forgotten that you agreed the menu yesterday. There is nothing that cannot wait until we have had our ride.' He came over and stood behind her, resting his hands lightly on her shoulders. If he noticed how she froze he did not show it. 'A little fresh air will do you good, Serena. I shall have the horses brought to the door in half an hour. Is that long enough for you to make yourself ready?'

His tone was perfectly amicable and his reflection showed he was smiling, but there was something in his eyes that told her he would not accept a refusal.

'Perfectly, my lord.'

'Good girl.' She felt the pressure of his fingers on her shoulders and he dropped a quick kiss upon her head before leaving the room. Even her heightened senses could detect no censure in him, only calm reassurance. When she was alone her shoulders sagged. Dorothea was right. She did not deserve such a man.

Once they were mounted, Quinn dismissed the grooms and escorted Serena into the park. She was on edge, last night's encounter hanging over her like a cloud, but a gallop across the springy turf did much to calm her. Quinn led the way to the northern boundary, drawing rein in a small stand of trees on the high ground and pointing out to her the fallow deer grazing in the sheltered valley below them. The scene was so peaceful and Serena felt the last of the tension draining away. A sigh of contentment escaped her and she was aware of Quinn's sudden, questioning glance.

'You have a delightful home, my lord.'

'It is your home, too, Serena.'

'Yes, of course.'

She felt the flush on her cheek, a sudden prickle of guilt, but Quinn was staring out across the park.

'This is one of my favourite spots,' he remarked. 'Look, over there is the tower, where we were standing yesterday.'

'Yes, I see it.'

She followed his pointing finger, but her thoughts were fixed on what had occurred last night. It had been such a good day and they had been in accord. Until the end, when she had ruined everything.

'My lord, about last night.'

His hand came up. He said, not looking at her, 'You do not need to say anything, Serena.'

'But I do.' She kept her own gaze straight ahead, her hands resting together on her leg and Crystal's reins held lightly in her fingers. Somehow it was easier to talk thus. 'I panicked. Suddenly I could think of nothing but that night. At Hitchin.'

'The memories will fade in time, believe me. I am sorry if you think I am rushing you.'

'No, no, it is not your fault at all. You have been most patient with me.' She drew a breath. 'I rarely have nightmares now and I thought… I wanted to prove I could be a…a good wife, but the memory was too strong, it blotted out everything else. After all your kindness.'

She stopped, her voice suspended, and he reached across, his large hand enveloping both of hers.

'Then we must make new memories. Happy ones to replace your terrors. Are we agreed?'

'Yes.' She raised her head and gave him a tremulous smile. 'Yes, indeed that is what we must do. So perhaps we should continue exploring the park, if you have time, my lord?'

He released her hands, flicking her cheek with one careless finger.

'All the time in the world for you, Serena.'

That surprised a shaky laugh from her. 'Why, sir, was that a compliment?'

'Aye, by Gad, I think it was. Whatever is happening to me?' He scowled, but beneath his brows there was a definite gleam of amusement in his hazel eyes. 'I shall have to insist upon your silence, madam, or I shall be losing my reputation as the rudest man in England!'

The drawing room was empty when Quinn walked in later that day. He glanced around him, a slight smile of appreciation curving the corners of his mouth. Everything was in readiness for the evening. The panelling glowed and the air was redolent with beeswax, decanters and glasses had been placed on a side table, and the empty fireplace was filled with a colourful arrangement of summer flowers. That must be Serena's idea, he thought, for it was not something he had seen in the house before.

Serena. He threw himself down in a chair, the smile growing. The morning's ride had somehow turned into a day's excursion. Neither of them had been in any hurry to curtail their outing and when they had finished exploring the park, he had taken her out into the surrounding countryside, where they had stopped to refresh themselves at an inn at the very limit of the Quinn estates.

The Bird in Hand was a small hostelry, more used to catering for local farmers and tradesmen, but Lord Quinn was well known and the landlady had hastily tidied her own parlour for their use and provided them with lamb pie and a rich fruitcake, washed down by a very palatable ale. The landlady had been mortified that she had nothing save coffee that was suitable for a lady to drink, but Serena had immediately assured her a glass of small beer would suit her very well.

The new Lady Quinn had put her hosts at their ease. There was nothing high in her manner, she had shown no reluctance to converse with them and when those locals gathered in the taproom expressed a desire to give a toast to my lord and his lady, she had suggested a fresh barrel of ale should be tapped and the reckoning sent to Melham Court.

The smile turned into a full grin. Nothing was more guaranteed to endear her to the neighbourhood and they had ridden away from the Bird in Hand to the huzzahs and cheers of the assembled company. It was difficult to describe the warm glow of pride he had felt for his bride at that moment.

'Sir Anthony and Lady Beckford, my lord.'

Dunnock's announcement interrupted Quinn's reverie and he rose to meet his dinner guests. Lottie did not stand on ceremony, she clasped his hands when he welcomed her, tugging him down so she might kiss his cheek.

'Are we unpardonably late, Quinn? Tony would insist on changing his coat before we set out.'

'Only because *you*, madam wife, complained the other was too shabby to wear out again, even for a cosy dinner with friends,' drawled Tony, following his wife into the room.

Lottie dismissed the accusation with an airy wave. 'We should give our friends no less respect than anyone else. In fact, we should give them more. Which is why you had to wear your good coat and I had to buy a new gown.'

'I am flattered,' murmured Quinn. 'As to being late... You are nothing of the kind. As you see, Serena is not yet downstairs. We went out riding today and were a little late returning.'

'Riding?' Lottie fixed him with her bright, inquisitive gaze as he escorted her to a chair. 'I did not think you had anything suitable for a lady in your stables.'

'I did not. I fetched a mare over from Pirton earlier this week.'

'From Hackleby's stables?' asked Tony. 'I had heard he was disposing of his cattle.'

'Aye, he doesn't ride much these days and decided it was time to sell almost everything.'

He broke off as the door opened. Serena stood in the doorway, a shy smile trembling on her mouth.

'I do beg your pardon that I was not here to greet you.'

Quinn crossed the floor and took her hand.

'A bride's prerogative, my dear.' He led her forward. 'And we agreed this would be an informal affair, did we not?'

'We did indeed,' cried Lottie, patting the seat beside her. 'Come and join me on the sofa, Serena, and tell me all about your ride today. Quinn says he has purchased a horse for you.'

'Yes,' replied Serena, making herself comfortable beside her friend. 'A beautiful dapple-grey mare.'

'I remember seeing Lady Hackleby out on her in the early part of last year,' exclaimed Lottie. 'That was before her illness. But, heavens, my dear, the creature did not look to be a quiet ride—nor an easy one. Why, she must be fifteen hands at least!'

Serena laughed at that. 'It is true. And she is quite a handful, but I like that. My lord could not have chosen anything better for me.'

Quinn felt a rush of pleasure at her words. He met her eyes for one smiling moment as he crossed to the side table to pour wine for his guests, then Tony was asking Serena what she thought of the park.

'I like it very much,' she responded. 'We rode to the tower. Do you know it?'

'The building at the end of the beech avenue? Yes, I have seen it when I have been riding here,' remarked Tony, taking a glass of wine from Quinn. 'Never been inside, though.'

Quinn smiled slightly. 'My wife has plans to hold dinners there.'

'Very small ones,' added Serena, when Lottie exclaimed in delight at the prospect. 'It will not hold more than half a dozen. More formal dinners will have to be held here.'

'I cannot recall any formal dinners at Melham Court,' remarked Lottie.

'No, my parents only entertained their closest friends here. And as a bachelor I have never felt inclined to host anything of that nature.'

'No, you have never been very hospitable, have you, Quinn?' Lottie wagged her finger at him. 'That must change now, sir!'

Serena shook her head. 'We may hold the occasional party here, but in the main we intend to live very quietly.'

Lottie said drily, 'You will have little choice, my dear, if you intend to rely upon neighbours to fill your table.' She looked up at Tony's muttered admonition and spread her hands. 'What have I said that is not true? There are not above a dozen families here to dine with.

For our ball you know we relied upon acquaintances making the journey from town.'

'Including the Downings,' added Serena. 'I am very grateful to you for that.'

Tony shifted in his seat and looked at Quinn. It was a fleeting glance, but Serena wondered what she had said to cause the look of consternation. Before she could ask, Dunnock entered.

'Ah, dinner is ready.' Quinn rose. 'Shall we go in?'

When the meal was over, Serena carried Lottie off to the drawing room, leaving the gentlemen to enjoy a glass of brandy. They remained in companionable silence for a while, Tony speaking only to compliment his host on the excellence of his wines.

He pushed his glass towards Quinn. 'You will need to restock your cellar, if you plan to entertain more.'

'Serena told you herself that she wishes to live quietly.'

'Yes, I heard that, but I am not sure I believe it.' He sat back, warming his refilled glass between his hands. 'Your wife is a society creature, my friend—it is in her blood, the way she converses, the quickness of her mind. She thrives on company. Mrs Downing said as much at the ball and I agree with her. How long do you think she will be happy, shut away in a quiet backwater?'

Quinn frowned. 'Serena is free to go to town whenever she wishes. She only has to tell me.'

'But will she, knowing that gossip will be rife? You should take her to London, Quinn. Show the *ton* that you are not ashamed of your wife.'

'Of course I am not ashamed of her!' The frown

deepened to a scowl as he recalled Jack Downing's disparaging remarks. He said curtly, 'I will not force her to go to town until she is ready.'

'She will never be ready if you keep her hidden away here, my friend.'

Quinn drained his glass and pushed back his chair. 'Shall we join the ladies?'

Chapter Ten

The golden glow of the evening sun had been replaced by candlelight by the time Quinn and Tony returned to the drawing room, although the long doors to the terrace were thrown wide to allow in the balmy night air. The gentlemen's quiet entrance went unnoticed and they both remained by the door, unwilling to cause a distraction. Serena was at the piano, playing a sonata, while Lottie sat beside her, turning the pages. Quinn had not seen Serena play before, although he had occasionally heard the melodic strains of the piano filtering through the house, but Serena always left the instrument as soon as he appeared.

He stood now, entranced by the performance, until the final note died away.

'Bravo, my lady.' Tony applauded enthusiastically.

'She is very good, isn't she?' said Lottie. 'I could never play Scarlatti.'

'That is because you will not take the trouble to practise,' retorted her fond spouse. 'But Quinn here is an excellent pianist. Has he played for you, Serena?'

'Not yet, but I had guessed he was musical because

this is such a beautiful instrument.' She ran her hands over the keys. 'It is kept in tune, too. Do you do that yourself, my lord?'

'No. Houston's send someone out from town to do it.'

Lottie said mischievously, 'I think the two of you should play a duet for us.'

Serena quickly vacated her seat at the piano, blushing and shaking her head.

'Perhaps we shall,' said Quinn, 'when we have had the opportunity to practise together.'

Serena said hastily, 'Lottie, you were telling me about the new Italian songs you have purchased. Perhaps you would sing one of them?' She glanced at the clock. 'We have time, before I order the tea tray.'

'Yes indeed,' declared Tony. 'Since you made me send for the sheet music, at vast expense, may I say, I should like to see what we get for our money!'

Knowing that Tony would not deny his wife anything, Quinn laughed at that.

'Yes, come along, Lottie,' he said, taking Serena's arm and drawing her down on the sofa beside him. 'It is your turn to entertain us.'

Serena tried to concentrate on the singing, but all she could think of was Quinn sitting beside her. He was at his ease, one arm along the back of the sofa. Surely it was mere imagination that she could feel the heat of it on her spine. If she were to relax just a little, she was sure she would feel his hand against her shoulders. The thought was strangely exciting, but frightening, too. After last night, would he think she was teasing him? He might be offended. He might even move away and that was the last thing she wanted.

Serena remained rigidly upright, fixing her attention upon Lottie's performance and trying to forget how close Quinn was, his muscular thigh almost touching hers, his fingers only inches from her back. She thought she would be pleased when the song was over, but when it ended and Quinn sat up to applaud she found herself wishing she had taken advantage of the situation, had settled herself against her husband and enjoyed a moment of closeness with him. He might even have welcomed it. If only she had made the attempt, but now the moment was gone and all that was left was regret, bitter as gall. Nothing of this showed in her face, however, as she went over to the bell to ring for tea, but she was aware of Quinn's eyes upon her and could not help wondering if he, too, was regretting the lost opportunity.

Conversation was desultory while Serena prepared and served tea to her guests. When Sir Anthony came over to take his cup from her, he remarked cheerfully that he hoped she had not found her first dinner party at Melham Court too onerous.

'Not at all,' she told him, smiling. 'It has been a pleasure.'

'And for me, also,' declared Lottie. 'It is the first time I have ever dined here.'

'Truly?' Serena's brows lifted in surprise.

'As a bachelor I could not invite respectable females to dine here,' explained Quinn.

'Not that he invited *any* females to dine here,' Tony added hastily.

Quinn was grinning and Serena felt emboldened to reply.

'No, he told me he had not moved here to be sociable.'

'Which makes this quite an occasion,' added Lottie. She threw her husband a triumphant glance. 'And therefore merited my buying a new gown!'

'Not that you ever require an excuse,' said Tony.

The loving smile he gave his wife sent a tiny dart through Serena. It felt very like jealousy. Not that it was Sir Anthony she wanted to look at her in quite that way, of course. She glanced from Lottie's canary-yellow gown to her own grey skirts.

'When I looked at my wardrobe this evening I realised that it is all a little...sober. I must remedy that with all speed. Is there a reliable local seamstress, ma'am, or should I look to town?'

'Oh, it must be London, without question,' replied Lottie. 'There is not enough business here to provide a living for a good seamstress.'

'Then I shall send to town in the morning—'

'No need for that,' Quinn interrupted her. 'I shall take you there myself.'

Serena was so surprised that she almost dropped her teacup. She carefully lowered it back into its saucer before turning a questioning glance at her husband. He met her eyes with a smile.

'I think it is time I showed off my wife to the world.'

'Did you mean what you said last night, about going to town?'

Serena and Quinn were at breakfast and, with servants in attendance, she asked the question with as casual an air as she could manage.

'Of course. Johnson is already looking for a suitable house for us. You need any number of gowns and it will be much more convenient than having dozens of seamstresses coming to Melham Court. Mrs Talbot must remain here, of course, but we will take Dunnock with us and he will ensure we are comfortable. Many families will have removed from London by now, but I hope there will be sufficient amusements to entertain us.' Quinn paused to select a bread roll from the proffered basket and waited for the footman to withdraw before he continued. 'We must face society sooner or later, Serena.'

She flushed. 'You mean I must face up to the scandal I have caused.'

'Yes, but you will not be alone. I shall be with you.'

She glanced towards the door, to make sure they could not be overheard.

'I have seen the newspaper reports. I know what they are saying of me. That I, that I—'

'That you eloped with your lover, but forsook him when a wealthier catch appeared. The wealthier catch being myself, although names were not spelled out.'

Her head dropped. 'Yes.'

'Do not be too downcast. Newspapers are notorious for giving too much space to gossip and speculation and not enough to serious matters, such as the riots in East Anglia and the atrocious weather, which will cause food shortages throughout the country.'

'That will affect us all, will it not?' she asked him, momentarily diverted. 'What will you do if your tenants have a bad harvest?'

'I can forgo the rents, although I can do nothing about the rise in the price of bread.'

'But perhaps you should be here, if there is likely to be unrest?'

'Johnson has been my steward and secretary for

years, he knows my ways and can deal with everything in my absence. We will leave at the end of the week, if that is convenient to you?'

'Perfectly, my lord.'

She could not keep the doubtful note from her voice. Quinn pushed back his chair and came to stand behind her, resting his hands lightly on her shoulders.

'We will face down the gossips, never fear.' He gave a short laugh. 'The newspapers are currently speculating on the end of the world, following reports of the earthquake in Scotland! There can be no interest in our little scandal.'

'I devoutly hope you are right, sir.'

Lord Quinn's travelling coach bowled into London on a rainy late-August day, when the sky was dark with lowering grey clouds. There had been little for Serena to do regarding the arrangements. Quinn's excellent steward had found three houses that were available for the summer and Quinn had suggested they take the most fashionable and expensive.

'There is only one detail you might not approve,' he had explained, when they went over the details together. 'There is a connecting door between our bedchambers. However, you have my word I shall never come into your room unless I am invited. You will have to trust me on that point, Serena.'

Serena had agreed to it because she knew enough of Quinn now to believe he would keep his word. However, as they pulled up at the steps of the elegant town house in Berkeley Square, she experienced a little shimmer of apprehension, although it had little to do with the sleeping arrangements. She would much rather be in a quiet street than in such a busy square. Gunter's tea shop was situated close by and it was a popular destination for the *ton*, who could even order ices to be brought to them in their carriages. There would be a constant stream of the rich and fashionable walking or driving past their door.

Quinn gave her fingers a squeeze as he helped her down from the carriage.

'Head up and smile,' he murmured, pulling her hand on to his arm. 'If we are going to cause a stir, then we are well placed here to give everyone something to talk about.'

One of Serena's first tasks was to write to her sister-in-law. Dorothea replied by return, making it plain that the seaside was proving so beneficial to little Arthur's health that she would not be cutting short her visit. However, a note to Elizabeth Downing was followed up almost immediately by Mrs Downing and her daughter calling in person and they left Serena in no doubt of their continued friendship.

This was comforting, but since neither Serena nor Quinn had made efforts to contact anyone else in London, she expected her arrival in the capital to pass almost unnoticed. However, during those first weeks, while she was still, in Quinn's words, *making herself fit to be seen*, a steady trickle of calling cards appeared at the house and the invitation cards lining the mantelpiece grew apace.

Not that Serena had much opportunity to dwell upon the number of invitations. She spent her days visiting warehouses, where she picked out ells of exquisite materials which were then taken to the modistes to be made up into gowns for every occasion. There were also trips to milliners, glovemakers, shoemakers and anyone else who could provide the accessories so essential to a lady of fashion.

Quinn had ordered that Serena was to have the finest of everything and no expense was to be spared. He even accompanied her on some of her outings, including an early call he insisted that she pay to Mrs Bell, to choose a new walking dress. When that celebrated seamstress suggested a pastel blue twill for Lady Quinn he was quick to reject it.

'No, no, such washed-out shades drain her of colour,' he barked. 'Try that one.' He pointed to a bolt of rich turquoise cloth on a high shelf.

Serena's eye had already been drawn to the material but she had allowed herself to be persuaded to look at the pale pinks and blues that Mrs Bell assured her were all the rage. Quinn's brusque intervention made the seamstress bridle a little, but she was too sensible to take umbrage at the interference of such a wealthy customer. However, when Serena stood before the looking glass with a length of the material draped across her shoulder, Mrs Bell was the first to admit that it was the perfect colour for my lady.

'It is merino wool, madam, although not at all heavy. It will make up beautifully into the military style that you have requested.' She stood behind Serena, gazing over her shoulder into the mirror. 'We shall add epaulettes, frogging and braid, and I suggest half-boots of kid, dyed to match. You will need a shirt of the finest cambric, of course, and a cravat. And on your head, we should have something simple, I think, such as a small round hat of moss silk. What say you to that, my lord?

If you prefer we might have a jockey cap, or a silk cap
and ostrich feathers...'

'As though you were suddenly the foremost connoisseur of female attire,' Serena told him as he escorted
her back to their carriage. She giggled. 'I do not know
how I kept my countenance when you told her you knew
nothing of such things.'

'It is the truth,' he replied. 'I leave such details to you
to decide.' As he handed her into the coach he added
darkly, 'As long as the result does not make you look
like a dowd.'

'I shall do my best to make sure of that, my lord.
But I think you may be assured that Mrs Bell will do
her best to please.'

'Good.' He paused in the doorway, one booted foot
on the step. 'Now, what are your plans for the rest of
the day? Do you wish to visit more warehouses? Or
mayhap you wish to go to Bond Street. If that is the
case I shall send you back to Berkeley Square to collect your maid. I, on the other hand, believe I deserve
a reward for spending the morning discussing frills
and furbelows.'

'You do indeed.' Serena smiled, wondering which
of the clubs he would visit. She was therefore surprised
at his next words.

'I thought I might look in at Somerset House. The
Royal Academy. Perhaps you might like to come with
me.'

Quinn was busy rubbing at a mark on his boot and
not looking at her, so she had no clue as to what he
wished her to say.

'I would like that very much.'

'Excellent.' Quinn threw up a word to the driver and

climbed into the carriage. 'I thought you might enjoy it—I remember your interest in the Titian.'

Serena turned to gaze out of the window as a tell-tale flush burned her cheeks. She had not forgotten her first morning at Melham Court, coming downstairs in her ruined gown and feeling more than a little shy. They had discussed the Venus and he had conversed with her as an equal. He had made her forget, for a short while, her disastrous situation.

A sigh escaped her. 'I fear you have paid a high price for your kindness to me that night, my lord.'

To her surprise he smiled. 'I think it might cost me a grand tour. Now the war is over we could travel extensively on the Continent. Would you like that, Serena?' He raised his brows. 'What have I said to make you look so shocked? We rub along quite well together, do we not? And if you dare to tell me you do not deserve such kindness then I shall box your ears!'

That made her laugh. 'Then I shall say nothing of the kind. Instead I will tell you that I should like nothing better than to make the grand tour.' Her laughter died. 'I wish we were doing so now, rather than being in town.'

'I am sure you do, but there are some in London who are determined to destroy your reputation and I will not allow that.'

He looked so fierce that she clasped her hands before her. 'You will not challenge anyone to a duel?'

'Not if it can be helped.' It was not the assurance she was hoping for and she bit her lip. 'Well?' he prompted her. 'You had best tell me what is on your mind.'

She looked down at her fingers, writhing together in her lap.

'You are not renowned for your good temper. If you should become angry, you might forget yourself.'

Quinn stared at her, swallowing the sharp retort that would have demonstrated the truth of her words.

'Are you afraid I shall embarrass you, madam?'

'No, never that,' she replied quickly. 'But I know how you abhor town. You do not like society and you are forcing yourself to endure it for my sake.' She fixed him with a look, her dark eyes full of concern. 'If we are to quell the gossip, you will be obliged to squire me to all sorts of parties, most of them full of tiresome people vying for the notice of the *ton*.' Her shoulders lifted in a faint shrug. 'I have no illusions about the fashionable world, Quinn. Hostesses will be so grateful to have you in their house that they will fawn over you in the most embarrassing way. Sycophants will latch on to you because you are wealthy and you will hate it. How will you bear it without losing your temper with them all?'

I will bear it because you are there.

Where the devil had that thought come from? Quinn harrumphed and shifted uncomfortably in his corner.

'My temper is not so ill controlled as you think, madam. Have I ever given you cause to fear me?'

Her face softened. 'Oh, no, you have always been the kindest of men to me. And for so little reward, too.'

He saw the pain in her eyes. She was recalling how she recoiled from his touch. He wanted to reach out, to enfold her in his arms and tell her it did not matter, that everything would come right, in time. But she would flinch from his embrace and he could not bear that. He kept his hands by his sides and looked out of the window as the carriage slowed.

'Ah. Somerset House. Let us go in.'

* * *

The first weeks in London passed in a whirl of activity for Serena. There was little time to rest. When she was not buying clothes or being fitted for another new gown, Quinn took her out and about with him. She enjoyed these excursions, not only to the Royal Academy and the theatre, but also to small, select gatherings of artists, musicians and authors. It was a world away from the glittering ballrooms of the *ton*. The talk was all of art or literature or even politics and Serena loved it.

'I especially like the fact that my opinion is respected, even if they cannot agree with it,' she told Quinn as he escorted her home late one night. She glanced up at him. 'Do they know who you are?'

He laughed. 'But of course.'

'And yet, no one entreats you to sponsor them, or seeks out your support.'

'Because I have made it plain I will not tolerate that. If I choose to become patron to a young artist, or to donate to some worthy cause, that is my affair. I go there for the company and the conversation.'

'Very different from the Drycrofts' ball, which we are engaged to attend tomorrow,' said Serena. 'Our first official engagement. Are you sure we must do this?'

'I thought you wished to go.'

She sighed. 'I was resigned to the fact that we must do so. But I have had word from Lizzie Downing that she has a slight chill and will not be attending, and now...'

He reached out and caught her hand, holding it warm and safe in his own.

'Do you wish to withdraw from the lists, Serena?'

'Why, yes, if you must know. We might live retired until our situation is completely forgotten. Heaven knows there is enough calamity in the world that no one will remember one little scandal in a year's time.'

His grip on her fingers tightened. 'The danger is that by then Forsbrook and the other vicious scandalmongers will have set in stone their version of what happened and it will be a hundred times more difficult to persuade everyone of the truth.'

She sighed. 'Is that so very important?'

'Yes, confound it!' He turned towards her, pulling her close, so that the street lamps and flaring torches illuminated their faces. 'You are made for pleasure, Serena. For laughter and balls and assemblies and dancing until dawn. If you retire to the country it should be because it is what *you* want, not because you have been driven away.'

Serena felt the breath catch in her throat at his fierce determination. He was willing to do this for her sake! At that moment the carriage swung around a corner, throwing her off balance, and she quickly placed her free hand on his chest to steady herself.

'You are a good man, Rufus Quinn.'

Their faces were only inches apart and the devil danced in his eyes. Serena held her breath, waiting for him to pull her close and kiss her. Instead his mouth twisted.

'I am here to show to the world that my wife is beyond reproach,' he said gruffly.

He released her and drew back into the corner, into the shadows. Serena crossed her arms, hugging herself, but it was nowhere near as comforting as having Quinn hold her.

Chapter Eleven

The Drycrofts' reception rooms were filling up when Quinn and Serena arrived, fashionably late. Serena was already acquainted with Lady Drycroft, a plump, kindly soul but an inveterate chatterbox. She was beaming as they came up the stairs towards her.

'Serena—Lady Quinn, I *should* say, how delightful you look, my dear, that watered silk is charming, quite charming, and the colour! What do they call that, my love, old rose? Yes, I thought so. My dear, I have never seen you looking so well. And how is your dear brother? No, not Lord Hambridge, for dear Dorothea writes to me regularly and I know they are going on very well in Worthing. No, I mean the other one. Russington. *Such* a rogue, but a charming one. And his lady, how is she? She has recently been brought to bed, I hear. Do give her my regards when you write.'

The purple ostrich feathers in her turban nodded as she turned to Quinn, eyeing him a little warily as he bowed over her hand.

'How delightful that you could join us, my lord.' Serena did not miss the doubtful note in the lady's voice. 'I do hope you will enjoy our little soirée. My husband has set up cards in the small salon over there, if that is your pleasure. Not that you are obliged to leave the ballroom, of course. After all, dancing is the reason for a ball, is it not?' She gave a nervous little laugh. 'No, no, you are not to be thinking for one moment that we are wishing you otherwise. You will want to dance with your wife, which is quite natural, and another gentleman is always welcome, is that not so, Lady Quinn?'

She continued to chatter, offering to come now and introduce Serena to new partners if his lordship wished to go off and play cards, or indeed to present suitable dancing partners to Lord Quinn, if that was his desire. Serena's lips twitched when she glanced at her husband. His features were schooled into a look of indifference, but she was sufficiently well acquainted with him now to recognise the impatience, nay, horror, growing within him as he listened to his hostess. However, he said nothing and Serena took pity upon him. As soon as their hostess drew breath she broke in.

'Thank you, ma'am, but there is no need for you to quit your post, for I see more guests arriving. I know we must appear very unfashionable, but I would much rather have Lord Quinn with me on my first social outing in town since…since my marriage. If you will excuse us, we shall go and find our way about.'

With a smile she led Quinn away.

'What a gabster,' he muttered. 'I do not know how Drycroft can tolerate such a chatterbox.'

'I believe he spends a deal of time at his club,' Serena murmured.

'No doubt he sleeps there, too. If I had to face such

a chinwagger over breakfast, I would cheerfully throttle her!'

She choked back a laugh. 'No, no, she is perfectly good-natured and I am sure if she knew her chatter irritated you she would be quiet.'

'I would not wager on it,' he muttered darkly.

He led her into the ballroom where the first dances had just ended. A liveried servant announced them in stentorian accents and the chatter died quite away as all eyes turned towards the door.

Serena recognised many of the guests. Hostesses who had welcomed her, gentlemen she had danced with, debutantes and their mothers who had been eager to count the popular Miss Russington among their friends. Now their faces displayed either disapproval or curiosity. Even those matrons she had seen at the Beckfords' ball regarded her with more open hostility than they had shown in Hertfordshire. One young lady, Beatrice Pinhoe, smiled at Serena, until her mother nudged her and muttered something that made Beatrice flush and drop the hand she had raised in greeting.

Only pride prevented Serena from turning and running from the room. Pride and Quinn's presence beside her. His elbow was pressing her arm tight against him, so that she was unable to remove her hand from his sleeve. Not that she wished to do so. She was grateful for his support, it wrapped about her like a shield and gave her the strength to keep her smile in place, to raise her head a little higher and meet the cold stares with at least the appearance of complaisance.

A portly gentleman with bushy side whiskers and claret-coloured cheeks pushed his way through the crowd. He came towards them, saying jovially, 'Quinn, my lady. This is a surprise. Didn't expect to see you here, my lord. Thought you'd be at Melham, delighting in that Titian you stole from under my nose!'

'Instead I am delighting in the company of my new bride,' replied Quinn calmly. 'My dear, let me present the Earl of Dineley to you.'

Quinn's voice and the faint squeeze he gave her fingers dragged Serena's attention away from the censorious looks and she managed to curtsy without wobbling. The momentary hush that had fallen over the room ended. People were chattering again and attention had moved back towards the dance floor, where the musicians were tuning up for another country dance.

'Delightful, quite delightful,' declared Lord Dineley, taking her hand. 'I am very glad now that I decided not to leave town just yet.' He winked at Quinn. 'If I had a nabbed me a beautiful young wife I, too, would want to show her off. In fact, I have a mind to claim her for the next dance—'

His grip on her fingers tightened. Panic flared as Serena wondered how she could refuse without offending the Earl. In the past she would easily have dealt with the situation. Indeed, she had done so dozens of times, but now her brain refused to work.

Quinn rescued her, saying coolly, 'In that case, Dineley, I should be obliged to call you out. I mean to dance with my wife myself.'

'What? Oh, quite. Quite so, sir.'

The Earl's face registered surprise and disappointment but he gave in with good grace and stepped aside. With a nod, Quinn led Serena towards the dance floor.

Relief made her want to giggle. She murmured, 'I

did not expect such aplomb from you, my lord. I am all astonishment.'

'Did you think I would relinquish you to that old roué? We are here to *restore* your reputation, madam, not destroy it completely.'

Serena winced inwardly as they took up their places in the set. She wanted to cry at his harsh words. Instead she kept her head up and her smile in place as the dance began. She skipped forward, put her hand out to her partner.

'Forgive me,' he muttered, pulling her closer. 'It seems my new-found aplomb does not extend to those I hold most dear.'

Serena's step faltered and only by the most strenuous effort did she keep dancing. Had he really said that? Had she heard him correctly? A swift glance up at his unsmiling countenance gave her no clue, but all the same she felt the nerves ease. As they progressed through the familiar movements her smile became genuine and she began to enjoy herself.

Quinn danced the first two dances with his wife, after which the Grindleshams came up to congratulate them upon their marriage and Lord Grindlesham carried Serena off to dance with him. Quinn would have preferred to remain as a spectator, but he knew his duty and solicited Lady Grindlesham to join him on the dance floor. That seemed to give the lead to other couples to approach and although Quinn did not dance again he had the felicity of seeing Serena stand up for every dance.

When supper was announced he was waiting to escort her downstairs. Her eyes sparkled as she left the dance floor on the arm of her partner and there was a becoming flush to her cheek. Quinn's jaw clenched when he saw how the young cub was gazing at Serena and he was obliged to curb his impatience while she thanked the fellow prettily before turning to accompany Quinn out of the ballroom.

'You appear to be enjoying yourself,' he remarked.

'Yes. Yes, I am.'

'And your last partner looked particularly enamoured.' Something dark and uncomfortable stirred within him. 'No doubt he wanted to take you down to supper.'

'He did, of course, but your dreadful scowls frightened him away.'

She was twinkling up at him and the darkness evaporated like smoke.

By the time the carriage carried them back to Berkeley Square Serena was exhausted, but happier than she had expected to be. After the initial reserve, very few of the Drycrofts' guests had kept their distance. She was cynical enough to know that much of this was due to her new position as the bride of one of the richest men in London. They might disapprove of the new Lady Quinn, but they would not cut her acquaintance.

She glanced across the darkened carriage to where she could just make out the black shadow that was Quinn. His renowned incivility had not been evident this evening. She had witnessed first-hand the way some of the guests had fawned over him and would have forgiven him for uttering a sharp set-down. Even when he had been subjected to the inane chatter of ladies who were even more loquacious than their hostess, he had endured it calmly.

'Thank you, my lord.'

The black shape in the corner shifted.

'For what?'

'Oh, for escorting me to the ball, for looking out for me all evening and especially for keeping your temper, when even I found some of the company tiresome in the extreme.'

'Did you?' He sounded surprised. 'You never showed it.'

'Ah, but I had you beside me for most of the evening, ready to carry me away before I could give vent to my impatience. I am only sorry that you did not enjoy yourself.'

'Actually, I *did* enjoy it.'

'What,' she teased him, 'all that toadying and silly chatter?'

'No, not that, of course not. But I took pleasure in some of the company.' She saw the flash of white teeth as he grinned. 'Whenever I wished to escape I could always say I needed to find you. Also, I admit that I enjoyed the music. And dancing with you.' He stretched out his hand. 'We make a good team, I think.'

Smiling, she put her hand into his. 'I am glad you think so, my lord.'

The carriage slowed and Serena recognised the elegant portal of their London house. Quinn handed her out and escorted her into the hall. He gave his hat and gloves to the butler and turned to remove the cloak from Serena's shoulders. His touch through the thin silk set her nerve ends tingling. Little arrows of heat pierced her body, pooling somewhere deep inside. She wanted to lean against him, to turn and put her arms around him, but Dunnock was hovering nearby and such a display would shock the poor man to the core.

Quinn walked with her to the stairs, his hand resting lightly against her back. She hoped he would escort her up to her room. She hoped he would kiss her. Perhaps it was dancing together, or the wine she had drunk, but every fibre of her body ached for his touch. The thought brought on a little quiver of excitement, of pleasurable anticipation that at last she might truly become his wife. She watched silently as he took one of the bedroom candles from the table and lit it.

'You must be tired.' He handed her the candle. 'Goodnight, my dear.'

With a flicker of a smile and a nod, he turned and strode away to the drawing room.

'Damn, damn, damn.'

Quinn shut the drawing room door and leaned against it. He closed his eyes, but all he could see was Serena looking more beautiful than he had ever seen her, with her eyes sparkling and the flawless skin of her shoulders rising from the deep dusk-pink silk gown. Serena dancing at the ball, talking with her acquaintances. Laughing with her partners. Laughing up at *him*.

By heaven, how much he wanted her, but he had given her his word that he would not make love to her until she was ready. When that lecher Dineley had leered at Serena he had seen the panic in her eyes. The woman she had once been would have laughed it off, sent the fellow on his way, but she had lost her confidence and he had stepped in, carrying her off to dance with him, and thereafter he had kept an eye on her, making sure she danced only with gentlemen who could be trusted not to go beyond the line of what was pleasing.

And his efforts had been rewarded. By the end of the evening she had regained much of her sparkle and self-assurance. That pleased him but it had also roused his desire. He shook his head. Much as he wanted to make love to Serena, he dared not rush her.

Exhaling, he pushed himself away from the door and crossed to the side table to pour himself a brandy. Upstairs was his wife, the most desirable woman in London. And he could not have her.

The shadows flickered alarmingly as Serena climbed the stairs and halfway up she stopped, blinking to keep the tears from filling her eyes. The evening had been such a pleasure, she and Quinn had been getting on well, but then, when she wanted him to sweep her up and carry her off to his bed, he had walked away!

'Odious, *odious* creature, how dare he do that?'

How was he to know what you wanted?

She glanced up into the darkness of the landing above her, then down towards the drawing-room door. Dare she do this?

She breathed deeply, trying to calm her nerves and steady the hand that was carrying the candle, then she turned and went back down the stairs. Dunnock had retired back to the nether regions and the hall was deserted. Serena left her bedroom candlestick on the side table and crossed to the drawing room.

Quinn was lounging in an armchair beside the empty fireplace, his eyes fixed upon the brandy glass cradled in one large hand. The draught of the opening door caused the candles in the room to flicker. Quinn glanced up and Serena found herself subjected to a brooding stare. Not only her body, but her mind froze.

'I am not tired,' she managed to say at last, then cringed inwardly. She sounded more like a petulant schoolgirl than a seductress.

Quinn's brows went up a fraction.

'I am pleased to hear it.' He pushed himself out of the chair. 'Would you care to sit down?'

Well, at least he had not thrown her out. Yet. She closed the door and moved to a sofa, grateful for all those years of deportment training that allowed her to glide across a room even when her legs felt like jelly.

He glanced at the assortment of decanters and glasses arranged on a side table.

'May I pour you a glass of something. Ratafia, perhaps. Or claret?'

'Brandy.' Sir Timothy had tried to intoxicate her with red wine and she wanted no reminders of that now. 'I will drink a little brandy, if you please.'

'Very well.'

Quinn poured out a small measure and carried it across to her. He looked wary but intrigued and after handing her the glass he sat down beside her, his large frame filling the satin-covered space. He touched his glass against hers, then settled himself back into the corner, turning slightly so that he might look at her, his free hand resting along the back of the sofa.

A stillness settled over the room, broken only by the occasional flicker of a candle and the rhythmic tick, tick of the French ormolu mantel clock. Serena took a sip from her glass, remembering far-off days when she had smuggled brandy into the school for a midnight feast with her friends. She needed to find a little of that daring spirit now, for Quinn seemed determined to wait for her to break the silence.

'I enjoyed this evening, my lord,' she said, running her tongue over her dry lips. 'I did not want it to end. Not the dancing,' she added hastily. 'I mean... I mean *us*.'

Her eyes were on the glass in her hand, yet she was aware that Quinn's attention was fixed upon her. She lifted the glass to her lips again, but the heat spreading over her neck and face had nothing to do with the brandy. A little bubble of hysterical laughter escaped her.

'I am at a loss, my education d-did not include how one should d-discuss these things with one's husband, but you s-said that *when* we c-consummate our marriage must be up to me, that it m-must be my decision and I...what I am trying to say...'

The sofa creaked as he sat up suddenly.

'You are babbling, Serena.' Gently, he took the glass from her fingers, putting it down beside his on the sofa table behind them.

'I know, but I am very much afraid that if I do not speak now I will not have the courage again and then it will be too late—'

'Hush.' He put a finger to her lips. 'I understand. I have already told you, there is no hurry.'

He put his arm about her and pulled her close, until her head was resting on his shoulder. He stroked her hair, his large hand surprisingly gentle. Serena relaxed against him with a shuddering sigh.

'Oh, but there *is*,' she muttered, one hand clutching at his lapel. 'I *want* it to happen. I want it quite *desperately*.'

'Desperately?' He put his fingers beneath her chin and, obedient to the pressure, she looked up at him. He was smiling. 'Then let us see what we can do about that.'

He lowered his head, his lips gently brushing hers. She slipped one hand around his neck, pulling him closer. Her lips parted, she was relaxing, melting against him. He shifted his position and pulled her on to his lap while she curled her fingers in his hair. The silky strength of it excited her, as did the complex scent of the man, the smell of his skin mixed with spices and soap, and the taste of him, overlaid with just a hint of brandy. His arms tightened, she could feel the taut muscle of his body pressed against her, but despite the curl of pleasure deep in her core, panic began to gnaw at her.

No. She would not be defeated. She *wanted* this and would not be denied.

'Take me, Quinn,' she muttered against his mouth. 'Take me now. Quickly!'

The last word was an entreaty. Quinn raised his head. He was still holding her against him and she could feel the frantic thud of his heart. His breathing was rapid and she put a hand up to his cheek, feeling the rough stubble against her palm.

'I want you to do this, Quinn.' She was begging, afraid of the insidious terror creeping up on her. 'Please, before it is too late!'

He stared down at her. Then, as his breathing steadied he put his hand over hers and drew it away from his face. He settled her back on the seat beside him, but kept a firm hold of her hands.

'Tell me what you mean by that.'

'I w-want to please you,' she murmured, looking away from him.

He said gently, 'This is not how it should be, Serena. There must be pleasure for you, too.'

'No, no, I have to do this, Quinn. It is my duty, as your wife.'

'Your duty!' His grip on her fingers tightened. 'Duty be damned. If I wanted only *my* pleasure I could have taken you weeks ago, is that not so?'

She bowed her head. 'You have been too good, too kind to me, b-but it is no use. I c-cannot enjoy a man's embrace. I thought I could but…fear engulfs me and…and I w-want to run away.'

She blinked rapidly, but could not prevent a rogue tear dropping on to her lap. Her heart sank. Any moment now he would send her back to her room.

Quinn did indeed release her, but only so he could cradle her face in gentle hands.

'Let us do this another way,' he said, wiping her cheeks with his thumbs. 'You shall tell me what you want me to do.'

A fiery blush burned Serena's cheeks. 'I—I cannot. I have no idea. I do not know how…'

She twisted away and sat beside him, her arms crossed as if to shield herself.

Quinn cleared his throat. 'Very well, let me make a suggestion. I am no rake, Serena, but I know that most ladies like being kissed. You appeared to enjoy that.'

'Yes,' she said shyly. 'I d-did. I do.'

'Good. Then let us start again.'

He put one arm about her shoulders and kissed her, a long, slow, languorous kiss that melted her bones. When he lifted his head, she remained with her head thrown back against his shoulder.

He smiled down at her. 'Did that frighten you?'

She gave a little shake of her head.

'And do you think you might like me to kiss your neck?'

'I think I might,' she said cautiously.

'Good.' He brushed his lips across hers, then his mouth trailed light, butterfly kisses along her jaw until he reached the spot just below her ear. A little sigh escaped her as he gently nibbled the soft skin. She closed her eyes and tilted her head to one side to give him more room. The caress of his lips was soothing, relaxing. No dark fears stirred within her.

'How is that?' he murmured, his tongue flicking over her ear.

'It is very...pleasant.' He stopped and she added quickly. 'I l-like it. Very much.'

'Excellent.' She gripped his shoulder as his teeth grazed her earlobe. She snuggled closer, aware of a sudden urge to purr. He breathed softly, 'Shall we move on a little?'

'Oh, yes.' She sighed. 'If you please.'

He settled her more comfortably against the sofa before his lips moved slowly down the side of her neck in a series of featherlight kisses. She gave a little moan when he reached the hollow between the collarbones.

Quinn raised his head. 'Do you not like it?'

'Yes, yes, I do. But I have never felt like this before,' she said, greatly daring, 'Could we begin again, perhaps?'

'Of course.'

This time she returned his kiss, her lips parting, and

she eagerly tangled her tongue with his in a sensual dance that left them both breathless. By the time his mouth had worked its way back to the hollow at the base of her throat, she had thrown back her head and her eyes were closed.

'What would you like me to do next?' he murmured.

'Wh-what else do ladies like?' she gasped, her body arching as he trailed one finger down her breastbone.

'Let me see if I can remember.' His finger ran around the neckline of her gown and she shivered with delight. 'But a word will stop me, do you understand?'

She nodded and he dropped a kiss on her shoulder, then returned his attentions to her mouth. She responded eagerly, tingling beneath the warmth of his palm as his hand slid over her silk gown. When he caressed her breasts, they strained to break free of the confining bodice. His expert kisses made her senses reel as his tongue teased and explored, stirring up the pool of latent desire that was steadily growing deep in her core.

She was dimly aware of his hand moving down over her waist and her hips, then he was gently pulling up the silken skirts, but she was too intent on enjoying his kisses to care, until she felt his hand on her bare thigh. She tensed and immediately Quinn stopped.

'Would you like this to end now?'

He breathed the words against her cheek and she sighed, her fears melting.

'No.'

Her reward was another deep, penetrating kiss, made all the more thrilling by the way her body was reacting to his fingers on her thigh. Heat coursed through her, an aching need for more. His hand moved upwards and Quinn continued to caress her, gently brushing over and around the sensitive skin until at last his fingers slid gently into her and she welcomed him with a little moan of pure pleasure. She moved against him restlessly as excitement rippled through her, a trickle at first, but building, like waves pushing against a dam. It was too much. She broke away from his kiss and dragged in a long, gasping breath.

'Enough?' Quinn ran his lips over her neck.

'I d-don't know.'

His soft laugh sent a shudder of need running through her and she clung to him. His fingers began to work again, stroking, teasing, drawing responses from every nerve in her body until all the attention was fixed on the aching core that was pulsing with a rhythm all of its own. Serena was no longer in control. The dam broke and her body bucked and writhed while Quinn continued his relentless pleasuring, unpenetrating, until she tensed and arched and cried out. Then his large hand cupped her, holding her fast as the last shuddering spasms racked her exhausted body.

Serena clung to him, eyes closed and breathing ragged.

'There,' he murmured at last, gently straightening her skirts. 'Did that frighten you?'

'Yes.' She looked up at him in wonder. 'Yes, but in a good way. I never knew...'

He kissed her nose. 'I am aware of that. Now, would you like to finish your drink?'

Serena leaned against Quinn and sipped her brandy. He kept one arm about her, and the comfortable, companionable silence that enveloped them was as unexpected as her reactions to this evening. When she had followed Quinn to the drawing room she had expected a hasty coupling that would satisfy a need, rather than the raw, all-consuming delight she had experienced.

'I am confused,' she said slowly. 'It seems I have taken all the pleasure this evening and not given anything in return.'

'I wouldn't say that.' The smile he gave her sent the blood pounding around her body again.

She looked away, blushing. 'I w-would like to repay the favour, Quinn.'

'I shall insist upon it, one day, but not now. You need to rest.'

He stood up and drew her to her feet. She was not sure she could stand, but with his arm to support her they made their way without mishap up the stairs. At her bedroom door they stopped.

'Goodnight, Serena.'

She clung to him and forced herself to voice the question that was rattling around in her head.

'Do you n-not w-want me?'

Her eyes searched his face. With a sigh Quinn drew her into his arms and kissed her gently. 'More than you can ever know, Serena, but there are fears and memories to be expunged. We must take our time.' He reached behind her and opened the door. 'Now, off to bed with you.'

More than you can ever know.

Serena hugged the words to her as she allowed Polly to help her into her nightgown and when at last she snuggled beneath the covers, she sank into a deep, contented sleep.

Quinn was in no very good temper when he allowed Shere to help him into his dark blue evening coat. He had not seen Serena since last night, when she had come to him, wanted him to make love to her, but so very afraid. It had tested him to the limit, demonstrating to her the pleasure of man's touch while denying himself a similar release.

He wished now that business had not kept him out of the house all day, wished they were not engaged to go to the Beddingtons' this evening. Damnation, it would be the sort of evening he disliked most. Hot, crowded rooms where one could scarce make oneself heard, the women vying to outshine one another with the latest fashions, men looking for social or financial advancement and all of them eager to share the latest gossip and scandal.

Serena had told him Mrs Downing had called and offered her a place in their carriage, so he need not have gone to all this effort. It was another wet evening and the last thing he wanted was to drive a dozen miles to mix with people he barely knew. He stood pensively before the looking glass as his valet gave his shoulders a final brush. Why the devil had he allowed himself to be sucked into this?

The answer was in his head even before he had finished the question. Serena. She needed him, not only the protection of his name, but his support. It would not be for ever. Once she had regained her confidence he could leave her to attend such parties without him.

'Will that be all, my lord?'

'Yes. Thank you.' He turned away from his own scowling image and took the hat and gloves Shere was holding out to him. 'Don't wait up for me—it is likely to be late.'

He strode out of his bedchamber and ran down the

stairs, his mood as grim as the weather. Once Serena had recovered, what use would she have for the over-large, unsociable man she had married?

Serena was waiting for him in the drawing room and the iron fist about his heart tightened at the sight of her. She was wearing another of the new gowns, a glowing emerald shot silk. He was dazzled. Not by the diamonds that winked at her throat and ears, but by her smile, the luminosity of her eyes. He stopped in the doorway, staring at her.

She was more than beautiful—she was radiant. No man would be able to resist her. Would she still need him once she realised that?

'Will it do?' she asked, glancing nervously down at the shimmering skirts. 'The gown arrived less than an hour ago from Mrs Bell.'

He came forward and took her hand. 'I have never seen you looking better.'

'Thank you.' The anxious shadow left her eyes and she twinkled up at him. 'You must take some of the credit, Quinn. This colour was your choice.'

For the briefest instant he regretted his part in making her look so fine, until it hit him: even in sackcloth and ashes she would be irresistible. She was like a butterfly, emerging from its chrysalis. Once her wings were dry she would want to test them.

'So it was and a good choice, too.' He pressed a light kiss upon her fingers and felt them tremble. He might not be able to keep her, but she was his for a little longer yet. 'The carriage is at the door. Shall we go?'

Beddington Lodge blazed with light as the carriages drove one by one under the soaring, pedimented portico where the guests might alight, safe from the weather. Serena left Quinn in the marble hall while she went off to the retiring room. As she entered a group of ladies gathered there drew closer together, like a flock of colourful birds alarmed by the presence of an intruder.

Serena handed her cloak to the attendant and sat down to put on her dancing slippers, trying to ignore the murmurings of the other ladies.

'It's not that I blame her for marrying a fortune,' declared one, in a whisper that reached every corner of the room. 'But 'tis the manner of it. Quite shameless. Sir Timothy was heartbroken when she cast him aside. Not that I condone his behaviour in eloping, but still, he did it in good faith.'

'Just like her mother,' said another.

'At least her mama had the decency to wait until she was widowed,' tittered a third.

'Poor Lady Hambridge, no wonder she has retired to the coast. Too ashamed to show her face in town, I suppose. It must be such a blow, to have harboured a viper in one's bosom.'

'As I have always said, spare the rod and the child is spoiled.'

'And her poor husband! Besotted, I suppose...'

Serena straightened, an angry retort upon her lips, but the little group was already disappearing out of the door in a rustle of silk. She should have spoken out as soon as she heard Sir Timothy's name and denounced him for a scoundrel. Her shoulders sagged as she realised how unlikely the truth would sound. Tears started to her eyes and she hunted for her handkerchief.

'Serena, are you quite well?'

Elizabeth Downing was approaching with her mother and Lady Grindlesham. Serena made haste to wipe her eyes.

'We were just coming in as Mrs Pinhoe and her cronies left,' said Mrs Downing, sitting beside her. 'We heard something of what they were saying. Have they upset you?' She patted Serena's hands.

'Pay them no attention, my dear,' declared Lady Grindlesham, hovering around her. 'They are merely jealous because you have married well.'

'But Quinn,' Serena whispered, pulling her handkerchief between her fingers. 'I had not realised how this must look for him.'

'Now don't you worry your head over that,' returned Lady Grindlesham in hearty accents. 'Lord Quinn has never cared a jot what is said of him. Come along, my dear, you dry your eyes while Mrs Downing and I change our shoes, then we will all go out together and woe betide anyone I hear making disparaging remarks about you!'

Serena was grateful for their support and she endeavoured to put the incident out of her mind. Quinn was waiting to escort her into the ballroom and the warm admiration in his gaze did much to restore her confidence. They danced the first two dances together and when their host requested Serena's hand for the next set, she was pleased to see Quinn stand up with Lady Beddington.

As always, dancing helped Serena to relax. Frosty stares and sly comments were forgotten and by the time she met up with Mrs Downing and her daughter during a break in the music, she felt very much like her old self.

'I think your fears of the evening have been allayed now, Serena, is that not so?' said Mrs Downing, twinkling.

'Yes, thank you, ma'am. Your kindness and that of Lady Grindlesham has done a great deal to help.'

'Nonsense, my dear, your own good manners and quiet dignity have won over all but the most spiteful of the tattlemongers, I assure you.'

They chatted for a few moments, before Serena excused herself and went off to find her husband. She could not see him in the ballroom and thought he was much more likely to be enjoying a quiet hand of piquet in the card room. She had almost reached the big double doors when someone stepped in front of her and flourished an elaborate bow.

'Lady Quinn. Your most *obedient* servant, ma'am.'

Serena stopped, the blood turning to ice in her veins.

Chapter Twelve

Sir Timothy was less than arm's length away. He was smiling, but his eyes glittered with angry menace. Serena glanced quickly around, but there was no one in sight she could call friend. She must deal with this alone.

She fought down the dark terror churning inside and said with icy disdain, 'We have nothing to say to one another.'

'Ah, how that cuts me to the quick.' He clasped his hands over his heart. 'Oh, cruel, cruel Beauty.'

Anger and panic were rising in equal measure. The flow of guests in and out of the ballroom had all but ceased as people stopped to witness the interchange. Serena tried to step past Sir Timothy but he blocked her way again.

'Ah, fair tormentor,' he declared with a sigh. 'Can you deny you have shattered my life?'

'I do deny it,' she retorted. 'You tricked me—'

He spoke over her, his bright, malicious gaze flickering around the room. 'My heart is broken. Irrevocably. I sacrificed *everything* for you, madam.'

'You sacrificed nothing,' she hissed at him, aware

that the crowd around them was listening with obvious relish to every word.

'You call it nothing, when the lady of your dreams begs you to elope, to go against all the precepts of good breeding and risk the censure of society—'

He sighed and cast another anguished look around him. Serena heard someone mutter 'shameful'. She wanted to hurl herself at him and claw the spiteful gleam from his eyes, but she kept silent. She would not lower herself to bandy words with this villain.

'But I am not vindictive,' he continued, assuming an expression of deep melancholy. 'I will not blame you for passing me over in favour of another.'

Her lip curling, Serena pushed past him.

'I am pleased—aye, *delighted*—that you are now so comfortably established,' he called after her. 'You will always hold my heart, Lady Quinn. Now and for ever!'

Serena was shaking, but somehow she managed to leave the ballroom with her head up. As she crossed the marble hall, Quinn walked out of the card room. He frowned when he saw her.

'What is it?' he demanded. 'Who has distressed you?'

Serena used every ounce of willpower not to run to him.

'Sir T-Timothy.' She caught his arm, 'No, no, I pray you will not go in search of him. He...' She leaned against him. 'He is still pretending it was my idea to fly from town. Th-that he did it all for me...'

'The devil he is!'

'Everyone believes him,' she muttered, blinking away a rogue tear. 'I am lost. But what I regret, most bitterly, is that I have dragged you into ignominy, too.'

* * *

Quinn stifled his rage. He needed to think rationally. Much as he wanted to thrash Forsbrook to within an inch of his life, he knew that would only fuel the fires of speculation that were burning so brightly around his wife.

He said now, 'We have a choice, Serena. We can run away and leave the field clear for Forsbrook to spread whatever vicious slander he pleases. Or we can stand our ground. I am not ashamed of my wife. In fact, I am exceedingly proud of you and I want the world to know it. However, if you would prefer, I can order our carriage now and take you home.' He glanced down at her. 'Well, what do you say? Can you face returning to the ballroom?'

Quinn watched the colour ebb and flow from her cheeks. Her shoulders straightened and her head came up.

'I can do it, if you are beside me, my lord.'

Quinn led Serena back towards the ballroom and paused momentarily in the doorway, his eyes travelling around the room. There was no sign of Forsbrook, but it felt as if all the guests thronged beneath the blazing chandeliers had turned to look at them. He kept a faint, unconcerned smile on his face, ignoring the sly nudges and whispers. Serena's clutch on his sleeve revealed her anxiety, but she, too, was looking about her with apparent indifference. Damme, but he admired her courage!

The scrape of a fiddle was the signal for couples to take their places on the dance floor. A cheerful young gentleman with artfully disordered curls and shirt-points almost reaching his eyes came bounding up.

'Ah, Lady Quinn, I was afraid—that is, you may recall you did me the honour of agreeing to dance the next with me!'

'Then you will be disappointed,' replied Quinn. Belatedly he tried to soften his blunt words with a smile. 'I shall be dancing the quadrille with my wife.'

'Ah.' The young man fell back a little. 'Well, then. Perhaps the Scotch reel, Lady Quinn?'

'I'm afraid not,' replied Quinn, leading Serena on to the dance floor. 'My lady dances with no one but me.'

His announcement caused a ripple of surprise among those close enough to hear his words and a great many eyes watched them as they danced. Serena was a little pale, but her grace and composure never faltered. By the time the lengthy quadrille was over, she was glowing from the exercise and readily agreed to his suggestion that they should forgo the next dance and instead seek out a little refreshment.

The supper room was situated a little distance from the ballroom and as they approached the open doors it looked deserted.

'It shows the popularity of the Scotch reel that there is no one here,' remarked Serena as they went in. 'I—'

She broke off and Quinn felt her shrink closer. There was someone in the room, after all. Forsbrook. He cursed silently.

Sir Timothy was standing by one of the sideboards, pouring himself a generous glass of their host's brandy. He looked up, his florid countenance darkening when he saw them.

'Lord and Lady Quinn.' He raised his glass in a mock salute.

'I am sorry I was not present just now, when you spoke to my wife.' It took all Quinn's willpower to keep his voice level. 'Perhaps it was for the best. I might have been tempted to call you out.'

'For what?' Forsbrook sounded confident, but there was wariness in every line of his body. 'I was quite sincere.'

'We all know that is a lie.'

'Ah, but can you prove it?'

Forsbrook's purring response made Quinn want to cross the space between them and throttle the villain.

'I am afraid the evidence is on my side,' Sir Timothy continued smoothly. 'After all, it was not I who duped her friends, neither did I force the lady to go with me. Her reputation was ruined the moment she stepped into my chaise.'

'You know very well I thought we were going to Vauxhall!' Serena put in angrily.

'You see how she holds to her story?' Forsbrook shook his head, saying sadly, 'I fear she has you, too, under her spell, my lord.'

A chill ran through Serena. What if Quinn believed that plausible rogue? She felt rather than heard Quinn's angry growl.

'By God, Forsbrook, I shall take pleasure in exposing you for the villain you are.'

Sir Timothy retreated a step, but he said with a sneer, 'Really? And how will you do that, my lord, without making public just how you came upon Miss Russington that night at Hitchin? Will you admit that her reputation was so compromised you had no choice but to marry her? That she was soiled goods? Then everyone will know that you and I have shared her charms—'

With a roar Quinn launched himself at Sir Timothy. The brandy glass went flying as a single blow from Quinn's fist sent him crashing to the floor. The noise brought servants running into the room, but they stood, irresolute, while Quinn towered menacingly over the cowering figure on the floor.

'Quinn, no more, I pray you!' cried Serena, clinging to his arm.

She could feel the iron of his bunched muscles beneath the fine wool sleeve, hear the rasp of his heavy, angry breathing, but to her relief he stepped back. The servants helped Sir Timothy to his feet. His coat and breeches were stained with spilled wine and candlewax from the floor and he brushed at them angrily, throwing Quinn a look of pure hatred.

'That was very foolish of you, my lord. Attacking me can only increase the speculation.' He glanced down at himself. 'You have ruined my clothes, sir, but it is nothing to the dirt that will stick to your wife if you try to avenge her, Lord Quinn. Remember that.'

Serena held her breath, wondering if Quinn might yet shake her off and attack Sir Timothy. Instead he put his free hand over her fingers, where they still clutched his sleeve.

'Believe me, I will ruin more than your clothes if I find you anywhere near my wife again, or if I hear you have been maligning her. Come, my dear.'

Even as they walked away Serena heard Sir Timothy's mocking voice following them.

'Now why should I malign Lady Quinn, when everyone knows she will hold my heart for ever?'

* * *

Serena was shaking so much she was afraid her legs would not carry her. She did not object when Quinn suggested they should leave and was profoundly relieved when they were at last bowling north in their elegant carriage.

'I beg your pardon,' said Quinn. 'I should not have allowed the villain to accost you. I should have been with you.'

'You cannot be beside me every minute of the day,' she replied miserably. 'It is I who should be apologising to you, my lord. I have brought nothing but shame upon you.'

'Nonsense. This is but a little setback.'

He gathered her into his arms and she clung to him, burying her face in his coat. Gradually she began to relax, soothed by the gently swaying of the carriage and Quinn's large, calming presence.

'You must regret you ever met me,' she whispered.

'Not at all.' He drew off his gloves and tilted her chin up towards him. 'There are many...compensations.'

He kissed her, his mouth working over her lips gently but insistently until she forgot about the ball and Sir Timothy. Forgot everything but the pleasure of his touch. His tongue darted and teased, drawing up a fine thread of excitement from somewhere deep within and she returned his kisses, revelling in the taste of him.

Her body melted against him. His hands began to caress her and she felt the heavy longing tugging at her thighs. His hand found its way beneath her skirts and his fingers were assuaging the aching need. She was hot, excited, as pleasure welled up inside her. She explored him with her own hands, revelling in the contained, muscled strength of his body.

She ripped off her gloves, the better to feel him, yet running her fingers through his silky hair and over the rough stubble of his cheek was not enough, she wanted to feel his naked body pressed against hers. But it was too late, she was losing control and could do nothing but gasp as her body arched and strained, wave after wave of exquisite pleasure pulsing through her.

Afterwards Quinn pulled her on to his lap and cradled her in his arms. The carriage rattled on through the darkness and at length she gave a long, contented sigh.

'Serena?'

His voice was a rumble against her cheek and she smiled in the darkness, clinging to his coat.

'You held me thus when we first met. I feel so, so *safe* with you.'

'Good.' He dropped a kiss on her hair. 'I see moonlight glinting on water. We must be crossing the Thames. Time to make ourselves respectable, if we can.'

Serena giggled, but she tidied her clothes and tried to straighten Quinn's crumpled neckcloth.

'There,' she said, pulling on her gloves and sitting down beside him. 'That is the best I can do.'

'Thank heaven I told Shere to go to bed,' he muttered. He reached for her hand. 'Did I hurt you?'

'No.' She blushed in the darkness. 'I—I would have liked…more. I wanted you. All of you.' The blush deepened at the admission.

Quinn squeezed her fingers. 'That is not something for a cramped, rocking carriage. The first time I take you I want it to be in comfort, in a feather bed with silken sheets and glowing candlelight shining on your golden body.'

'You make it sound wonderful, Quinn.' She rested her head against his shoulder. 'But I have come to associate bad things—terrors—with the bedchamber.'

'I hope we can eradicate those memories, given time.'

'I hope so, too. But, Sir Timothy—' She broke off. 'Perhaps we should return to Melham. Just for a while.'

'I think not. To withdraw now would hand victory to Forsbrook. No, we shall stay, if you can bear it. I believe in time the world will know just who is telling the truth. Sir Timothy wishes to be seen as the jilted lover, but he is too much of a philanderer to maintain that pose for long.'

'Very well. If you think it best.'

'I do.' He raised her hand to his mouth and kissed it. 'Be brave, Serena. I will look after you. I give you my word.'

When they reached Berkeley Square Quinn escorted Serena directly up the stairs. Her body was still thrumming and she leaned heavily on his arm, unwilling to trust her legs to support her. She wondered if he would take her to his room. To his bed. Unbidden came the memory of a darkened room, heavy, carved bedposts and black, black shadows. It reared up so suddenly that she stumbled.

'You must be tired,' he said, holding her up. 'It has been a long day.'

She wanted to contradict him, but try as she might, the words would not come. At her door they stopped and Quinn looked down, his face shadowed, unreadable.

'Remember, I am only in the next room. You have only to walk through the door, if you want me.' He kissed her gently. 'Goodnight, Serena.'

He was gone. She wanted to run after him, but instead her legs carried her into the room. Polly was waiting for her and as the maid helped her out of her gown and into her nightshift, Serena recalled Quinn's parting words.

You have only to walk through the door, if you want me.

I do, she thought desperately. I do want you, Quinn!

Once Polly had left, Serena remained sitting before the mirror. Silence closed about her, thick and heavy. Finally, she pushed herself to her feet and walked across to the connecting door. She only had to open it, to go to Quinn. He would take care of her.

Her trembling fingers hovered over the handle, then with a sigh she rested her hand against the polished wood and bowed her head. She couldn't do it. Not yet.

Chapter Thirteen

A week of social engagements followed, with Quinn dutifully escorting his wife everywhere. Timothy was not in evidence, but his spiteful tongue had been busy and the altercation at Beddington Lodge was the subject of much gossip. No one gave Lord and Lady Quinn the cut direct, but several of their acquaintance were distinctly cool. Serena presented to the world a smiling face, but inwardly she raged and could not feel other than guilty at what Quinn was having to endure for her sake. When she tried to speak of it he brushed it aside, telling her not to worry, but the injustice gnawed away at her and cast over her days a cloud that rivalled the overcast skies.

A week after the Beddingtons' ball she was alone in the morning room, when Dunnock came in to announce a visitor.

He gave a slight cough. 'Mr Charles Russington, ma'am.'

'Russ!' Serena jumped up from her seat. 'My dear, dear brother, what brings you to town?'

'You,' he said promptly, holding out his arms.

Serena did not hesitate. With a sob she ran into them.

'And now I know I was right to come,' he contin-ued, holding her close. 'I have never known you to be blue-devilled before.'

'Oh, Russ, I am so unhappy. I have made such a mull of everything.'

'So it would seem, if the reports that have reached Compton Parva are even half-correct. You had best tell me the whole.'

Quinn walked quickly along the streets, the rain dripping from his curly-brimmed beaver. Damn this weather, he thought sourly. He had spent the past hour with his lawyers, freeing up funds. The poor summer had resulted in a disastrous harvest and his tenants would not be able to pay their rents at Michaelmas.

He had discussed the matter with Serena and knew she agreed with him that payment should be waived for anyone in hardship. He had always kept his own counsel but over the past few months it had become his habit to share business matters with her. He had come to value her opinion and as he turned into Berkeley Square he found himself hoping that she was not entertaining visi-tors. That he might have her to himself.

The lack of carriages outside his house was encour-aging. It was unlikely anyone would have walked here today to pay a morning call. A footman opened the door to him and he quickly divested himself of his outer gar-ments as he demanded where he might find his wife.

'She is in the morning room, my lord.'

Quinn strode away through the hall. He expected to find his wife alone, and it was a surprise—nay, a damned shock!—to find Serena had company.

The gentleman sitting on the sofa beside Serena was everything Quinn was not. The fellow was lean and darkly handsome with black hair curling fashionably about his head. He was dressed impeccably in a morning coat of blue superfine and there was not a spot of mud on his gleaming Hessians or pantaloons. Quinn's mood darkened even further. That would suggest he had arrived some time ago, before the rain started. Which meant he had been alone with Serena for at least half an hour. Damn him.

Quinn stood in the doorway, taking in the scene. Serena was leaning against her visitor and looking forlorn, but when she heard the door open she jumped up, her face brightening.

'Quinn! Do let me present my brother Russ to you.'

He felt his hackles settling and moved further in to the room to greet Serena's half-brother.

'I came to offer my congratulations on your marriage,' Russ said to him. 'However, from what Serena has now told me, I think commiserations are more in order. The minx has dragged you into the devil of a fix.'

'Russ!'

'Well, you cannot deny it, Serena.'

Russington's plain speaking surprised a laugh from Quinn.

'It is not wholly Serena's fault,' he said. 'Forsbrook is a dashed scoundrel.'

'Yes, I am acquainted with the fellow,' replied Russ. 'A nasty piece of work and always has been—'

He broke off as the butler came in with a tray and there was a pause in the conversation while the butler withdrew and Quinn filled three glasses. He waved Russ back to his seat beside Serena.

'I take it my wife has apprised you of everything?' Quinn dropped into a chair opposite them. 'Including how we met?'

'It was necessary, if I was to make sense of it all,' said Russ. 'I pray you will not be angry with her.'

'On the contrary, I am glad of it. I have never liked prevarication.'

'Good.' Russ grinned. 'I always suspected the explanation Henry sent me at the time of your marriage was not the whole truth, but at that point I was not in any position to post south and find out for myself.'

'Ah, yes.' Quinn nodded. 'I trust your wife and the baby are now going on well?'

'They are, I thank you. I was telling Serena that Molly has invited you both to come and stay. Immediately if you wish.'

'While the gossip dies down, you mean?' Quinn finished his wine and got up to recharge the glasses. 'If it becomes unbearable we may well do that, but my instinct is to ride it out.'

'That is just what I said,' Serena put in, showing more fire than Quinn had seen before. 'I do not see why we should run away because of Sir Timothy, the little toad. But we will come north soon, Russ. I am longing to see baby Emma, and little Charles, of course. Why, he must be three years old by now.'

Quinn was happy to let the conversation move on, and when Serena asked Russ to stay for dinner he quickly added his voice to the invitation. He said very little during the meal, taking pleasure in the way Serena chattered happily to her half-brother. At one point she threw her head back and laughed, a full-throated, delightful sound that caught at his chest. This was Serena as she was meant to be. As he wanted her to be, not anxiously worrying over what the world might say.

At length Serena rose from her chair, saying she would leave the gentlemen to their brandy.

'But not too long,' she warned him. 'I expect to see you both in the drawing room well before the tea tray is brought in.'

'You have my word on it,' replied Quinn, his mouth twisting into a grin. 'Now, off you go, baggage!'

The twinkle in her eyes told him she was not at all offended by this style of address and his grin widened as he watched her glide out of the room.

'You appear to be very fond of my half-sister.'

'I am.' Quinn turned back to his guest. 'Your visit has made her the happiest she has been since our return to town.'

'The gossip is that bad, then?'

'Aye.' Quinn scowled as he poured brandy for himself and his guest. 'Some of the town tabbies have very long memories.'

'Ah,' said Russ. 'They have raked up stories about Eleanor, I suppose. Serena's mother.'

'Yes. I must have heard something of it at the time,' said Quinn, 'but around that time I had my own troubles. Was she as bad as they say?'

'Oh, yes.' Russington stared moodily into his glass. 'Eleanor married my father for his fortune. She was very charming to Henry and me until the knot was safely tied, then she ignored us, and once Serena was born she was left in the care of nurses and governesses. Eleanor craved company. When Father died, she lost no time in finding herself another rich husband.' His mouth twisted. 'Conte Ragussina, a handsome Italian with deep pockets and a nature as restless as her own. She ran off within months of my father's death, and was married before the year was out.'

'And Serena?' Quinn prompted him.

'Left to learn of her mother's defection from her governess. She was not quite nine years old.'

'Poor Serena.'

'Poor Serena indeed,' muttered Russ, taking a long pull at the brandy. 'She should have gone to live with Hambridge, but Dorothea wouldn't have her. Serena was sent to a succession of establishments, seminaries, academies for young ladies—not that she ever settled at any of them. My own dear Molly has proved as good a friend and guide as anyone. I regret now that we did not take her north with us when we married, but Henry insisted she must have her come-out. And what a mull he and Dorothea have made of it.' He looked up suddenly. 'Your marriage to my sister seems to be the best thing that has happened to her. And it was none of Henry's doing, I'll wager.'

'Not at all,' replied Quinn, unruffled.

Russ frowned. 'They should be here, supporting Serena, not hiding at Worthing.'

Quinn refilled his glass and pushed the decanter across the table. 'It doesn't help that Forsbrook is enacting the broken-hearted suitor. If I call him out the gossip will only intensify, yet while he is in town Serena cannot be at ease. I am tempted to have him abducted and pressed into service on one of his Majesty's frigates.'

Russ sat back in his chair. 'Oh, I don't think you need do that,' he drawled. 'I have a plan, which I hope will do the trick as far as Sir Timothy Forsbrook is concerned.'

* * *

Serena looked towards the door as she heard voices in the hall and moments later the gentlemen came in. The room seemed to shrink upon their entry, for they were both big men. Her half-brother was tall, but Quinn was a few inches taller, his broad shoulders and muscular body making even Russ's athletic frame look slender. Quinn was not conventionally handsome, with his craggy features, his crooked smile and not quite straight nose, but over the past few months she had come to regard him as the most attractive man of her acquaintance. She was shaken to realise how much he now meant to her.

Quinn was smiling at something Russ had said and Serena was pleased the two men were getting on so well.

'There is great sport to be had in Yorkshire,' remarked Russ. 'As you will see when you visit.'

'And we shall, as soon as our business in town is finished,' said Quinn. 'I cannot think it will take too much longer now.'

A glance passed between the two gentlemen, but Serena was distracted by the arrival of the tea tray and thought no more about it.

It was midnight before Russ rose to take his leave.

'Will we see you tomorrow?' asked Serena, walking with him to the door. 'Perhaps I might take you for a drive in the park. Quinn has bought me a new phaeton and the prettiest pair of match bays to pull it. I venture to think you would not be ashamed to be seen with me.'

'I should never be ashamed to be seen with you,' he told her, smiling. 'Unfortunately, I have another engagement tomorrow and must then return to the north. This was only ever going to be a fleeting visit.' He kissed her cheek. 'Bring this showy equipage with you when you come north and you can drive Molly in style around Compton Parva!'

With that he was gone.

'I was very pleased to see Russ,' said Serena, when Quinn escorted her upstairs to her bedchamber soon after. 'I was glad, too, that you liked him.'

'He is very different from his brother.'

'He is indeed. Russ has always been my favourite. That is why I thought—' She broke off, flushing.

'Why you thought a rake would make a good husband?' Quinn finished for her. Serena bowed her head, too mortified to respond and Quinn laughed softly. 'Goodnight, Serena.'

She watched him walk away, heard his firm tread going back down the stairs and misery cut through her like a knife. They had been getting on so well and she had ruined everything.

Serena entered the bedchamber, closing the door with a snap that made Polly jump out of her chair.

'Good evening, ma'am. I have your nightshift all ready for you.'

Serena looked at the garment laid out on the bed. It was made of the finest linen and decorated with mother-of-pearl buttons and exquisite Brussels lace. It had been vastly expensive, Dorothea insisting that a man of Lord Quinn's wealth would expect to his wife to wear only the best.

Serena thought of the painting of *Venus with a Mirror* that was now hanging in the library at Melham, the Titian she had seen that first morning. Quinn might find the naked form much more alluring than being covered neck to toe. Her mouth dried at the thought, but a sudden excitement fizzed through her blood like champagne. There was only one way to find out.

Somewhere in the house a clock chimed the hour. Serena paced her room and pulled the wrap closer, not so much from cold as nerves. The excitement and determination she had felt earlier had evaporated and if Quinn did not go to bed soon then she would not have the nerve to go through with this. Then she heard it. The firm tread along the passage, the rumble of voices from the next room that told her Quinn was in there with his valet.

She retreated to the bed and sat down on the edge, pleating the skirts of the raspberry silk between her fingers. When she heard the soft pad of Shere's feet in the passage she moved again towards the connecting door and pressed her ear against the panel. Silence. Perhaps Quinn had drunk too much brandy and was already asleep. She moved to the long mirror to rearrange the thin robe. The red silk, almost black in the candlelight, was wrapped snugly around her and tied with a single ribbon under the breast. Apart from her hair, which she had brushed out and left to fall loose down her back, she looked perfectly respectable. Until she moved, when the front edges of the robe fell away to reveal the nakedness beneath.

'If he is indifferent to me now,' she whispered, 'then I shall never try again.'

Straightening her shoulders, Serena crossed to the connecting door. It opened silently and she saw that Quinn was in bed, propped up against the bank of snowy pillows, reading. The shadows from the single candle enhanced the rippling contours of his bare chest and shoulders.

He did not notice her at first. She took another, tentative step into the room and he looked up. Serena was watching him closely, his face registered surprise, but not displeasure. He threw back the covers and slipped to the floor. In one fluid movement he pulled the banyan from the end of the bed and shrugged himself into it, but not before Serena glimpsed his athletic form, wide shoulders and deep chest, narrow hips and strongly muscled thighs. There was a shield of dark hair on his chest. It arrowed downwards over the tight, flat stomach. She recalled the sketches and paintings Henry had shown her of statues he had seen on his grand tour.

A Greek god, she thought wildly. He is built like a Greek god!

It was not the smooth, boyishness of Michelangelo's *David*, but a much more adult, muscled figure. A warrior. A champion.

'Did you want me?' There was a hint of amusement in his deep voice.

Serena forced her eyes back to his face. Nervously she ran her tongue over her lips.

Oh, yes, I want you!

Her cheeks burned.

'I—' She swallowed, trying to force the words from a throat that felt too tight.

Smiling, he leaned back against the edge of the bed and held out his hands. 'Come here.'

Slowly she moved towards him, trying not to think of the way her own robe parted as she walked, displaying a leg from toe to thigh. He was her husband. Who else should see her thus? She *wanted* him to see her. Besides, he had seen her naked before, when he had helped her from the bath. Her step faltered as the black terror of those memories resurfaced.

'I c-can't—'

Quinn reached out and took her hands. She clung to him, as if she was drowning, and he pulled her close.

'Come and sit with me.'

He guided her to a large chest with a padded top that was placed at the end of the bed. Very little light from the single candle reached this far, but even so her hands clutched at the edges of the robe, pulling them together as she sat down beside him. He made no attempt to stop her, merely keeping one arm about her. His forbearance was too much. She gave a little sob and buried her face in his shoulder.

'I thought I could do this,' she mumbled as her tears soaked his silk banyan. 'I beg your pardon, Quinn. I have failed you.'

'No, no.' He cradled her cheek and gently turned her face up towards his. He said softly, 'Now, what is it that frightens you?' She glanced past him. 'Ah, of course. The bed.'

She nodded and hid her face in his shoulder again. 'The shadows. He held me down. At the inn. He threw me down and t-tried to...' She shivered and his arm tightened around her, holding her firm, giving her courage. Her fingers clutched at his dressing gown. 'I want to please you, Quinn. I w-want to be your wife in more than name.'

'And so you shall be, Serena, in time. We need not rush this.'

She relaxed against him, sighing.

'Will you…?' She took a breath and looked up at him. 'Would you kiss me, please?'

Even in the shadows she saw his eyes gleam. 'It would be a pleasure.'

He pulled her to him, one hand about her neck as he lowered his head and captured her lips. He kissed her slowly at first, gently, until she began to respond. He teased her lips apart, his tongue exploring her mouth. She yielded, her body softening, melting against him as his hand caressed her neck, easing away her tension.

His mouth moved, light as a feather, along her jaw. She put back her head, closing her eyes as he continued those delicate, tantalising kisses along her neck. He tugged at the ribbon tie of her wrap and she felt the satin sliding away. Her body tensed when he stroked her breast but she did not flinch away, rather she pushed herself against him. His thumb began to circle the tip, oh, so slowly, then his mouth closed over its fellow and Serena gave a little cry. Heat shafted through her blood from her breasts to somewhere deep between her thighs, into an aching pool of desire.

He stilled and she clutched at him, begging him to go on. With a soft laugh he teased one hard nub with his thumb and forefinger while his teeth caught the other. Serena's body pulsed and shuddered beneath the onslaught. She had slipped to the edge of the seat, her body instinctively arching towards Quinn. When she opened her eyes, she was staring up at the shadowed canopy of the bed, but the darkness no longer frightened her. There was no hint of panic. Instead she felt more alive than ever, the blood singing through her body.

It was a revelation, so absorbing that she barely noticed Quinn had moved. He was holding her firm, one arm about her waist, and his free hand gathered both her breasts while his mouth roved lower, down across her ribs and on to the soft skin of her belly. He eased her legs apart and, glancing down, she saw that he had shed his banyan and was naked, on his knees before her.

'Quinn!'

At her whispered cry he looked up. 'Do you want me to stop?'

'Yes. No. I do not know.'

His eyes glinted wickedly in the candlelight. 'Then I shall go on.'

His hands slid down to her hips and he lowered his head, his mouth moving from one side to the other, then back to nestle in the curls at the hinge of her thighs. Her body froze with shock, but only for a moment. Then she was opening for him, shifting restlessly as his tongue flickered and teased. Another cry escaped her, but lest Quinn should think she did not like what he was doing to her she pushed her fingers through his hair, clutching at the thick, silky locks.

He gave a soft laugh. 'Do you like that, Serena?'

'Yes, yes,' she panted, offering herself up to him again. 'Oh, don't stop now.'

He obliged her with his mouth and tongue while the rippling excitement built inside her. She arched back against the bed, her hands thrown out on either side and gripping the covers as he continued the exquisite torture, holding her firm as she writhed against him. The ripples became a flood that carried her higher until she did not know if she was flying or drowning. She cried out, her body bucking and shuddering as wave after joyous wave swept through her.

At last the tide receded, leaving her sated and barely

conscious. All she could hear was her own gasping sobs. Quinn gently removed her silk wrap, then he gathered her up and carried her around to place her in his bed. He climbed in beside her, snuffed the guttering candle and pulled the covers over them both. With a sigh she reached for him and he took her in his arms.

'No more terrors?' he murmured, his mouth against her hair.

'No,' she whispered, one hand pressed against his chest, her fingers threading through the crisp, dark curls.

'Good,' he pulled her closer, 'because there is more.'

'More?' She managed a shaky laugh. 'Oh, Quinn, I do not think I could...'

He stopped her words with a kiss.

'Not yet then,' he murmured, pulling her into his arms. 'Sleep now.'

Serena stirred. Something was different. She opened her eyes and the grey light of dawn creeping in through the unshuttered window showed her that this was not her bedroom. This was Quinn's room. Quinn's bed. There was nothing to fear.

But, glancing up at the canopy, all she could see was an inky blackness. Icy fingers ran down her spine, fear gripped her. She could hear Quinn's deep, regular breathing beside her. She wanted to cling to him and let him comfort her, but black terror was enveloping her and she could not breathe. She could feel again cruel hands around her throat, choking off her life.

Trembling, she slipped silently from the bed. Without waiting to find her dressing wrap she fled back to her own room.

Chapter Fourteen

Serena sat up beside Quinn in the phaeton, doing her best to keep her distance, but it was difficult not to bump against him as he swung the carriage around the corners and negotiated the traffic.

'I am glad you accepted my invitation,' he remarked as he guided the bays into the park. 'We need to talk. About last night.'

'Yes.' She clutched her hands tightly in her lap.

'I thought it would be better done in private, and it gives me an excuse to drive your bays and be seen in this vastly fashionable equipage!'

Serena knew his attempt at levity was to set her at her ease, but it only made her feel more wretched. She had failed him. Again.

'It was very kind of you to buy it for me. Very generous.'

He said, 'You were gone when I awoke this morning. I want to know what I did to make you run away in the night. Did my passion frighten you?'

'No! It—it was not you, Quinn. You were all kindness.' He gave an exasperated hiss and she hurried on. 'I... I enjoyed your attentions. More than I can say. I have never known anything quite as wonderful.' She was thankful for the veil covering her cheeks, hiding her blushes. 'I thought the bad memories had been exorcised, but when I woke, it was so very dark. All I could see was shadows. And I panicked.'

She bowed her head, remembering how cold her own bed had been. How empty. She had curled up beneath the covers, shivering and feeling thoroughly wretched.

'I thought as much.' He tipped his hat towards the occupants of a smart barouche coming the other way, but did not stop. 'That is why I sent a note up with your breakfast, rather than coming in person. Your room is your sanctuary, Serena. I will not enter uninvited.' He reached out and briefly put his huge, gloved hand over hers. 'As long as it was not my...*attentions* that distressed you.'

Serena felt another swell of gratitude for his understanding. She tucked her hand in his arm and leaned against him.

'No, Quinn, you have never done anything to distress me. I just wish I could be a...a proper wife to you.'

'We have all our lives to work on that.' He flashed a smile at her. 'But for now, we shall continue as we are. I am yours to command, madam. But you must trust me, Serena. I will never ask more of you than you wish to give.'

She squeezed his arm and rubbed her cheek against his sleeve. 'You are a good man, Rufus Quinn.'

'Nonsense.' His gruff response was followed by a growl of annoyance. 'By heaven, let us get out of here. Damned crowds and it is not even the fashionable hour. The devil only knows how you stand it!'

* * *

The worsening weather brought more families back to town. Hostesses began to find their reception rooms filling up again and Quinn persuaded Serena that they should hold a party of their own.

'It need only be a small affair,' he told her. 'You may invite whomsoever you wish. Although we should include your brother Henry and sister-in-law.'

'Yes, I suppose we must.' A shadow of uncertainty flickered over her face. 'Dorothea has written to tell me they are returning to town at the end of the week.'

'You are not looking forward to that?'

'Dorothea disapproves of any sort of scandal.' Her hand fluttered. 'She disapproves of *me*.'

'If she had taken better care of you in the first place, there would be no scandal.' Quinn finished his coffee and rose from the table. Serena was still looking pensive and he stopped behind her and dropped a hand on her shoulder. 'You are Lady Quinn now, Serena. If your sister-in-law annoys you, tell her to go to the devil.'

That made her laugh. 'Yes, that is what you would do, Quinn, is it not? One would expect nothing less of the rudest man in London!'

She looked up at him, her dark eyes alight with merriment, and he caught his breath. He wanted to bend and capture those smiling lips, to kiss her senseless, then carry her off to bed and make love to her for the rest of the day. Even as his body reacted at the thought he saw the laughter die from Serena's face. And she shrank away from him, blushing violently.

'G-goodness, is that the time? I promised Cook I would discuss tonight's dinner with her, so I had best hurry and finish my breakfast...'

She began to cut the toast on her plate into tiny squares. Quinn stepped away. She had shown him more clearly than any words that his passion frightened her. Oh, she had denied it when he had asked her outright, but if that was the case why did she shy away from him? Every day he looked for some sign that she desired him. Every night he strained to hear the sound of the connecting door opening, but it remained firmly, obstinately shut. He had promised he would not rush her and he would hold to that, even though it was becoming more and more unbearable.

'I have correspondence that requires an answer,' he muttered, turning to the door. 'If you will excuse me.'

Serena kept her eyes on her plate, listening to Quinn's footsteps as he went out and closed the door behind him. How had she ever kept her seat, when she wanted so desperately to throw herself into his arms? The impulse had been strong and so sudden that it frightened her. Even now she was trembling so much she could hardly wield her knife.

And the worst part of it all was Quinn's disappointment. He wanted her, she read that quite clearly in his eyes. She was his wife and he had every right to expect to take his pleasure, but he was too much of a gentleman. It must be her wish to go to his bed and she *did* wish it, although for some reason she could never put it into words or actions. Every evening when she retired to her room she looked at the closed door between them, wanting desperately to walk through to him, but fear held her back.

Fear of the dark shadows that reminded her of Sir Timothy choking the life from her, fear of the terrifying panic that welled up, that made her want to scream and rip and tear at Quinn, to reject him and run away rather than allowing him to love her. And something else, too. The fear of irrevocably committing herself to this marriage. To committing to Quinn. Until it was truly consummated he might still walk away, find a wife who was worthy of him.

Serena pushed her plate away, her appetite quite gone. She had panicked again, blushed like a school-girl and shrunk away from Quinn. She closed her eyes. If only she had shown him by a word, a look, how much she wanted him then he might even now be covering her with kisses and making her body sing.

'I beg your pardon, Lady Quinn.' She looked up to find Dunnock hovering in the doorway. 'Cook was asking if you were ready to see her, because she was hoping to go to the market later.'

'Yes, yes of course.' Serena rose, pushing her own concerns away. 'I will go to her now.'

By the time Serena finished discussing menus with Cook, Quinn had gone out. He left word that he was dining out but would return in time to escort her to the theatre. She was disappointed, for the desire she had felt earlier was still there, a nagging whisper deep down. Heavens, she thought, a wry smile tugging at her mouth, how unfashionable, to yearn for a husband's company!

When she saw the clothes laid out on the bed, her new coral-coloured silk gown and the velvet opera cloak, Serena felt a *frisson* of excitement, as if this was her very first ball. Perhaps tonight would be different. She and Quinn both enjoyed the theatre and she was hopeful that afterwards…anticipation made her stomach swoop. Hope. She was *hopeful*. How long had it been since she had felt like this?

Serena stared into the looking glass as Polly dressed her hair and found herself smiling. It was as if she was waking from a bad dream, rediscovering the zest for life that had once been natural to her. And she had Quinn to thank for it. The curl of desire was still there, working its way around her body.

'There, my lady.' Polly stood back to admire her handiwork. 'You look as fine as fivepence, if you don't mind me saying.'

'Not at all.' Serena laughed.

She turned her head this way and that, regarding her reflection in the mirror. Her thick tresses were gathered up into a neat topknot with a few guinea-gold curls framing her face.

'Indeed,' said a deep voice behind her. 'As fine as fivepence!'

'Quinn!'

Her smile grew wider as she turned to see him standing in the doorway. He had changed into his evening attire of blue frock coat and white satin waistcoat, his muscular legs straining against the tight-fitting breeches and silk stockings. As he walked towards her a diamond sparkled from the folds of his snow-white cravat. That and the heavy gold signet ring, were his only ornaments, but Serena thought this only enhanced the magnificence of his physique.

'I had no idea it was so late.' Her hand went to the ties of her wrap. 'I have yet to put on my gown—'

'We have plenty of time yet.'

Serena glanced at her maid. 'Leave us, Polly, if you please. I will ring when I need you.'

When they were alone, Quinn came closer and held out a velvet box. 'I thought you might like this.'

Intrigued, she took the box and opened it.

'Oh.' She gazed down at a full set of coral and gold jewellery. 'It is a perfect match for my robe. How clever of you.'

'I saw this parure in Rundell's today and since I knew you intended to wear your new gown...'

She put the box down on the dressing table and lifted out the comb. Carefully she nestled it against the top-knot, the coral enhancing the deep gold of her hair. The ear drops followed, but when she reached for the necklace, three strings of fine coral beads, Quinn stopped her.

'Let me.' She kept very still as he placed the necklace about her neck. His fingers brushed her nape as he fastened the catch and her mouth dried. 'There. I hope you are not offended that I did not buy you more diamonds? I could have done so, I know that some women would settle for nothing less, but I thought that you—'

She lifted one hand to the necklace—the coral was warm against her fingers.

'No,' she said softly, meeting his eyes in the mirror. 'I have the diamonds you gave me as a wedding gift— I do not need more. This parure will set off the gown perfectly. Thank you.'

His hands moved to her shoulders and this time she did not shy away. Instead she turned her head and dropped a kiss on to the back of his fingers. His grip tightened and she felt his lips on her neck.

'Mayhap we should forgo the theatre this evening,' he murmured, his breath warm on her ear.

'Perhaps we should,' she whispered, amazed at her own daring.

He met her eyes in the mirror. 'Surely it would be a pity to waste all this effort. I know how much you wanted to see Macready playing Othello.'

'I think...' Serena swallowed. 'I think I would prefer to go to bed with you than see Mr Macready.'

Laughing, he pulled her up into his arms and kissed her, a long, unhurried kiss that turned her bones to water.

'Very well then. If you are sure.'

The blaze in his eyes set her heart racing even faster. She touched his cheek. 'I am sure, Quinn.'

He dragged her close for another searing kiss that left her dizzy. How could she have ever thought herself safe with this man?

'Well, madam, should it be your bed, or will you risk the shadows of mine?'

Held close against Quinn's chest she felt light-hearted and reckless.

'I think it must be yours, sir. Let us not waste time moving everything from mine.'

He threw back his head and gave a shout of laughter. 'You are quite wanton, Lady Quinn, and I love you for it.'

Her senses reeled. She felt quite faint. Love. Had he really said that?

He had his arm about her and was leading her through the connecting door. Pressed close against him, she could feel the barely contained power of the man. It was, she thought, like being too close to a powder keg.

Serena's cheeks burned when she saw the valet was in the room and she looked down, shrinking closer to Quinn.

He said coolly, 'You may go, Shere. I shall not need you again tonight. And you may tell Lady Quinn's maid she need not wait up.'

She heard the door close softly behind the valet, then Quinn was pulling her round into his arms. Slowly, with infinite care and myriad kisses, he unlaced her stays and removed every scrap of clothing until she was standing before him, naked save for the coral jewellery. Slowly he removed the comb and pins from her hair, watching as the heavy silken curtain fell about her shoulders.

'My Venus,' he murmured, gazing at her in a way that sent a delicious shiver running through her body.

He dropped his head to kiss her breasts, but Serena felt at a disadvantage. She scrabbled at the buttons of Quinn's coat and soon his clothes joined hers in an untidy pile on the floor. At last only the snowy shirt was between Serena and Quinn's glorious body. She plucked at it impatiently, feasting her eyes on him as he drew it off over his head. He pulled her close, skin to skin, then scooped her up into his arms.

'There is always the daybed,' he murmured, nodding towards the couch in one corner of the room. 'If you would feel safer there. It is your choice, Serena.'

A vague image of the inn flickered through her head, but she blinked and it was gone, it had lost its terror because this was not Hitchin. This was Quinn's room and when she looked towards his bed now all she remembered was the pleasure of his caresses. She slid an arm about his neck, smiling up at him.

'The bed, if you please.'

Holding her eyes with his own, he laid her gently down on the covers. She reached for him and he measured his length beside her, bringing his mouth to hers for a long, languorous kiss that drew out her very soul. Her hands roamed over him, marvelling at the silky skin over iron-hard muscle, and when he began a series of tantalising kisses down her neck she drove her fingers through his hair, clutching his head as his tongue worked its magic on her breasts.

They swelled, tightening beneath the teasing attention of his mouth, but this time she was not prepared to lie passive while he pleasured her. She began her own exploration, using her hands and her mouth, revelling in the salty spiciness of his skin as she worked her way across his chest and downwards, exploring, teasing, learning what excited him and how to make him groan with pleasure beneath her touch. He reached for her, drawing her close, sliding his fingers over her skin and down to the aching heat between her thighs. Urgent desire spiralled through her and she moved restlessly against his hand.

'Go on,' she pleaded. 'Go on, Quinn. Finish this!'

He rolled her on to her back and covered her. His fingers slid away and she felt him enter her. She bit her lip, anticipating pain, but there was none. Quinn was moving gently, slowly and Serena lifted her hips to push him deeper. She moved with him, matching his rhythm, her fingers digging into his shoulders as the now-familiar excitement took over. With each thrust he was carrying her higher. She was flying, soaring, and as she reached her pinnacle he tensed and held her there. They shared a brief, wondrous moment of ecstasy when his shout of triumph mingled with her own cries before she fell into joyous, heady oblivion and beyond. She subsided at last, trembling against him, and Quinn held her, a gentle giant, keeping her safe, cocooned against the world.

* * *

Serena stretched luxuriously and opened her eyes. It was not yet dawn. Quinn's naked body was wrapped around hers, his regular breathing soft against her neck. She felt a rush of emotion, a mix of happiness and affection so strong that tears filled her eyes. Wonderingly, she reached out and touched his cheek. It was rough with morning stubble.

'I love you,' she murmured.

He did not stir. She kissed his lips and his arms tightened around her. Smiling, she snuggled closer and sank back into a deep, dreamless sleep.

When Serena woke again, the sunlight shining into the room told her it was morning. A delicious thrill ran down her spine when she remembered how they had spent the night and she turned towards the large, warm body beside her. Quinn. Her husband. A smile tugged at her mouth as she watched him sleeping. His eyelids fluttered, the dark lashes lifted and his hazel eyes stared at her. He raised himself on to one elbow.

'Can you not sleep? Is anything wrong?'

'I was merely thinking how good you have been to me.'

One eyebrow went up. 'And that prevents you sleeping?'

'No,' she said, smiling. 'That is because I am not accustomed to sharing a bed with a man.'

'Ah, I see. And you find it an unpleasant experience?'

'On the contrary.' She felt a blush spreading through her, even to her toes as she added daringly, 'I should like to do it a great deal more.'

'Then you shall,' he muttered, pulling her against his hard, aroused body. 'As long as it is only with me!'

* * *

The following week passed in a happy daze for Serena. It was mid-October, but the sun seemed brighter, the days warmer than they had been all summer, and she found herself singing as she went about the house. Something had shifted inside her. There was no longer a black cloud of despair weighing heavily on her spirits and she began to take pleasure in living. She knew it was due in no small part to her husband.

Just the thought of Quinn made her smile, but it was not only the nights spent in his bed. She delighted in his company and could only regret that the more she was accepted into London society, the less she saw of Quinn. At first she had barely noticed the change in attitude towards her, but her own notoriety had been eclipsed by fresh gossip about Sir Timothy, as Miss Downing lost no time in explaining when Serena took her up in her phaeton for a drive in the park.

'He is pursuing the widow of a wealthy mill owner,' Elizabeth told her, with obvious relish. 'It is the talk of the town. They were at Covent Garden Theatre last week, for Mr Macready's *Othello*. Perhaps you saw them?'

'We did not go, after all,' said Serena, a rosy blush stealing through her as she thought of what she and Quinn had done instead.

'Well, I have seen her,' declared Elizabeth. 'She is a handsome creature with quantities of black curls and a passion for jewellery. One cannot help but notice her, for she is very loud and...and *flashy*. She is from the north, you see,' she went on, as if this explained everything. 'You will not find them at any respectable society parties. But he takes her to the Subscription Balls, where positively *anyone* can buy a ticket.'

'But who is the woman?' Serena was unable to resist asking. 'Is she so very unsuitable?'

'Oh, yes. Her name is Mrs Hopwood and she positively *reeks* of trade and bad breeding,' said Elizabeth cheerfully. 'Mama and I saw her shopping with Sir Timothy in New Bond Street and one could not help but overhear their conversation. Her voice is quite coarse, you know, her style of dress designed to attract attention and she was *dripping* with ornament! She looked like a jeweller's trade card! Sir Timothy was fawning all over her.' She shuddered. 'It was truly grotesque.'

Serena knew her friend was enjoying relating the story to her, but she could not share her amusement.

'Poor Mrs Hopwood. Someone should warn her about Sir Timothy.'

'What, when they are providing the *ton* with such amusement?' Elizabeth laughed. 'I am sure the widow can look out for herself and as Mama says, Sir Timothy's determined pursuit is turning opinion in your favour. No one believes he was ever in love with you now, Serena. No,' Elizabeth concluded, 'this little development can only be to your advantage.'

Serena knew it was true, but her new-found happiness brought with it a wish that others should be happy, too, and when she sat down to dinner with Quinn that evening, she could not help but mention her concerns.

'I do not like to think of any woman being duped, as I was, by Sir Timothy,' she told him, when the covers had been removed and the servants had withdrawn. They were in the habit of sitting together at one end of the table when dining alone and she cast an anxious glance up at Quinn, who turned his head to smile at her.

'Your kind heart does you credit, my dear, but I doubt there is anything to fear. If the widow is as wealthy as people say, then she will have an army of lawyers to advise her.' He grinned. 'Sir Timothy is certainly burning his boats in setting his cap at the woman. I saw him at Tattersall's today, buying a showy pair of greys on her behalf. It would appear this Mrs Hopwood means to drive herself about town in a phaeton and a high-perch one at that.' He glanced at her. 'Perhaps you are afraid she will cast you into the shade.'

She laughed. 'She may do so, with my blessing!'

He reached out and briefly covered her hand with his own.

'She won't do it,' he told her. 'You are a nonpareil. I have never seen a woman handle the reins better than you. And you may believe it. You know I will never lie to you.'

'Th-thank you.' She blushed, inordinately pleased by his praise. 'Nevertheless, I cannot be easy about this. Sir Timothy is a scoundrel and I do not like to think of him preying on anyone.'

Quinn growled. 'You know that nothing would give me greater pleasure than to call the fellow out and put a bullet through him,' he said, 'but that would reflect badly upon you, which is something I want to avoid at all costs.' His hand tightened over hers. 'Try not to be anxious about Mrs Hopwood, Serena. She will not come to any harm.'

With that she had to be satisfied, but it seemed that Serena could not avoid hearing about Sir Timothy and his new flirt. Her own escapades appeared forgotten, which pleased her, but it meant that Quinn no longer felt obliged to escort her everywhere. Serena missed his company at the balls and parties, but she tried not to complain, knowing that he did not enjoy such gatherings.

However, he would have to attend their own party.

Knowing Quinn would not enjoy a ball, Serena had decided upon a musical evening, where they could invite some of the young musicians with whom Quinn was acquainted to perform. But even here Serena could not avoid the latest gossip concerning Sir Timothy. During a performance by a promising young harpist, Lady Grindlesham dropped down on the sofa beside her, declaring, 'It must be a match. He is for ever in her company.'

'Yes, I have seen them driving out in the park,' murmured Serena.

'They are *everywhere*,' exclaimed Lady Grindlesham. 'Of course, she may not have entrée into the best houses, but they are together in every public place.' She leaned closer. 'They attend a great many private card parties and it seems the widow's luck is much greater than that of her escort! I understand he is so much in debt that only a rich wife can save him now. Yet he continues to live high. The word in town is that it can only be a matter of time before they are married.' She gave a little tut of displeasure. 'I hope she does not think that will make her any more acceptable in polite circles. Sir Timothy's standing is quite diminished, you know, which I am sure must be a great relief to you, my dear. Any man who could so shamelessly pay court to such a vulgar creature, however large her fortune, *cannot* be a true gentleman!'

Lady Grindlesham patted Serena's hand and moved

away as the company politely applauded the harpist's performance. Nothing more was said of the matter, but Serena relayed to Quinn all she had heard once the guests had departed.

They were alone together in the drawing room, where Quinn had persuaded her to sit down on the sofa and enjoy a glass of wine with him.

'Naturally, I am relieved that people now believe me rather than Sir Timothy,' she said unhappily, 'but it has nothing to do with truth and everything to do with the fact that the widow is not considered worthy of their notice.' She gave a little huff of disgust. 'Such hypocrisy!'

'Now you see why I dislike town so much.'

'I do, but...' she tucked her hand in his sleeve '...I thought it was also because Barbara died here.'

For a moment she feared she had offended him, that he would not reply, but at length he sighed. 'I have never been a great one for society, but I realise now I used her death as an excuse to withdraw completely.'

'Then it is very good of you to come back for my sake.'

'I confess I have enjoyed it more than I anticipated,' he said, relieving her of her empty glass.

'I am glad.' She sighed. 'But I cannot expect you to remain in town for ever, Quinn.'

'Of course not. We shall return to Melham Court in due course.'

Serena wanted to tell him that she was ready to leave town immediately, but at that moment he took her in his arms and kissed her, driving all coherent thought from her head.

Despite the exigencies of hosting her first social event in town, Serena was up and about early the following day. Now she was most truly Quinn's wife she felt much happier and much more alive. Perhaps it was the new closeness she felt with her husband. Having completed her household duties, she went to look for him and was a little disappointed to discover he had gone out and would not be back until dinnertime. Serena wondered what to do in the meantime and, looking out of the window at the fallen leaves dancing about the square, she decided a brisk walk would serve to use up a little of her restless energy. She ran upstairs to change into her walking dress and set off with Polly running to keep up with her.

'Where are we going, my lady?'

'Oh, I am not sure yet. I know,' she said, struck by inspiration, 'we shall go to the Pantheon Bazaar.'

'You've no need to go there, madam.' Polly sniffed. 'You don't need to watch the pennies.'

'Perhaps not, but I have not been there since I was a schoolgirl. It might be amusing.'

The exercise, and browsing the tempting counters in the Pantheon Bazaar, proved a perfect way to while away a few hours. Serena could not find anything she really needed, but she bought a pair of white evening gloves while Polly was looking about her, wide-eyed at the cornucopia of treasures. Serena took out her purse and gave her a handful of coins, ordering her to go off and treat herself.

'Ooh, madam, thank you, but I can't take this.'

'Of course you can,' Serena told her. 'Now off you go and find yourself something you would like. I shall be happy enough wandering around here. We shall meet back here, in half an hour.'

Polly went off, her money clutched tightly in her

hand, and Serena returned to browsing the selection of gloves laid out before her.

A flurry of activity caught her attention and she looked towards the doors in time to see a lady enter, a tall, striking figure in a modish promenade dress of scarlet wool decorated with quantities of gold frogging. It was Mrs Hopwood, Serena recognised her from her drives in the park. She took the opportunity to study her more closely. She had a pleasant face, although it was painted and powdered too heavily for Serena's taste. Her countenance was framed by an abundance of thick, dark curls that peeped out beneath her stylish bonnet with its scarlet ostrich feathers. She was accompanied by her maid, a dour-looking woman in a severe black gown and jacket, a complete contrast to her flamboyant mistress.

Serena bit her lip and after a brief hesitation, she approached the widow.

'Mrs Hopwood.' The woman turned, her brows rising, and there was a definite wariness about her. That was not surprising, thought Serena, for she was being accosted by a perfect stranger. 'Forgive me, we have not been introduced.' She coloured slightly. 'I am Lady Quinn.'

'Are ye now?' said the widow. 'Well, I've heard a deal about you, my lady.'

The voice was rough, uncultured and had an unmistakable northern burr, but a smile hovered about her carmine lips and her unmistakable friendliness caused Serena to relax a little.

She said, 'Can we talk, privately?'

Mrs Hopwood regarded her for a moment, then she nodded to her maid, who withdrew to a discreet distance. The widow turned towards the embroidered stockings displayed on the counter.

'Let's look at these and we'll be less conspicuous, perhaps. Well, Lady Quinn, what is it you wish to say to me?'

What indeed? Serena sought about for words that would not be insulting, or misconstrued.

'I have seen you driving in the park.'

'Have you now?'

'You are always escorted by...' Serena could not help her lip curling in distaste '...by Sir Timothy Forsbrook.'

'What of it?'

Serena's colour rose, but she had come too far to turn back now.

'I wanted to put you on your guard.' The widow gave her a searching look and Serena hurried on. 'I may be wrong. Perhaps he is indeed in earnest and means you no harm, but—' She stopped, her cheeks burning. 'You say you know of me. If you heard my story from Sir Timothy then it is lies, but I do not ask you to believe that. All I can say, all I would urge, most strongly, madam, is that you should be careful in your dealings with that man.'

There was a long silence and Serena wondered if she had offended the widow. After all, they were not acquainted, what business was it of hers? Serena was about to apologise and walk away when the widow spoke.

'Thank you for your concern, dear, but I know exactly what I am about.'

'I beg your pardon,' murmured Serena. 'It was presumptuous of me—'

'No, no, I understand and I am grateful. Truly. But

I pray you will not be anxious for me.' The voice had softened and lost its strong north-country accent, but the next moment it was back again. 'Now, you'd best move away from me, my lady, before anyone can remark upon our meeting.'

Serena nodded. She had half-turned away when Mrs Hopwood touched her sleeve.

'Bless you, my dear. It was good of you to warn me.'

With a swirl of scarlet skirts the widow went off to join her maid and Serena was left wondering if she had been wise to address a total stranger. But she could not regret it. Mrs Hopwood might be in thrall to Sir Timothy, but at least she had tried to warn her of the danger.

It was a Monday morning, overcast but dry, and Quinn was already in the breakfast room when Serena entered. His smile was intimate, reminding her of the night they had spent together. Of every night for the past few weeks, she thought, her stomach swooping delightfully, but his voice when he spoke was perfectly calm.

'Well, my dear, what are your plans for the day?'

'Why, nothing very much, my lord. I thought perhaps you might like to drive out with me later? November is upon us and I doubt we shall have many more fine days.'

'Alas, I have business in the city today.'

'Oh.' She tried to hide her disappointment.

'And I shall not be at home for dinner this evening.'

Serena looked up from pouring her coffee. 'You will be out all day?'

'I am afraid so.' He added, as an afterthought, 'It is Settling Day at Tattersall's.'

'Good heavens.' She laughed. 'Have you been playing deep, my lord? I had not thought that was your style.'

He bared his teeth at her. 'You know it is not. But I thought I would look in today.'

'But you will be back in time to come with me to Lady Yatesbury's rout tonight? We do not need to be there until later.'

'Alas, I fear I shall not.' He glanced across the table. 'Do you really wish to go? It will be a dreadful crush,' he told her. 'Yatesbury has no discernment and lets the world and his wife through the door. I would much rather you did not attend.'

'Then I shall not do so.' Serena bit her lip, more disappointed at not seeing Quinn than missing the rout.

'Good.'

He turned his attention back to his plate, indicating that the matter was closed, and Serena felt a little stir of alarm at his reticence. She had never known Quinn to gamble recklessly and she could not believe he had done so now, but there was something he did not wish to share with her. Dunnock came in with the post on a silver tray. Serena drank her coffee while Quinn sorted through the letters. He pushed his chair back.

'There is one for you,' he said, coming around the table to her. 'From Lady Hambridge. You may tell me later what she says. I must deal with my correspondence before I go out.'

He bent to drop a light kiss upon her hair and was gone, leaving Serena feeling restless and uneasy. Quinn was as kind and affectionate as ever, but he went out a great deal these days and rarely told her too much about where he was going. Perhaps he was developing a taste for town life, just when she had decided she would prefer to return to the country.

The day dragged. In the afternoon Serena sent for her phaeton and took a drive around the park at the fashionable hour. However, the house felt even more silent and empty when she returned. She went upstairs and while she waited for Polly to come and help her to change her dress, she stood at the window, looking out at the square. There was no doubt about it—she missed Quinn. Whenever he was away from her she was impatient for his return. It was foolish. It was definitely unfashionable, but there it was.

She went downstairs and instead of going to the morning room, where she usually spent her time alone, she made her way to the library in an effort to find some small crumb of comfort. There was no study in the town house and Quinn worked at the large mahogany desk in the library. She went in, smiling when she saw everything on the desk top was in order, inkwells full, a supply of pens trimmed and ready for use, the accounts journals piled neatly on one side.

At Melham she had been in the habit of helping Quinn with the estate business, but although they still discussed such matters, there was little to be done from London and she felt excluded. How foolish, she thought, going around to sit in his chair. She ran her hands over the carved arms, as if trying to feel some sense of Quinn from the polished wood.

He had never excluded her and, if he currently appeared preoccupied, it was because he was immersed in town life: dinner at the clubs, sparring with Gentleman Jackson at his famous boxing saloon in Old Bond

Street, perhaps even attending cockfights, although Quinn never mentioned such things. He must know she would not approve.

A sliver of paper protruded from the top right-hand drawer of the desk. Careless of Quinn and probably indicative of his hurry to be gone this morning. She pulled open the drawer. The offending sheet was the top one of a sheaf of opened letters that had been hastily pushed into the drawer. This morning's correspondence, she guessed.

As she reached forward to flatten the top sheet she noticed the flowery heading. Rundell, Bridge & Rundell. It must be the bill for her coral parure. She lifted it out, mildly intrigued to know how much the set had cost. The figure at the bottom of the page made her gasp, until she realised that beneath a detailed description of the parure were three further items: a diamond bracelet, ring and necklace.

Serena stared at the page, an icy hand squeezing her insides. Perhaps Quinn planned to give them to her later, but a far more persuasive answer presented itself. Quinn had bought the diamonds for his mistress.

Some women would settle for nothing less.

No. There must be some mistake. But she could not resist pulling the rest of the bundle from the drawer, bills from London tradespeople, mantua-makers, milliners, haberdashers and shoemakers. There were even two more bills from Rundell's. She scrutinised each sheet, but recognised none of the items listed. She reached over and took out the last document. Spreading it open on the desk Serena gazed at it in dismay. It was the lease of a house in Devonshire Place.

Carefully Serena put everything back in the drawer,

blinking away the tears that threatened to drop and smudge the elegantly written accounts. She had not even considered it, yet now she berated herself for a fool. Quinn was a man, was he not, and it was years since the love of his life had died. Why would he not have a mistress? And why would he give her up, merely because he had married? He had wed Serena to save her reputation and she was so damaged that it was only recently that she had welcomed his advances. It was quite understandable that he would want someone to give him the comfort that was lacking in his marriage.

It was too much. She collapsed on to the desk, sobs tearing at her body. The pain was intense, as if indeed her heart were breaking, but such powerful emotions could not continue and at length she dried her eyes. There might be another explanation for these purchases. She should ask Quinn. But even as she wiped all signs of her tears from the library desk she knew she would not do so. He had promised her he would always tell the truth and she was afraid that his answer would be too painful to bear.

Chapter Fifteen

As instructed, Quinn's driver turned the closed carriage into Devonshire Place and brought it to a halt a few yards along, from where Quinn had a good view of an elegant town house with its black-painted door, iron railings and ornate wrought-iron balcony on the first floor. He glanced at his watch. Ten thirty.

He looked up as another carriage rattled into the street, a hackney, which stopped outside the house. The cab drew away and Quinn watched a fashionably dressed gentleman run up the steps and into the house. Quinn picked up his hat and fixed it firmly on his head, then he waited a full five minutes before jumping down from the carriage and, after a brief word with his driver, he made his way towards the black door.

The manservant who admitted him answered Quinn's questioning glance with no more than a nod. Silently Quinn handed him his hat and cane then lightly ran up the stairs to the drawing room. There was only one person present, the fashionable buck who had preceded Quinn into the house. He was standing by the window, staring out, an open letter dangling from one hand.

'So, she is gone.'

Sir Timothy Forsbrook swung round.

'You!' He waved the paper. 'Are you behind this?'

'You have been duped, I presume.' Quinn ignored the question and stripped off his gloves, dropping them on to the small dining table in the centre of the room.

'You know damn well I have.'

Forsbrook's voice shook and Quinn noted that his usually florid face was very pale.

'Actually, I know very little. Why don't you tell me?'

'That high-flyer tricked me finely, the bitch!'

Quinn walked over to the side table and poured out a glass of brandy.

'Here, sit down and drink this.' For a moment he thought Forsbrook would knock it from his hand, but after an inward struggle he snatched the glass and tossed the contents into his mouth. Quinn took the glass. 'Sit down,' he barked again, waiting until Forsbrook had complied before turning to refill the glass and then pouring a brandy for himself.

As Quinn returned to the table Forsbrook looked up at him.

'Did she dupe you as well?'

'On the contrary.'

Forsbrook's face contorted and he swore viciously. 'I knew it. The moment I saw you here I knew you were behind this.'

'I am sure you did,' replied Quinn unmoved. 'The thing is, what are you going to do about it?'

'Devil take you, what *can* I do? If I don't show at Tattersall's and settle my account...' He trailed off, his hand grasping the brandy glass until the knuckles glowed white. Then with another curse he pushed himself to his feet. 'But you will meet me for this, Lord Quinn—'

'Oh, I don't think so, Forsbrook. I have a much better plan for you. One that will allow you to pay your debts of honour, at least.'

Quinn sipped his brandy, seemingly relaxed but alert, should Forsbrook attack, which the murderous look on his bewhiskered face indicated he would like to do. A minute went by. Quinn was aware of the noises from the street, the rattling of a carriage over the cobbles, dogs barking, the shout of a hawker crying his wares. At last Forsbrook lowered himself back into his chair.

'You have no idea how much I owe.'

'Tell me,' Quinn invited him cordially. 'I should imagine your debts are extensive.'

'They are.' Forsbrook emptied his glass, went over to pick up the decanter and brought it back to the table. 'That damned whore gave me to believe she was sweet on me. She was dressed like a swell and very free with her blunt. By Gad, I'd never seen so many jewels on a woman and all of 'em real, I swear.'

'Oh, they were,' murmured Quinn, but Forsbrook did not hear him.

'Naturally, I had to keep up with her. She was determined to be seen about town, too.' He threw another venomous look at Quinn. 'No doubt that was your plan, to provide fodder for the town tabbies. Well, it worked. They were scandalised. There was no hiding her inferior breeding, but I did not think that would matter overmuch to me. She might be as common as the hedge but once we were married I planned to set her up in a snug country manor and come to town without her.'

'Chivalrous.'

'Well, what do you expect? I knew I would be marrying beneath me, but we are not all of us born with a fortune!'

'So you did not tell her you were already living on the edge?'

'Of course not. She was very generous, so how could I be otherwise? Whenever she asked me to purchase some little trifle or go to Tattersall's subscription room and place a wager on a horse she favoured, how could I refuse? And she always paid up, next time we met. And at the card parties...' He shook his head. 'She would ask me to stake her, if she had not brought sufficient funds, but more often than not she won it all back that same evening.' He reached for the decanter and slopped more brandy into his glass. 'We'd talked about marriage. She didn't want a fuss, said her people might not understand about her marrying out of her own sphere. She asked if I could obtain a special licence, even gave me the blunt to cover it there and then!' He dropped his head in his hands. 'I arranged the whole for this morning...'

Quinn's lip curled. 'And no doubt you were going to take your blushing bride direct from the ceremony to Tattersall's.'

'No, damn you, it wasn't like that! I admit much of what I owe at Tattersall's is to cover bets placed—mine and hers!—but almost half of it is for those damned nags of hers. She wanted to set up her stable and asked me to buy the cattle for her. The first team didn't suit, so last week she asked me to purchase her another. Prime goers and damned expensive, too. What could I say? She told me she would have the money here for me today. And after that I was going to settle all my obligations. I would be home free.'

'Instead of which you face ruin. And worse,' said Quinn softly, 'disgrace.'

Forsbrook glared at him, hatred bright in his eyes, but behind that something else. Fear. He thought little of his fellow man—even less of women—but he set great store by his own standing. Gambling losses were debts of honour and if Forsbrook could not pay them, he was finished. Quinn was unmoved. It suited his purpose very well that the fellow considered himself at *point non plus*.

He said now, 'What sum would you need to clear your debts?'

Forsbrook slumped in his chair. 'It will take nothing less than eight, nine thousand pounds. How am I to come by such a sum without surety?'

'I will give you ten thousand pounds.' Forsbrook's head came up, hope and suspicion warring in his face. Quinn continued, 'I shall, of course require you to fulfil certain conditions.'

'Go on.'

Quinn fetched pens and ink from the writing desk, then he went back and pulled a thick sheaf of documents from the drawer and placed them on the table before Forsbrook.

'First, you will sign these letters for publication by the main London newspapers, to wit, the *Gazette*, the *Morning Chronicle*, *The Times* and the *Morning Post*. You need only read one—they are all identical.'

'You have gone to a great deal of effort for this,' sneered Sir Timothy. 'You must have been very sure of me.'

'Read it,' ordered Quinn. 'I will not have you say afterwards you did not know what you were signing.'

He watched as Forsbrook's eyes skimmed the neat lines.

'You would have your wife exonerated from all blame and at the expense of my good name.'

Quinn shrugged. 'We both know this is a man's world. Society will not think much worse of you for admitting you abducted an heiress.' He watched as Forsbrook scrawled his name on each copy of the letter. 'Your being duped by the woman calling herself Mrs Hopwood will do far more harm to your reputation.'

'I am aware of that.' Quinn heard the unmistakable sound of grinding teeth. 'I shall be obliged to remove myself from town for a while.'

'Which brings us neatly to the next condition.' Quinn moved the letters out of the way and replaced them with two more sheets. 'I will grant you the sum of ten thousand pounds, on the understanding that you quit England for the next five years, and never—mark my words, Forsbrook—*never* come near Lady Quinn or her family again. If you break either of these conditions, I shall serve a writ upon you for the repayment of this sum and pursue you mercilessly for it.'

'Leave England!' Sir Timothy sat back, his face suffused with anger. 'And what the devil am I to do for the next five years?'

'I neither know nor care. There is a chaise waiting at the Golden Cross to take you to Dover and thence to France. We are no longer at war, so you may travel the Continent, as many of our compatriots are doing.'

'Preposterous,' Sir Timothy blustered. 'I shall do no such thing.' He waved an accusing finger at Quinn as he folded each of the letters and placed them safely inside his coat. 'And do not think I shall allow those letters to be published without challenge. I shall refute them. I shall say you coerced me.'

'Then I shall be obliged to call you out,' retorted Quinn. 'Believe me, I should like nothing better than to put a bullet through you.' He paused another moment, then reached out for the agreement. 'Very well. If you are not minded to take up my offer...'

'No.'

Forsbrook stopped him and Quinn drew back, waiting. Forsbrook looked about the room, as if hoping the rich widow would appear suddenly and tell him it had all been a joke designed to tease him. At last he sighed and picked up the pen.

'Very well, since I have no choice.'

It took most of the day to settle Sir Timothy's affairs and the clock was striking ten when Quinn finally brought him to the Golden Cross.

'Damn it all, Quinn, there is no need for you to come with me like a blasted gaoler,' Forsbrook exclaimed wrathfully. 'We are agreed I will leave the country. Confound it, you heard me tell my landlady to have my things packed up and sent after me.'

'You are a slippery customer, Forsbrook, and I shall not be content until I have word you are safely in France.' He watched Sir Timothy throw his portmanteau into the chaise. 'You know the consequences of breaking our agreement.'

'Aye, I know it, damn you. By heaven, Quinn, this has cost you a pretty penny! I hope she is worth it.'

'Oh, I think so.'

Quinn pushed him into the coach and closed the door. Forsbrook leaned out of the open window.

'You are a fool, if you think you can keep her, Quinn,' he declared. 'Her family has always courted scandal and Serena Russington is no different. A beautiful pleasure-seeker.' His last, sneering words stayed with Quinn as the chaise drove out through the arch. 'A man such as you will never hold her!'

As his coach rattled towards Berkeley Square, Quinn leaned back in the corner, gazing out at the dark streets. He was dog-tired, but satisfied with his day's work, and he looked forward to telling Serena all about it. Serena. Just the thought of her revived him and when he reached the house he sprang out and hurried to the drawing room. It was empty and he went back to the hall, looking for Dunnock. Serena's maid was about to disappear into the nether regions of the house and he called to her.

'Is your mistress in her bedchamber?'

Polly turned and took a couple of steps towards him before bobbing a curtsy.

'She is gone to Lady Yatesbury's, my lord.' She observed Quinn's frown and twisted her hands together. 'A new gown was delivered and my lady said 'twould be a pity not to wear it out.'

Quinn dismissed the maid and went upstairs. When they had spoken at breakfast, Serena had not seemed eager to go out. In fact, she had told him she would not go. Yet she had changed her mind, just because her new gown had arrived. As he strode to his bedchamber, Forsbrook's words floated back to him.

A man such as you will never hold her.

Serena's head ached from the noise and chatter in Lady Yatesbury's overcrowded, overheated rooms. In truth, she wished she had not come, but when she had discovered that Mrs Bell had sent round her new evening gown, the angry rebellion simmering beneath her despair had erupted. Why should she remain in Berkeley Square, lonely and lachrymose, when Quinn was out who knew where, enjoying himself?

Some part of her, the dutiful wife she had tried to become, argued that she had no right to object if Quinn had a mistress. She should be grateful for all he had done for her. But the truth was that Serena did not *feel* grateful. She felt...jealous. Jealous of this unknown woman upon whom Quinn had spent a small fortune. She had donned Mrs Bell's white and silver gauze creation and set off for Lady Yatesbury's rout in a mood that could only be described as high dudgeon.

Serena took a surreptitious peek at the mantel clock and her heart sank. It was not yet eleven. To leave so soon would give rise to comment, but to remain, when it was an effort to raise a smile, was unthinkable. She would seek out her hostess, make her apologies and slip away with as little fuss as possible.

Lady Yatesbury was by the door, greeting two late arrivals. They made a striking couple, the gentleman tall and dark, with pomaded black curls and thick whiskers, his lilac coat heavily laced, and while Serena could only see the back of the lady, is was clear that her scarlet gown was heavily embroidered with gold thread. Fixed into her fair curls she had two bejewelled combs that matched the sapphires and diamonds around her neck. It could not be better, thought Serena. The appearance of such an ostentatious pair would mean her own absence would barely be noticed.

Serena drew closer and hovered, waiting for the newcomers to move away so that she could take her leave of her hostess, but Lady Yatesbury appeared to be in no hurry. She was waving her fan and blushing at something the gentleman was saying to her. Then she caught sight of Serena and called to her.

'Lady Quinn, well, how fortunate! Come closer, my dear, do.'

The lady in the scarlet gown turned and as Serena approached she found herself staring at a face that looked strangely familiar.

The lady held out her hands, beaming. 'My darling girl. Have you a kiss for your mama?'

Chapter Sixteen

Serena's world rocked. There could be no doubt. The petite frame, the chocolate-dark eyes and guinea-gold curls—it was like looking in a mirror. True, the face was a little more lined than Serena's, but the woman was still beautiful and when she spoke her voice was soft, musical and full of warmth.

'You must let me present my Eduardo to you, my love. Conte Ragussina.' She gave a tinkling laugh. 'I suppose he is your step-papa, now.'

The Conte made a flourishing bow and picked up Serena's nerveless hand.

'But I beg my Lady Quinn will call me Eduardo,' he crooned, kissing her fingers.

Serena gently withdrew her hand, murmuring something incoherent in reply.

'So, it is true,' marvelled Lady Yatesbury, looking from Serena to the Contessa. 'You had no idea you would meet here tonight?'

'None at all,' purred the Contessa, 'I had written to advise of my return to England, but one knows how easily letters go astray.'

'Indeed, indeed,' cried their hostess. 'And for this

happy reunion to happen in my house!' She clasped her hands in delight and Serena could imagine how the tale would have spread by the morning. 'But you will wish to talk privately with your daughter, Contessa. I shall take you to my boudoir on the next floor. You will not be disturbed there, I assure you.'

'Yes, yes, we must talk.' The Contessa slipped one hand through Serena's arm and waved the other imperiously at her husband. '*Caro mio*, you must go away and enjoy yourself while Serena and I become acquainted again.'

In a daze Serena allowed herself to be carried away from the overcrowded reception rooms and up the stairs to a comfortable little sitting room decorated in shades of powder blue. The Contessa Ragussina sank down gracefully on to a sofa and patted the seat beside her.

'Come, my dear, I will not bite, I promise you. How long is it, seven, eight years?

'Twelve,' replied Serena coolly, choosing a small chair opposite the sofa. 'I was but eight years old when you left me.'

A shadow of something that might have been guilt flickered across the Contessa's features.

'Ah, do not hate me for that, my darling. What was I to do? I knew your brother would never allow me to take you and I would be the first to acknowledge that the life Eduardo and I lived would hardly have been suitable for a little girl.'

'You have no other children, madam?'

'Good heavens, no. One was quite enough.' She gasped and put her hands to her mouth. 'Oh, my darling, pray do not think I did not want you. Nothing could be further from the truth, but I had such a *horrid* time of it, you see, and children are quite disastrous for one's figure, as you will discover soon enough, for you are married now. Lady Quinn. Well, I declare! And I am quite, quite furious with Hambridge for not informing me.'

'Oh?' Serena's brows went up. 'Does Henry correspond with you?'

'He does not, but he should. The Conte's *avvocati* have written to him upon occasion, so he cannot say he does not know how to contact me. Neither did he inform me of Russington's nuptials. I learned of that and of your own good fortune when I reached London. We have been here, what, four weeks now.' She made a little moue of distaste. 'I had forgotten how cold and miserable it is. We came at the invitation of the Hollands, you see, but it would not do to impose upon Lord and Lady Holland for too long so we have hired Kilborn House, near Hampstead. I know it is a little out of town, but it was the only house big enough for us to entertain in any style.'

'And do you intend to stay long in England, ma'am?' Serena marvelled that she could make such a calm, polite enquiry when she was still reeling from this unexpected meeting and her mind was seething with conjecture.

'Oh, no.' The Contessa chuckled. 'Although it would annoy your brothers immensely, which would be amusing! We remain another se'ennight only. But that is long enough for you and I to become acquainted.'

Serena arrived back at Berkeley Square just as the watch was calling two of the clock. She and her mother had remained closeted together in Lady Yatesbury's sitting room for over an hour and by the time they emerged

Serena had learned a great deal about the Contessa Ragussina, but felt very little affection for the woman who was her mother. Papa she remembered as a bluff, jovial man. Her mother was a much more elusive memory, a golden creature whose painted cheek the young Serena had been allowed to kiss, after first being warned that she must be careful not to crush her gown. When Papa died and Mama had quit the country, the eight-year-old Serena had experienced no sense of loss. It had made little difference to her life, except that her half-brothers were anxious that no whiff of scandal should be attached to Miss Serena Russington.

She had remained at the rout for another hour or so, and by that time she had formed a pretty accurate assessment of her mother. The Contessa Ragussina was a charming, spoiled beauty who cared for nothing but her own pleasure. Her delight in coming so unexpectedly upon her daughter appeared genuine, but Serena thought it was more for the sensation it would cause rather than any maternal affection. The Conte was an inveterate flirt, but he seemed genuinely fond of his wife and was rich enough to provide for her every wish. They were louche, loud and most definitely scandalous, and she had no idea what Quinn would say when he knew she had met them.

Quinn. Serena crossed the hall and made her way slowly up the stairs. She very much wanted to go to him. Twenty-four hours ago she would not have hesitated to go to his room, to wake him up if necessary and tell him everything that had occurred at the rout. But the fact that Quinn might have spent the day—and most of the night—in the arms of his mistress gnawed away at her. Knowing it was jealousy and might well be unfounded did not help one jot. It just made the night spent in her own, lonely bed that much longer.

When Serena went into the breakfast room the following morning Quinn was already there, finishing off a plate of ham and eggs. She bade him a polite good morning and received nothing more than a considering stare in return. A servant served her with coffee and hot rolls, but once they were alone Quinn asked her if she had enjoyed herself last night.

'Thank you, it was interesting.'

He threw her a glance. 'You did not come to my room.'

'No.' She concentrated on buttering her bread roll. 'It was very late.'

'I missed you.'

The words were quiet, almost off hand, but they increased her inner turmoil. Did he really care about her, or did she merely feed some insatiable appetite? That thought produced a prickle of anger.

She said with ill-concealed bitterness, 'I thought you would be exhausted. After a day spent enjoying the pleasures of society.'

'What the deuce do you mean by that?'

'For one who professes to dislike town so much you are very reluctant to quit it.'

Quinn frowned. He put down his knife and fork and pushed away his empty plate.

'What is this about, Serena—have I offended you in some way?'

Tell him, Serena. Ask him to explain the bills, the lease of another house. There should be no secrets between you.

'*Something* has occurred, and I want to know what it is.' He bent a searching look upon her. 'Well, madam?'

The butler's cough interrupted them.

'I beg your pardon, my lord. Lord and Lady Hambridge have called. They wish to see you immediately.' Dunnock's sombre tones were overlaid with a hint of anxiety. 'Lord Hambridge says it is a matter of some urgency.'

For a moment she thought Quinn might tell the butler to go to the devil. Instead he nodded and pushed his chair back.

'Very well, we will come now.'

'I have shown them into the drawing room, my lord.'

'We will finish this later, Serena,' muttered Quinn as they followed Dunnock through the hall.

But she barely heard him. She was wondering about the revelations that awaited them in the drawing room.

When Dunnock opened the door for them to enter, Quinn saw immediately that something was seriously wrong. Henry was pacing up and down the room, while his wife was perched on the edge of a sofa, pulling a lace handkerchief between her hands with quick, jerking movements. His first thought was for Serena. He guided her to a chair and gently pressed her to sit down before greeting the guests.

'Good day to you, Hambridge, Lady Hambridge. When did you return from Worthing?'

The butler had withdrawn by this time and Henry wasted no time on pleasantries.

'Last night,' he replied shortly. 'And we were devastated by the news that awaited us. Poor Dorothea has been quite prostrate.'

Serena tensed and his hand tightened warningly on

her shoulder. 'I am sorry to hear that. I take it this concerns us?'

Hambridge stopped and fixed Quinn with a solemn gaze. 'Serena's mother is in London.'

'I see.'

'Such a dreadful shock,' exclaimed Dorothea, tugging at the unfortunate scrap of lace between her hands. 'She has been in England for a full month with that disreputable husband of hers! That foolish clerk of Hambridge's should have sent the letter on to us, but no, he must leave it for our return. I vow I was almost carried off by a seizure when Henry read it to me. They have hired a house out of town, thankfully, and there is little chance of them being invited to the sort of gatherings *you* will attend, Serena, so all is not lost.'

Henry nodded solemnly. 'And if by some mischance you should meet, on no account must you acknowledge them, Serena.'

'Indeed not,' declared Dorothea. 'I vow if I should happen to see that dreadful woman I shall not hesitate to give her the cut direct. That is, if I should recognise her.' She gave an angry titter. 'I have no doubt she is quite hideously raddled by now, with the debauched life she has been living.'

'Oh, I do not think you will have any difficulty knowing her,' remarked Serena. 'I do not believe she is much changed. And the likeness between us is quite unmistakable.' She added coolly, 'I met the Conte and Contessa, you see. At Lady Yatesbury's rout last night.'

So *that* accounted for her strange mood this morning, thought Quinn. His surprise at the announcement was nothing compared to that of Lady Hambridge. She shrieked and fell back on the sofa, while Henry scrabbled in her reticule for her smelling salts to wave under her nose. Quinn and Serena watched in silence.

'Thank God you don't subject me to such histrionics,' he muttered.

'You have met the Contessa?' Henry's outraged stare moved from Serena to Quinn. 'What the devil were you about, sir, to allow such a thing?'

'I was not at hand to prevent it,' Quinn retorted.

'Do you mean to say Serena was there *alone*?' cried Lady Hambridge, sitting up.

Quinn ground his teeth. 'I am not her keeper, madam.'

Dorothea sucked in a scandalised breath. 'You are her *husband*, my lord, and it is your duty to protect her reputation. What's left of it!'

Quinn saw Serena's hand come up, as if to ward off a blow, and he bit back a scathing reply. Dunnock came in, bearing a sealed letter on a tray. With admirable aplomb he fixed his eyes on his master and ignored everyone else.

'A note has arrived for you, my lord. The messenger insisted it should be delivered to you immediately and he awaits your answer.'

Quinn took the letter and dismissed the butler. He glanced about him as he broke the seal and opened the letter. Serena was sitting pale but composed in her chair, while Hambridge fussed about his wife, who had relapsed on the sofa.

'We must see how best we can resolve this situation,' declared Hambridge, plying his wife's fan as she lay back with her eyes closed. 'A single chance encounter at Lady Yatesbury's may not be so very bad, but we must ensure there are no further meetings. It would be best if you were to withdraw from society, Serena, until the Conte and Contessa have returned to the Continent. You must cancel all your engagements and Quinn shall take you back to Melham Court. Dorothea and I will make sure everyone knows the meeting was not of your making. I am confident that by next Season this will all be forgotten and you need think no more about that scandalous female.'

Serena sat up a little straighter in her chair. 'You forget, Henry, that *scandalous female*, as you call her, is my mother.'

'And a most unnatural parent,' declared Dorothea in scathing accents.

'But Serena's parent, nevertheless,' put in Quinn, coming forward. 'It is therefore up to my wife if she wishes to continue the acquaintance.'

'Out of the question.' Dorothea sat up. 'Serena's reputation is already damaged. To accept the connection with the Contessa, to be seen in her company, would put her beyond the pale.'

'Calm yourself, my dear,' Henry said as his wife snatched back her fan. 'The Contessa may not wish for the connection. After all, she has shown no interest in Serena until now.' He looked suddenly much happier. 'I doubt if she truly wants to acknowledge the daughter she abandoned more than ten years ago.'

'I hate to disappoint you,' drawled Quinn, glancing at the paper in his hand, 'but the Contessa wishes very much to see her daughter. She has invited us to dine with her at Kilborn House this evening.' There was a stunned silence. Quinn continued, 'Dinner, followed by a little dancing.'

'Out of the question!' The Hambridges both spoke at once.

'I will not allow it!'

'It is not a question of what *you* will allow, Hambridge,' barked Quinn. 'My wife is quite capable of deciding for herself.'

Henry's face flushed. 'Think, man. This is not only her reputation at stake, but yours, too, as her husband!'

'Reputation be damned,' Quinn snapped. 'I have never cared for society's good opinion and I am not about to start now.' He turned to Serena. 'Well, my dear, shall we accept the Contessa's invitation?'

Serena saw only understanding in Quinn's hazel eyes and it steadied her. She ignored Dorothea's gasp of outrage and her brother's angry mutterings and spoke directly to him.

'You would come with me?'

'Of course.'

'Then I confess I should like to go.' She wanted to tell him her first impressions of the Contessa, but she was loath to do so in front of Henry and Dorothea. It smacked of disloyalty to the woman who had borne her.

'Then I shall give the messenger our answer now.'

Dorothea barely waited for Quinn to leave the room before she gave a loud huff of disapproval.

'You have shocked and disappointed me, Serena. I thought we had taught you better than this. If you persist in your wayward behaviour, then I wash my hands of you!'

'Now, now, my dear, 'pon reflection I think 'tis natural Serena wishes to know a little about her mother and a private dinner is perhaps the best thing for it.'

'With dancing! How can it be private? The entire Holland House set might be present!' Dorothea's eyes went back to Serena. 'Never tell me Quinn mixes in that company!'

'I have no idea.' Serena looked towards Quinn, who had just come back into the room. '*Do* you visit Holland House?'

'I have dined there, in the past. The conversation is always stimulating. But I do not go there now.'

'Well, that is a small mercy, I suppose,' Dorothea conceded. 'The scandal surrounding Lizzie Webster has never been forgotten.'

'Surely it is to his credit that Lord Holland married her,' reasoned Serena.

'That merely shows he is as bad as she is,' flashed Dorothea.

'Poppycock,' said Quinn. 'If I do not go to Holland House it has nothing to do with the fact that Lady Holland is a divorcee, but because the Hollands are such avid supporters of Bonaparte.'

'But you are sure to meet them at Kilborn House and heaven knows what other scandalous company the Ragussinas may keep.'

'Then we shall soon find out,' replied Quinn, with what Serena thought was admirable calm.

Dorothea rose in a crackle of silks. 'I see there is no arguing with either of you. Come, Henry, we shall take our leave.'

'You must see our position, Serena,' said Henry, escorting his wife to the door. 'We cannot grant you more than a bow in passing, if we see you out and about in your mother's company. And what Russ will say when he hears of it…'

Dorothea gave a snort of derision. 'Knowing your brother, he will merely laugh!'

Serena caught the glimmer of amusement in Quinn's eyes and she said, 'Thank you, Dorothea, that gives me some comfort.'

'Well it was not what I intended! Come, Henry, take me home, if you please.'

'Oh, dear.' Serena sighed when the door closed behind them. 'I fear they are seriously displeased with me. I only hope they do not cut all acquaintance with us.'

'They will come about,' said Quinn. He grinned. 'You are a very rich woman now, Lady Quinn. That counts for a great deal with your brother and his wife.'

'But not if I continue to cause a scandal.'

'You won't.' He pulled her into his arms. 'We shall be the very model of marital harmony.'

Serena's heart skittered at the warm glow in his eyes, but she could not forget the bills stuffed into the drawer in the library. How could she lose herself in his kiss if she was sharing him with some unknown mistress? With a little laugh she twisted out of his arms.

'Heavens, Quinn, how droll that sounds,' she said lightly. 'But you must excuse me, if you please. This unexpected invitation to dine with the Contessa has thrown me into complete confusion. I must go and find Polly to help me decide what to wear.'

She made her escape and managed to avoid seeing Quinn again until they set off in the carriage for Kilborn House. When they arrived, she handed her cloak to the hovering footman and Quinn glanced at her coral gown.

'Beautiful,' he murmured. 'But why are you not wearing the parure?'

She put a hand to the diamonds at her neck. She had no heart to wear the coral set—it reminded her of the expensive gifts he had bestowed elsewhere.

'I thought these were more fitting,' she replied at last, adding with a touch of bitterness, 'after all, diamonds are what every woman loves most.'

She moved quickly away towards the lackey waiting to show them into the drawing room, leaving Quinn to follow her.

The Contessa greeted them regally before making them known to their guests. There were some half-a-dozen people in the room and Serena recognised only two of them: Lord Fyfield and Mrs Medway, a dashing widow with a reputation for stealing husbands. They were greeted with an enthusiasm that bordered on the obsequious, which Serena disliked as much as Quinn. Neither did she like the Conte's familiar attitude towards herself, but she hid her unease beneath a cheerful smile, accepted the glass of wine pressed into her hand and did her best to join in with the conversation, wondering how soon after dinner they might take their leave.

Quinn's countenance was impassive as he watched his fellow diners. This was just such an evening as he detested, inconsequential small talk and malicious gossip. The flight from England of Lord Byron and Brummell earlier in the year had been followed by a storm of speculation and even now the Contessa's guests were eager to pick over the bones of the scandals. Quinn took no part, neither did he respond to the advances of the widow on his right. Serena, he noted, was turning away the flirtatious remarks of the Conte and Lord Fyfield with a smile, but her cheeks were more flushed than usual. He wondered how much wine she had drunk.

A question from his hostess claimed his attention, but he answered it briefly and went back to watching Serena. She appeared to be avoiding his eye and unease flickered. Was he mistaken in thinking her liveliness was forced? Was she indeed enjoying the dissolute company? An icy hand clutched at his guts. Perhaps Forsbrook was right. How could he hope to hold the interest of such a vibrant, lively creature as Serena? She had wanted a rake for a husband, not a serious, unsociable fellow who preferred books to parties.

Throughout dinner, Serena felt Quinn's eyes upon her. He was seated between the Contessa and Mrs Medway but he made little effort to engage them in conversation. He was living up to his reputation, then, as the rudest man in London. She did not look directly at him, afraid to read disapproval in his face. The wine had made her a little light-headed and she had been flirting with the gentlemen sitting near her. Well, she thought angrily, if Quinn was jealous she was glad. It could be nothing to the pain she was suffering.

With each glass of wine, the idea that Quinn had a mistress became more fixed in her mind. It must be so. There could be no other explanation. He probably considered it a kindness to keep the fact from her. How strange, she thought, that she could laugh and talk as if she had not a care in the world, when inside her heart was breaking.

The Contessa rose to lead the ladies from the dining room and as Serena passed Quinn he reached back and caught her hand.

'Are you all right?'

No. I want to rip and tear and scream. I want to throw myself into your arms and cry my heart out, but I will not do that because I am sure those arms have been wrapped about someone else.

'Oh, Lord, yes. I am enjoying myself vastly.'

She gave him a glittering smile and walked on. This was to be their life from now on. A pretence of happiness.

The ladies disposed themselves around the elegant drawing room and the Contessa invited Serena to join her on the sofa.

'You do not seem to be at ease, my dear,' she said, taking Serena's hand. 'Are you wishing yourself elsewhere?'

'No, indeed, ma'am. I very much wanted to come this evening.'

'Then perhaps it is your marriage. Ah, I can see by the way you have coloured up that I am right.' She sighed. 'I cannot say I blame you.'

'I do not know what you mean,' Serena replied coldly, pulling her hand free.

The Contessa was in no way discomposed. She said, 'Lord Quinn is not easy in society. Why, he said barely a half-dozen words to me during dinner.'

Serena saw no reason to be polite. 'I doubt the insipid conversation was to his taste. He has never been one for tittle-tattle.'

'But, my dear, gossip is the most entertaining kind of conversation! Do not tell me your husband is a prig as well as a bore.'

'You must admit, Contessa, he does have a magnificent physique,' giggled Mrs Medway, overhearing.

'Does he have a mistress—oh, no need to look like that, Lady Quinn, we are all women of the world here. Of course he does. What rich man does not?'

Serena wanted to deny it, but jealousy swirled about her like a hot red mist and kept her silent. This could not go on. She could not bear it. She would talk to Quinn, discover the truth, however painful. But for now she could only pray that the subject would soon be dropped.

The Contessa touched her arm and gave a soft laugh, shaking her head at Mrs Medway. 'Now, now, Edith, you are putting my daughter to the blush. She and Quinn may still be very much in love.'

'Charming, but quite unfashionable,' smirked another of the matrons, disposing her skirts more becomingly. 'However, it will pass, it always does.'

'Not for the Conte and Contessa, apparently,' remarked Edith Medway. 'Do tell us your secret, madam.'

'That is easy. Constant amusement, including lovers! Wherever we are we surround ourselves with young people who entertain and divert us.' She reached up to caress Serena's face. 'With your looks I could make you the most sought-after woman in Rome or Paris. How amusing that would be!' The Contessa laughed. 'What do you say, Serena, why not quit this dull marriage and come to the Continent with me?'

Serena blinked, startled.

'I—I am flattered but, but it is quite out of the question.' Her eyes slid away from the Contessa's considering look. 'I c-cannot... I do not wish to leave my husband.'

'No, of course not. No need to colour up so, my love, it was merely an idea.' The Contessa sent a smiling look around the room. 'Enough of this. Let us talk of fashion before the gentlemen come in. I saw the most exquisite bonnet in New Bond Street today. A new milliner...'

Serena would have liked to leave as soon as the gentlemen joined them, but the room had already been cleared for dancing and good manners dictated they remain a little longer. Besides, she would do anything to put off the evil hour when she must talk to Quinn. She pinned on a smile and pretended an enjoyment in the evening that she was far from feeling.

She danced first with the Conte, then with the elderly roué whose wife was consigned to the pianoforte. After that Lord Fyfield approached, but Quinn cut him out.

'My turn, I think.'

Serena eyed him warily. She was feeling a little dizzy, which was possibly the wine, for her glass had constantly been refilled throughout the evening. Quinn was not smiling, but she could not make out if he was angry or merely bored.

She said, a little recklessly, 'I hope you are not going to scold me, Quinn.'

'No, why should I? You flirt very prettily.'

She felt a flash of anger, irrational, but too real to be ignored. Did he not *care* that she had been flirting? The dance separated them, but when she passed him she took her chance.

'Sauce for the goose, my lord!'

His brows snapped together. 'What the devil does that mean?'

They changed partners, skipped and pirouetted their way through the dance until they were facing one another again at the end of the line.

'Are you angry with me, Serena?'

'I suppose I should be grateful for your company

tonight. You have had so much *business* to attend to recently.'

'Yes. But this is not the place to discuss it.'

Serena knew that. Of course she did, but some demon was prodding at her and before the dance separated them again she sent one last, Parthian shot.

'Oh, no explanations, I pray you. How dull that would be!'

She saw Quinn's face darken as she turned away from him for the final movements of the dance and barely had they made their courtesies before he grabbed her hand.

'A word in private, if you please.'

There was confusion as everyone regrouped for another dance. With the iron grip on her hand Serena could do nothing but accompany Quinn out of the room. He spoke to their host in passing and the Conte's knowing smile made her blush vividly. In the hall, a footman directed them to a small sitting room, where candles burned and a cheerful fire blazed in the hearth.

'We cannot talk here,' she objected. 'What if we are interrupted?'

'We won't be.' His voice was scathing. 'A household like this will have plenty of private little rooms ready for use.'

'But you do not want to make love to me.'

'No, I don't,' he growled. 'I want to know what the devil is wrong with you tonight.'

Serena panicked. She was not quite sober and she needed all her wits about her when she confronted Quinn about his mistress.

'I am put out, that is all,' she said. 'Because you do not like my mother, or her friends.'

'And you do?'

Not for the world would she agree with him! She said airily, 'They are most entertaining.'

'Is that what you call entertaining? Gossiping, pulling reputations to shreds, flirting—'

'Hah, now we come down to it, my lord.'

'To what?'

Again, she retreated, hating her cowardice in not asking him the one question that was eating away at her soul.

'You object to other men taking notice of me.'

'Not at all.' His mouth twitched. 'Although I would object to you taking notice of other men.'

It was an attempt to lighten the mood but she ignored it.

He said at last, 'Are you sorry you married me?'

Yes, if you do not love me and only me.

When she did not speak his mouth twisted, he said heavily, 'I am not at ease in society, Serena, you know that. You appear to enjoy it.'

'It is the life I was brought up to expect.' The words sounded haughty, even though she meant it as an explanation.

His face darkened and he walked away from her.

'Idleness and indulgence,' he retorted. 'I thought you wanted more than that, Serena.' At the window he stopped and looked back, saying bitterly, 'Ah, but I was forgetting. You intended to marry a rake.'

'You are not a rake and nothing like one!'

'No, nor do I wish to be.' He sighed and turned to the window, staring out into the darkness. 'Perhaps you would be happier with your mother's set. Parties every night, touring the grand cities of Europe, with as many rakes as your heart desires.'

'Then you should leave me here!'

It was like watching herself from behind a glass wall. Serena wanted to scream at herself to stop, but instead she could only watch herself parcelling up the happy life she had been building with Quinn and pushing it towards a precipice.

'You should go,' she said, shaking with hurt and anger. 'Go away and leave me here with my mother. She has already suggested I go with her when she sails for France next week.'

'Then you must do that,' he barked, keeping his back to her. 'If it makes you happy.'

'It cannot make me any more miserable!' She threw the words at him, wanting only to wound.

'Very well,' he said, his voice brittle. 'I shall leave you to enjoy the company of your new friends.'

'You may tell Polly to pack up my things and send them to me.'

He had reached the door by this time, but her words stopped him and he turned to look at her.

'If that is what you want.'

She tried to glare at him defiantly, but the mixture of hurt and anger burning in his eyes made her look away.

'No, 'pon reflection, you need not bother,' she said icily. 'Pray do not send me anything from Berkeley Square. I shall require far more dashy gowns for living with Mama.'

For an instant she thought he would pick her up and carry her bodily from the house. Hope flared as she realised just how desperately she wanted him to do that. Instead he nodded silently and went out.

'I will not cry.' Serena muttered the words to the empty room. 'I *will not* cry.'

Blinking hard, she made her way back to the drawing room, where the Contessa gave her a searching look.

'Lord Quinn has left,' she said, keeping her head up and her tone cool.

'That is excellent news, *cara*.' The Conte took her hand and lifted it to his lips. 'We shall enjoy ourselves much more without him. *Che stupido*—he is a man most tedious!' She felt his hand on her back as he escorted her across the room to the Contessa. '*Tua madre* says you are coming to the Continent with us, no?'

She was surrounded by eager, inquisitive faces. Mrs Medway and Lord Fyfield would make sure the story would be all over town by the morning and what a titillating piece of gossip it would be. Henry and Dorothea would be scandalised, but that did not worry her. Only the effect on Quinn.

Suddenly she was no longer trapped behind the glass wall. She knew exactly what she wanted to do. What she wanted to say. Gently but firmly, she freed herself from the Conte's grasp and addressed her mother, her voice clear and steady.

'No, I am not going with you. You will think me unfashionable, but I love my husband, very much. And if it is not too late, I am going back to fight for my place in his life. If you have any feeling for me at all, Mother, I pray you will order a carriage to take me back to Berkeley Square with all possible speed.'

Chapter Seventeen

Quinn had told the driver to make all haste, but his rage was abating long before they had covered the four miles to Berkeley Square. He handed his hat and gloves to Dunnock, ignoring the old retainer's questioning glance. Time enough for them all to learn that Serena was not coming back.

It was only a few paces to the drawing room, but it was long enough for a lifetime of thoughts to race through his head. He had lost her and it was only now that he realised how much she meant to him. Over the past months he had watched the fragile, broken creature he had rescued from the inn at Hitchin recover her spirit. He had always known the docile, timid woman he had married was not the real Serena.

He had never wanted it to be. He wanted the fearless, passionate woman he had seen at their very first meeting, the woman who had ripped up at him, not caring for his wealth or rank. She had faced him as an equal, even though she barely reached his shoulder!

He had always known such a vibrant, pleasure-loving creature might not be satisfied with his quiet way of living. He had thought that once she had recovered her confidence he would go back to his books and his estates and they would live their separate lives. There was nothing unusual in that. He had thought himself prepared for it. Looking forward to it, in fact. Until tonight, when he had seen the old Serena, beautiful, alluring, irresistible, and he had discovered he could not bear to live without her.

The silence in the drawing room pressed in on him. He paced up and down, going over the events of the evening. He should not have lost his temper. Serena, too, had been in a rage, although at the time he had not seen that. He raked a hand through his hair. He had promised to look after her. He should not have left Serena at Kilborn House. Whatever she decided to do, he should not have abandoned her in such company.

Quinn glanced at the clock, then dashed out to the hall and past the astonished butler. He had been home barely ten minutes. If he ran to the mews he might be in time. They might not yet have unharnessed the team.

As he wrenched open the front door, the postillions of a travelling chariot were bringing the four sweating horses to a plunging halt outside the house. He stopped in the doorway, blinking to make sure he was not dreaming, but there was no mistaking the golden-haired beauty who stepped out of the carriage. She did not see him until she had hurried up the steps, then she stopped, uncertainty in her face.

'Quinn. I—'

'Not here.' He reached out for her hand. Gently, as if she would break. The initial soaring relief and elation he had felt had subsided a little, for the travelling chariot had not driven away. She was not yet his. She might never be. Silently he escorted her to the drawing room.

Once the door was closed, Quinn turned to look at her. 'You came back.'

'For the moment.' Her eyes were dark and troubled. 'There are things we must discuss. They will not wait.'

He said, clutching at the only straw he could find, 'If it is the thought of meeting Forsbrook in town that has made you want to leave, you may be easy—'

'Sir Timothy?' She looked faintly surprised. 'No, he no longer concerns me, but in any case, Lord Fyfield told me tonight that he has fled the country. No one knows the whole story, but it would appear the wealthy widow gave him his *congé*. I am relieved for Mrs Hopwood,' she added. 'I would not want to see her tied to such a man. I would not wish anyone to be condemned to an unhappy marriage.' Her eyes flickered towards him again. 'That is what we must discuss.'

Quinn said nothing. He squared his shoulders and waited for the blow to fall.

Serena moved restlessly about the room and drew off her gloves. She must choose her words with care.

'I am not leaving England with my mother. I have no wish to join her set.'

'Then why is her carriage still at the door?'

'In case I have to leave this house tonight.'

'Are you afraid of me?'

'You know I am not! I owe you such a great deal, Quinn. Even my life, I think. Perhaps we should never have married, but it is done and cannot easily be undone. We may not be able to live together, but I have no wish to disgrace you more than I have already. I thought, perhaps, you might put one of your properties at my disposal. Somewhere remote, where I might live quietly and cause no more scandal.'

'Wait.' He stopped her, frowning. '*Why* can we not live together?'

She took another turn about the room, fighting the urge to burst into tears.

'I thought I could do this, Quinn. I thought I could live with you, share your world, to help you with your estates, your people.' She stopped, knowing what must be said, and forced herself to look at him. 'I have fallen in love with you, Quinn. I know now that I cannot share you. If I cannot have you to myself, then I prefer to retire to the country and, and n-never see you again.'

He straightened, as if a great weight had been lifted from his shoulders.

'There is no one else, Serena.'

He reached for her but she held him off.

'Truly?' She looked up, her eyes searching his face. 'Do you not have a mistress?'

'No. I never have. Oh, I admit, after Barbara died there were others, but not recently. And certainly not since I found you.' He smiled. 'I did not know it until tonight, when you sent me away, but you have my heart, Serena. All of it. The thought of living without you is intolerable.'

She swallowed. 'But... Barbara?'

'I loved her, very much. She was my friend and my first love, and I will never forget her. But there is room for another in my heart, Serena. One last and enduring love.'

She shook her head at him. 'Quinn, I have tried to be a conformable wife—'

He put his fingers to her lips, silencing her.

'That is not what I want, my darling. I want the *real* Serena, the lady who will stand up to me, argue with me if she thinks I am wrong. I fear we will have battles royal, but is that not better than a life spent constantly in calm waters?' He smiled, his burning gaze turning her very bones to water. 'I love you, Serena. I love you for your warmth, your spirit, your courage, and if you will stay with me I shall do my utmost to prove it for the rest of our lives.'

'Oh, Quinn!'

He stifled the words with a kiss, swift, hard and impatient. Serena responded, but after a moment, and with a supreme effort, she pushed him away. She wanted to believe him. She wanted it so much that her heart ached, but she had to be sure.

'I have to know, Quinn. I f-found several bills and receipts in your desk...'

'Ah.' His brow cleared. 'Perhaps we should sit down.'

She allowed him to pull her down beside him on the sofa, but he had done nothing to ease her anxiety and she said impatiently, 'Explain to me, if you please!'

He grinned. 'Those, my dear, are the consequence of a highly improper deception I agreed with your half-brother Russington.'

'Then, you do *not* have a mistress in Devonshire Place?'

He lifted her on to his lap. 'Why would I want a mistress when I have you?' He kissed her. 'No. I set up the glorious Mrs Hopwood.'

'Sir Timothy's rich widow!' Relief flooded through her and a laugh bubbled up. 'So she was never in danger of being duped.' She sighed. 'And you planned it all for my sake?'

He shook his head. 'I cannot take the credit for it—that was Russ. His was the plotting and planning. I, er, merely insisted upon financing the whole. The lady is a friend of Molly's, one of the, er, unfortunate women from Prospect House. The cook, in fact.'

'Nancy! But I have met her. She is an earl's daughter.'

He chuckled. 'Not the drab that Forsbrook took her for at all. When Russ explained the situation, she was more than willing to play the role. She was confident no one would recognise her.'

'She was quite correct. I certainly did not! I spoke to her, you see, at the Pantheon Bazaar, but even then, I had no idea—what a good actress she is.'

'Aye, she drew Forsbrook in nicely. Dangled the bait before his eyes: a northern fortune that was not tied up in trust. She was very convincing, the more so because she was rigged out with no expense spared.'

'So that explains the bills,' she murmured. 'If only I had asked you about them.'

'I should have told you what was afoot. I beg your pardon.'

'It does not matter now. And Nancy has gone back to the north—she is safe?'

'Yes. She disappeared in the night, leaving Forsbrook open to…er…persuasion.'

'You paid him off?'

'I thought you would not be in favour of my murdering him.'

'No indeed, but all this must have cost you a great deal.'

'A trifling sum, when you think what Lady Hambridge would have had me spend on a grand wedding.' He kissed her. 'I forbid you to worry about it. The yellow phaeton and carriage horses are now stabled in the mews ready to be sold on, but I let Nancy take everything else with her. Most of it will be sold to provide funds for Prospect House. I hope you do not object? The gowns would be far too big for you and I did not think the trinkets were quite your style. Whenever you wish, I will take you to Rundell's and buy you all the jewels your heart desires.'

She sighed and snuggled closer. 'For now all I want is to stay here with you.'

'Truly?' His arms tightened around her.

'Truly,' she said, turning her face up to his, her eyes shining. 'I love you, Quinn. I want to live with you as your wife. As your lover. I want to have dinner with you in the stone tower, alone or with our close friends. I want to learn to play duets with you on the piano and sing with you. It would be wonderful to take the grand tour with you, but I do not need a life full of parties or a host of admirers. Only you, my darling. I want only you.' She drew his head down towards her for another kiss. 'Send the coach away, Quinn, and take me to bed.'

* * * * *